WHAT THE HEART CAN HOLD

What the Heart Can Hold

By Charlotte Symonds

Cover Graphic Design:
Manuel Beltran and Margaret Huck

ISBN-13: 978-1499295801
ISBN-10: 1499295804

Dedication

To my daughters, Samantha and Jessica, whose hearts first beat within me which I carried with unfathomable love and whose hearts I hold most dear. Although, years ago the cords were detached, no matter how far in distance we may become, their hearts I will always hear.

Acknowledgments

My heartfelt gratitude to Dr. Jeanne Loysen and Lisa Marie Sterling for their collaboration with the editing of this book.

Special Note: Author available to be a guest at book clubs, bookstores and libraries. For more information contact the author at chatwiththeauthor@gmail.com

DAY ONE

Day One, Saturday, June11th Marissa's Story

Little did she know when she closed the door gently behind her, that the events about to occur would change her life forever. The sun had barely peeked over the horizon as Marissa was getting into her old, beat up red VW bug. Her routine was always the same. Say a quick prayer that it would start, turn the key, and then thank God when the engine turned over. Her friends laughed at this ritual, but it always worked. Her grandmother would say it was her strong faith that made her old car keep running.

Daybreak was her favorite time to work out, whether she was home in the city or here at the Hamptons. From the house, the drive to the beach only took a few minutes, as there was little traffic at this hour. When she would arrive at the beach, it was as if it was her very own. She was its only inhabitant; at least until the hoards of sun worshipers would invade the neatly combed sands. As always she would lock her purse in the trunk. It was as if she could actually still hear her father telling her not to leave any valuables in plain sight that might invite a break in. Would she ever stop hearing the advice he gave her in her head, she wondered. She hoped not, for as long as she could still hear him telling her what she should do, then he was still with her. She kicked off her polka dotted red and white flip flops, slipped off her old worn out denim shorts, and threw her white eyelet poncho onto the back seat. She grabbed the extra car key with the red spiral cord, which she always kept in the ash tray, and put it around her wrist. She grabbed her Wonder Women beach towel, which she received as a gag gift on her last birthday, from the passenger seat and off she went. She loved the feel of the cool sand as it slipped through her toes as she ran towards the ocean. A much better feel than it would be hours from now when you would see children jumping about like grasshoppers to avoid its unbearable temperature.

This early in the morning the only sounds she would hear were from the squawking seagulls and the crashing of the waves onto the shore. As her toes reached the wet sand a slight chill would run through her. She would always rush right into the ocean, not tip toe in like most. Like ripping off a band aid quickly, she felt it was the best way. The ocean always gave her a sense of peace. It was cold but invigorating. It was much more of a workout than swimming in a pool, but Marissa was always up for the challenge. She could swim at a slow pace and glide through the water or she could push herself harder and really feel her muscles burn. But the best part was that while she swam she could think. Swimming seemed to clear her head, and answers to any problem she might have seemed to easily come to her. The taste of the salt water would bring her back in time to when as a child her family would visit Coney Island. She could almost smell the hot knishes she would eat on the beach and could almost see the airplanes pulling the Coppertone ads flapping behind them across the blue sky.

She had very good recall for the moments of her life that she wanted to remember. On her seventh birthday, her father had given her a beautiful long stem pink rose. She had put it into a bud vase and placed it on her bedroom night stand. When her grandmother had come to tuck her into bed that night Marissa had explained she would leave the rose there forever. She was upset and started to cry when her grandmother informed her that in about a week it would wither and die. Her grandmother wiped away her tears, took the rose out from the water and dried the stem on her apron. Handing the rose to Marissa she told her to look at the rose, to examine it closely. She was instructed to pay close attention to every detail of the petals. She was to make herself aware of the shape and scalloped edge of each one, of their velvety appearance, how tightly packed together they were, and to notice their different shadings of pink. Her grandmother wanted her to note the deep green color of the stem and how at the top of the stem where the bud had opened, it appeared to be in the shape of a star. She told Marissa to feel the soft velvety texture of each petal and the smooth sleekness of the stem, thorn free. She then told her to close her eyes and deeply inhale the fragrance of the flower, while continuing to touch it and picture in her mind what she had just seen. "That", she told Marissa, "is how you make a memory, and anytime you want to see the flower again, all you have to do is to close your eyes". And ever since then, for as long as Marissa could remember, she had been making memories that way of all her favorite moments in her life.

Marissa was visiting with her lifelong friend Rita and her husband George, at their beach house at the Hamptons this week. The Hamptons were quite different from Coney Island, the difference being hundreds of thousands of dollars for the cost of real estate. What a difference a few miles can make, she thought. George worked for a successful investment company and bought the house at the Hamptons "at the right time in the market" he would say. Rita and George knew the third anniversary of Marissa's father's death had just passed, and with her grandmother's death only two months earlier, she needed some time at the beach to relax and reflect. Marissa always had an open invitation, but this week Rita had insisted that she come out. Rita was aware of Marissa's struggle finding work during the past year. With all of the city's budget cuts, the schools were just not hiring new teachers, and this was her third year on the substitute teacher list. Marissa was fortunate to have two long term substitute positions offered to her this year but who knew what lay ahead for the next school year. Marissa seemed always to be struggling to pay her rent and get caught up with her bills. That was her biggest frustration in life, money. Why did it always come down to money, she would often think? She hated that money had such power and control over peoples' lives, the lack of having it, that is.

Marissa had been blessed with Rita's friendship since kindergarten. She always knew if she was in a pinch, financial or otherwise, Rita would always be there. Realizing her financial situation, George would never allow Marissa to pay for anything when they would go out, and the three went out together often. It didn't matter if it was a hot chocolate at a Village café or dinner at a 4- star restaurant, George always paid. He would never accept money from Marissa in any amount, no matter how small. More importantly, he always made Marissa feel as if he and Rita enjoyed her company so immensely that it made them happy to pay her share, for having her accompany them.

Marissa had not received any calls recently to sub, so when Rita asked her to come out to the island, there really was no reason not to. Rita knew how soothing large bodies of water were to Marissa. When they were younger, whenever Marissa had a problem, Rita walked with her and sat under the Brooklyn Bridge for hours. Marissa would look out at the water while listening to the hum of the traffic above. It always seemed to help her find solutions to her problems. The ocean had a similar effect for Marissa. She would lay on a towel for hours with her eyes closed, deeply breathing in the smell of the salt air while feeling the soothing warmth of the sun caress her body with an occasional gentle breeze blowing across her face. She delighted in running her fingers through the sand and listening to the seagulls. She was able to mentally bring herself back to a time when she was a little girl with her family enjoying a blissful day at the beach. It was then that she could bring back the two people she loved the most, her dad and her grandmother.

Marissa was becoming tired from the swim. Her body was telling her that it was time to quit for the day. As she started to swim, towards the shore, a piece of seaweed swept by her face. It brought back a sweet memory of when she was ten years old. She had been playing in the ocean when she almost swallowed a piece of seaweed. The taste of it disgusted her. She ran to the blanket where her family was sitting. As her grandmother wiped away her tears she said "You have to take the good with the bad Marissa. You love the ocean, but everything has a flaw, nothing is perfect." She really missed her grandmother, especially her words of wisdom she would preach, spoken so delightful in her broken English with her comforting Italian accent. When Marissa would lose hope that she would ever find true love, her grandmother would remind her of the Italian proverb, "The right man comes at the right time", and insisted that she be patient. In fact it was a few days before she had died, when her grandmother had told Marissa she would shortly meet the man of her dreams. Her grandmother said that she could feel it. Italian intuition was no laughing matter. There were always tales told in her family of predictions that had come to pass. And actually, for as long as Marissa could remember, her grandmother's intuitions had always come true.

As Marissa was coming out of the ocean, she noticed some boys hanging around the area where she had tossed her towel. Why teenagers would be up so early on a Saturday morning puzzled her. All the teenagers she knew would surely not be awake on a Saturday until noon. As she came closer to her towel she realized that these boys were not randomly walking the beach but were waiting for her. They appeared to be about eighteen years old, dressed in T- shirts and jeans, looking like normal teenagers, but it was the look on their faces that concerned Marissa. They were the kind of faces that if you were walking down the street and saw them you would veer away. When she looked into their eyes a cold chill ran through her. It was as if she was looking into the eyes of wild animals on a hunt. She stopped, trying to collect her thoughts on how she should react. She decided to turn left and just walk away from them. After all, she had her car key on her wrist, so all she needed to do was get to her car. However, when she turned left, the three teens ran ahead of her, blocking her path. Being from Brooklyn she knew how to put out a strong verbal attitude, even if it was under pretense. She asked them annoyingly to move aside. One of the boys said as he held out her towel, waving it towards her face, "Don't you want your towel?" She ignored the question and attempted to move forward, then to the left, then to the right. But with each of her moves they would change their direction to continually block her escape. At this point tons of thoughts were rushing through her mind. How many times had her parents and grandmother given her unwanted advice? Don't swim alone. Never go down alleys for a shortcut in the city. Girls should travel in pairs. Don't walk alone in isolated areas and always carry your mace and rape whistle. The list was endless. Rules she had been taught and ignored for years were rushing through her mind. "NO!" she thought, "Now was not the time to panic. Now was the time to strategize." She looked all around; there were no lights on in the houses nearby. Was no one awake? Would no one see what was happening and at least call the police, she thought. She remembered stories she had heard over the years, stories of horrible things that had happened in the streets of New York City, where people had witnessed a crime and yet ignored it. New Yorkers, the newspapers said, "didn't want to get involved". She started to think of ways she could protect herself. She would at least get one of them to fall to his knees by kicking him in the groin. She started to recall some moves George had taught her, after he and Rita had taken a few self defense classes. "If you thrust the heel of your palm into a man's throat, with all your might, he will fall and gasp for air", George had told her. She decided she would scratch at their eyes and continue digging her nails into their skin. She would also use the car key around her wrist to rip into their skin. Her heart was racing, she was scared to death but she was ready to defend herself.

They were walking around her like a pack of dogs, taunting her. It was then in the distance Marissa noticed a jogger. At the same time, so did the teens. As the jogger came closer she could see in the teens' facial expressions they were thinking he might cause them a problem. She was pretty good at reading facial expressions, especially when emotions heightened. With many of her relatives speaking fluent Italian, growing up she would get the gist of many conversations through facial expressions and body language alone. She wondered if the jogger would stop or just run by. She decided she would scream, for surely that would make him stop and help her. Just as she was about to scream she noticed the jogger had picked up his pace and was heading straight towards them. There was no need to scream, he was coming to help. He stopped just a few feet in front of her and said, "Good Morning", surprising her with a charming German accent. Then looking at her with the deepest blue eyes she had ever seen, he said "Any problem here?" She wondered if he was asking the question to give himself time to catch his breath. At that moment one of the teens pulled out a knife from the back pocket of his jeans and said "No problem that concerns you man, just keep on jogging". Marissa noticed the jogger had removed the windbreaker that was tied around his waist and nonchalantly wrapped it around his left arm. She had watched a show on TV, that gave suggestions on how to protect yourself if being attacked by a dog. The jogger was definitely going to help her, she thought, or why else would he make an attempt to protect his arm from the knife. "Why don't you boys go home, you look like you've had a long night", the jogger said. They laughed, as if with three to one odds, he hadn't a chance. The jogger then said "This is your last chance boys. I suggest you leave now". It was at this moment when Marissa noticed the logo on the T- shirt of the jogger. He was a Navy Seal, or at least he had been one, as the shirt was a bit faded and worn. Her eyes gazed up to the sky, "Thank you God!" she thought to herself. The jogger was right. These boys looked like they had been partying all night. She hadn't before noticed their eyes were all bloodshot. The jogger told Marissa to leave and go to her car. There was something in the tone of his voice that invoked trust. As she started to leave, one of the teens jumped in front of her. The jogger instantly put himself in between Marissa and the teenager. He placed himself so closely to her that she was right up against his back. Marissa could feel him breathing, she could smell his scent. His sent gave her a sense of comfort. She couldn't explain it, but she felt safe, even though surrounded by the three delinquents and a knife. He turned, looking down at her and whispered "Run now to your car, I will distract them long enough for you to get there". As she turned to run she noticed a police car pulling up with its lights on. The teens notice this also and took off running. "New Yorkers do care", she thought to herself, "Someone had called the police!"

Marissa was so emotionally exhausted from the ordeal that she felt her knees give way. The jogger swiftly caught her. She started to shake. It was an incontrollable kind of shaking. The jogger put his wind breaker over her shoulders and held her. She pressed her face against his chest and held onto him. He held her tightly. She didn't know how long she had stayed in his embrace as his scent was intoxicating to her. Strong, strange unknown feelings were running all through her body. She had never before been so close to a potentially personal dangerous situation. She was safe now;

she continued to repeat to herself silently. If it weren't for the jogger she didn't want to think about what possibly could have happened to her. The police quickly apprehended the boys and put the teens into the patrol car. One of the officers approached the two of them, with the jogger still holding Marissa, inquiring if they were all right. After answering some questions for his report, the two were told they were free to leave. Marissa emotionally calmed down and her body stopped shaking. It all had seemed so surreal to her. She composed herself and released herself from the joggers embrace. "My name is Hans. Are you all right to walk yourself to your car? Would you like me to escort you?" Hans asked. "Yea, I would appreciate that. My name is Marissa, I can't thank you enough for stopping to help me" she replied, but before she could add another word he quickly interjected, "I'm glad I was here to be able to be of assistance". Hans walked over to where the boys had dropped the towel, picked it up, shook out the sand and tossed it over his shoulder. As they walked to Marissa's car she realized how handsome the jogger was, and his German accent added to her attraction to him. He was a bit older than her and had a great build. She had noticed that while he was holding her, and knew from the situation they had just encountered that he was a man of character. That was something you could not learn about a man on match.com. Hans inquired if she was all right to drive herself home and Marissa assured him that she was.

Marissa didn't want their meeting to end as there was something about this man that intrigued her. She suggested that after his heroic gesture, the least she could do was to buy him breakfast. When she offered he replied, "I'm not in the habit of allowing ladies to purchase my meals but as all I carry with me when I jog is my phone and ID, I suppose this once I could make an exception." As she attempted to quickly put on her worn out jean shorts one of her toes got stuck in a frayed hole in the left leg. Almost falling, she grabbed onto the car door. "Shit, now is not the time to be looking like an idiot" she thought to herself, while hoping that Hans hadn't noticed. After trying to cover up the apparent fall, she quickly put on her white eyelet poncho and flip-flops, as he got into the passenger seat. She was glad she had cleaned the inside of her car the day before, otherwise Hans would have been stepping on Starbucks cups and sneakers, and sitting on old lesson plans, and her gym clothes that had been piled up on her passenger seat for weeks. As Hans got into the car, he turned and put her beach towel onto the back seat while saying, "Interesting towel, a super hero. If you had those gold cuffs you could have summoned her powers". Marissa said jokingly "Ah, but I did. Didn't you notice me clicking my wrists together before you arrived, summoning extra strength? And there you were!" As she turned the key in the ignition, she said to herself "Please God, this would NOT be the time for this car not to start".

She drove down the street to a little diner she knew opened early. She stopped there often when visiting her friends to bring back coffee for the late sleepers. During the week days when she entered, she was always welcomed with the smell of freshly brewed coffee, the smell of bacon wafting throughout the air and the sounds of laughter and busy conversations. During the week-ends, without the daily commuters, the aroma was the same but the setting was more tranquil. Marissa had always been a take-out customer, staying at the front counter before today, and had never noticed the photos that lined the walls of the diner. As she made her way to a booth in the back she passed several beautiful photographs of Greece, proudly displayed, some of its beautiful ruins and others of its lush gardens with granite archways and stone paths.

The brown leather seats of the booth were soft and broken in from the thousands whom had sat there before. The seat was as comfortable as an old favorite chair. They talked for hours about almost everything as the time passed quietly forward. She told him about her work, her family and her friends. She shared stories of growing up in Brooklyn with her mom, dad and grandmother. She mentioned her grandmothers' recent passing and how much she missed her. She commented on some of the little things she missed the most about her. She missed her frequent quotes of words of wisdom, the warm freshly baked cookies she had out when she knew Marissa would be visiting, and how her grandmother always worried that she wasn't eating enough. Marissa even missed the meals, she would insist she didn't need, which her grandmother had frozen and would have ready for Marissa to take home whenever she'd visit.

Marissa listened intently when Hans answered her questions and surprisingly he was equally as engaged when listening to her replies. She thought perhaps she might have talked a little bit too much about work or the lack of it. She enthusiastically spoke of her passion for Shakespearean literature, and listed some of her favorites. During the conversation they discovered they both lived and worked in Manhattan, loved jogging, working- out, reading, attending the theatre, and socializing with close friends. Hans talked about growing up in Austria, comparing the differences and similarities to that of growing up in New York City. He loved classical music, while she favored country music. When Hans told her he knew of no one from the city who enjoyed Country music, Marissa replied, "Well I am from the south, South Brooklyn that is". They both laughed, she was pleased he got her sense of humor.

Hans was not a fan of TV but admitted to watching the History and Discovery channels as he was enthralled with documentaries, while she loved romantic movies and admitted to checking out old movies from the library on rainy weekends. His recent favorite documentary was one he had seen on the ruins of the Mayan civilization, which coincidently Marissa had seen also. She mentioned some of her favorite old romantic movies, *An Affair to Remember*, *Love Actually* and *Bridget Jones Diary*, none of which he had ever heard of, no less seen. Hans could not even recall the last movie he had seen at a theatre. As he hadn't any interest in movies, Marissa leaned the discussion to the Mayan culture for awhile. She was glad to learn he was more interested in their architecture, sculptures, paintings and hieroglyphs than of their human sacrifices, as Marissa deplored violence and it troubled her to see it or discuss it.

The discussion then turned to the large number of museums located in New York City. Hans mentioned he had been to the roof top garden at the Metropolitan Museum recently, when his friend Wolfgang had come to town. The museum housed a very strange piece of art work at the moment, which consisted of a bamboo structure that Hans confessed to not liking nor understanding its purpose. Marissa mentioned she had been to several of the Lincoln Center Festival nights listening to music with friends. They had both heard of a current exhibit at the Whitney Museum. The heiress to the Whitney family had a large collection of modern American art that she was displaying at the museum. They decided they would go to see it together. Marissa was thrilled he had an appreciation for the arts. As if his good looks, charismatic personality and great physique were not enough to attract her, it seemed the more he talked and the more she learned about him, the more desirable he became. She was hoping the attraction was mutual.

Hans mentioned he worked in the financial investment field, whose office was located in lower Manhattan. He spoke with such excitement of the thrill of discovering extremely talented individuals with fresh and innovative ideas and with his utilizing his investment know- how, he could be instrumental in instituting a successful business venture. Marissa was fascinated by his view of the financial workings of investments. She had been on many dates before with men who worked in the financial district in Manhattan but Hans was the first one to use the words ethical, principles, moral obligation or fairness during their conversations. She wondered what breed of man this was before her. He certainly was not the cookie cut out breed of financial bankers she had previously met. Marissa was intrigued with his perspective on how the financial world worked yet she couldn't help but hate the power money held over peoples' lives. Her own personal finances were always in a state of disaster and she could not remember the last time she had her checkbook balanced, a fact however that she didn't divulge.

Marissa could not remember ever feeling this comfortable or attracted to a man. When she asked him if he had been a Navy Seal, he answered "Yes, but that was a long time ago", adding no other information. When previously talking with men who had served in the Armed Services, including her cousin Joey, she noticed they were uncomfortable discussing it as well. She believed the cost of freedom lay heavy on the minds of some soldiers who had served during wartime and decided to not ask any further questions on the subject.

They were at the diner for hours and yet never ran out of things to talk about. But with Marissa, having something to talk about was never a problem. When he asked her if he could buy her dinner tonight, she remembered she had plans with her friends. Marissa graciously declined, as she was not the kind of person to ditch her friends for a man. Although she knew if Rita could see Hans she would have demanded that Marissa say "YES"! She told him she was going back into the city on Sunday and suggested they meet for dinner then. He was agreeable to the idea since Hans also was heading back to the city on Sunday. He asked her if she had a favorite restaurant in the city. She thought for a minute. Since Hans had never actually mentioned the name of a company he worked for, she wondered if he had a steady job or perhaps he freelanced as an investment consultant. Marissa knew some successful financial investment advisors and when they played racket ball at the Y they always dressed head to toe in all the latest fashions, looking as if they had just stepped out a current issue of GQ.

There sat Hans in a beat up T shirt and gray cotton basketball shorts that had seen better days. His sneakers looked as if they had been with him since college. Not knowing his financial situation, she picked a great spaghetti place near her apartment. The food was cheap but good. She replied that she liked *Antonio's* in Little Italy. They decided they'd meet there at 8. When she offered him a ride back to where he was staying on the island, he told her he preferred to jog back. Marissa got into her car, put the key into the ignition and couldn't help but wonder if this was the man that her grandmother had spoken of. Was he "The right man at the right time"?

When arriving back to her friends' house, she told them of her ordeal. They were of course horrified. But then she began to tell them about Hans. They were both elated to see her seemingly genuinely interested in a man, as it had been too long to remember since she had last been on a date, and it wasn't for Rita's lack of trying. That night when some friends came over for a dinner party, Marissa again retold the events of her day. Of course they were more interested about Hans than any other part of the story. She was the only one in her group of friends still unattached. That of course didn't include Carter as he was in a category all his own. He was currently in a relationship, but with Carter some force of nature would always occur and in the end he would inevitably be left alone. But being Carter, he was never alone very long. As Carter would say, "Men are like buses, if you miss one, just wait and another one will show up in five minutes". Marissa had actually lost count on how many relationships Carter had been in since they met, and she would use the word relationships in the loosest sense of the word. She wished he could have made it to the party, because she was dying to tell him about Hans.

Day One, Saturday June 11th Christian Hans' story

Hans was preoccupied this morning, and with the lack of sleep he received last night it was hard for him to focus. He couldn't seem to shut off his mind last night long enough to fall asleep. It was normal for his mind to be racing with concerns surrounding current investment opportunities that he was involved with. But, more than that, he was upset with himself for not introducing himself to the woman in red, whom he had seen three times on the beach this week. One minute he would be thinking about marketing possibilities and the next his mind would wonder off envisioning the lovely creature he had seen emerging from the ocean on Monday. She was the most beautiful woman he had ever seen.

He was usually involved with several company investments at the same time, delegating specific assignments, but with him always remaining at the helm. His current endeavor involved an investment opportunity with two recent graduates from a university in upstate New York. The two had started a new company whose product line involved holograms, which intrigued Hans. He was considering how much capital to invest and whether or not to invite other investors. Or perhaps he would wager the risk and potential gain alone. He thought during his morning run he would mull over the situation as the meeting with the owners was scheduled for early Monday morning. Hans enjoyed his work immensely and derived much pleasure from helping failing companies rise and new companies develop. He wondered at times, if he put all of his time and effort into his work because of his passion for it or for the lack of passion in his life. He spent more hours at work than at either of his homes, and when he was at home he was usually at his desk working.

He opened his dresser drawer and grabbed his old Navy T shirt and gray cotton basketball shorts. He had to retrieve these items out of the trash on more than one occasion. His housekeeper, Rosa, would try to get rid of them often when she would find them in his hamper. She believed that it was the clothes that made the man, a fact she would repeat to him often when she would see him wearing them. He would try to explain to her that it wasn't the clothes that made the man but rather his character. After then trying to convince her that the old clothes were broken in and comfortable, he would inevitably give up. Too late however as that would be about the time she would start lecturing him in Spanish. Rosa felt that with all Hans' wealth it was downright foolish for him to look so shabby. It was at times like those when he wished he hadn't paid such close attention during his college Spanish classes. But, as he knew she meant well, he would just smile, shrug his shoulders, pretend he didn't understand and leave to run. In fact, Hans felt fortunate that he was fluent in Spanish. Otherwise, he might have missed out when the opportunity had presented itself for him to meet Rosa. It was seven years ago, when Hans had decided he wanted a weekend retreat from the hustle of the city, somewhere where the view of the sky wasn't blocked by buildings and where trees grew freely and not from holes cut out of the concrete sidewalks. He was touring an estate in the Hamptons that he was interested in purchasing. The lot size was big enough for privacy, the neighborhood houses were equally as spacious in their lot sizes allowing for a great deal of distance between them, and the flower gardens were rich and diverse reminding him of his home in Austria. The house was a bit larger than he needed, but if he held work related gatherings and charitable events there, he could write off some of its upkeep expenses at the end of each year, making him feel it to be more than a frivolous purchase. Hans and the realtor were in the library when the realtor received a call, excusing herself, to go into the hall to take it. Hans was reading titles on some of the books on a shelf when he overheard a conversation of two women speaking in Spanish from the adjoining den. As the door was ajar, Hans could barely see the women through the small opening. He could tell by her tone of voice, facial expressions and content that Rosa, despite her younger age, was the senior house-keeper and dissatisfied with the coworkers work ethic. Apparently, Rosa had noticed the top shelves, and the top of the fan blades had not been dusted. When the older woman replied that it didn't matter, as the house was being sold and she would soon be out of a job, Rosa started to give her a lecture. She told the older woman if she didn't have pride enough in herself to do the best job that she could, that she was earning a fair wage to do this job and she owed it to the employer to have it done right. Rosa reminded her that she wasn't out of a job yet, and needed to earn her pay.

When the realtor returned, they finished touring the estate. Hans had decided to purchase the estate, but aware of the games realtors play, he told her he'd be in touch. Hans then asked the realtor if he could speak with the head housekeeper as he had some questions for her with regard to the house. When Rosa entered the room, Hans noticed she was a tall, slender woman, who was probably younger than her weathered face made her appear. Hans shook Rosa's hand, gave her his business card and spoke to her only in Spanish, to the realtor's dismay. He told her she would soon learn that the estate had been sold, and he wanted her to know he would be its new owner. He wanted her to also know that he desired to keep her on in his employment if she would agree. He asked if she would call him to set up an appointment to discuss the capabilities of the other staff at the estate, and told her that she would be monetarily compensate her for both her time and exper-tise. After seven years, Hans had become use to her lecturing, and Rosa had become use to his pretending not to understand Spanish.

As the sun was almost rising, he hurried downstairs. When he walked into the pantry to retrieve some dog treats from the box on the shelf, Greta asked him if he was going to have breakfast. As he put the treats into his left pocket, he told her he would eat after his run.

When he had bought the house in the Hamptons, he decided he would need to hire a cook, as it was not like New York City where you could order and have delivered anything you could possibly want 24 hours a day.

During one of Hans' weekly telephone conversations with his mother, she had mentioned her dear friend Greta and her son Boris, who wanted to move to America. Greta's husband had recently died and she wanted to leave Austria and all of the memories it held for her. Hans had tried on numerous occasions to convince his mother to visit America as he was confident she would love it. He suggested if he hired Greta she could come to help settle her in, but she declined as usual refusing to even consider a vacation abroad. As always Hans' assured her his jet was on call at any time, if she should reconsider. Hans tried to go home to visit his mother at least three times a year, always mixing his visit with business. However during his visits he never seemed to be able to completely relax and let go of business. After hours of his mothers convincing, actually of her wearing him down, he decided to offer them jobs, Greta as his cook and her son, Boris, as his driver. The couple happily accepted and came to America on work visas. Hans did enjoy being able to speak German again to someone other than himself if he were to stub his toe.

This morning, Boris drove Hans to the same patch of beach as he had done many mornings. Hans enjoyed running along the beach this early in the morning, as he was usually its only visitor, with the exception of a frisky yellow lab that would occasionally run with him. Hans always brought some treats with him in case the lab was there. But, he wasn't there this morning. Most people had gym memberships or a gym in their homes at the Hamptons and only went to the beach in the afternoons for social gatherings or sun bathing. Although Hans had a full gym at his estate, he much preferred the ocean air and the give of the sand under his feet. His routine was always the same, he would run his allotted distance for the day, then call Boris to come and retrieve him. As he started his run, he had hopes of getting a glimpse of the lovely lady in red he had seen a few times at the beach earlier this week. He reveled in the thought that she might be there again today. Perhaps today he would muster the courage to say hello. Strange how bold and assertive he could be in a board room yet how hesitant he was at approaching her. He never had a problem talking with women before, so he was perplexed as to why she was any different. He had met enough women at charity events, art openings, dinner parties, elevators, and just by walking down the streets of Manhattan to keep him busy. He was never starved for the attention of a woman. He had a way with women and he used it often to his advantage, yet never taking advantage of any of them. No strings, no attachments, no relationships and no heartaches. Every woman he dated would know up front that he was not monogamous and that he had relations not relationships and each woman accepted this. He never stayed long enough with any one woman to have her think she would be the one to change him. He had built a wall so high and so thick around his heart that no woman was ever getting a chance to get into it again, or so he thought.

Hans' first sighting of his lady in red occurred on Monday as she was coming out of the ocean approaching the shore. The waves were crashing upon her calves, and she glistened from the sun reflecting off her golden tanned skin. His pace slowed as he was mesmerized by the mere sight of her. As she toweled off he could see that her body was toned and perfect and her face was classically beautiful. She possessed the kind of beauty that didn't need make up to cover any imperfection or to exaggerate any asset. Just as she was, in that one piece red bathing suit, she was perfect. The second time he had seen his lady in red was Tuesday. As he jogged by her, he noticed she had the most beautiful smile and seemed to be enjoying herself immensely in the simplest pleasure of playing fetch with a dog and a piece of driftwood. She was so "in the moment" with the dog that she hadn't noticed he had circled back to pass her a second time. When he heard her speaking to the dog, he noticed a distinctive heavy Brooklyn accent, which he found alluring. It was a nice departure from the fake smug socialite New York accents that he would hear from the women he had met from the Upper East Side of Manhattan. He recognized the red bandana collar and the brown patch over the dog's snout. It was the same dog he would run with. She was playing with the same dog that would keep Hans company during his run. The dog also seemed to have been bewildered by her spell as he hadn't noticed Hans approaching, either by sight or the smell of the treats. His last sighting of his lady in red, and his favorite one was on Thursday. She was lying on her back on her towel with her eyes closed, knees bent slightly, sifting the sand slowly through her fingers. He slowed his pace to almost a walk as he passed by her to take in her beauty. Her skin appeared velvety soft and appeared radiant from the reflection of what Hans assumed was sun screen. Her still wet one piece red bathing suit hugged tightly to her body. Her hair was tossed across her face, with strands separating only slightly, allowing but a mere glimpse of her face. Around her neck she wore a dainty cross on a delicate gold chain.

Today would be like any other, or so he thought. The sun was just starting to come up over the horizon when he arrived at the beach to start his run. He could see that it was going to be a beautiful day. He inserted his ear buds, touched his music app on his smart phone, found his jogging playlist and put his phone back into his pocket. He enjoyed listening to classical music while he ran as it helpd to clear his mind and decisions seemed to come more easily. He had run only a short distance when slightly ahead he saw the lovely woman in red with some teenage boys. It didn't appear to be a good situation. As their distance lessened, he could see that the boys were taunting her, circling her like a pack of wolves. He quickly called 911 and picked up his pace to reach her as fast as he could. He was no longer jogging. He was running full speed. As he approached the boys, he could tell by their stance and attitude that they were indeed intending on harming her. She was soaking wet, apparently having just come out of the ocean, as he could see the beads of water still dripping from her suit. After he spoke to one of the boys, another one pulled out a knife. Hans untied the windbreaker he had around his waist and wrapped it around his arm. He knew the material would give some protection from the knife if a fight ensued. Hans could see his lady in red was shaking, and not from the chill of being wet. He did his best to disengage the situation but just as he believed a fight was inevitable, the police arrived. Hans had never been this close to his lady in red before. She was even more ravishing up close. She had striking features, a real natural beauty, not overly made up like so many women he had met in the city. He didn't actually know why she was so captivating. Her bravery during the encounter was certainly admirable. When he had first approached her on the beach he could see by her stance that she had put herself in the position and mind set to fight.

It was obvious to him that she was shaken up. He caught her as she almost fell to her knees when the ordeal was over. She held onto him for support and he seized the opportunity to hold onto her tightly. While holding her he could smell the slightest of fragrance in her hair. The ocean had washed out most of its fragrance, but still lingered was a light scent of strawberries. He was glad she had taken a long time to compose herself as he was savoring every minute he had to hold onto her.

As Hans walked Marissa to her car, he was trying to figure out how he could tactfully ask for her phone number. It was without a doubt the strangest of first meetings, but he didn't want it to be their last. What if the incident caused her to stop coming to the beach? He would then lose any chance of seeing her again. He decided if he was to ask her for her number it would make it seem as if he was taking advantage of the situation. When he looked at her car, glancing at her license plate number, he realized he could memorize it, make a few calls, find out her address and hope for a chance meeting if he were to frequent some local stores in her area. Slightly borderline stalker, he thought, but desperate times require desperate measures. So when Marissa him invited him to breakfast he was both surprised and relieved.

While getting into the passenger seat, he noticed Marissa had caught her toe in her shorts. He thought she looked adorable as she tried to cover up her apparent near miss fall. Here he was, just feet away from the woman he had been fantasying about for a week. With her eyes on the road he could easily look at her, taking in every detail, the dimple on the right side of her mouth when she smiled, the small scar on her left knee, the small beauty mark on the top of her right ear. It was hard not to stare. He loved the way she dressed, so carefree. Her polka dotted flip flops were definitely not the Milano Blahniks that the women he usually dated wore. Her cut off jeans were just short enough to be provocative, yet still being decent as she wore a bathing suit underneath. The interior of her car was understandably worn as it was an older model, but it was impeccably clean. The exterior had dings and chips in the paint but as she lived in the city that was inevitable. Its paint job wasn't very old as the color was still a bold bright red, which was set off nicely by the chrome that shined as if it had been recently polished. She broke all the myths he had heard about women drivers in America as she shifted her 5-speed with smoothness and ease. As she pulled into the parking lot of the diner, Hans was impressed with how well she squeezed her bug into a spot he had thought was too small.

The diner she had picked was perfect. It was both quiet so they could hear each other without distractions and had very few customers so they did not have to hurry their stay. It had been a long time since he was in a restaurant without linen table cloths, waiters in white shirts and black ties, and a wine list. It was enjoyable to be left alone to talk without waiters at your table constantly attempting to predict your every need. It was a nice change of pace.

During their breakfast he found himself talking with her for hours. That wasn't like him, as he never opened up about himself. What was it about her that made him want her to know him? He did not know, but he was compelled to learn why. As he was getting to know her, her personality deepened his attraction to her. While sitting at the booth Marissa's hair had dried naturally. With no primping, it was absolutely lovely with long loose curls framing her face. He could see that she wasn't wearing any makeup and that she actually had no need of it. The mere sound of her voice was extremely pleasing to him. He found the enunciation of her Brooklyn accent to be as captivating to him as was her beauty. Hans was thrilled that she possessed substance and not merely beauty, as she was fascinating to listen to. He never tired of any topic she discussed. She never seemed to have to search for a topic. As soon as one was exhausted she would easily segue to the next.

He had wanted to go to the Whitney Museum to see their new exhibit. When Marissa brought up the subject, he thought it would be perfect to ask her to accompany him to see it. She had been the first woman he had dated that actually watched documentaries and could discuss one with him. He wished he had seen at least one of the movies she had mentioned, but unfortunately he was not a movie enthusiast. As he listened to her talk about the romantic movies she had seen, he could sense that she was a true romantic believing in happy endings, and not a realist as himself. However, he thought, perhaps she could make a believer out of him. A full lunar eclipse was to occur in four days; and according to the radio station his driver was listening to this morning, lunar eclipses could speed up events and things that started could take on added significance. He did not believe in astrology, but who knows, he thought, perhaps the celestial bodies were in his favor.

When they left the restaurant, Hans called Boris to pick him up. Upon arriving back to his house Greta was about to start his breakfast. "Long run today Hans?" she asked. He told her he had already eaten and went upstairs to shower. After showering Hans walked into his closet to get dressed. As he surveyed the clothing on the shelves and on the hangers he decided he needed to go into the city a day earlier prior to his date to go shopping.

From the conversation with Marissa he learned that she refused to date men who had any substantial amount of money. It appeared that every man she had dated who had been well off had been an egocentric, conceited, egotist who expected a woman to be subservient and totally absorbed in his life, without any regard of her own self worth. Marissa had explained that her friend's husband George had been the only exception to this rule. He had kept the same values he possessed growing up in Brooklyn; he had no pretenses as his success had not changed him. It appeared that Rita had set up Marissa with many colleagues of George's and each ended in disaster. All the men had been handsome and well educated, but also shared another trait. They all believed because they were such a good catches financially that any woman, including Marissa, would be thrilled to sleep with them. Furthermore, they believed any woman to turn down their offer would be unintelligent. She had left her handprint on enough faces of that category of men to write them off her list as potential future dates. And as she put it, "She would never give any of them the satisfaction of sleeping with them".

So Hans, whose closet was full of handmade suits and shirts, the finest of silk ties, and a closet floor with rows of Italian hand -made shoes, had to purchase some off –the- rack clothing. He needed Marissa to believe he was not in that category of men. He was concerned if she found out he possessed a substantial amount of wealth before she got to know him, that she would never allow herself to know the real person that he was. And for some reason, which he didn't quite understand himself, he desired her to get to know the real him. During the summer months, traffic to and from the city was always at a standstill so Hans decided to call his pilot to ready his helicopter. So there he was on a Saturday afternoon, with his pilot heading for the city.

For Christmas and birthdays Hans always sent checks to his family members, as he hated shopping. Checks were easier to send than actually going shopping, he believed. It was on the rarest of occasions that he would even venture onto the internet to purchase something. For in actuality, he had people to do those tasks for him. Marissa unknowingly possessed such a mysterious power over him that here he was shopping on a busy Saturday afternoon in the city, in the midst of a crowded department store. He was pleased he had decided on Bloomingdales, for to his good fortune the men's department had a clerk, Stephan, who possessed both taste and style and a speed at assembling outfits with such ease which enabled Hans to have a quick departure from the store. All that was required of Hans was to explain that he didn't want to try anything on, that he wanted his stay as short as humanly possible and to give Stephan his sizes. It was hard for him to believe that in the time it would have taken him to pick out one ensemble that Stephan had picked out five suits with coordinating ties, handkerchiefs, shirts and shoes plus several casual outfits piled high on the counter and ready to check out. Hans decided if he needed any further items he would ask his secretary Mrs. Hobes if perhaps she wouldn't mind going online and ordering them for him. He was certain that she would be agreeable to the idea. She had been with him for years and although they had a strictly professional relationship, he knew she would help him, as she always had.

DAY TWO

Day Two, Sunday, June 12th Marissa's Story

On her ride back into the city Marissa started to think about what she should wear for her date with Hans. She was becoming frustrated with the possibilities. She decided to call Carter to ask him to meet her at her apartment to help her pick out an outfit. She told him she had just passed Nassau County and as there was no traffic, she would be home within the hour. Carter was her "go to guy" in this department, as he had better taste in fashion than anyone else she knew. He assured her he would be delighted to come over, as he was dying to hear all about this new man in her life. As she drove over the Brooklyn Bridge she called him to let him know she'd be home in five minutes. Parking was always a challenge in the city, but luckily with a VW bug she didn't need a lot of space to park. And with the car alarm her cousin Joey had installed, she never needed to worry that it would be stolen, as he had connected such a high pitch shrill that was actually painful to the ears.

Carter was there sitting on her stoop waiting with anticipation as she arrived; he wanted her to tell him everything. Who was this man she was going to dinner with and when and where the heck did she meet him? He could not believe that with only one missed dinner party he could be so far behind in the status of her social life? As they walked up the three flights of stairs, he bombarded her with question after question, wanting to know every detail and not wanting to wait until they got to her apartment for the answers. She insisted he wait, not wanting to give out any details per chance the prying neighbors might be within ear shot. When they reached her apartment she told him of her chance meeting with Hans and how attracted she was to him. Carter was fanning himself with his hand saying, "God this is such a hot story, it sounds like a Jackie Collins novel. I knew it was only a matter of time until my Ice Princess melted. Now tell me more about his hot sweaty body touching yours and his marvelous physique". Marissa ignored his further inquires and he followed her into her bedroom.

He looked through her closet picking several different selections. "It depends", he said, "Do you want to look sexy, flirty, or do you want to get laid?" Carter knew Marissa was still a virgin but when picking out outfits for her he always added that choice to his repertoire. "I want to take his breath away", she replied. Carter picked a cotton floral print strapless summer dress. The material was thick enough that she didn't need a bra, yet sexy enough that the slightest hint of her nipples would be apparent. He added a midriff length, red cotton cardigan with short sleeves to pull out the red in the tiniest of the flowers on the dress. He chose green sling back leather sandals, with a small heel to pull out the color of the leaves and added a small red clutch. Carter stayed while she got ready, helping her with her makeup and hair, but mostly for moral support. He put up her hair in a twist with wisps of hair draping down the back of her neck. The wispy bangs was a really sexy look on her. "No hairspray!" she demanded. She wanted her hair to be soft in case Hans put his hands through it. She sprayed on her usual cologne *Obsession*. Carter could not understand that with the thousands of scents to choose from, she always purchased and wore only *Obsession*. "It always makes me feel sexy" she replied. Carter could not understand why she needed to feel sexy if she never had sex; he supposed it was a girl thing.

It was 7: 30 pm and she was ready to go. Little Italy was only a few blocks from her apartment in Chinatown so she decided she would walk to the restaurant. Carter recommended that she be a little late. "Make him wait" he said. "It always entices men. The anticipation will make him wild, because there is always the slight chance that you could get stood up". As Carter knew how men's minds worked she listened to him and didn't leave the apartment till 7: 55 pm. Carter wanted to walk with her to steal a look from the window of *Antonio's* to see the man who had seemed to have swept Marissa off her feet.

She told Carter she wasn't so sure about the choice of dress he had picked for her. Marissa was always second guessing herself and Carter never understood why; as she always looked great, even in a pair of old jeans and a torn beat up T- shirt. Carter assured her that florals were "in" this year and that she looked stunning. "I can't take my eyes off you, and I'm gay, so imagine what effect you will have on him", Carter said trying to make her more confident. She could feel her heart racing as she neared the restaurant. Upon looking inside the window Marissa said, "He is the one in the back table with the silver box with the red ribbon". Carter said "Nice touch, flowers. To give a girl flowers in public is a powerful gesture. If you give flowers to her at her apartment no one sees it, but when you give them to her in public you are telling everyone that this lady is someone special to you." Marissa asked, "You can tell all that from a flower"? Carter said," Go get him Tigress and let me know how the night turns out. Call me anytime, wake me up. I want to hear all about this night".

When she entered the restaurant Hans noticed her entrance immediately and stood up. He pulled out her chair for her to sit.

When she was seated he picked up the silver box from the table and handed it to her. "This is for you. I hope you like them." Marissa opened the box and smiled. They were the most beautiful flowers she had ever seen. No one had ever given her orchids before; these were her first. There was one stem with eight orchids on it nestled in a bed of bright green ferns. The petals were white with light lavender streaks running through them. In the most inner part of the orchids was exposed the richest, deepest color purple. She lifted the box to smell their fragrance, "Umm, they smell like raspberries and cream. I never knew orchids smelled so delicious. It was so sweet of you, thank you". Hans replied "I wanted to give you a flower and thought a rose too common for someone as amazing as you." He was even more handsome than she had recalled. And his accent, well that was the cherry on the sundae to just how much of a turn on he was!

He wore a pin stripped tailored gray suit, pink shirt, lavender tie and a paisley print kerchief in his breast pocket. He cleans up well, she thought. They both ordered spaghetti with meat balls, the house specialty, and shared a bottle of Chianti. They split a piece of rum cake for dessert. The dinner couldn't have been more perfect. The conversation flowed as easily as the Chianti.

Hans was absolutely wonderful; she was becoming more captivated by him as the night went on. The wine was starting to affect her so she stopped after the third glass. When the bill came she noticed he had over tipped, which was a big plus on his side. Having been a waitress prior to teaching, she knew how hard it was to live on tips. She believed that when you received above average service it was nice to show it. So "point one Hans", she said to herself. Actually, if there were a point system in place, he would have already been well off the chart. When dinner was over, Hans asked Marissa what she would like to do. "I love walking in the city at night. Do you want to take a walk?" she asked.

They walked for miles and talked for hours. She was learning so much about him. He was born in Vienna, Austria, where his mother still lived. He came to America when he was nineteen to start a new life. He attended college as a business major, became an American citizen, and then joined the Navy when he was twenty-three. While in the Navy he tried out for and was selected to become a Navy Seal. When his enlistment contract had ended, he was honorably discharged and consequently started his career as a financial investment consultant. He has three true friends, two of whom he met in the Navy and one a childhood friend from Austria. She mentioned to him how she had always wanted to be a teacher and that she loved working in the city. She knew some teachers who didn't want to work in some of the schools where she had but she saw those assignments as challenging. In the three years she had worked as a substitute teacher in the city school district she never had any serious problems with a student.

She again spoke of her grandmother and dad, fondly recalling stories of them. She remarked that she and her mother were not as close as she would have liked. She never quite understood what the distance was between them. But there was something there that hindered the two from forming the kind of relationship she would have liked. She loved her mother but had never received the same affection or reassurance that she had constantly been given by her grandmother and dad. It was her grandmother who had been more of a mother to her, she believed. Marissa was impressed how intently Hans appeared to be listening to her.

Marissa hadn't really been paying attention to where they were walking, but when she looked up at a street sign, she realized they were two streets from her apartment. She then veered them in the direction of her apartment. Upon arriving in front of her doorway she asked, "Do you want to come up? I have a bottle of wine chilling". Hans smiled and said he would love to see where she lived. Entering her apartment he looked around noticing the eclectic style of it. He smiled, a cute boyish kind of smile, and commented that her apartment reflected her personality perfectly. He walked over to the rocking chair near the fireplace admiring the carvings of the grape vines into the headrest, saying it was his favorite piece in her living room. Marissa told him it had been her grandmother's rocker that she had brought with her when she moved to America from Sicily.

Hans handed Marissa the silver box he had been carrying since they had left the restaurant and she went into the kitchen to put the orchids in some water. She was thankful that it wasn't a bouquet of flowers as she couldn't recall where her large vase was. She did have one slim, 12 inch tall, clear glass vase that would be perfect for the orchids and ferns, in the cabinet over the stove. She returned to the living room with the vase and placed it on the fireplace mantle. She went back into the kitchen to retrieve the wine and two glasses. When she returned she realized that Hans had put on a CD. He had picked the only CD that wasn't Country from the pile on the table, Marianas Trench. She had felt compelled to purchase it after hearing the lyrics to the song "Beside You" at Rita's house for she believed it explained exactly how she wanted a man to feel about her.

They sat on the love seat, as her apartment was too small for a full couch, and drank their wine. Hans put down his glass and gazed into Marissa's eyes. He had the most beautiful blue eyes she had ever seen and when she looked into them she felt as if he could see right down to her soul. When he reached over and kissed her, she felt her heart stop. Their first kiss could not have been more perfect. He continued to kiss her, softly at first and then with more intensity. As he drew her nearer she could feel her heart racing, and for the first time she felt a titillating feeling in an area that had never been awaken by a man's kiss before. Her body was aching with desire. She had never gone pass merely making out with a man before as their kisses had never had this powerful affect on her. As he stoked her bare arm with the gentlest of touch she could feel her body's desire for him grow. "Yes", she told herself "he is going to be my FIRST". After all these years of remaining a virgin, she realized that it wasn't because she was a good Catholic girl. It was because she had never met a man before who released within her sensations of such intensity that their desire to be gratified was too overwhelming to ignore. Had it been like this with any other man, she would never have been able to resist. She decided she needed to tell him that she was a virgin. She wanted to make sure he would be gentle, although she knew innately that he would be. She released herself from his embrace for a moment and said, "There is something I need to tell you". He asked her if there was a problem. She said "I have never been "with" a man before. I realize I am twenty-six and it's probably an oddity, but it's just that no one until you has made me feel that I had wanted to". As she was saying the words she realized how lame it sounded, "twenty-six and still a virgin". He said, "Are you asking me to make love to you"? She replied in almost a whisper, "Yes". Marissa instantly became nervous and sensed Hans could feel the tension in her body. He again kissed her gently as he had at first and her body relaxed. Then the kisses became longer exchanges of pleasure. She had never known that kissing held the key to unlocking within her secret pleasures of which she was unaware. In her heightened state of excitement she couldn't recall exactly how they got to her bedroom.

While on her bed he undressed her slowly, seemingly savoring the removal of each garment. With the removal of her dress, she was happy she had chosen to wear the red silk bikini panties which she had recently purchased. For an instant she recalled the *big mother underwear* scene from *Bridget Jones Dairy* and was happy to not be repeating it. She lay there thinking for a moment how she no longer needed to recall that movie while fantasizing about Colin Firth. For now she had a man of her very own to pleasure her. No fantasizing needed, he was real. He kissed and caressed every inch of her skin. It was so erotic as he undressed her that she wished she had worn more clothing. He paid such attention to kissing and pleasuring her body that she lost track of time and of reality. As she lay naked on her bed she marveled how she was not cold. She was never able to walk around her apartment naked without being chilled, either due to drafts in the winter or the air conditioning in the summer. Yet there she lay naked on her bed, feeling as hot as if she was sitting in front of a raging fire. With each touch of his hands, lips and tongue she became increasingly more excited and equally as increasingly aware she was not going to be needing the K Y jelly that sat in her dresser drawer, which Rita had tucked in her Christmas stocking last year "just in case". Her body had never experienced this reaction to a man before, it was as if a faucet had opened and the waters had been set free.

Hans kissed her neck, her shoulders, her breast, her nipples and her abdomen staying at each destination for an extended amount of time. When his lips started kissing her thighs and his hand slipped between them, she thought perhaps she knew what his next move might be. She had heard stories of oral pleasures from some close friends, and stories of its distaste from friends whom just tolerated it from their lovers. But now she believed she would be experiencing it first-hand. Within seconds she realized she was correct on knowing the intention of his destination. His lips had now kissed a place where no man had gone before. His lips, tongue, breath, and fingers all played harmoniously to bring her pleasures she never knew existed, nor could have ever imagined possible. She felt like she should be responding, doing something to pleasure him but she was lost in her own ecstasy taking in every pleasurable sensation that he gave her, responding to his every touch. She could feel her toes curling and realized her fingers were clutching the sheets and thinking, this only happens in movies. But before she could even dwell on that thought she had the most intense string of unimaginable orgasms of her life. She could actually hear herself scream. She had heard over cocktails her friends discuss the topic of multiple orgasms. Those who had experienced, them relishing in the retelling of their marvelous lovers and the disbelievers, who had never experienced them had called them merely myths and dismissed their existence. Marissa now knew for a fact they existed. The experience left her totally exhilarated and exhausted. And then instantly, she felt embarrassed.

She realized this event was all about her. They did not have sexual intercourse, nor had he been sexually gratified. He had done all the work with her as the lucky recipient. As he came up to her, she didn't know what to say. Hans kissed her cheek and put his arm under her head and drew her near to him. She laid her head just under his left shoulder on his chest; where there seemed to be the perfect little nook for her head to rest. She could not remember ever being this relaxed or comfortable in her whole life. She deeply inhaled his scent, loving how he smelled. She wanted to make a memory. She could feel herself falling asleep. Was it too much wine, was it the orgasms? Was it the mixture of the two? She couldn't keep her eyes open. As she fought to keep awake, she glanced down and realized he had never undressed. The only items he had removed were his jacket, tie and shoes. She wondered, "If this was the most incredible experience of my life, how much more amazing will it be when we have sexual intercourse?"And with that thought she drifted into the deepest sleep she had ever known.

Day Two, Sunday, June 12th Hans' story

That night getting ready for his date, Hans found himself becoming nervous which was totally out of character. This was not like other dates when he would take a woman out and innately know he would end up in bed with her. This fact was not because of his wealth; it was that he had had a way with women, which he discovered he possessed during his teenage years. There was something about him women were attracted to, although he never knew exactly what it was. He knew he was handsome, as he was told this time and time again. He worked out quite frequently, so his body was always toned. But he also possessed a genuine appreciation for women and was always up front with them, never leading them on. Ever since he had his heart broken at the age of nineteen, he had never had nor wanted another serious relationship. Before he would go out with a woman, he always let her know up front that he was not looking for a relationship. So being nervous for a first date was not like him. But then again he had never met a woman like Marissa. He knew she was different as she stirred within him feelings that he was unable to identify. When he was near her he was strangely nervous and comfortable simultaneously. He was glad she had picked a restaurant in Little Italy, as there was little chance of running into someone he might know. He didn't want her to think he had lied to her if someone should come up to him and greet him with "Hi Christian". In actuality, Hans was his name, his middle name. As Christian was his father's name as well, everyone in his family called him Hans. But here in the States everyone knew him as Christian. When he had started his new life in America, he started with a new name; it was his way of starting over.

He stopped at a florist on the way to the restaurant to buy Marissa a flower. He didn't want a rose, as it seemed too cliché. He wanted something special, something exceptional, more like her. He asked the florist for the most unique flower he had in his shop. The florist brought him over to a section with orchids, explaining they were a strong resilient flower with the ability to adapt to its environment. He explained they didn't live in dirt, instead they attached their roots to the bark of trees, receiving all the nutrients they need from it. He further explained how orchids loved basking in the sunshine, so they only attach themselves to the highest part of the trees. Hans thought it would be the perfect flower for Marissa, as it seemed to be as unique as she was. When Hans inquired about their fragrance he was told some had the scents of fruits. Hans was hoping they had one that smelled of strawberries like Marissa's hair, but the closest the florist had was one with the scent of raspberries. The florist gave Hans its botanical name Paphiopedilum Lynleigh Koopowitz. They were placed in a rectangular silver box, one stem with eight orchids and two buds cushioned in a thick layering of ferns. The florist gently wrapped the orchids with beautifully glittered silver tissue paper. When asking Hans the color of ribbon he wanted affixed to the box he said without hesitation, "Red".

Hans took a cab to the restaurant, as he didn't want Marissa to see him with his driver. When Hans entered the restaurant, he could feel his heart beat begin to quicken. It had been a week since he had his first glimpse of Marissa, and here he was finally on a date with her. He wanted every detail of the night to be perfect. He arrived early at the restaurant to get a good table. Hans tipped the maître d' and asked him for a quiet table in the back of the restaurant. He sat at the table awaiting Marissa's arrival with the same effervescent anticipation of a child's awaiting the arrival of Santa on Christmas Eve. When she arrived he could hardly contain his excitement. She looked so radiant and had such strikingly beautiful features. She had worn her hair up exposing her neck, which Hans found extremely enticing. Hans was glad she wore only the hint of make- up, as he thought she needed none at all.

Again they spent hours talking, with Marissa doing most of it. It fascinated him how she never ran out of topics to talk about. It amazed him even more how he never grew tired of listening about anything she said. He found her Brooklyn accent charming and never tired of hearing the sound of her voice. At one point during their conversation, she was explaining the struggle some students had trying to pass the New York State Regents exams, which in itself would be a monotonous subject. However, she explained it with such passion in her voice and with such conviction, that he was actually fully engaged in the conversation.

When dinner was over Marissa had suggested a walk. Hans would go anywhere she had suggested, as he only wanted to be with her and it didn't matter where. After walking for what seemed hours they arrived at her apartment. He had promised himself prior to leaving his apartment, that at the end of the date, he would kiss her good night and politely leave, Marissa was different and he wanted to take this slow. But when Marissa mentioned she had chilled a bottle of wine for them, he felt she might be offended if he declined. And if the truth be told, he did want to go up to her apartment. After a glass of wine, and sitting close to her for about 20 minutes, he could not control himself any longer. The urge to kiss her overcame him. He leaned in and kissed her softly. He felt her respond with delight so he kissed her longer, and then harder. He brought her in closer to himself. He had to stop, for a moment, as he wanted to control himself. He moved away but still had the urge to touch her. He gently caressed her exposed arm. He could not believe that the mere touch of her bare skin excited him so. When she asked him to make love to her he could not refuse. He had hoped it would occur but had never imagined it would be that night. He gently made love to every inch of her body. With each touch he paid such close attention to every move of her body, every muscle twitch, and every sound she made, no matter how slight. He mentally made a map of what seemed to excite her most. Hans knew what he wanted to do, and where he wanted to go on her body, but wasn't sure if Marissa would allow him. As he started to kiss her thighs, nearing his desired destination, he paid even closer attention to her responses, hoping to sense the approval he needed to continue. He did not want to do anything that would make Marissa uncomfortable; he needed to listen to her body for consent. He could tell by the pace of her breaths, the ever so slight sounds she made, and the movements of her body that he would be a welcomed guest to the one organ on her body that's only designed function was for pleasure. An organ that although a mystery to many men, was one which Hans was well acquainted. He was thrilled that she seemed to be so engaged in the moment that she let herself totally accept every bit of pleasure she was receiving. He lost all sense of time, focusing totally on giving Marissa pleasure. As he felt her body tense, he noticed she was also clenching the sheets. He knew she would be climaxing soon. When she came to orgasm, he felt a rush of pleasure run through him. He had always enjoyed pleasing women, but this time the intensity of the pleasure was heightened to a degree that he had never experienced before, he felt totally selfless. He came up to her and held her tightly. He wanted her to relax and savor what she had experienced, especially since it was her first time being with a man. He held her close to his chest as she drifted off to sleep. This was so unlike Hans; he never slept over with his dates. Had this been any other woman he would have had sex, then after having stayed a respectable amount of time left her apartment. But this was not any other woman, this was Marissa. He had decided when she had asked him to make love to her that he would, but that it wouldn't include sexual intercourse. He wanted her to be sure she wanted to give up her virginity to him. If she had too much wine and it had affected her decision, it was one that could not have been reversed. As he held Marissa, he had a feeling of comfort that was extremely relaxing and he found himself falling asleep. The last thought he had before drifting off was that he hoped Marissa wouldn't regret this evening when she awoke in the morning. Because for Hans, he could not remember ever having a better time with any other woman, ever.

DAY THREE

Day Three, Monday, June 13th Marissa's day

When she awoke in the morning Hans was not in her bed. Marissa got up, put on her robe and looked around the apartment for him. He was nowhere to be found. She looked for a note; surely he would have written one. She frantically looked in every possible place where one could be left, the night stand, the bathroom mirror, the coffee table, her desk, the refrigerator door, but nothing. When she went to make herself a pot of coffee is when she saw it. There it was, a pink post-it note that he had stuck to the kitchen faucet. It read "Call me" and had his phone number written under it.

She quickly called Carter, as he was the expert in this field and she needed for him to come over now. Carter arrived to her apartment in record time, as he wanted to hear every intimate detail. Of course she wouldn't divulge the details, but what she did tell him was she had the most amazing orgasms of her life, but that she was still a virgin. Carter looked confused, he asked "Did you come when he was dry humping you"? She quickly replied, "God, no!" He then asked, "You mean he went down on you?" She lowered her head, and in a faint voice responded, "Yes". Carter said, "And did I hear you correctly? Did you say orgasms, inferring to more than one?" She again answered in a faint whisper, "Yes". "That a boy, he went down on you!" said Carter. "I hear that is a very important aspect of love making in the straight society. Girls seem to love it, disgusting visual for me however. So why aren't you happy, you have finally been to bed with a man, and had a multi orgasmic experience, an exceptional lover it would seem, so why do you look distressed? You should be beaming with delight!" She explained how she didn't reciprocate, she merely allowed him to please her, with no gratification given to him at all. Carter assured her to no end that if Hans had wanted to do more he would have. She showed Carter the pink post-it note. Carter laughingly said, "Usually guys that write on pink post it notes don't enjoy going down on women." She immediately said, "Very funny Carter, it's probably all he could find in the apartment to write on." Carter told her she should call him and make arrangements to meet again immediately. She told him she had no intention of calling him, as she was too embarrassed that she hadn't reciprocated. Carter told her straight out she was nuts and that she should call him that day, that hour, that minute. But she didn't that day and she didn't know if she ever could.

Day Three, Monday, June 13th Hans' Story

As his overnight stay at Marissa's was both unplanned and unexpected Hans had not set the alarm on his phone. He was fortunate when the sun shone onto his eyes from a slight opening of her bedroom curtain and awoken him. He remembered he had an 8:30 am meeting with the inventors of the hologram product line. He instantly looked at her night stand clock and was relieved when it said 6:10 am, as it meant he hadn't overslept. He got up with as little movement as possible, not wanting to disturb

Marissa. This was after all her summer vacation; she should get to sleep in. Hans was amazed at how rested he felt. He couldn't remember the last time he had slept so well. He went into the living room to retrieve his tie, jacket and shoes as quietly as possible. He looked for paper to write Marissa a note. He didn't want to open her desk drawer or snoop around her things while looking for paper. He then noticed a package of pink post it notes and a pen on top of her phone book, on the bottom shelf of her bookshelf in the living room. There was not a lot of room on the post it note so he only wrote "Call me" and added his number. He wanted to place it somewhere in the apartment where she would be sure to see it when she awoke. He looked around her apartment for the perfect place. He decided to put it on the kitchen faucet. Every American makes coffee when they awaken, he thought, surely she would find it there. He quietly turned the knob lock on the inside of the door and closed the door tightly, checking to make sure it locked behind him. On the way down the stairs, he called Boris to come pick him up.

When he arrived back at his apartment he ran on the treadmill before taking a shower. As he ran, visions of the evening he had spent with Marissa filled his head and he enjoyed recalling every moment. He hoped she would call him later in the day, as he had forgotten to ask for her number. But he did have her address and her apartment number so he wasn't totally without being able to contact her.

When Mrs. Hobes arrived at the office Hans was already at his desk working. This surprised her, for in the 10 yrs she had worked with him, he had never arrived before her. Every Monday she greeted him saying "Good morning Hans, how was your weekend?" and each Monday he would respond, "Fine, Mrs. Hobes, do you have the "such and such" file done yet?" This Monday was different. When she greeted him with her usual question, he responded, "Wonderful. Isn't it a lovely day? The sun is shining so brightly and the city looks magnificent today. Do you have the file ready for the hologram investment meeting?" She knew something was very different. There was a sparkle in his eyes, and a cheerier tone in his voice than usual. When she handed him his usual coffee and Danish he had a peculiar smile. She could hear him humming to himself as he worked. This was not like him; something must have happened over the weekend. Then it dawned on her, he must have met someone special. The mere thought of that possibility made her smile. He was such a sweet man, but he worked way too many hours for such a young man. In all the years she had known him he never had a girlfriend. Ladies, oh yes, there were many ladies, but not one girlfriend. A man that good looking never wants for female companionship, she knew.

Hans called Mrs. Hobes into his office around 10 am. "How would you feel about shopping for some casual attire for me on the internet"? Mrs. Hobes replied, "Excuse me?" He explained he needed a pair of sneakers, some T-shirts and jogging shorts. He told her he had gone shopping on Saturday but had forgotten to get sneakers and some running attire. He explained that he wanted nothing too expensive, only average costing items. Now she KNEW something happened this past weekend, Hans never went shopping. And for him to be shopping on a busy Saturday afternoon, she knew something was definitely going on. In all the years she worked for him she had never denied him a request. Over the years she became very fond of him and doted on him like a son. She would make sure he never skipped lunch; she made appointments for him to have a massage when she could see he was overworked, and she refused to leave before he did to ensure he never left later than 9pm. So she said yes of his request for her to shop.

Hans gave Mrs. Hobes a list of some items, including his sizes, and she went back to her office. In about an hour she returned to his office announcing the list had been purchased and was being shipped over night to his Manhattan apartment. He thanked her and she assured him it was nothing and went back to work, secretly wishing she could find out the reason for this sudden change in his behavior. But inquiring about his personal life was not the relationship they had. They were cordial and respectful of each other but they never pried into each others' private lives.

On his drive home from work, Hans was surprised that Marissa had not called. When he arrived at his apartment, he went through his mail, worked out, ordered some take-out food to be delivered and spent the night going over figures for his new investments. Pretty much, the same routine as always, but keeping his phone by his side as he didn't want to miss a call from Marissa. When he went to bed around midnight, he couldn't help but wonder why she hadn't contacted him. He fell asleep that night, not thinking about work but counting all the reasons why Marissa wouldn't have wanted to call him back. Perhaps she did not enjoy their dinner together, or perhaps he was inadequate as a conversationalist. Could he have come on a bit too strong? Was his note too short; should he have written a note explaining how great the night had been for him? Was it possible that after going out with him, the thrill was over for her? Was he not as competent in the bedroom as he thought? Or did he not meet her expectations for a first time experience......the list went on and on until he finally fell asleep around 2 am.

DAY FOUR

Day Four, Tuesday, June 14th Marissa's Story

This was the next day after the "event" and Marissa still couldn't seem to find the courage to call Hans. She tried on several occasions, picking up the phone and touching in the numbers onto her phone, but was not able to touch the send button. She thought of him often, but kept herself busy to try to keep him out of her thoughts. She had spent last evening with Rita discussing the situation over and over but even Rita couldn't get her to make the call.

To further add to her embarrassment about the "event", she learned from a phone conversation with Rita this morning that after she had left Rita's apartment; Rita had discussed the situation with George. Rita explained that both she and George thought Hans to be a true gentleman. George believed since wine was involved, it was chivalrous of Hans to have not gone all the way with Marissa with the possibility of her judgment being impaired. Rita swore she only gave George the briefest of information. However limited the information, Marissa was mortified with the realization that the next time she would see George, she would know that he knew. Well it seemed the jury was in; her three best friends all agreed not only that she should call him, but that he was a true gentleman.

That afternoon there was a delivery for Marissa, a small two inch square box. When she opened the box inside was a silver key ring and a note. On the front of the key tag was engraved "Call Me", and on the flip side was engraved Hans' phone number. Marissa read the note, "Dear Marissa, I am sending you my phone number in hopes you will call me. I want to assume that you either never found my note or you have misplaced it. Otherwise, I will have to admit to myself you don't want to see me again, and that would cause me a dilemma as I am so anticipating our next date. Fondly, Hans." She was impressed how well he expressed himself with words, which gave her an idea. She decided to text him.

She wasn't sure if he even received text messages but she was going to find out. Her text message read, "I apologize for not call-ing you. It was wrong of me. I am embarrassed, as I left you totally unsatisfied when we last met. We did not make love". Two hours went by with no reply. She assumed he must not text. With that thought her phone vibrated. It was a text message from Hans, "You did satisfy me the other night. You have no idea of the immense pleasure you gave me. Making love is a journey and some journeys take days to complete. You must savor every stop along the way. Each stop has its own excitements and delights. I am hoping the other night was just one of the destinations we shall encounter to-gether. I am earnestly looking forward to our next. Never for a sec-ond believe that I did not thoroughly enjoy myself."

Day Four, Tuesday, June 14th Hans' story

This was the second day without a call from Marissa. Hans started to obsess as to why she hadn't called. This had never hap-pened to him before; that a woman would not want to see him again. He started adding reasons to his list as to why she didn't call him. Should he have woken her up to say good bye? She hadn't given him her number so he could not call her, should he have stopped by unannounced to see her? He was certainly perplexed; she was a type of woman he had not yet encountered.

As he was walking to a meeting, he passed a jewelry store. In the window was a display of key rings, which gave him an idea. He finally had a plan, something he could do to coax her to call. This waiting, doing nothing, was getting to him. He would buy the key ring and have his phone number engraved onto it. Then it hit him, perhaps she had lost the pink post it note or perhaps she never saw it. He remembered the window behind the sink being open, perhaps it had blown away. When he went into the store, he told the jeweler he needed the key ring to be engraved and delivered by noon that day; he didn't care how much it would cost. When leaving the jewelry store he felt confident now she would call. He then went to his meeting hoping his plan would work.

Hans had a very productive and busy day. Around 4 o 'clock he remembered he had forgotten to turn his phone back on after his first meeting. He quickly turned it on. He checked to see if Marissa had called. He was elated! His plan had worked, as there it was...a text message from Marissa. After reading her text, he was relieved to know now why she hadn't called him. It was definitely not one of the reasons he had come up with while making his list. He never would have guessed that one. He wanted to respond to her right away, but he took his time to carefully choose his words. He hoped Marissa would agree to see him again as he desired her more than any other woman he had ever been with.

Day Four, Tuesday, June 14th (The Day Continues)
Marissa's Story

Marissa contemplated how she would reply to his text. She had been wrong all along; he wasn't upset about not having been sexually gratified. She longed to see him again and ached at the mere thought of him. Whenever Hans would come to mind, she would desire him, but she had been pushing those feelings deep within herself and not allowing them to resurface. When she read his text message she was elated. She decided to text him to see if he was free tonight, "How about dinner tonight at the Chinese restaurant under my apartment? Dress is casual. Eight o'clock sound good to you?" It seemed as if only seconds had passed when her phone vibrated. "Sounds great. Pick you up at eight", was his reply.

Marissa quickly called Carter, to update him on the situation with Hans. But her real reasons for calling were to elicit his help picking out an outfit and for morale support. When Carter received her call he was on his way to Connecticut for dinner, after receiving an impromptu invitation from his newest boyfriend Roberto's parents. As Carter spoke Marissa could hear the excitement in his voice. His past relationships were usually short lived. This was the first time any of his boyfriends had brought him home to meet the parents. Carter was giddy with anticipation as he told her which wine he had just purchased as a gift for Roberto's dad and the type of bouquet he had handpicked from the florist for Roberto's mother. Marissa was thrilled for Carter. He seemed to have finally found someone who genuinely cared for him. His making it to the "meet the parents" stage in this relationship was an outward sign for him that Roberto's feelings for him were sincere.

With no assistance from Carter, Marissa was uneasy about what to wear. He assured her if she went with her gut instincts she would look fabulous. She tore through her closet looking for just the right outfit, tossing the rejected items on top of her bed. The clothes on her bed were piled so high it resembled a clearance bin at Macy's bargain basement floor on 34th street. With every possible combinations examined, she decided to go with her favorite denim mini skirt. It was short and would bring attention to her tanned legs. She also chose a white midriff cami trimmed with lace and her red short-sleeve waist length cotton cardigan. She picked her red sandals with the thin ankle strap and her red clutch. She wondered if it was perhaps too much red. But she was feeling very sexy and she felt her best whenever she wore red. And after all, Carter had told her to go with her gut, and her gut was screaming "Wear RED!"

As it was getting late, she hurried into the shower. As the warm water down cascaded her body she had thoughts of Hans. She shaved her legs and primped hoping they might make love after dinner. After her shower she lathered lotion on every part of her body making herself silky smooth. She decided to wear her hair down, and flat ironed it, which made it appear longer than with its natural curls. She only wore a touch of make- up and of course her *Obsession*.

For the first time ever she sprayed a little cologne on her thighs. It made her feel naughty. If the nuns at her former high school could see her now, in her red bikini underwear and short white cami with her navel exposed spaying cologne on her thighs they'd be saying, "Catholic school girl gone wild!", she laughed to herself.

When she was completely dressed, she checked herself out in the mirror. She took a picture with her phone and sent it to Carter. His reply text message was complimentary expressing how fabulous she looked. He suggested she try wearing her large gold hoop earrings and the new necklaces she had bought last week with the skeleton keys and heart charms attached to it. He also mentioned to try pushing back her hair over one of her ears. She tried his suggestions and was happy with the results. Carter texted he was getting nervous as they were nearing the parents' home. Marissa texted, "You have nothing to worry about. The parents will fall in love with you, just as Roberto obviously has. You are FABULOUS! Enjoy your dinner!". Carter texted back "Thanks, I love you too." Noticing the time she quickly went into the living room to start the gas fireplace. She thought it would give a romantic start to the evening to have it lit. Just as she was going to give herself one more look in the mirror the, she heard the door buzzer.

She panicked. The memory of Hans having seen her naked and having sex with her came rushing back to her consciousness in an instant. The feeling of embarrassment returned for not having satisfied him sexually. Now here he was and she would soon be face to face with him again. "Breathe, just breathe" she told herself. She buzzed him up and waited partially paralyzed at the door for his knock. He must have run up the stairs as it seemed only seconds had passed when she heard the knock on her apartment door.

When she opened the door and took one look at him those titillating feelings she had felt the other night reemerged allowing the flood gates to again open freely. How was it possible Hans could make this happen to her with just a glance, she thought. He looked absolutely delicious wearing a pair of perfectly fitted jeans with black boots, black leather waist cut jacket, black shirt, black tie and the most beautiful smile. He was picture perfect. Carter himself could not have dressed Hans any better, she thought.

As he walked by her entering the apartment she caught a hint of his scent. She was losing control. She was afraid she would not be able to control her urges until after dinner. She had to have him NOW. She was totally out of her element, and she was definitely not herself; at least not the self she thought she was. This was not her field of expertise. She wished she could somehow text Carter; he was the artesian in matters such as these, he could tell her what to do. Realizing it would be impossible to text Carter at this very moment, she accepted the fact that she would have rely on her gut instinct.

As Hans closed the door behind him, without even a second thought, she pressed him up against the door and started kissing him. She could not resist, for being with Hans released passions within her that she never felt before. It was as if her body was on fire. She hadn't even given him the chance to say hello before she slammed him against the door. Luckily for her he had the next move as she hadn't a clue what to do next. Within minutes they were on the floor in front of the fireplace. She thought perhaps he wanted her as badly as she wanted him. Why else, she thought, were they on the floor and not in the bed. The heat of the fire added to the excited state she was in. Hans was just as gentle and attentive as he had been the other night, taking such care while removing each article of clothing. She unbuttoned his shirt, but not with the same finesse as he had taken off hers. She fumbled while trying to undo his belt. He must have felt her awkwardness while kissing her; for in one swift movement, he removed it himself. Marissa could feel her hands tremble as she started to unzip his pants. Her heart was racing as she removed them. She was apprehensive to look while removing his underwear, and hesitated a moment before partaking in the magnificent view. This time, it was not only she that was undressed, they were both naked.

Marissa had never seen a man naked before. She had taken an art history class when she was a junior in high school and the memory was fresh in her mind of the first time she had seen a photograph of the sculpture David by Michelangelo. That night she had spent hours in her room exploring the mysterious anatomy in the numerous views provided in the photographs of the David in her art book. The sculptor had such vivid details that seemed to bring to life a subject Marissa so wanted to learn more about. She studied the photos with such attention to the muscles in his neck, chest, abdomen, arms, thighs and calves. The intricate details of the hands were carved with such precision that the veins appeared as if they would be capable of carrying blood. The back view of the statue was equally as memorizing to her. The muscles of the back, arms and legs were so dramatic and the buttock was sheer perfection. The photos of the uncircumcised penis and pubic hair were the most captivating to her as these were the most religiously forbidden. At the end of the school term, Marissa had reported the book as lost. She thought it was probably a double sin to lie to a nun, but there was no way she was giving up the picture of her perfect man now that she had found him.

Marissa had upon occasion nonchalantly looked at guys on the beach, and guys playing basketball at neighborhood courts with their shirts off, but the scenario playing in her apartment was much different. Right before her was a naked man of her very own to explore visually and tactility. She wanted to examine his body as closely as she had the photos of the statue of <u>David</u>, but now instead of a photograph made of paper she was staring at flesh and blood. She moved back a bit from him to get a better look. She gently touched his exposed chest and delighted in the sensation of his hair against the palm of her hand. When he pulled her closer to kiss her, the tickling feel of his chest hair was a pleasurable sensation against her breast. She kissed him on the lips, the neck, and his chest working her way down to the one area that she coveted most.

Marissa's anticipation heightened her enjoyment of her exploration. The excitement of her arriving at her desired destination inhibited her from staying at each area for as long a period of time as Hans had done with her. After gently caressing and kissing his thighs she found herself at the one organ that held the most sensual pleasure for Hans. She savored learning the new sights, tastes and textures of this newest of discoveries. She made mental pictures so she would be able to recall this moment again in her mind whenever she wanted.

Marissa felt Hans gently bring her back up to him. This was the moment, she knew it. While kissing her she was aware that Hans had put on a condom. She wasn't nervous as she thought she would be; she was relaxed. She breathed in deeply as she felt him enter her. It didn't hurt as she had heard it would. It was absolutely wonderful! She had places touched inside of her that she never knew existed. She tried to pay attention to the sounds he made as it heightened her excitement but she was going into her own state of euphoria and could only feel and enjoy her own pleasures. She heard herself scream and almost simultaneously she could feel his body tense and then relax telling her that he had climaxed also. They laid there for quite awhile in each others' arms exhausted and satisfied. As they laid there, she felt the soft fake bear skin rug underneath them, so comfortable against her skin. She was happy that Carter had convinced her to buy it and wondered if this situation was what he had in mind when he persuaded her to purchase it.

Hans told Marissa he would be back in a minute. Luckily, she had a box of tissues on her coffee table. She hadn't noticed when he had wrapped the used condom in the tissues, but she watched as he picked up the crumbled up tissues from the floor and walked to the bathroom. What do you do now, she thought? As she sat up, Hans came out of the bathroom and sat next to her on the floor. The glow of the fire reflected off his tanned body beautifully and made him look even more gorgeous than ever. He grabbed the blanket that was thrown across the back of the love seat and covered them both as he laid back on the rug with her. As they laid there in silence, she was afraid she was falling in love with him.

He kissed her ever so gently. "Would you like to go to dinner?" he asked. She was hungry and had certainly worked up an appetite, so she replied "Yes". She felt that Hans could sense her being uncomfortable about being naked. He gathered her clothes and while handing them to her suggested she get dressed in the bathroom while he would stay in the living room to get dressed. When Marissa looked into the bathroom mirror she noticed her face was flushed and she had red splotches on her chest. She was still weak from her orgasms, "God, he is good", she thought to herself. She got dressed and applied make-up to cover her flushed face when she thought, "How can I face him now, after having attacked him. Two dates, two embarrassing moments, was this a pattern"?

When Marissa came out of the bathroom Hans was sitting on the love seat. He had turned off the gas fireplace, replaced the blanket over the loveseat and was ready to go. She sat next to him. "Hi" she said, "I never did get to say hello. Sorry for attacking you at the door like I did." "No need to apologize" he said. "It's nice to occasionally have dessert before dinner". She smiled. He always seemed to say just the right thing. After Hans used the bathroom, they left. She was more relaxed now as they walked down the stairs to the restaurant. It was then Marissa realized that she wasn't falling in love with him; she was in love with him.

Hans requested a table in the back of the restaurant where it was quiet and more conducive to conversation. Usually Marissa was at such ease while conversing but not tonight. Here she sat across from the man to whom she had just given her virginity to and she found herself at a loss for words. She felt as if she was in a whole new ball game; one which she didn't have a rule book for or even know which ball to use.

As Marisa looked at Hans face, remembering where it had just been she could feel herself blushing. As soon as they sat down Hans took her hands and held them, a sweet gesture she thought. Hans gently touched her face, which beckoned Marissa to look at him. "Marissa, I know this might seem sudden to you. And I am not certain you would want this, but I wondered if you would consider us being exclusive. What I'm trying to say is that I would like us to get to know each other better. And I am hoping we could do it while not dating others." Marissa didn't reply, she was numb, for the first time in her life she was speechless.

Minutes went by without any conversation at all. They just sat there quietly with Hans looking at Marissa and her looking down at his hands that were holding hers. Fortunately, Hans started a conversation as Marissa was becoming uncomfortable with the silence and feared the dinner might be eaten without a word spoken. Marissa realized perhaps they should have stayed at her apartment and ordered take out. Although what they had just experienced to-gether was routine for Hans, for Marissa it was a momentous event, one which she was still playing over and over in her head. She was trying to pay attention to his words but her attention kept on going back to her own thoughts. As she looked at him while he spoke, his words sounded as if they were off in the distance, faint at best as she was in a dream like state. Her body was sitting there but in her mind she was reliving the wonderful event that had just taken place. She was remembering every detail of how he had just held her, touched her, kissed her and made love to her. Here sitting before her was the man of her dreams, who was everything she had ever prayed for.

To complete her romantic fantasy, the man to whom she had just give her virginity, had asked if they could be in an exclusive relationship. Was this too good to be true? She had friends who had searched for such a love, and who had failed time and time again. She had known girls who had given away their hearts and their virginities only to be used and tossed aside like trash. Could it be possible that the first love of her life would be the one she would marry and grow old with? She tried to think rationally, but with each question she asked herself to bring her back to reality, her heart's answers were the only ones she was listening to.

With each story of his childhood that Hans shared, she could see he was letting her deeper into his world, perhaps deeper into his heart as well. As she looked deeply into his strikingly bright blue eyes she wondered how it was possible that someone this wonder-ful could still be single. Her grandmother had told her that every-thing had a flaw, and she couldn't help but wonder what his was?

The food they ordered was the catalyst for Marissa to finally join in on the conversation. Food was one of her favorite topics to talk about, both the preparing and the eating of it as well. Watching Hans enjoy the taste of the items she had selected seemed to help her break through the contemplative state she had been in, as it brought her great pleasure to introduce him to spices he had yet to explore.

When dinner was over Marissa wanted to sit on the bench near her bridge to reflect on the events of the evening. There was a lot for her to think about and she still had yet to respond to a question that needed to be answered.

Day Four, Tuesday, June 14th (The Day Continues) Hans' story

While Hans showered he thought about what to wear on their date. As he walked into his closet, remembering that Marissa had said to dress casual, he decided on his leather jacket and jeans. He still was trying to figure out how Marissa had such a hold on him. They had only just met and yet he found himself thinking about her on and off throughout his day. It was if she had magically put a spell on him. In the middle of a meeting he would think of her smile, the smell of her hair, and the feel and taste of her skin. It had been a long time since he wanted to spend more than just a few dates with a woman. His intuition was telling him she was different, and everything he was learning about her was deepening that belief.

Hans decided he didn't want to come on too strong, as he didn't want to scare her off. He decided that after dinner, he would walk her to her door but not go upstairs. He would kiss her good night and say he had an early meeting and leave. But he would definitely make plans for another date before leaving. He realized he was falling for her, and hard. He didn't want her seeing any other men, while getting to know him. With that realization came the acknowledgment of how much he cared for her already. And he was powerfully aware that he wanted to spend as much time with her as he could. He decided if he could find the right moment he would ask her how if they could date exclusively, so they could see where this was going.

Hans didn't want to take the chance of Marissa seeing Boris drop him off so he took a cab to her apartment. As he rang her door bell, he repeated to himself "Control yourself. Control yourself". He did not want her to think all he wanted from her was sex, so he would not put himself in any situation that would allow it. She buzzed him in, and he climbed the stairs in record time. As he got closer to her apartment door he could feel his body starting to sweat. His face was flushing, he was sure.

When he knocked on the door he felt as if his heart was beating through his chest. No woman had ever had this affect on him. When Marissa opened the door she was so stunning it took his breath away. How was it possible she was more beautiful each time he saw her? Her legs looked fantastic in her skirt, so toned and tan. The skirt was just the right length to drive a man wild. Her shirt did not touch the top of her skirt, leaving a hint of skin exposed, which he desperately wanted to touch.

She was so breathtaking that it left him speechless. He walked into her apartment trying to get the word "Hello" to come out of his mouth, but the word wouldn't come. As he turned to her after closing the door he was shocked as she pushed him against it and started kissing him. "My plan is not going to work. Definitely not going to work!" he thought to himself. There was no way he could resist this advance from Marissa. Her body was so close against his and he could feel her pressing even closer. She was bombarding all of his senses at once. With her provocative appearance, the close-ness of her body, the scent of her hair and her perfume, the sound of her rapid breathing and the taste of her kiss it was impossible for him to stop her. He remembered that out of habit he had put a few condoms in his jacket pocket. He was pleased at this moment that he had, as there was no way he would want to stop this activity to make a run to a drug store.

His hands were up her skirt within seconds. He felt like a teenager groping her as they were against the door. He could feel the moisture of her lace panties which heightened his pleasure immeasurably. As he picked her up making his way towards the bedroom, he noticed from the corner of his eye there were clothes thrown all over her bed, so he decided to bring her in front of the fireplace.

He wanted to consummate this act as soon as they reached the rug, as he didn't know how long he could last in this intense heightened state of arousal. She ignited within him desires to a depth of which he had never before known. He took a few deep breaths realizing he needed to pace himself for the adventure that lay ahead. He carefully undressed her, noticing that she was undressing him also. He found it amusingly charming how she fumbled with the buttons of his shirt. When he noticed she was having difficulty removing his belt, not wanting her to become frustrated, he removed it himself.

He watched her face while she undressed him, noticing her expression as each piece of clothing was eliminated. It was as if she was a child opening birthday presents. With each gift opened a more delighted smile would appear until the realization that there was but one gift left, and so the hesitation of unwrapping it immediately for not wanting the unwrapping to end.

As they lay naked, Hans noticed that Marissa was looking at him with exploring eyes, appearing to examine every detail of his anatomy. He had never been so visually scrutinized before. He had never had a woman's face appear to be so genuinely pleased at what she discovered. Hans immensely enjoyed himself as Marissa systematically surveyed every inch of her new domain. She went places he thought she might have avoided for a first encounter. He was amazed how skillful she was, as this was her first time. She seemed to know instinctively what enhanced his pleasure and how to make it linger. When he could not take anymore of her exploration, as his state of arousal was near peaking, he brought her up and kissed her.

Hans was careful as he entered her for his not wanting to cause her any pain or discomfort. However, when the deflowering occurred, the soft sounds she made, assured him she was still receiving pleasure and delighting in the moment. Hans had never enjoyed a sexual encounter more than he had tonight. It was an experience like no other. Making love to her was different than sex with any other woman with whom he had been with; there was an unspoken connection. As he laid totally satisfied holding her, he realized that when he was with her he felt wonderful and he wanted to feel this way forever.

After making love, Marissa became deep in thought. He held her for awhile savoring each minute enjoying her scent, her touch, and just being with her. The sound of her stomach growling reminded Hans that they hadn't yet eaten dinner. When Marissa appeared to be a bit quieter than usual, Hans wondered if it was because it was her first time with a man or possibly that she had regretted what had just occurred. He hadn't had a moment with her yet where she had seemed to be at a loss for words, that was until now.

He suggested they go downstairs to the restaurant to eat. When they arrived at the restaurant they sat at a table in the back to avoid the noise of the people waiting for take-out. Hans thought perhaps this would be the time to ask her to be in an exclusive relationship with him. He hoped she was still basking in the glow of the great sex he believed they had just shared and that would encourage her to agree. She seemed dazed when he brought up the subject. In fact she didn't even reply to it. Minutes went by with no conversation. Hans didn't know what was wrong; they had never before sat in silence. He remembered that Marissa had explained to him why she loved teaching, so he thought perhaps he would share his reasons with her for working with finances.

He began, "When I was a young boy my parents owned a piece of land that they farmed. It wasn't a big business but it paid the bills. When my father died, my mother was having difficulty keeping the mortgage loan current. She had been behind in payments when the bank starting foreclosing on the property. My mother was heartsick as she didn't want us to lose our home and our land. She told me that if we lost our home our only option would be to move into her parent's home. I vividly recall her telling me that as her sister lived with her parents, she would do anything to not let that occur. I remember the look of dread in my mothers' face as she read the letters she received from the bank.

Then one day a man from the bank came to our door. He had a friendly face and looked different from the other bankers that had come to visit. He told my mother he had noticed my father's name on the list of properties that were being made ready for foreclosure and he decided he wanted to help. My mother didn't trust any man who wore a suit. She believed that they didn't earn their living by their hands but earned their living off the sweat from other men that did.

The banker told her a story of himself as a young foolish boy, on a hot summer day wanting to cool off in a stream even though he couldn't swim. He told himself he would only go waist high. The problem with his plan was that he wasn't aware the stream had a ravine about 20 feet into it. When he slipped off the edge he knew he was going to drown. Out of nowhere, a man swam out and brought him back to land. He told her that man was my father. He had been swimming in the stream that ran beside our property, and fortunately for him her husband was walking by. He told her if it hadn't been for my father he would have drowned. He explained how he felt obliged to help us as my father helped him. He found a few investors willing to take a chance on her small business. She would remain owner but the investors would share in the profits.

My mother had been praying for a miracle and believed that this man was the answer to her prayers, so she signed the papers. When the banker left my mother told me she remembered clearly the day of the incident of the near drowning. She had just finished mopping the floor when my dad had come in sopping wet. As she yelled at him for ruining her clean floor he told her of the near drowning of the boy. She said she proudly dried him off and thanked God the little boy was all right." Hans ended the story by saying, "That is why I went into investment consultation work. Yes, you can make money, but you can help hard working people who just need a little capital to keep their business afloat and you can help others who have a great idea and just need someone to back them. You can make a difference in people's everyday lives, a big difference"

Hans could not believe that he was still talking. How did she get him to open up so much? Marissa seemed to be more herself now. She told Hans his reasons for working in the financial industry were honorable. She added that she was sorry he had lost his father at such an early age, and expressed how hard growing up without a father must have been.

The food at the restaurant was excellent. Marissa had ordered some dishes that were new to Hans. He tried them and was impressed with the flavors. The conversation then turned to food. Marissa mentioned some of her favorite things to cook and she bragged about her family's recipe for lasagna. Marissa said she wanted to cook a meal for Hans and he graciously accepted. She spoke with such enthusiasm while explaining how important food was to Italians and the joy they took in preparing it. "Cooking is one way how an Italian woman expresses her love to her family", she said. He couldn't help but wonder how it was Austrian women showed their love to their families. Growing up he remembered his mother doing all the cooking, the washing, and the cleaning, but he never remembered any joy in her face, nor the look of love.

Surely, she must have loved him but she never told him. He remembered when his father had died; his mother told him to be strong and that he mustn't cry. At his fathers' funeral his mother didn't shed a tear, nor did she even hold Hans' hand. He stood alone and frightened at the grave site, at the tender age of nine. He remembered having a cold childhood. It seemed that when his father died something inside his mother died as well. Perhaps that was why it was so easy for him to move to America. Perhaps he just wanted to get out of the cold.

After dinner they walked to the waterfront. Marissa's apartment was only a few blocks from the Brooklyn Bridge. They sat on a bench in a park near the entrance to the bridge for about an hour, quiet not saying a word, just staring at the beautiful night, the bridge and the lights of the buildings on the other side of the water. Hans felt so fortunate to be with her. He enjoyed her company even in the silence. He broke the silence and asked her if she would like him to spend the night. She looked up at him. He could see a tear welling in her eye. She said, "That would be perfect." They walked back to her apartment in silence. Hans wondered why she had a tear in her eye, what could be wrong? When they arrived at her apartment Marissa unlocked her apartment door. She looked up at Hans and he noticed that tears were falling down her cheeks. "Yes", said Marissa," I would like us to be exclusive". Hans held her closely to him. He promised himself he would never do anything to make her cry, unless they were tears of happiness, as tonight.

Marissa was brushing her teeth readying herself for bed, when Han took a long hard look at her. He realized having sex with him tonight must have been an emotional event for Marissa, as he had never seen her so quiet or pensive for such a long period of time. He decided he would take off from work to spend the day with her. When she entered the bedroom he asked, "Marissa I was wondering, if you are not busy tomorrow I would like to take off from work and spend the day with you". The beautiful smile that came across her face was the only answer he needed. The kiss that followed assured him he had made the correct decision.

DAY FIVE

Day Five, Wednesday, June 15th Marissa's Story

Some summer days in NYC were sweltering, but today was one of the hottest that Marissa could remember. The city was in the middle of a heat wave and it had been reported on the news this morning that there wasn't an air conditioner for sale to be found anywhere in the local area. The stores it seemed had been sold out for two days. Libraries and other city facilities were extending their closing times to allow people who did not own air conditioners a respite from the high temperatures.

Why did she have to pick today of all days to tour the city with Hans and look at its architecture she wondered? Then she remembered last night when Hans suggested he take the day off from work to spend it with her. She wanted to do something special with him. Knowing how interested he was in architecture and never having had a tour from a native New Yorker, she seized the opportunity to show off her hometown. She had gotten up early, took out her map and made a route for Hans to see exactly what it was about New York architecture that made it unique. She picked just the right buildings to make her case, that her city was a one in a million gem.

During their walk they saw several fire men attaching sprinkler units to fire hydrants so the children could cool off. It would have been a refreshing break if she and Hans could have joined the children standing in front of the fire hydrants as well. She remembered as a child constantly complaining how she wanted to grow up. Her grandmother would always tell her, "It's not always fun to be an adult. Some days you will wish you were a child again." Marissa thought to herself, "I guess this was one of the times she meant".

When the temperature would soar, the high heels of your shoes would actually leave indentations into the asphalt. They also would leave black marks on the tips of your heels rendering them useless to wear again unless you were quick enough at cleaning them off, and fortunate enough for them not to be a light color as they would stain. Today had been one of those days. They had just walked by the New York Public Library when Marissa was explaining this fact to Hans. He displayed a look of skepticism, so Marissa took a penny from her purse and said, "Oh Yee of little faith. You doubting Thomas". To which Hans replied, "Oh so I suppose you are going to report me to Pope Benedict XVI for my lack of faith". After saying that, it occurred to her he might be Catholic. Why else would he know the name of the current pope? Just when she thought he couldn't be more perfect, she proved herself wrong. Marissa pushed the penny into the asphalt heads up, stepping on it to make sure it stuck, to prove her point. She said, "There, I told you that would happen. Now every time you cross E 42th and 5th Ave. you will see this penny and think of me".

Marissa had several buildings left on her list to show Hans when lunch time came around. As they neared a pizzeria, Marissa suggested they stop for a slice because it would be quicker than going to a restaurant. They fortunately found a table even though the place was crowded. Marissa asked Hans if he would mind sitting at the table to save it for them, as she went on line to get the pizza. She commented that since she had invited him to lunch today, she would be paying. She always kept her I Pod Nano in her purse. After her morning runs she would keep it in there for when she had to ride the subway alone to both lessen the boredom and the noise of the train cars. She handed them to Hans saying, "Here, you will have some music to listen to so you won't be bored while you're waiting". The line was long, but that was normal during lunch hour in the city.

When Marissa returned to the table and put down the slices of pizza and bottles of water, Hans gave a slight laugh and a smile when he handed her back her I Pod Nano. Instantly she remembered she had recently given Carter her I Pod Nano to download some new music for her to jog with. Carter was always finding sexually suggestive music to slip into her playlist to spice up her workouts. She remembered a song he had recently added to her playlist whose subject matter was the act of fellatio. She wondered if perhaps that was the reason for his playful smile. She could see that Hans was trying to keep a straight face when he said, "Interesting music you have on your playlist Marissa. There is one in particular I found rather intriguing. I can only guess from the lyrics that the title might be "Addicted To You". Marissa could feel her face flush. He had heard the song that she was hoping he hadn't. She quickly responded, "Carter occasionally adds songs to my playlist to try to get a rise out of me". Hans picked up his slice and said "Interesting choice of words you used Marissa; I could see it getting a rise out of me". They both laughed. Marissa thought to herself, "Third date, third sexually embarrassing moment. That is three for three. This is definitely becoming a trend".

They continued with their walking tour after lunch. The pizzeria had air conditioning so they were refreshed and ready for the rest of the afternoon. When they walked in the East Village, Marissa noticed a small, frail, older Italian woman, dressed totally in black passing by them. The woman reminded her so much of her grand-mother. It was not only the woman being totally dressed in black clothing, but the way she wore her gray hair up in a bun, the weathered look upon her face, the wooden cane she used to walk in one hand while carrying a shopping bag with a loaf of Italian bread sticking out of it on the other. When she passed by Marissa and they made eye contact, the woman gave her the sweetest smile. Marissa could never understand why that after their hus-bands died some Italian women often wore only the color black for the rest of their lives. Marissa's grandmother had moved to Brook-lyn from Sicily to live with them after her grandfather died. Marissa had never seen her wear any color but black. When Marissa inquired one day why, her grandmother's only reply was, "We wear black to show honor and respect for those who we love who have passed." On hot days, such as these, her grandmother would tell her stories of how comfortable the temperatures were in Sicily during the summertime, due to the breezes that blew across it from the sea. She would tell Marissa she had heard the extreme heat in NYC was due to the absorption of the suns ray by all the blacktop on the city streets and all the black tar paper on its rooftops. Marissa tried explaining to her that it was not scientifi-cally accurate and merely an urban myth, however she would in-evitably give up realizing that being Sicilian, her grandmother was bull headed at times.

By 4:30 that afternoon, they had certainly had their fill of archi-tecture. All they had eaten for lunch was a slice of pizza, so Marissa suggested they go back to her apartment to cool off and get something to eat. She shortened their tour by leaving out some important buildings, due to both the heat and her hunger. She real-ized there was no hurry to show Hans all the buildings in one day. They could always see more tomorrow, the next day and the next for she had an inkling that Hans was a keeper.

The subway air was hot and stale. The smell of the ordinarily tolerable but distinct subway air was intensified by the heat and humidity of the day, making its smell unpleasant. The subway was not overly crowded and Hans found them two seats together. During the ride home Marissa talked about some additional unique places she wanted to show Hans in the city. She mentioned that in spite of all the wonderful places there were to visit in Manhattan, her favorite of them all was the bench near the Brooklyn Bridge. The bridge had been her favorite place ever since she was a child, only then she was viewing it from the other side of the East River. During her childhood, when she would open the front door to her home it was the first site that greeted her each morning. It was a comforting scene for her with its magnificent arched towers of granite and its interwoven ropes of steel so powerful and majestic. Its mere existence was a true testament to one man's vision and hundreds of men's sweat. The bridge always gave her a sense of hope, for if in the 1800's they could connect two boroughs, over a river, despite tremendous surmountable obstacles and its surviving over 100 years, she could certainly conquer any problem she might face. She enjoyed being mesmerized by its beauty, while listening to the hum of the traffic and gazing into the water as it drifted by underneath.

Marissa felt at times she tended to dominate their conversations, not allowing Hans equal time to converse. She was genuinely curious to find out the places Hans enjoyed visiting in the city. When she inquired where his number one, all time favorite place was, he suggested that instead of telling her he would show her. He asked if she was free for lunch tomorrow, and if yes, he would bring her to visit his favorite spot. For the duration of the ride, Marissa asked questions trying to pry out of him where he would be taking her, but Hans refused to play the twenty questions game with her. No clues, no hints. He adamantly refused to budge on revealing its location. Becoming frustrated with not being able to persuade his decision Marissa said, "Fine!, Then the day after tomorrow I will take you to my second favorite place in the city, as you already have been to my bench near the bridge, and I am not giving you a hint as to where it will be." Marissa marveled how Hans didn't inquire for further details. Men were certainly strange creatures, she thought, not a curious bone in their bodies.

Marissa noticed Hans had felt the heat of the day as much as she had, because he wasn't walking at his usual quickened pace. On the walk to her apartment from the subway Hans told Marissa he would not be staying over this evening because he had work he needed to catch up on. She assumed he would be sleeping over, but understood that work had to come first, especially as he had skipped out of work today to be with her. As they continued their walk to the apartment all she could really think about was getting into her air conditioned apartment and taking a shower. She was dripping with sweat and wondered if it had been such a good idea to do a walking tour today.

Walking into her cool apartment was a welcome relief from the heat of the day. As she entered the apartment she immediately started to undress walking directly into the bathroom, leaving a trail of clothes behind her that started at the front door. She was delighted when Hans knocked on the bathroom door to ask if he may join her. She immediately answered yes as every adventure with Hans was a memorable one. He seemingly had anticipated her response as he entered the room naked as soon as she answered. Hans adjusted the water and allowed Marissa to enter first. He had made the temperature cooler than what she was use to, as when she entered the shower she quickly backed up. Hans instantly said, "Let me make it warmer if you'd like, I just thought perhaps it would feel favorable after the heat from the day". The cooler temperature actually was more refreshing, and Marissa did not attempt to alter it. They soaped each other up and as with any time they were naked, they took their time. Rinsing off, was

Marissa's favorite part. Hans had a way with her handheld detachable showerhead, with its multi changeable massage settings that drove her wild. Hans stopped with Marissa highly aroused. "Tease!" she coyly said. "Never a tease, Marissa, it's called foreplay", he said while stepping out of the shower. As she gazed at the showerhead back in its resting place, she realized that if the manufacturer added to its packaging information suggestions for usages which Hans had performed with its product, the showerhead would certainly fly off the shelves. When Marissa had purchased the showerhead she honestly had no idea it could have been used to elicit such pleasure.

Marissa stayed in the bathroom longer than Hans as she had more primping to attend to. She lotioned every inch of body, to assure its smoothness wherever he might touch her. She could see out of the corner of her eye that Hans was watching her from the bedroom, so she was careful to apply the lotion as erotically as she possibly could. He made her wait, so she was going to make him wait as well. Although being new at this "trying to be sexy" thing, she wasn't sure if she was turning him on or just looking stupid. She entered the bedroom in her towel and saw Hans sitting on the bed in his black boxers that she personally found to be a "turn on". When she had first seen them she thought they were cotton bicycle shorts. It wasn't until she was "up close and personal" that she noticed the opening in front, discovering they were underwear. She loved the way they snugly fit, especially how they hugged his derriere, one of her favorite features of his body. Of course, she loved his eyes, his face and that boyish grin, but she really loved his butt. And it looked just as good in a pair of jeans as it did naked. She had fixated on the statue of David for so long, she was elated to have her own real life version. Actually anything he wore was a turn on to her. She loved him in and out of everything. But she did have her favorite items. His black waist length leather jacket was another item she thought he looked rather sexy in. The leather was extremely soft, plus the smell of the leather combined with his own scent drove her wild.

He was sitting on the bed with his ear buds in while holding his Smart Phone. She wondered if he was going to listen to some music while falling asleep. When he beckoned her to the bed she knew he had a different idea. She could tell when he flashed her that boyish smile he was planning on seducing her, but she wondered what music he was going to use while accomplishing that feat. He handed her the ear buds saying, "You shared some of your music with me today, so I want to share some of mine with you". Marissa chuckled. He told her he wanted her to let the music take her wherever it went. She wondered if he was going to try to have her listen to a classical piece, as he had spoken previously on how much he enjoyed that genre of music. Actually she felt that as long as he was making love to her, it didn't matter what music was in the background, she could always block it out.

He told her to get comfortable. She adjusted the ear buds, fluffed up some pillows, sat back and told him she was ready. At the same time Hans started to brush away her hair from her neck and started to kiss it as he turned on the music. When the music started she was startled. When she thought of classical music she thought of elevator music, this was definitely not light and fluffy music. She hadn't expected the reaction that her body had to it. She had always enjoyed pumping up the music if a favorite song of hers was being played, but this was different, so very different. This music "moved" her. The music started strong, producing such a powerful sound. He gently pressed her down onto the bed removing her towel with such finesse. He softly kissed her forehead, her eye lids, her nose, her cheeks and her ears. He always took such time and care at whichever part of her body he was making love to as if each were of equal importance. As he worked his way down her neck and shoulders, he then made his way to her breasts. She could feel her body reverberating from within with the strong sounds of each instrument. It was as if Hans knew which section of the music was being played in her ears, for it seemed that with each of his caresses, kisses and breaths, he was in perfect synchronization with the music in both duration and intensity. He was orally pleasing her and performed as if he was part of the orchestra and she was his instrument, and he was playing her magnificently well. As the music came to a peak so did Marissa.

She had never enjoyed classical music before, but at this epic orgasmic moment she was quickly changing her mind. This expanded the pleasure of her sense of hearing during lovemaking. The music had helped to bring her to a level of excitement that even rose above the already heightened enjoyment she had always achieved whenever she was made love to by Hans. She had heard and paid attention when her friends would talk about using vibrators, but never had used one herself. This music was intensifying her pleasure, as she had heard a vibrator would do. However, this intense reverberating sensation was felt from within her whole entire body, not only one isolated area as a vibrator would do. And the whole time while her entire internal body was being reverberating by the music, on the outside her body was being equally as excited by Hans. She couldn't explain it and didn't think anyone of her friends would believe her if she told them. And in any case, she hadn't any intention of sharing the story anyway.

When the musical piece ended, Marissa was so satisfied and comfortable she didn't even put on her chemise that night. She just snuggled up into her special nook under Hans left arm and fell asleep. It was the first time Marissa had ever slept naked. She always had something on, even if only a T- shirt and underwear. Hans on the other hand always slept in the nude, which Marissa enjoyed immensely. It wasn't until she was almost asleep when she realized once again Hans had pleasured her without having achieved an orgasm himself. She was too tired to open her eyes, no less to pleasure Hans at this point. The heat of the day, all the walking and the great sex had exhausted her. She would make it up to him tomorrow, she told herself as she drifted off to sleep.

Day Five, Wednesday, June 15th Hans' Day

Hans was looking forward to seeing which buildings Marissa would pick to show off her city. He secretly hoped that one day she would accompany him to Austria, where he would show her an abundance of architecture that would delight her senses, especially when she toured their castles. Not that he wanted to prove his hometown of Vienna was better in its architecture than her city. However her city had no castles and he couldn't help but speculate her enjoyment when she would see that his did.

The news report on the radio stated the city was still in a heat wave. One advantage to living in the city during the summer months was the abundance of visible bare skin on the lovely women walking about. The city was a virtual museum of beauty on every avenue. As in any museum the variety was vast. The city had an endless array of women to choose from to look upon. There were blondes, brunettes, red heads, raven haired, tall, short, with practically every ethnic group represented, and clothed in an assortment of small, thin summer attire. This summer was different. Hans had noticed he wasn't partaking in the usual glances of the women he would pass by on the streets. These days he was focusing only on the beauty he had on his arm, and when she wasn't with him, she was still all that he could see.

Hans was pleasantly surprised and impressed with the buildings Marissa had selected to show him. She hadn't picked the classic architecture as he had predicted that she would, such as City Hall or the Flat Iron Building. Instead, she picked small buildings and private homes. He had to admit to passing many that she had shown him, yet having never looked up or turned his head as he walked by, missing their appeal. There were many brownstones with intricate details in their carvings of moldings, brackets, and architraves with spectacular veins of various colors within its stone. There were wide brownstone stoops, where the brownstone itself was used instead of iron for railings. He was stunned at the amount of superlative stain glass windows which she had shown him, with such quality in their designs they would be suitable to be displayed in any museum.

Marissa pointed out various antique doors which were made of deep rich mahogany, oak, and redwood, from what Hans could tell. There were several which had been painted over in red, blue, or enamel black so the wood was not revealed. There were many with vintage hardware while others sported new highly polished brass doorknobs. Many had striking arched beveled windows above them containing antique glass.

One of Hans' favorite features of many of the buildings was the range in variety of the wrought iron work. There were gates, fences and railings with such artisan craftsmanship of swirls, bends, twists, dagger like spikes and pickets. Behind some of the high wrought iron fences, Marissa had revealed several beautiful gardens in the city that were hidden from view. It amazed him how she knew where they were, for behind the fences had been thick, tall, fully leaved bushes to insure their privacy from the street. As they got close up to the fences, she would show him a small opening in the bush from where he could see the most magnificent gardens with a remarkable array of flowering plants for such small amounts of space. They were small oasises in the midst of the busy city.

Hans enjoyed walking along the city streets with Marissa. She was so interesting to listen to, and had at times the oddest of known facts. Hans was in disbelief when the penny that Marissa placed into the asphalt had actually stuck. When she mentioned that each time he passed it he would think of her, he smiled. If she had only known how many times in a given day his thoughts would turn to her, she would have been stunned.

Marissa had them walking half the island of Manhattan, visiting the Bowery, the Lower East Side, Gramercy, Chelsea, Tribeca, and the East and West Villages looking at homes. Due to the heat and being hungry she decided they would end their tour for the day, just as they were passing 5th and Park Avenues. Hans had not expected Marissa to want to walk along Park Ave to look at architecture. He had also not been prepared for them to pass by his building. Fortunately, as they did, the doorman was behind the front counter in the lobby on the phone. He knew he was safe from being spotted when Marissa turned and headed towards the subway.

On the subway ride home Marissa asked Hans which buildings he saw today were his favorite. He commented that his first pick had to be the home of Edgar Allan Poe's at 85 W. Third Street, for the mere fact of seeing the home where the man lived who wrote some of the darkest words Hans had ever read. His second favorite was the Thinnest Building with its interior at 8½ feet wide at 75 ½ Bedford St. He was perplexed while trying to imagine how they could have accommodated furnishings into such a confined space. When he had seen the "For Sale" sign on the property he told Marissa they would have to call and see it, to quench his curiosity. She assured him he would not get an appointment to tour the house. She had heard on the news the asking price was 4.3 million dollars and that "regular" people would never be shown the house. He asked her if he could finagle a way to get a peek at the house would she accompany him, and she enthusiastically said she would, but there was a look of disbelief on her face. His third favorite house was the Merchants House Museum, at 29th and E. 4th Street. It was a magnificent older building in mint condition, which Hans thought interesting. Marissa mentioned if she had to pick one street in the entire city that displayed the full flavor of New

York it would have to be Leroy St. Hans agreed, for the street was lined with rows of beautiful, well kept brownstones with phenomenal wrought iron work. If these images were represented on a post card none receiving it would miss it as having been sent from the Big Apple.

Hans had not used the subway system for years and had forgotten how hot and foul the air could become in the summer months. Hans had wanted to take a cab, but Marissa did not want him to waste his money. He needed to tell her soon about his financial situation, if for no other reason than the mere comfort it would afford them in their travels. They had been in the subway more times in one day than he had been in the last seven years. But Hans had to admit that no matter where he was with Marissa he was enjoying himself, even if it was standing on a crowded subway platform, breathing in the stale hot air, awaiting the arrival of a train.

When Marissa asked Hans to tell her his favorite place in the city, tons of places ran through his mind. He did have one special place in Manhattan in mind, but wondered if he should appear cultured and perhaps tell her the Guggenheim or the Metropolitan Museum of Modern Art. But if he was going to be truthful, he would have to tell her Central Park. There was a special place in the park where when life became too complicated he would go and sit to sort things out. You couldn't see the skyline from that vantage point. The trees and brushes in the area, strangely enough resembled so much the woods near his childhood home. He could imagine he was back in Vienna and could have himself believe that only several hundred feet from where he was sitting, stood his home. He came upon it quite by accident during one of his morning jogs. He frequented this area more often when he had first arrived to America and had not really been there much lately. He had sat there often years ago contemplating his future and making important decisions. It was there where he decided to open his own financial investment company and it was there when he decided to ask Mrs. Hobes to leave the company they both worked for, to join him. He was glad that Marissa had only asked for his favorite place in Manhattan. For, if she had not been specific to the area of Manhattan, he would have had to admit to his house in the Hamptons. And, he wasn't ready to divulge that information about himself quite yet. He needed a bit more time for Marissa to get to know the real him before he would reveal that side of himself.

It was pleasurable for him to see Marissa trying to get information out of him as to the location of his favorite spot in Manhattan. As he watched her try to wrangle any detail she possibly could from him, he thought it adorable how upset she became when she failed. At one point she actually whispered into his ear a sexual favor she would grant him if he would divulge the location. Knowing full well the particular act mentioned seemed to be one which she seemed to favor and would most likely perform anyway, Hans had to keep from laughing out loud at her attempt. If she was this much fun watching while attempting to pry out information, he couldn't imagine how enjoyable it would be during the Christmas season when there would be a wide assortment of boxes under a tree for her to try to guess the contents of.

When she turned the key to her apartment door, Marissa said "Do you know how I know there is a God"? Hans believed the conversation was about to turn philosophical when he replied, "How"? Marissa cheerfully remarked, "Because he gave someone the idea to invent air conditioning." Hans replied, " It was a gentleman by the name of Carrier and he invented it in 1902 one year after graduating from Cornell University. He was raised on a farm in New York near Lake Erie. He worked for a company in Buffalo, N.Y. that owned a printing plant in Brooklyn. The company was having problems with its paper due to the humidity in the air due to the season. He invented the air conditioner to solve their paper problem". She looked at him laughing saying, "Some of the stuff you know amazes me". Little did she know where Hans had picked up that tidbit of information. A repair man had recently been called to Hans' office to repair the air conditioning unit on his floor. When he realized that it could not be repaired a new one was installed. When Hans had returned from a meeting he noticed the repair man had left a brochure on the Carrier Company on his desk. Prior to tossing it out, Hans noticed a biography written on the back of the founder of the company. He was intrigued with the history he read. When he informed Marissa of his needing an early departure from her apartment tonight due to some overdue paper work, he could see the disappointment in her face. He knew however, when she learned the real reason for his leaving she would understand.

Marissa's apartment was a nice haven from the sweltering city. Hans was surprised at Marissa's undressing as soon as her foot touched her living room floor. He followed her discarded clothing when she announced she was taking a shower. It was a trail on the floor starting with her purse, then one sandal, then the other, her cotton dress, her bra and just outside the bathroom door, her undies. No sooner had the words left her mouth, than Hans was asking permission to join her. If he had answered her question honestly, being naked with Marissa anywhere in the city was his favorite place to be.

After a few moments of just standing under the water to cool off, Hans started to lather up a face cloth to wash Marissa. Hans observed the water as it cascaded over the curves of her body. He couldn't help but stare as it was a more beautiful site than he had ever seen painted on any canvas. Since he was the first man that Marissa had ever been with, Hans delighted in showing her new heights of pleasure with the use of the simplest of things. He was actually surprised to learn that she had never thought to use the showerhead as he had, "Catholic girls" he said, "you really do need to be taught how to be bad". Marissa laughed and they continued to enjoy their shower. Hans left the shower when he realized

Marissa was building in intensity of arousal, as he did not want their finale to occur in the shower. He had plans for Marissa.

Hans wanted to share a classical piece of music with Marissa. She had shared her music with him this afternoon and he wanted to reciprocate. He wanted to expose her to a classical piece and see if she would enjoy it. He thought the best way to introduce her to his favorite music would be during an activity she seemed to enjoy immensely, so that she would associate the two together. Sex was the first thing to come to his mind, oral sex in particular, as she would be a captive audience. He hoped that the addition of a powerful auditory enhancement of such magnificence as a requiem would add to the pleasure she would receive and it would be a welcomed facet to her enjoyment.

As he was trying to locate the piece of music he wanted on the app on his Smart Phone, he noticed Marissa lathering lotion onto her body. She drove him wild as he watched her touch herself in areas that he longed to be soon be visiting. The way she caressed her legs with long stokes made his desire run wild. When she came out of the bathroom, he was sitting on the bed with his Smart Phone in hand. "There is a classical piece I would like you to hear", he said. He tapped on the bed lightly and asked her to come and sit down. He instructed her to close her eyes and allow herself to flow with the music. She stood in front of him, still wrapped with the towel around her. He was in his cotton form fitting boxers, his usual pre bed attire. "I think this is the best way to introduce one of my favorite selections to you". She tucked the towel in tighter at the chest so it would not fall off before she sat on the bed. Hans found this act humorous as he knew it would not be on her for long. He handed her the ear buds and told her the piece she would be hearing was a Mozart Requiem. As he turned on the music, he could see the shocked expression on her face. He realized she hadn't expected something this powerful. He was hoping he had picked the right piece for her first experience. He could hear the music escaping ever so faintly from the ear buds. He knew where each selection was at every moment of his pleasuring her. He felt the music was having the effect he had hoped it would on her body. He could feel her body move with delight at certain sections of the musical selection. He enjoyed hearing the sounds of enjoyment she made which were louder than usual. Due to the ear buds she could not hear herself, so she did not quiet her responses. As he played the music in his head he tried to create the right pressure and timing to match the sensation of his touch with her sensation of the sounds. He knew he had timed it perfectly when he felt Marissa's body tense and heard her scream as she climaxed. Hans worked his way back up the sheets and upon arrival Marissa looked at him with an impish smile on her face. That was all the confirmation he needed to know he had done well. Marissa said, "Any time you want me to listen to any additional selections from your collection, I would be happy to accommodate you. That is, as long as you bring them to bed." He could see in her eyes that she was tired. When she laid her head onto his chest, he knew she was about to fall asleep.

Whenever Hans made love to her, she would respond so positively to his every touch. She had no idea how her reactions excited him. Hans received such satisfaction from bringing her pleasure. He realized she was tired. He was tired as well, and was totally satisfied to have her just fall asleep in his arms.

He looked around her room, as she was drifting off. Her bedroom décor was so much a reflection of her personality. He noticed a paperback copy of Romeo and Juliet on her nightstand with the pages spread apart due to frequent readings. "She is such a hopeless romantic", he thought. As Hans held her tightly as she slept, he realized that he never wanted to be without her. Wherever she was, was where he wanted to be. He would rather be with her in her tiny apartment in Chinatown with it leaky kitchen faucet, a bathroom with a broken window frame that would refuse to open, noisy upstairs neighbors and a front door that required four locks for safety, than be in his penthouse apartment on Park Ave. with its impressive address, lavish décor, a view overlooking Central Park and 24 hour security without her.

Looking at the time on the clock on her nightstand Hans realized it was time for him to leave. He needed to make lunch to bring to the park tomorrow. When he was sure she was totally asleep, he quietly left for home. He needed to go food shopping for items for tomorrow's lunch and he wondered where the nearest hardware store was to get a washer and a wrench to stop the leaky faucet.

DAY SIX

Day Six, June 16th Marissa's Day

Marissa was looking forward to meeting Hans for lunch this afternoon. He hadn't stayed over the night before and she had been wondering why. Perhaps he did have to work, just as he had said. She believed she was possibly reading too much into his not staying over. After all, it was not as if he had left her unsatisfied before his departure. That reminded her, he had left unsatisfied last night, a situation she told herself she would remedy later in the day.

Marissa was staring into her closet attempting to visualize an outfit for the day when Carter dropped by. He came bearing gifts, toting with him several small shopping bags from his boutique Understated. Rita and Carter had opened the small boutique in the East Village together two years after graduating from the fashion institute when neither was able to procure work. George used his financial savvy to get them a prime location in the city and a silent partner to back them. Marissa loved the design they picked for their shopping bags, believing they perfectly matched the risqué atmosphere of their store. The bags were shiny black, with a black paper lace cut out over lay attached. The handles were made of black braided ribbon. Attached to the handle was a small two inch silver toned shiny tag with the stores' name embossed in calligraphy styled writing. The silver sparkly tissue paper that peeked out of the top edge of the bag added a touch of excitement to its appearance.

Their boutique was stocked with handmade lingerie using the finest satins and lace. All of the items in the store were either black, or red, with some one-of-a-kind pieces. They originally focused only on lingerie but had recently tried to branch out and include other items made of satin or lace to their line. Carter was always giving Marissa new designs he was working on to try out before adding them to their shelves. She opened the bags to find five pairs of matching bras and panties. The items they stocked in their boutique were always of the highest quality and above reproach. However, their prices well exceeded what Marissa's budget would allow. Fortunately for her, Rita and Carter would often bring her bags of goodies when they visited.

At the bottom of the last bag she opened was an English to German translation dictionary. She looked up at Carter who at this moment was grinning from ear to ear. In an instant she realized Rita had shared with him the conversation they had earlier this morning, when Marissa shared with her how sexually alive she felt with Hans. Carter smiled and said " I thought your escapades of the last few days deserved some celebratory lingerie. And check out chapter 3 in the dictionary, it's a section on sexual phrase translations. I highlighted some phrases you might be particularly interested in. You want to make sure you are clear on what you want him to do and not to do with you". As Marissa kiddingly hit Carter on the shoulder with one of the empty bags, they both laughed as she said, "You are so bad!" Marissa thought to herself, "Only in NYC could you find a translation dictionary that has a chapter on sexual phrase translations and Carter would be the one person who would locate it."

Carter wanted all of the details from the previous night's event, but Marissa would only acknowledge that it was MAGNIFICENT! Carter was disappointed with the lack of details, but assured Marissa that one night while under the influence of one too many glasses of wine she would surely proudly explain in full detail about her conquest.

Marissa told Carter she was going to lunch shortly with Hans and didn't have a lot of time to chat. Carter assured her he had to get back to work, and would be gone before Hans' arrival. Looking her over he asked, "You're certainly NOT wearing those jeans and top are you?" "Don't be silly, I put these on to go down to pick up my mail?" she replied. She informed him she hadn't planned on dressing up as Hans was surprising her with the location of their lunch and had suggested she dress casual. She showed him the simple white sun dress she was thinking of wearing and mentioned she was planning to accompany them with her favorite red sandals with the ribbon that wrapped around her lower calves. Carter hated those sandals. He was with her when she purchased them and mocked her lack of style every time she wore them. It had been awhile since he teased her about them. She assumed either he was accepting that she had a style different than his own, or else, he was giving up trying to convert her to wearing only trendy styles made by the best designers, realizing they were too pricy for her budget. He cringed after asking her where she bought a particular item, if she would respond Pronto.com or any other website. "You live in New York City. You do not need to shop on line. Those sites are for people who live in Jersey", he would always say. However, he did approve of her latest online purchase, a simple white linen sun dress with the fold over envelope type flaps on each side of the neckline and the tiniest white buttons that went from neckline to hemline. It was thick enough not to need a slip and her favorite part was that it had pockets on the side seams near the hip. She loved to slip her hands into pockets whenever she was standing, and often the presence of pockets would be a deal breaker when choosing an article of clothing to purchase. Carter smiled with approval on the dress. He helped her pick out the right necklace and earrings, and of course, a small red handbag with a long strap that she could wear across her chest leaving her hands free. He also rearranged her straps to the sandals so they doubled up and wrapped only around her ankles. She was impressed how much better they looked that way. But, then she wondered why she was surprised, as Carter always knew how better to enhance any article of clothing or accessory.

It was almost time for Hans to arrive; she always got a bit excited before their dates. Carter commented on how this was the first man he had ever seen her go *GA GA* over. The door bell buzzed and she buzzed him up. Carter was looking forward to meeting this mystery man, as he had only caught a glimpse of him through a restaurant window. When Marissa opened the door, Hans leaned in and kissed her and smiling at her asked, "Are you ready or do you need more time? I have a cab downstairs." Marissa said she was ready, but wanted him to come in for just one minute to meet Carter.

As Hans entered the apartment he saw Carter standing near the fireplace. He walked over to him, shook his hand, introduced himself and then immediately apologized saying, "I would certainly have invited you to join us for lunch on any other day, however, I have something special planned for today and didn't know you would be here." Carter told Hans it was not a problem, and he wouldn't think of intruding. He had only stopped by to give Marissa something. "I find the musical selections that you download for Marissa to be quite interesting" Hans said. Carter recalled which songs he recently added to her nano and knew which song he was referring to, and was surprised Marissa had actually played it for him.

It was then when Carter realized Hans was breaking Marissa well out of her comfort zone, which was something she had long needed. "Well, you know, I am always trying to keep her workouts interesting. I try to throw a song in here and there that I know she hasn't heard which would go along with her already racing heart-beat". Hans told Carter it was nice meeting him and that he was looking forward to spending time getting to know him better soon. Carter responded "As soon as Marissa is finished getting to know you better and is willing to share you I will certainly also be eager to get together as well".

The three of them then left. While Marissa was entering the cab, Hans shook Carters hand saying how nice it was to finally get to meet him. Marissa wondered where they were going. Where was Hans' favorite spot in the city? Then she felt her purse vibrate. It was Carter texting her he totally approved of Hans. His text message read, "He looks even better close up. Nice manners, firm handshake. Smells great and couldn't help but notice he has a nice package and a great ass. Two thumbs up." Marissa looked up at Hans after she read her text message and smiled, "It's Carter. He says he likes you." Hans told her Carter seemed nice and was looking forward to meeting him for a longer length of time. "You have told me some colorful stories about him. I can only wonder what you might be telling him about me", Hans replied. Marissa got a bit red, "Hans, nothing like THAT. No, I don't share intimate details with anyone". Hans smiled. "I hadn't suspected that you had spoken of THAT Marissa".

It was another beautiful sunny day in the city and Marissa was enjoying the cab ride. When the cab turned into Central Park, Marissa was perplexed as to where they were going to eat. She knew there were hot dog venders in the park and concession stands, but couldn't think of any other places to eat. Tavern on the Green was too fancy for him to have told her to dress casually. After a few minutes of driving into the park the cab stopped. As they got out of the cab, Marissa was even more puzzled. All that surrounded her were trees and grass, and there was not a hotdog vender in site. Hans walked to the back of the cab and returned carrying a picnic basket. She was totally surprised as she had never expected he would be taking her on a picnic. Her first picnic date, how romantic, she thought. He never ceased to amaze her. Marissa had never been in this part of the park before. Hans told her it was the Cherry Hill section and that down this path their destination was Wagner Cove. How was it, she wondered, he knew more about her city's park than she did. He certainly always seemed to be surprising her with one fact or another. She was fully engaged in listening about its history when they finally arrived to a secluded area near the water. Hans took her hand as they walked a bit down a path to where there was a clearing, a perfect grassed area for a picnic lunch. It was absolutely breathtaking. Who knew this spot even existed, Marissa thought. There was a small antique gazebo with benches that dated back to the 1800's close to where they had their picnic. Hans explained this area was used as one of the stopping points when people traveled by boat up and down the lake in the park. Hans unhooked the leather strap and laid out the red and white checkered blanket down on the grass. He looked up at Marissa saying "I hope this is ok"? Marissa was beaming with delight. "This could not be more perfect", she replied with a soft kiss.

She sat on the blanket, untied and removed her shoes while Hans took off his jacket and loosened his tie. When he opened the picnic basket she asked him which restaurant he had purchased the lunch. When he told her he made it himself, it confirmed what Marissa had believed, she was special to him. He first opened the wine and poured them both a glass. He then got out the plates and put two in front of each of them. On one he put a sandwich and on the other he put a small amount of the pre-made salad adding the tomatoes, carrots and crotons, taking such care as he removed each from out of its individual zip-locked bag. He handed Marissa a bottle of red vinaigrette dressing. She was so impressed she didn't know what to say. "This chicken salad is absolutely delicious", she said. He explained, "This is why I left your apartment last night Marissa, I needed to make the chicken salad. I cut up each carrot, pepper and piece of romaine lettuce" he said with his boyish smile.

"This is your favorite place in the city? Of all the places you could have chosen, why this one?" Marissa asked. He replied, "When I jog in the park I take pleasure in going off the path in search of unexpected areas. From here you cannot see the skyline. When I am amongst the trees and flowers I feel like I'm home. There are seldom any people here. Those people you see over there sitting on the blanket, you can't hear them speaking. It's the same with the couple over there on the bench kissing. I cannot hear anyone speaking English so it's as if I could be back home in Austria. If there are times when life or work gets a little too overwhelming, I like to come here. Of course, I come alone and not with a picnic basket". Marissa smiled. "Oh this isn't your picnic basket? You didn't steal it from Little Red Riding Hood?" "No, it's my secretary's Mrs. Hobes. You are safe with me. I am not the big bad wolf. I may have been a wolf in the past, but to you I am merely a domesticated canine. Feel free to rub my belly at any given time", he added jokingly and with that delicious smile of his. The two sat on the blanket sharing stories of their childhoods, exploring both similarities and differences as the afternoon drifted by.

One similarity they shared was both having one true friend they had known since kindergarten. For Marissa, that friend was Rita, but through knowing her came two additional friends. Of course when she married George, he had no choice in the matter but to add Marissa as a friend. Rita met Carter in fashion school and the two became close. When Marissa first met Carter it was an instant bonding and she had grown to love him in the seven years she had known him. So, Marissa, Rita, George and Carter had been the four musketeers ever since. Hans was very interested when she spoke of her friends, as she spoke of them with such love. He could tell by how she talked of them she was a good friend to have; someone who was loyal, and would be there any time day or night for them.

Hans had told Marissa that his best friend was Wolfgang. They had met in kindergarten and became like brothers over the years, doing everything together. Wolfgang had even talked Hans into performing the "blood brother" bond once with a Swiss army knife Hans had received from his mother on his 10th birthday. Of course, being children they didn't know how deep to cut, and Hans showed the scar from the stitches he received after that foiled plan of theirs. He told her he had two other friends he had met when he was a Navy Seal. He was close to them but Wolfgang was still his best friend. She didn't know if it was the second glass of wine, the heat, the fact Hans had opened up so much to her or that he had put so much effort into this lunch, but she had the strongest urge to have sex with him right there at the park. She acted on her impulse and pounced on him. Hans returned her kiss but politely reminded her of where they were and of the proximity of the people around them. What was it about this man that made her lose her sense of control? She immediately became embarrassed. She could see that Hans sensed her embarrassment. He reached into the picnic basket and pulled out one single silver foiled wrapped candy *Kiss*. As he handed it to her he whispered in her ear. " I want you just as much as you want me right now . For dessert, I brought you one *Kiss*. It is the preview of what I had in mind for after lunch. Having sex with you would be the best dessert I could think of. Should we to go back to your apartment?" Marissa smiled. They were in sync. Hans was the most romantic man she had ever met. She felt like she was living a fairy tale and knew they always ended with "and they lived happily ever after."

They packed up the picnic basket and walked back to the road. They strolled on the path towards the exit of the park. It was a peaceful, beautiful walk. The sun was shining brightly, the birds were singing and squirrels and chipmunks scampered all about. They didn't talk. They walked holding hands while taking in all the ambiance of the park. Hans saw a cab and hailed it down. As Marissa entered the cab she couldn't help but feel her and Hans were becoming closer with every minute they shared.

When the cabbie asked, "Where to"? Hans replied "75 ½ Bedford St". Marissa was instantly shocked. When she asked Hans how he ever was granted a showing of the Thinnest House his reply was, "Oh Yee of little faith". She couldn't believe he used the same line that she had thrown at him yesterday. She checked her phone for the time and asked, "Are we on time for the showing"? Hans assured her they had plenty of time. When the cab pulled up in front of the building, there was a man waiting in front of the house on the sidewalk. After letting them into the house, he then waited outside. Marissa was in total disbelief this was occurring. She continued to ask Hans how he got an appointment and how it was they were allowed to go through the house unescorted. He told her not to concern herself and replied, "It's not what you know, but who you know in this town". As Hans looked around, Marissa was taking pictures of everything on her phone and sending them to Rita and Carter. She called Carter at work from the house and he and Rita couldn't believe that Hans had actually been given a showing of the house. However, with picture after picture being sent, there was an abundance of proof for her friends.

After touring the first floor, Marissa being impatient wanted to see the third floor. She heard there was a magnificent skylight, and ran up the stairs to see it. After touring the third floor they walked to the second floor. While Marissa was busy taking pictures Hans told her he wanted to check out the first floor again. When she was texting Carter a caption to one of the pictures, she heard a familiar voice, shouting "Juliet" from the backyard. As she opened the French doors and walked out onto the balcony with the wrought iron fencing, she saw Hans standing down below reciting in a rather loud voice, "What light through yonder window breaks? It is the east, and Juliet the sun! Arise, fair sun, and kill the envious moon, who is already sick and pale with grief that thou her maid art far more fair than she." Marissa smiled as she looked upon the man she loved quoting Shakespeare. She quickly ran down the stairs to kiss him. When he had given her the chocolate *Kiss* she beleived he couldn't do anything more romantic than that, and here he was proving her wrong again.

When they finished their long kiss and embrace, Marissa noticed an elderly woman sitting in the back of the garden. The woman said, "Lovely, you two are just lovely. It is nice to see such a romantic boy. But I would not suggest you purchase this house. It is too small for little ones and I suspect you will be having many children that will need room to grow". Marissa smiled but didn't know how to respond. Hans, however, always seemed to know just the right thing to say at the right time. As he took Marissa's hand he looked at the elderly woman and said "I suspect you are correct. This house would be far too small for a family. We will continue in our search. Although I doubt we will find a garden as beautiful as yours. Good day, Miss." The garden was beautiful so it was not an empty compliment. There were three houses that shared one large backyard. It was designed perfectly for the space with an eating area, a secluded meditation area and a garden with an array of colorful flowers. When they reentered the kitchen, Hans asked Marissa if she was ready to leave. She kissed him and replied "Yes". As much as she enjoyed touring the house, the balcony scene was her favorite part and she couldn't wait to get her Romeo home.

When they arrived at Marissa's apartment, she couldn't wait to rip off his clothes. Hans put down the picnic basket, and from what he pulled out of it, she realized that she was on his mind as much as he was on hers. As if she hadn't already wanted him badly enough in the park, his quoting of Shakespeare with her on the balcony drove her to an even higher state of desire. She realized she probably was appearing to be "easy" to him, but she didn't care. It seemed as if with each day that passed, she was falling deeper and deeper in love with him and deeper and deeper in lust with him as well. She loved each moment they spent together, but felt the closest to him when they were making love. That was when she felt they were truly connecting, and words weren't needed. Their bodies would connect in a way that seemed as if each already had known the other forever. Whenever they went on a date, they would inevitably always return to her apartment. That was when Marissa would partake in her favorite part of their dates, the "dessert".

Day Six, Thursday, June 16th Hans' story

It was 12:05 am when Hans left Marissa apartment. He knew he needed to go home and make food for their lunch at the park. He was fortunate to find a cab. During the ride home he started to make a list of items he needed for their lunch. As the cab neared his apartment he had it stop at the corner store that was open 24-hours a day. He recalled that in his college days his roommate would always devour his chicken salad whenever he made it. So, with that one positive response, and including that it was his favorite sandwich, he decided to make that recipe. There were few things he could make well yet that seemed the best suited for a picnic lunch. With list in hand he went down each and every aisle. He needed chicken breast, mayonnaise, celery, onions, lettuce, carrots, tomatoes, peppers, croutons, a bottle of salad dressing, bread, zip lock bags, a can of whipped cream and paper napkins.

He didn't need to buy any spices. When he purchased his apartment, the decorator that he hired, added a fully stocked spice rack to his wall. There must have been at least twenty spices if he recalled correctly. He never actually read the labels, but was sure the basic ones would be there. When he went down the last aisle he saw a stack of Styrofoam ice chests. He realized he needed something in which to bring the items to the park. But, a Styrofoam container just seemed to lack any sense of class. He stood there trying to think of where he could purchase a picnic basket this late at night. He was stumped. Then he had an idea. He would call Mrs. Hobes, for certainly she would know where he could find one. He searched the contact list on his phone and found her home number. As he hit send he realized it was late and probably shouldn't have called her, but she answered before he could hang up. She was surprised to hear his voice and assured him he was not disturbing her, although he could tell he had woken her up. "Mrs. Hobes, I have a question for you. If you needed a picnic basket, where would you find one?" Mrs. Hobes thought it was an odd question but responded, "In my pantry, bottom cabinet, next to my large punch bowl". "No, Mrs. Hobes, you misunderstood, I need a picnic basket", he said. She replied, " Hans do you need it now or will the morning do?". "Well the morning would be fine", he answered. Mrs. Hobes told him she would bring hers into work in the morning.

Mrs. Hobes could hear a cash register in the background. "Where are you?" she asked. "At the corner store" he replied. "Well don't buy any plates, cups or silverware" she said, "The picnic basket comes equipped with those and also it has a red and white checkered blanket that attaches to it with a leather strap. It also has a plastic side container attached to add a bottle of wine". Hans thanked her and continued to the checkout counter. He hadn't thought of borrowing a picnic basket. He couldn't remember the last time he had borrowed anything.

While waiting in line to pay for his items, he remembered that he had borrowed something once. He was a teenager with a new drivers' license. He asked his mother if he could borrow her car for a date. When she said no he then asked his aunt, knowing full well the two hadn't spoken in years. The night he borrowed his aunt's car he took a young lady to a road in a wooded area. He parked it to the side of the road to make out. As they were in the heat of passion in the back seat, someone drove by and sideswiped the car. By the time Hans got up to the drivers' seat the car was too far ahead to chase down. That night he had to admit to his mother what he had done. It was then when his mother told him "You should never borrow anything that you can't afford to replace". His mother paid his aunt for the damages and she had Hans work hours in the hot fields that summer to earn enough money to pay her back. She had doubled the cost of the damages that he needed to pay her back, calling it interest. But he knew his mother was hurt because he went behind her back and asked her sister. Hans never borrowed anything since.

The clerk asking, "Is there anything else?" brought Hans back to reality. He said, "Do you happen to know where there is a hardware store in the area?" The clerk told him where the nearest one was but that they would not be open this late. Hans looked down at the counter and noticed a bag of Hersey *Kisses*, then added them to his items on the counter. When he informed Marissa he wouldn't be sleeping over, he saw the disappointment in her face. He knew however, when she learned the real reason for his departure, she would surely be happy.

When Hans arrived at his apartment building the doorman was there to greet him, asking Hans if he needed any assistance with the bags. Hans assured him he did not, however he did need to know where he could acquire a wrench and an assortment of sizes of kitchen faucet washers. The doorman said he would report that he was having a problem with his kitchen faucet and it would be fixed first thing tomorrow morning. Hans explained that it wasn't for his apartment, he merely wanted those items. The doorman told him he would procure the items requested and have them delivered to his office first thing in the morning. Hans tipped him handsomely and took the elevator up to his apartment.

Hans entered his apartment and immediately put on some classical music. He played the piece he had recently played for Marissa, as he enjoyed the memories it brought back. He turned up the Requiem and with the music surrounding him he started the task of making the chicken salad. As the chicken cooked, he went to his wine rack and picked out two of his favorite bottles of Austrian wine and placed them on the counter next to his keys and money clip so he would be certain not to forget to bring them in the morning. He wondered when they started adding wine holders to picnic baskets. When he was younger they never had them. A brilliant idea, he thought. It was then he realized this was the first time he had actually cooked in his apartment. When he purchased the apartment the decorator had it fully stocked with pots, pans, utensils, plates, silverware, and storage containers. But, all that he had ever made in his kitchen was a mess, with take-out containers or pizza boxes. The only time the coffee maker was used was when Wolfgang used of it. Hans had his driver stop at Starbucks on the way to the office each morning, and he didn't drink coffee on the weekends. So there was never the need to brew coffee himself. So here he stood, breaking in his virgin kitchen. The chicken salad turned out well. He couldn't have been more pleased with himself if he had prepared a Thanksgiving dinner. When he was making the side salad, he carefully washed all the vegetable and lettuce. He cut the pieces very small so that a knife would not be needed to cut the food, as the plates would be on a blanket. He put the tomatoes and peppers in separate bags, so they wouldn't get the lettuce mushy. He opened the bag of Hersey kisses and removed one silver foiled wrapped chocolate kiss and put it in a zip lock bag. When the meal was complete he gathered all the zip lock bags together and put them all into the refrigerator. When he went to open his refrigerator, he noticed the shiny stainless steel door that stared blank before him. Marissa's fridge had no empty space on it, as it was covered with photos of loved ones, clippings from newspapers, poems, post cards and magnets. When he looked at the front of his refrigerator all he saw was his own reflection. When he opened the door he saw all it contained was a six pack of Heineken and the only items in his freezer was a bottle of Vodka and ice cubes. Totally a bachelor's fridge, he thought to himself. He much preferred Marissa's fridge with its overly covered door and its shelves over stuffed. It had more of a feel of home to it, than his lowly 6 pack, Vodka and ice cubes. Actually he felt that Marissa actually had a home, he merely had a place to live.

Hans went to bed thinking of lunch with Marissa and hoping she would enjoy the food he had prepared and also the place he would bring her to. He missed having her next to him when he fell asleep but, he knew it would be worth it when she saw the romantic lunch he had planned. As he was drifting off to sleep, he thought about the choice of Wagner's Cove. When Marissa asked Hans to take her to his favorite place in NYC, he knew it had to be that spot. But he wondered if this in fact would be a romantic place for lunch or only where he thought a romantic lunch should be. He wondered if he had made a wrong decision. Perhaps there would be kids playing kick ball near his area, or that bugs might be annoying to Marissa. Hans realized he was over thinking the situation way too much. It made him realize just how deeply he cared about what Marissa thought.

When Boris arrived in the morning, Hans arrived at the car heavily armed with his briefcase and three bright yellow plastic grocery bags which he got from the corner store. The bags were full with the items for lunch accompanied with an abundance of ice so everything would remain cold. Mrs. Hobes as promised, had her picnic basket at her desk upon his arrived. Mrs. Hobes could see Hans was struggling with the bags and took them from him. "No need for the ice", she explained, as she showed him the blue frozen ice blocks she had already placed in the picnic basket. Mrs. Hobes arranged it so everything fit into the basket neatly. "There is only enough room for one bottle of wine", she told Hans. "I know Mrs. Hobes, the other one is for you to say Thank you" he responded. "Hans that wasn't necessary, but thanks", she replied.

The other employees of the company always thought it was odd how Mrs. Hobes when talking to Mr. Von Geirscher would call him Hans and yet when he spoke to her he always called her Mrs. Hobes. No one in the office knew of their prior relationship. He always spoke to her with the same respect he gave to her when he was a rookie investment advisor straight out of college and she was the assistant to the CEO of the company he worked for. She had put him under her wing and guided him through the ruthless business he was about to venture into; and in the two years she had led him through the shark infested waters where he was left without as much as a scratch. She had seen instantly the potential he possessed for success with his brilliant financial ideas, but more importantly she recognized something she hadn't seen in quite some time in men who worked in the financial world. She saw a man who cared, a man with a heart, someone who would make a difference for good, not only for profit. When he was ready to start his own company, after making enough contacts and successful ventures, she happily went with him, with her Rolodex in hand.

At 11:40 am Mrs. Hobes went into Hans' office, interrupting a meeting, to remind him he had another appointment to attend. As the gentlemen left, Hans texted Marissa that he was leaving work and would be there shortly. Mrs. Hobes had a cab waiting outside the building for Hans. She was getting seriously curious about this girl he was seeing. It was obvious to Mrs. Hobes that the new woman in his life was unaware he was a man of wealth, or else he would have had his limo drive them. She was secretly happy about that fact, as she had seen Hans with too many women for whom she had been suspicious of their intentions. Yes he was handsome, and he was kind, but to some women the allure of money is what they sought, not the character of the man. This woman he was seeing, Mrs. Hobes had a gut feeling, was "The One".

Hans had a map of Central Park that he showed the cabbie as he explained exactly where he wanted the cabbie to let them off. When he told the cabbie he wanted the picnic basket in the trunk, the cabbie explained there would be an extra charge for use of the trunk and it would be cheaper for him to just keep it on the seat. Hans had a hard time getting the cabbie to understand the price didn't matter. He wasn't sure what language it was the cabbie was speaking, but he knew it wasn't one of the four languages that he knew how to speak.

When Hans arrived at Marissa's he was surprised she had company. He felt an obligation to invite her friend to go with them but it would not be suitable for a picnic. Hans did not want to appear rude, apologized and then let Carter know he would love the opportunity to meet him again. He instantly liked Carter. He could see what Marissa saw in him, as he had such an effervescent personality.

Hans enjoyed that Marissa had no clue as to their destination. When they arrived at the park and Hans approached Marissa with a picnic basket, the smile that came across her face was priceless. He had totally surprised her, and that was what he was hoping for. He was happy to see there were only two other couples in the area, and they were at a great enough distance to give them privacy.

The lunch went well. Marissa said it was all delicious. However, it wasn't until she ate her whole sandwich that he believed she wasn't just being polite. They conversed for hours. His mind was usually going a mile a minute with ideas and thoughts about work rushing through it. However, it was amazing to him, how time flew by so fast yet seemingly stayed still both at the same time whenever he was with her. His mind would just focus on her. Work never entered his thoughts and the world seemed to be far off in the distance. He still was in awe as to how Marissa would get him to open up. He had only known her for such a short time and yet he felt as if he had known her forever.

He was relieved when nothing had spilled on Marissa's beautiful white dress, as he would have felt responsible because she had no idea she'd be eating on a blanket. He really liked her dress. It had two folds downward at the neckline stopping just above the bra line, which exposed more of her chest, which he found very alluring. Although from what he could see, she was not wearing a bra. The folds folded over like a turned down bed at a hotel inviting the guest to enter. The dress had the tiniest buttons. They seemed to stare at him teasingly, as if they knew they would be impossible for him to undo. What designer would pick such small buttons for a dress he thought, knowing how long it would take for a man's large fingers to fumble them through such tiny button holes. He hoped that when they had gotten back to her apartment the dress would slip over her head, for he knew in the heat of the moment those tiny buttons would be rolling all over Marissa's hard wood floor and he would be owing her a new dress. Those buttons would not be standing in the way of his dessert.

With each meeting with Marissa, he became more captivated. Everything about her enticed him. Plus, she was always surprising him. When he least expected it, she would be there to pounce on him, throwing him totally off guard. He totally would enjoy it, but he wasn't used to being the prey, as predator was his usual role. Today was no exception. They finished their lunch and were in a deep conversation, when out of the blue, at least to Hans; Marissa threw him down on the blanket and started kissing and caressing him. He thought for a moment perhaps she had forgotten where they were. Hans thought this was the perfect moment to give her the candy *Kiss* he had brought for her. He was glad she also wanted to have sex after lunch. It was intriguing to Hans to re-member how recent her first sexual encounter with him had been, and yet how she seemed to have surpassed even his high sex drive. She was the most amazing woman he had ever met, and became more amazing with each passing day.

Hans enjoyed the surprised look on Marissa's face when she learned they were going to see the Thinnest House. He hoped she would assume that someone in the financial investment community owned him a favor, and was glad when she didn't press too hard for details. For actually, all he had to do was have Mrs. Hobes call the realtor and have one of his employee's pick up the keys. He marveled at how thrilled she seemed while taking pictures of the house and sending them to Carter and Rita. She was like a child in a candy shop. Hans was busy investigating how they made 8 ½ feet into viable space. Keeping the same antique oak floors throughout the house extended the linear feel to the rooms adding depth, as did the ceiling to floor French doors at the back of the first and second floors. He thought the two cleverest ideas to utilize space were in the kitchen. Instead of a four burner stove with two burners on each side, this house had its four burners all in a single row. The kitchen floor also had a trap door on the floor that led to a finished basement. The extra large windows that faced the street also helped to make the space seem less confined. Hans was amazed at the amount of natural light that permeated the house, but perhaps not such a feat at only 32 feet in depth. The third floor skylight was a nice way to extend the feeling of not being closed in. The balconies of wrought iron extended the usable space and overlooked a beautiful open garden with shade trees that were shared with the neighbors on both sides. As Hans stood on the balcony of the second floor looking down onto the garden he had an idea and left Marissa taking pictures to go to the backyard. He remembered her favorite play by Shakespeare was <u>Romeo and Juliet</u>. He went out into the garden and started to repeat the lines that he recalled from the balcony scene. Since he had taken English literature in high school, he did remember some of the lines, but was thankful when Marissa left the balcony as he wasn't sure how much more he could recall.

On the cab ride to Marissa's apartment, Hans believed he had done a good job of surprising her twice during the day, the picnic then the Thinnest House. He wondered where Marissa would bring him tomorrow for her second favorite place in the city. He grinned to himself, as he wondered if any pouncing would be involved.

When they arrived at Marissa's apartment, Hans could tell by the look in Marissa's eyes she wanted to have sex. She had been toying with him the whole ride home lightly rubbing his thigh so he was eager as well. Hans put the picnic basket down on the table. He opened it and dug under all the items and pulled out a wrench and a package of assorted sized washers that had been wrapped in a yellow grocery bag. "First, I'm doing you and then I'm doing your leaky faucet". They both broke out in laughter. He loved that she had a sense of humor and that she got his.

When they went to sleep that night, Hans fell asleep quickly. It wasn't that he was so totally satisfied physically by Marissa, which he was, it was that he didn't have to hear the incessant dripping of her kitchen faucet which he would try to ignore each night. As he laid there with Marissa in the nook of his shoulder, he couldn't have been more pleased with himself. In one day he had pulled off surprising Marissa with a great picnic lunch, a tour of the Thinnest house, and fixing her leaky faucet. He wondered if perhaps the best surprise of the day might have been when he pulled out the can of whipped cream from the picnic basket on the way to the bedroom to make love to her. "Life is good" he thought to himself as he fell asleep, "and getting better every day".

DAY SEVEN

Day Seven, Friday, June 17th Marissa's story

Marissa had been sleeping in lately. She didn't know if it was the fact that Hans' love making would inevitably push back her bedtime or the fact that after making love with Hans, Marissa would be so relaxed and physically exhausted causing her to drift into a much deeper state of sleep than she had ever known before. This made her totally unaware of Hans getting out of bed in the morning.

She realized that since she met Hans she had been neglecting her morning run, so last night she had set her alarm for 6am. When her alarm when off, she could hear Hans in the bathroom. She demanded herself to get her ass out of bed. When Hans opened the door to the bathroom she could tell by his facial expression he was surprised to see her standing there fully dressed with sneakers on, spiral key ring with apartment keys attached to her wrist, I Pod Nano attached to her arm, and smart phone tucked under the left pant leg of her spandex shorts, apparently ready to jog. As he went to kiss her, she told him to hold on as she wanted to brush her teeth. As he walked out of her bedroom with keys and wallet in hand, she approached him she saying, "Now with brushed teeth I can give you a proper send off". Their kiss was lingering and delicious.

Hans told Marissa she made it difficult for him to want to leave her and go to work. She broke their embrace and with a smile saying "Nope, you gotta go, one person in this apartment not working is already one too many". She walked him down the stairs going first, knowing full well he would be checking out her derriere in her spandex shorts. As they left the building and entered the sidewalk, Marissa turned and lightly kissed Hans good bye reminding him not to forget their lunch date. She turned towards the direction of Little Italy and started to run.

When Marissa ran it was always the same time of day, as she loved the city as the sun rose, for it casts such a beautiful glow on the buildings. Today, for no apparent known reason, she seemed to take notice of things she hadn't been aware of before. Her senses seemed heightened. The sun seemed brighter, the sky looked bluer, the colors of the leaves on the trees seemed sharper, her sense of smell seemed more sensitive, and even with only a few hours of sleep she had never felt more alive in her whole life. She somehow felt energized. She noticed she was jogging at a much faster pace than usual with no added effort. She wondered if perhaps her senses were heightened due to the fact that she was now in love. She had heard of people refer to love as addicting as a drug. Perhaps being in love just makes everything better, she thought. Or was it the great sex, or a combination of the two? Whatever it was, she had never physically felt better than today.

She was about a half a mile into her run when she slowed up due to a yellow street light she was approaching at the next corner. She noticed as the light had just turned red, a black limo was about to make a turn. Limos were a common sighting in the city but not usually this early in this part of town. Marissa also saw at the curb, a small boy who was struggling with his mother attempting to release himself from her grip, screaming that he did not want to go to daycare. As Marissa reached the curb she noticed he had broken free and had darted into the path of the turning limo. The mother froze as if in shock. The boy stopped dead in his tracks as a deer in headlights when he saw the limo coming towards him. Marissa sprinted full speed, picking up the boy, while hearing the screeching of the limos breaks, never stopping till she hit the other side of the street. The boy was crying as the ordeal had frightened him. The mother ran to the other side of the street, took the boy from Marissa's arms and thanked her profusely. The driver of the limo made eye contact with Marissa and smiled at her. She knew he had done nothing wrong, as his light was green. The driver was probably as shaken up from the incident as she was, and she smiled back. He rolled down his window and in an accent very similar to Hans' he asked, "Is everything alright Miss?" Marissa yelled back, "Fine, the boy's fine", then continued with her run. The adrenalin rush pushed Marissa to hasten her already fast pace.

At 6:30am her phone rang. She pulled the phone out of her spandex and saw that it was Carter. Marissa mentioned to him yesterday that she wanted to run this morning and hoped she had the stamina to get up. He was calling her to make sure she had. She assured him she'd already been running for a half an hour. He told her "I just wanted to make sure you got your ass out of bed. Can't have you getting out of shape now that you have finally found a guy you will actually let see you naked". He insisted on her taking a picture of something she was near as proof that she was actually up and out of her apartment. She laughed at his commitment of trying to help her keep her promise to exercise and sent him a picture of a Calvin Cline billboard with a picture of a very sexy man in a pair of underwear. Carter texted her "Thank you for the image, it has totally woken me up and I am ready to start my day". Marissa continued her run and returned to her apartment about 7:45am.

Before showering, Marissa wanted to clean out her two flower boxes outside her living room windows. She needed to cut off the dead blossoms and leaves and then fertilize the soil. The red tulips she planted would come up each spring beautifully, but only would last a short time. When they died this year, she planted some red geranium plants to continue the vibrant red color she loved to see when she looked outside her windows. Her window boxes were lush with color as she packed in as many plants as she could possibly fit into those two rectangular three feet long black, thick plastic window boxes. After cleaning out the flower boxes she decided to dust her apartment and vacuum before taking a shower. She was meeting Hans at 12:30 pm for a lunch date and didn't want to be late. She told him to meet her at Barclay St. near Ground Zero.

As it was another hot day in the city, Marissa decided to wear another sun dress. Cotton dresses were so much more comfortable to wear in the summer than pants. The red dress she picked to wear was strapless with an empire waist, which she wore with a strapless push up bra. This gave the illusion of having larger breasts. The length was perfect, short enough to be provocative and show off her toned thighs. Her favorite part of the dress was the red eyelet overlay of material, making its texture more interesting. She wore white sandals with a red small hand bag whose strap laid across her chest leaving the purse lying against her hip. As it was only a five minute walk from her apartment she didn't leave until 12:20 pm.

Marissa was sitting on the steps of St. Peters church when she saw Hans walking towards Barclay St. She walked over to meet him at the corner. As he stood in front of her, he looked over his shoulder at the site of Ground Zero, "Haunting", he said. Marissa showed him the metal beams that resembled a cross which the rescue workers from 9/11 had saved from the rubble of the Twin Towers. It was now kept behind a tall wrought iron picket fence on the side of St. Peters church. She took his hand and led him up the many steps that led to the entrance of St. Peters church. As they neared the top step, Hans asked "This is your second favorite place in the city"? She put her hand on the brass handle to pull open the door, looked at him and smiled "Yes, this is it". I want you to know there is a custom that every time you visit a Catholic Church for the first time, you get three wishes. So pick your wishes wisely". She then led him to the pews to the right side of the church near the back. They sat down at the third pew from the back. Marissa told Hans that whenever she felt troubled or needed to center herself this was where she came. She told him it was here she felt protected. It was her safe haven from the world. She pointed out the front of the church near the ceiling where the paint was peeling and also where there were other places where the church needed repairs. It certainly was a weathered church but it was also the oldest Roman Catholic Parish in all of NYC. As she kneeled, she turned to Hans and whispered, "Go ahead and make your three wishes. My Grandmother would say to be careful how you word what you wish for, as you might get it." She then added with a smile, "Don't waste any of your wishes for me, I'm a sure thing." They stayed at the pew silently for about ten minutes, with Hans sitting and Marissa kneeling in prayer.

After leaving the church they walked a few streets to a hot dog stand. Marissa ordered two hot dogs and two bottles of water and despite Hans' insistence on paying, she said, "Remember whoever invites is the one who pays". Hans asked, "This is our lunch date?" "Yes", replied Marissa, "The only place you would find a better hot dog would be at Nathans and that's up near Times Square. I knew you only have about an hour for lunch, so I thought we'd eat here". Marissa walked over and sat down on a stoop. "Bonus", Marissa said, "We can people watch at the same time". Hans laughed as he sat down next to her with his hot dog. They sat there on a strangers stoop and ate while discussing the colorful people that walked by.

When Hans left to return to work Marissa got on the subway to visit her mother in Brooklyn. She didn't want too much time to go by between visits, although her mother kept herself busy with her clubs and was rarely at home. Marissa did not call first to see if she was home as she secretly hoped she wasn't. Then all she would need to do was to leave a note stating she had been in the area and stopped by; for as her grandmother would always say "It's the thought that counts". She would then get the credit for trying without having to actually visit her mother.

It was uncomfortable since her grandmother had died whenever Marissa returned home. As she turned the key in the lock, she realized there wouldn't be the overzealous welcome that would embrace her when her grandmother saw her come into the house. As she entered, the house seemed darker, perhaps because the light of her grandmother's warmth was no longer there. She called out for her mother and there was no reply. She went into the kitchen and looked out the back window to see if perhaps she was in the backyard. Her mother was not there, but she noticed her grandmother's vegetable garden was overrun with weeds. It broke her heart to see it so uncared for.

Marissa went upstairs to her old bedroom to find some clothes to change into to work in the garden. As she passed her grandmothers room she couldn't help but stop in to sit on the bed once more and feel the hand embroidered linen comforter and smell her grandmother's scent on her throw pillows. When she opened the door she was shocked to see her mother had taken out all of the furnishings and made it an exercise room. She sat on the floor crying, missing her grandmother terribly. It was then she realized it didn't matter that her mother had gotten rid of everything in the room because, just as her grandmother had taught her, she had made so many memories to hold onto while in that room, that all she needed to do was close her eyes to see them. So that's exactly what Marissa did. She sat on the floor with her eyes closed, tears running down her face, remembering her grandmother and how she looked as she was holding her hand when she died.

As Marissa opened her old bedroom door, she wondered if perhaps her room was transformed as well. But it wasn't. It was just as she had left it. She found a T-shirt, shorts and an old pair of sneakers and got to work on the garden. As she knelt weeding she realized if her grandmother's spirit was anywhere it would be there in the garden that she loved so much. So Marissa decided it would be there where she would tell her grandmother all about Hans. There were no more tears. They had been replaced with a smile as Marissa told her grandmother of how her life was now unfolding. The two hours she spent weeding passed quickly. Marissa was pleased with how well the garden now looked. She had picked a bunch of vegetables. She left some in a bowl on the table for her mother and put the rest in two plastic grocery bags to take with her.

Since her mother was still not home she decided to shower and put back on her red dress. While in the shower she realized she needed to see Rita. She was upset about her grandmother's room and knew she would feel better if she could talk to Rita. After she dressed she called Rita to see if she could stop by Understated to see her. Rita of course was never too busy to see her, and told her to come by. When she mentioned to Rita about her grandmothers room, Rita suggested she look in the basement for the items. Marissa ran down the steps in seconds and was thrilled to see all the items piled high in the corner of the basement. She found a large cardboard box next to the headboard where she found her grandmother's quilt and throw pillows. She opened the box and took out a throw pillow and inhaled its scent deeply, with a smile coming to her face. Then looking up to heaven said "Thanks God", and then carried the box upstairs.

She left her mother a note on the kitchen table, "Mom, thanks for keeping grandma's things for me. I sincerely appreciate it. I weeded the garden and left some veggies for you in a bowl. I am taking grandma's bedspread and pillows with me. Will check with cousin Joey to see when he can move her furniture to my place in his truck. I will see you soon. Love, Marissa". That being done, Marissa found three large shopping bags in the kitchen closet and stuffed the comforter into one and the two pillows into the other. In the third she placed the vegetables. Just as she was about to leave she thought she should text Hans and let him know she would be with Rita and perhaps he could come over after dinner. Then off she went to the subway to see Rita carrying three large Macy's shopping bags in tow.

Shopping bags were so much easier to handle while traveling on the subway than a cumbersome box. However, when her phone vibrated as she was walking down the subway steps, she didn't have a free hand to answer it. She could hear the train pulling into the station and didn't want to miss it. Marissa decided she'd check her message when she got to Manhattan. She hated that cell phones didn't get reception in the subways. For if you are ever running late there is no way to let a person know it.

Marissa was happy to see Rita and Carter. Rita suggested they go to the office to chat. Their business was doing quite well and they had recently added two sales clerks to their staff. Leaving Rita and Carter to do more designing and sewing than being on the floor in sales. "Being a boss is fun, you can stop work any time you want" Rita said. They all laughed as they walked to the office in the back of the small shop. Rita and Carter were very sympathetic to Marissa's feelings. They knew her mother well and tried to put her actions into perspective for Marissa. She gave them both some of her grandmother's vegetables, just as her grandmother would do every summer. While Marissa was there, George called to see how late Rita would be coming home tonight. When he heard that Marissa was there, he suggested they all go out to dinner. Marissa realized she hadn't checked her phone since she entered the subway and quickly opened it. She had a missed text message, it was from Hans. It read, "Hope you have fun with your friends. After dinner would be fine. I have some work at the office I could catch up on. How about I come over at 10:30." Marissa texted back "Sorry for the late reply, got busy, forgot to check phone. 10:30 would be great. See you then".

The four went to a small, relatively unknown restaurant in Brooklyn. Apparently George recently found some investors to help the chef open it and wanted to try out the Thai cuisine. They had a wonderful dinner as the chef brought out samples of everything on the menu for all of them to try. He also sent over bottle after bottle of wines for them to try as well. He told them to eat, drink and enjoy for it was all "on the house". It was apparent he was appreciative of all of George's help with the opening of his new business.

Marissa was having a marvelous time with her friends, just as she always had. She was partaking in a little more wine than she usually did. Perhaps it was the festive occasion with all of the bottles being sent to the table. But, more likely it was due to the fact of her seeing her grandmother's room was void of any trace of her having existed. It would not have been so bad if her mother had actually exercised and needed that room. But she knew in her heart, it was just her mother's attempt to remove the memory of her grandmother from her home.

Marissa noticed it was 10:00 pm. George and Rita wanted to stay to have one more drink, so Carter and Marissa said their good byes' and left for the subway to go home. On the way to the subway station, Carter hailed down a cab. Marissa asked "What are you doing? Let's take the subway. This is too expensive". Carter showed her the two twenty dollar bills, "George slipped this to me as we left. He said he doesn't want you taking the subway tonight, as we've been drinking". Marissa loved that George cared as much as he did for her. He was like the brother she never had. As they sat in the cab on the way home, Marissa couldn't help but think how perfect a fit Hans would be to their group. She was positive once they met him, they would love him just as she did.

When the cab pulled up to Marissa apartment she saw Hans standing near her front door waiting for her. She looked at her phone and it was 10:28. She wasn't late yet, but she should have realized he was always a bit early. As she opened the door to get out of the cab, Carter said, "Hi Hans, nice to see you again. Sorry but Marissa has had a little bit too much to drink tonight. Hope it doesn't ruin your plans for the evening." Hans approached the cab to help Marissa out and carry her shopping bags. He assured Carter that it was fine. As they reached the door to her apartment Marissa asked, "Would you mind if we just laid in bed together and called it a night?" Hans replied it would be fine with him. Hans put the shopping bags on her bedroom floor. Marissa took out the bed-spread and threw it across her bed, and then took the pillows out and put them on as well. They were obviously not new and was glad when Hans didn't ask whose bedspread it was as she didn't have the emotional strength tonight to explain the whole story.

Marissa was starting to feel comfortable with her body when she was with Hans. He had a way about him that did not make her feel self-conscious. He was getting ready for bed, changed out of his clothes and was brushing his teeth. Marissa had just finished brushing her teeth and put on her red silk chemise and red silk un-derwear. She sat on the bed Indian style, looking through her I Pod Nano searching for a special song she wanted Hans to listen to. When he came to bed he looked so adorable. She just loved the black cotton boxers he would wear; of course he would slip them off before getting under the sheets each night. He sat on the bed Indian style facing Marissa. "What are you doing?" he asked. "There is a song I want you to hear by a band, Marianas Trench, called "Besides You". It expresses how I want a man to feel about me someday". She put the ear buds into his ears and played the song. Her hands were in front of her, her fingers interlocked with her face looking downward. Hans opened her hands and started to lightly and slowly stroke the palm of her hands softly with his fingertips. It was interesting how he knew of some erogenous zones she possessed of which she hadn't been aware of. Hans put his right hand and cupped it to the back of Marissa's neck. He brought her head to his chest and held her. "I will be there for you Marissa, right beside you," he whispered into her ear. He put his finger under her chin and lifted her head gently towards his face and kissed her. Marissa loved how Hans would always make her feel protected and secure. She felt as if nothing could harm her if he was by her side. When she first heard this song at Rita's she remembered wishing she had a man to feel that way about her. She didn't realize in only a few short weeks she would meet someone with whom she would share this song with. Marissa didn't know if it was because she was over tired, or had a few extra glasses of wine, or had just seen her grandmother's room transformed, or the fact she had just shared a personal part of herself with Hans. It could have been a combination of all four, but no matter what the reason, she could feel herself start to cry. Hans held her tightly and kissed her softly on the top of her head. "Whatever it is that's distressing you, Marissa, I can help you work it out." Marissa never answered. Hans pulled down the sheets and they went to bed. Hans held Marissa while she cried. Thoughts of her grandmother continued to sadden her. Today had been a very emotional day for her. Not only had she been missing her dad and grandmother terribly, but she was disappointed they would never get to meet Hans. She was certain she knew if her grandmother had met Hans what she would have said about this whirl wind romance. It was the same thing she had said every time Marissa was hesitant about taking a risk, "Don't question life, just live it". She drifted off to sleep holding onto her grandmother's quilt, hoping she might dream of her tonight.

Day Seven, Friday, June 17th Hans' story

Hans set his alarm on his smart phone to low volume so he wouldn't wake Marissa in the morning. He tried to get out of bed as quietly as possible as there was no reason she needed to be up this early. Hans grabbed his clothes that were tossed over the chair near the window and his socks and shoes from the floor and quietly left her room. He didn't mind having to go home to shower and change before going to the office, but he was thankful he had a toothbrush in her bathroom as he felt better with his teeth brushed. He was a bit more tired this morning than most as Marissa had awoken him about 3 am in a very playful mood. He felt as if he had just fallen back to sleep when his alarm went off. He was thankful he texted Boris to pick him up outside the subway station near Marissa's apartment before he had gone back to sleep for the second time. Now he wouldn't have to deal with the hassle of the trains.

He was startled when he opened the bathroom door and there stood Marissa. He couldn't believe how beautiful a person could be upon just waking up and extremely sexy as well. She had on the tightest hot pink midriff running shirt, a pair of black spandex shorts and hot pink sneakers. Her hair was in a pony tail with a hot pink elastic band. She brushed her teeth while he went to retrieve his wallet and keys from the top of her bedroom dresser. When he returned he was still taken aback by her natural beauty. He leaned in to kiss her, and as their kiss lingered he wondered if perhaps she would be willing to put off her run, but she would have no part of it hastening him to leave for work. He reminded her of the Nike slogan "Just Do It" and she quickly corrected him saying "See the cats on these sneakers? They are Pumas and this kitten is going to run". Hans so badly wanted to tell her he owned his own company and he could show up as late to work as he wanted. Now was not the time to come clean, soon, but not yet.

As Hans followed Marissa down the stairs from her apartment, he watched as her pony tail swayed back and forth. He also could not help but admire her physique in those spandex shorts. She definitely had a spring in her step this morning he thought and wondered if he had anything to do with that. When they entered the street Marissa kissed him and told him she wouldn't be walking him to the station as she had a jogging routine and always ran through Little Italy. Hans was thrilled when she disclosed that information as he did not want the chance of her to seeing him getting into a limo.

Boris was already outside the station before Hans arrived. He greeted Hans with his usual tall coffee from Starbucks. Hans thanked him saying "You have no idea how much I need coffee this morning." As they drove down the street Hans noticed they were approaching Marissa. He saw that they were alongside of her as they were nearing the corner. Hans had no concern that she would see him due to the tinted windows. Hans noticed a little boy dart out into the street and instantly felt the car come to an immediate halt. It seemed simultaneously Marissa had sprinted to the boys rescue. He was impressed on how quickly she had responded and to what end. He instantly thought "Wow, she does spring like a cat in those Pumas", but that was a statement he couldn't share with her, not yet.

When Hans reached his apartment he changed into his jogging clothes to go across the street for a run in the park. As he tied his sneakers, he wondered why Mrs. Hobes had purchased Nike's'? Was it the adds that were plastered all over the media "Just Do It"? He wanted to ask her. He also wondered why he had never heard of the company Puma. They definitely need a better ad agency, he thought.

Hans felt more awake now that he was jogging. He much preferred running in the park to using his treadmill, but it did have its practical uses. If Hans only had a short amount of time due to scheduling, or if there were too much ice coverage on the sidewalks, the treadmill was a good second choice. But, this is what he loved, running among the trees and greenery with the earth beneath his feet. Before he met Marissa he would have an earlier start for his run and the park was almost uninhabited. He was amazed how many people he passed with his later arrival time. After about a mile into the park is when he left the walkway to go into the more wooded area. He looked forward to the challenge of having to dodge fallen branches, ruts in the ground, large rocks or puddles and avoiding animals that might dart across his path. It was like adding a game to his workout. Listening to classical music while he ran seemed a perfect match to him. The melodic pieces he chose would blend nicely with the other information his senses would be taking in, the calm blue sky, the beautiful foliage and the peacefulness of being in a wooded area. Hans had long ago stopped attending Mass, but he never lost contact with God. It was here in the wooded areas of the park where Hans would thank God for the plentiful gifts He had bestowed upon him. And today was the day that Hans thanked God for giving him his best gift ever, meeting Marissa.

As Hans shaved, he looked into his bathroom mirror looking at the reflection of his huge bathroom behind him with its gray and white streaked marble walls, walk in shower with its three shower heads and the skylight above. He looked down at his long marble countertop with its two glass sinks and brass faucets, with a perfectly placed vase as an accent piece. It looked as if it were a picture straight out a magazine. It didn't have the lived-in look as Marissa's bathroom had, with its limited footage, crowded counter surface and abundance of hooks for hair dryers, flat-irons and towels. As he returned the razor to his medicine chest he saw the emptiness of it. There were only a few colognes, a toothbrush, toothpaste, razor, shaving cream, and an emergency kit. He realized he had never even opened the medicine chest over the second sink. When he would put his toothbrush away in Marissa's cabinet, she had given him a case to put it into as it would have to be jammed in among the countless make-up products, tampons, and nail polishes. He realized he had tons of room in his cabinet for her, and tons of room in his life for her as well.

When Hans arrived at work this morning, he informed Mrs. Hobes he would be leaving today at noon for a lunch appointment. As she had nothing work related scheduled for him at that time, she smiled and asked what restaurant he would be at in case she needed to contact him. He knew she was on to his secret of being in a relationship. He simply replied, "It's of a personal nature and you have my cell number", and smiled back at her. His morning went by quickly. He was surprised when Mrs. Hobes came into his office to announce that it was 11:45. Hans thanked her as he had lost track of time. As he left the office, she smiled and said "Enjoy your lunch, Hans". He just flashed his charming boyish grin, shaking his head and said "You too, Mrs. Hobes.

Hans' office was close to where Marissa wanted him to meet her, so he grabbed a cab. There was no way he was going to take the chance of Marissa seeing him get out of his limo, and he didn't want to take the subway. He was surprised that Barclay Street and Ground Zero was where she had wanted him to meet her as that was where the attack on the Twin Towers occurred. If this was her second favorite place in the city, it intrigued him as to why. Whenever he drove by the area it always gave him an ominous feeling. The mere thought of being so close to a place where three thousand innocent people were murdered gave him an uncomfortable feeling in his gut. He believed all terrorist to be cowards. For only cowards would kill unarmed civilians.

Hans looked for Marissa at the corner of Barclay and Ground Zero and didn't see her at first. Then he noticed her sitting on church steps. When she took his hand to walk him up the church steps, he was taken aback realizing that this was her second favorite place in all of NYC. But, she was always surprising him, so it shouldn't have come as a shock to him. When she explained her reason for picking the church, it did make perfect sense. As she kneeled in prayer he just stared at her, trying to figure out who this wonderful girl was. With his now knowing her two favorite places, he deduced two things. First, she wanted peace in her life. When things were chaotic she needed the Bridge and the water to quiet things down. Second, she needed to feel secure and safe. Hans believed he could fill the void that made her feel exposed and vulnerable. He could be her pillar of strength when she had seemingly overwhelming problems, and he could protect her when she was scared. With this in mind he made his three wishes. Remembering to word them carefully as Marissa had suggested. He bowed his head and prayed silently, "Dear God, here are my three wishes. First, I want Marissa to marry me. Second, I want her to bear my children. And third, I want to be with her until the day I die."

After making his wishes he started to have thoughts of making love to Marissa. He was staring at her buttocks while she was still kneeling in front of him. He tried not to, as he was raised Catholic and felt a church is not where he should be thinking of the things he wanted to do with her. He hadn't notice that a priest was nearing as he was in deep thought while still staring at Marissa buttocks. As their eyes met, the priest just shook his head. Hans was slightly embarrassed, but his embarrassment increased when the priest said "Good afternoon Marissa". Hans was glad Marissa had stayed a few more minutes as Hans did not want to be introduced to this priest at this very minute, as it would be an uncomfortable moment at best.

Hans knew the time was nearing when he would have to divulge the truth about his financial situation as it was definitely interfering in the amount of time he was able to spend with Marissa. She thought he had only an hour for lunch so she planned on eating from a hot dog stand. If she had known he was the owner of his company, they could have gone to any restaurant that she had wanted for lunch. However, Hans was pleasantly surprised at how much fun he had while eating his hot dog on the stoop while conversing with Marissa and people watching. He didn't want his wealth to change anything. He wanted things to stay exactly as they were, and hoped that the knowledge of his wealth would not corrupt the innocence of their times spent together.

When Marissa texted Hans, he was in the middle of a meeting regarding a wind turbine project in Pennsylvania and it didn't seem like the meeting would be ending soon. After the meeting he had piles of folders to go through with possible potential investments which Mrs. Hobes had reminded him he had been putting off going through for a week now. So when Marissa wanted to have dinner and drinks with her friends, Hans was pleased to have the time to be able to catch up on his work. If she hadn't asked for a later time to meet, those folders would still have been unopened on his desk in the morning. For when it came to Marissa, she always would come first.

As Hans worked through his pile of folders, he would get an occasional picture sent by Marissa showing all the fun she was having with her friends. He welcomed the interruptions. She sent him a photo of George and Rita, then one of George, then one of Rita and Carter and the last one of herself holding a glass of wine, each photo attached with a text below. Hans had an inkling that perhaps she was drinking a little more wine than usual, as the spelling and grammar under each photo was understandable but not correct.

He decided to walk to her apartment as it was a beautiful night and his office was close to her apartment. He arrived a few minutes early and when she didn't answer her buzzer he stood by her door waiting for her arrival. When the cab pulled up and Marissa had got out, he could tell she had been drinking, not too much, but perhaps one glass too many. She looked adorable in her slightly intoxicated state. When they walked up to her apartment he walked behind her to catch her if she lost her footing.

Marissa brushed her teeth first and left the bathroom before Hans finished. When Hans entered the bedroom Marissa had on a low cut red chemise. She was sitting on the bed seemingly searching her I Pod Nano for a song. Hans sat down in front of her. He could see she was distressed. She told him there was a song she wanted him to hear. As he listened to the lyrics, he looked deep into her beautiful brown eyes. He couldn't help but wonder what sadness lay behind them to have caused her to have chosen this song to be the one to express how she wanted a man to feel about her. She had always seemed so happy and carefree.

But something was behind those walls that she built up to protect herself and he wanted to find out what it was. Hans realized he was correct in his assumption at the church earlier in the day. She needed to feel protected and cared for. If she only knew how much he cared for her she would realize he certainly would be there for her. He thought perhaps he wasn't as transparent as he believed he had been to her about his feelings towards her. Or perhaps he was and that's why she wanted him to hear the song. He felt closer to her after listening to it. Marissa was opening up herself to him little by little. He lifted her chin and kissed her. He wanted her to know he would always be there for her. And then she did something he wasn't prepared for, she cried. Hans was out of his element. He had never stayed with a woman long enough to have her cry in his arms. The only relationship he had was as a teenager with Gretchen. And she was such a cold hearted wrench he was sure she had never shed a tear, only caused them to flow from others. Hans wasn't quite sure what he should do, so he just held her. And as he held her, he noticed she held on tightly to the bedspread she had just put on the bed, clutching it close to her face. He wondered if perhaps it had been her grandmothers as it appeared to be old and weathered. He held her tightly and just kept on holding her until she fell asleep. He hated the way it felt to have her cry and not be able to help her. He hoped she would feel more comfortable soon with him to be able to ask him for help. He wished she realized that he would do anything for her.

DAY EIGHT

Day Eight, Saturday, June 18th Marissa's story

Marissa awoke feeling completely rested after a great night's sleep and decided to make waffles. She slipped out of bed and went into the kitchen quietly. She bought home some large plump strawberries from her grandmother's garden yesterday that would be a perfect addition to the waffles. Plus, there was also a can of whipped cream left from the other night's escapade. She felt badly for Hans having to work on a Saturday, and decided to send him off with a hearty homemade breakfast. She put in a CD and started to gather all the ingredients she needed. As she was cracking the eggs into a bowl one of her favorite songs by Carrie Underwood, "Some Hearts', started to play. Marissa turned it up only slightly, as she didn't want to awaken Hans before his breakfast was complete, as she wanted to surprise him with breakfast in bed. It dawned on her that although she had sung along to this song hundreds of times this was actually the first time she could truly relate to it. Marissa loved listening to music as she cooked as she seemed to really get into the music more deeply. While removing the waffles from the waffle iron and transferring them onto the plate, she noticed Hans had been watching her from the doorway. She was slightly embarrassed as she didn't sing well and had been totally uncensored with her movements to the music, believing she was alone in the room. She glanced at Hans leaning against the archway and he said to her with his boyish grin, "I think I am going to have to expand my range of acceptable music genres. Watching you has totally peeked my interest in Country music." Marissa blushed and continued to complete the task at hand.

After cleaning up the kitchen from breakfast, she declared to herself this was to be the day she would start her search for a new career. The local schools had another run of layoffs, so a teaching position was not within her grasp. With her bills starting to pile up she realized waiting until September to work as a substitute teacher was not a viable option. After making a pot of coffee, and feeling a bit disheartened she got right to work searching the internet. She located tons of web sites devoted to available job listing. She first searched to see which careers had the most prospects of hiring at the moment. All of these required computer technology training which she didn't possess. She realized June was not the best month to be looking for work. Thousands of recent college graduates had already been hitting the pavement, and there was an abundance of undergraduate students on internships.

Marissa was fully aware she should have started this task sooner, but when her grandmother became gravely ill in February the last thing on her mind was looking for summer work. The days she hadn't subbed she spent taking care of her grandmother. The days she did work, she would go directly home after school and spend the rest of the day and night at her grandmother's bedside. But now, Marissa realized it wasn't summer work she needed, it was a real job.

Never having thought before of what she else she might like to do besides teach, it was a tedious process searching the web. She enjoyed working with people and didn't want to be stuck working in an isolated cubicle. But at this point, she had to settle for what-ever she could get. The hours seemed to creep by, for time does fly when you're having fun and does drag on when you're not. With each web page she searched, increasing put forefront in her con-ciseness how she might never get a teaching position. One pot of coffee and four hours later, a chance meeting with a woman at Starbucks popped into her memory. This occurred several months ago when she was updating her resume on her laptop after getting a cappuccino. A woman sitting at the table next to Marissa noticed her working on her resume, on her laptop, and struck up a conver-sation. She mentioned to Marissa that she worked for a pharma-ceutical company. The woman explained how invigorating her job was, because she met new people and faced new challenges every day. She slipped into the conversation how substantial the salary was. When the woman gave Marissa her business card she tucked it into her purse. At that time she was still hoping to be able to find a teaching job, and not wanting to appear rude, accepted the card.

Marissa sat there trying to remember which outfit she was wearing that day so she could figure out which purse the business card in. Then it came to her. It was the black purse with the enve-lope style front closure. She opened her closet and looked across the wall of screwed in hooks, that were flesh colored and shaped as bent fingers, that she had neatly arranged to place all of her purses on. When she purchased the flesh colored finger screw in hooks in a novelty store in the Village, Rita thought she was nuts, but Marissa believed they were "campy". And besides, no one would see them except for her, as they would be in her closet out of view. After she sorted through the bags she finally located it. She unzipped the inside pocket and there was the business card, exactly where she had placed it. As she held the business card in her hand, the conversation she shared with Miss Weston was all coming back to her.

She brought the card to the computer and starting drafting an email to Miss Weston when her phone rang. It was Hans. He called to invite Marissa out to dinner, but wanted to surprise her with the location. When she asked him if she should wear something casual or dressy, he responded that he was wearing a suit and whatever she wore would be perfect. Not helpful she thought, but it was very much like Hans to be mysterious with his answers. They agreed on 8 o'clock and Hans cut the conversation short as he needed to get back to his meeting. After he hung up, she realized how nice it was to hear his soothing voice after feeling so stressed out from worrying about finding work. She finished up her email and decided she had spent long enough on the job hunting process for one day.

She decided to check out her closet to see what she would wear to dinner. As she opened the closet door and saw the jam packed closet she thought to herself, "No time like the present to clean this out". She was still on a caffeine high; it was a good time to take on the challenge. She wanted to make room for some of Hans clothing and she realized that was the real catalyst to the starting of this project. It was a deep closet with two rods for clothing and two shelves above the rods. Even some of her friends who had much bigger apartments were envious of her spacious closet. On the back rod she kept clothes she didn't wear often, and on the front rod she put clothes which were her favorites. She took everything off the rods and placed them on her bed. She could not believe all the clothes that were lodged in there. She looked at the high stack of clothes on her bed and decided this would be a good time to weed through her clothes and make a pile for the Goodwill Store. She picked up each hanger, examining each piece of clothing carefully. There were some clothes she rarely wore either because they were out of style, didn't fit or she no longer liked how they looked on her. She was deciding whether or not to keep each article of clothing, before putting it in the Goodwill pile. She played around with mixing different pieces together to change up her wardrobe. Then she found a dress that would be perfect for this evenings date. It was a simple black dress, very classic. She purchased it at a vintage clothing store in the Village about a year ago. Rita needed a cocktail dress for a dinner party being given by George's boss and asked Marissa to go shopping with her. Rita found nothing she liked after several hours of shopping. But the day was not a total loss as Marissa bought this little black dress. She had forgotten all about it because over time it had been shoved way to the back of her closet. She had fallen in love with it the moment she tried it on in the store. When she saw herself in the mirror, the front of the dress reminded her of Audrey Hepburn in the movie *Breakfast at Tiffany's*. It was sleeveless, the neckline was cut straight across just above her cleavage. It had two inch straps at the shoulders, and the back was cut down into a large V shape exposing most of her back. The V shape stopped about one inch from the lowest point of her back, which was a bit risqué for Marissa. But every now and then she had to push the limits to the restrictions she had placed on her as a Catholic school girl. Sister Agnes would stand with her yardstick at the entrance to the Most Holy Child High School and measure all the girl's uniform skirts as they entered the building each morning. It was a daily ritual that she would scowl at Marissa while having her unroll her skirt to its respectable length each day. She thought of how Sister Agnes' face would exhibit a look of horror if she could see this extremely low cut black dress she was about to wear tonight. "How would you like me now Sister Agnes?" she laughed as she said to herself. She hung the dress on the closet door and continued the task of organizing her wardrobe. When she came to her black silk shawl with the tiny red threads woven into the material, she decided to wear that with the dress and hung it over the closet door as well. Finally, she was finished going through all of the clothes. The next task was to tackle the shelves in the closet until she noticed the time.

It was 5:30 pm and she wanted to take a bubble bath to relax before getting ready for her date. Not having a job, and with her savings account dwindling, stress was creeping into her life. She didn't want thoughts of money to ruin her date. She drew the water for her bath and added the most delicious smelling strawberry milk bath lotion.

She had two favorite things she loved most about her apartment. They were her fireplace and her oversized claw foot tub. Her tub was so roomy that she could stretch her body all the way out and still have room left over. She put on some music, lit a few candles and laid there enjoying the warmth and silkiness of the water. As she closed her eyes, all her problems seemed to drift away. She would not allow the thought of money, or lack of it, to enter her mind. She just laid there with visions of moments she had shared with Hans playing in her mind. The moments she decided to replay were the hottest and steamiest ones that she could recall. She was sure these were not the moments that her grandmother had in mind when she taught her how to make a memory.

As she tucked her towel around her chest she sat on her bed wondering what to wear with her dress. She looked through her jewelry box and decided on her long strand of white faux pearls. Even when stranded twice around her neck they still reached her mid section and they would look fabulous against her solid black dress. She picked her dangling pearl earrings that she received from Carter last year for her birthday. Whenever she would come across them in her jewelry box she would smile. For almost as long as she had known him, Carter often teasingly called Marissa "Wonder Woman". He first called her this when they were at a bar one night and she happened to point out two men who were there, whom she had dated. He thought she must have had extraordinary powers to be capable of not having sex with such gorgeous and well built men. Carter had stuck the studs of the earrings through the ears of the "Wonder Woman" towel he had given her last year for her birthday. When she opened the box and saw the towel she got the joke instantly, but never noticed the earrings. When she turned to thank him, Carter laughingly said "How cheesy do you think I am sweetie, to think I'd give you only a towel"? Then he showed her the earrings.

She put her hair up in a French twist, with whips of hair falling down her neck, as she wanted to make good use of the V cut back. She decided not to wear her usually *Obsession*. Instead she wanted to smell of the strawberry milk bath she had taken. She had also used a strawberry scented shampoo and conditioner. She smiled as she thought, "Perhaps Hans will think I am good enough to eat". She decided to wear her open-toed black heels which would expose her red toenails she had just freshly polished to match her fingernails. She recently purchased a new tube of lipstick and decided to try it tonight. The advertisement promised its color would last all night and tonight was going to be its test. It was the reddest of reds and when she applied it, it made her lips appear as if they were wet. She liked the effect and thought its price was worth every penny.

She looked at the clock, 7:50pm. Perfect, she thought. She just finished putting all her things in her clutch when she heard the door buzzer. She went over and buzzed Hans up. As she unlocked the door she realized she left her shawl on the closet door and went back into the bedroom to get it. She heard Hans knock on the door and yelled "Come In". He was standing at the doorway when she entered the living room. As she walked over to him she could see that he was checking her out. She hadn't planned on making an entrance but was pleased when it turned out that way. When she saw the look on his face, she knew all of the effort she put into getting ready had been well worth it. She leaned into him and gave him a hug. She didn't know if the red lipstick would actually stay on when kissed so she decided to wait until later to try out its lasting power. "I'm ready to go" she said as she was discretely checking him out as well. He looked absolutely delicious to her. He had on a perfectly-fitting black suit with the thinnest of blue stripes. His shirt was baby blue, with his silk tie a deeper blue matching the thin stripes of his suit. When she hugged him, she noticed he had not put on cologne. She was happy he never wore cologne, as his natural scent was more of a turn on than any cologne she had ever smelled. She loved it when he was freshly shaven, because his face felt so smooth and she could smell the slightest hint of his shaving cream when he came in close to her.

Marissa was curious about where they were going to dinner. Hans had a cab waiting downstairs and told the driver ahead of time their destination so when they entered the cab it just took off. Marissa was in deep conversation with Hans and didn't notice where they were driving. Ten minutes later the cab pulled up to a brick building with a bright red door, with oversized brass numbers 462 on the top of it. A uniformed doorman opened the door, welcoming them. When they entered through the door, Marissa was shocked to see the door opened to a long narrow hallway. As they made their way to the end of the hallway there was a staircase that led to a lower floor. The walls of the hallway were papered in an ivory and gold flocked pattern and were very elegant with several small chandeliers hanging from the tall ceiling to guide their way. At the bottom of the staircase she was pleasantly surprised to see a small restaurant with a décor of the 1940's. It was not a big room. It had about 25 round tables, with no table seating more than four. There was a four piece ensemble playing slow, melodic music. The songs they played were older yet seemed oddly familiar to Marissa. Then she recalled when Carter had gone through a blue period for about a month after one of his break ups. He was hooked on Barry Manalow's album "Love Songs", which he listened to repeatedly. Marissa realized some of those were the songs the band was playing.

Hans held out the chair for Marissa to sit down. They had a cozy table in the back of the room, far enough away for the music to be heard and not to be a nuisance when they were in conversation. When Marissa looked at the menu she mentioned to Hans that there were no prices listed on hers. Hans told her in this restaurant women always got the menus without the prices. He added, "As I invited you, I get the menu with the price list. Remember, whoever invites pays. Your rule. Don't worry, dinner won't cost more than the pizza and hot dogs", he said with his cute boyish grin. Marissa was always conscious about the price of things and not having a price list made her uncomfortable. She didn't want to order something too expensive and sabotage Han's budget, so she decided to order chicken.

After they finished dinner, Hans asked Marissa if she'd like to dance. He took her left hand and with her behind him led her through the rows of tables to the dance floor where there were several couples dancing. The band only played slow dancing music throughout their stay there. Marissa was looking forward to being close to Hans. When they reached the dance floor Hans pulled Marissa in close to him, she could tell instantly he was a skilled dancer. She however, was not. He led her with such ease and confidence. As his warm hand touched her bare back, she actually felt herself quiver. It was such a pleasurable sensual sensation as she felt his hand move lower and lower down her back, inching its way to the bottom of the back of the dress. By the second dance he had entwined their fingers and brought them to rest against his shoulder. Marissa closed her eyes, making a memory and feeling as if they were the only two people in the room. Time froze when she was in his arms and she wasn't aware of how long they had been dancing. Perhaps, she thought, he was enjoying himself as much as she and time was standing still for him as well. She noticed that Hans' body was pressing even closer to hers now, and that his movements had slowed up their pace. When he would move his leg he would lightly rub against her in a way that brought her such sexual pleasure. She wondered if he was consciously trying to excite her or if it were merely a happy coincidence. Strangely, Sister Beatrice came to mind. She had been one of the chaperones during Marissa's senior ball. She went around the dance floor during the slow dances, actually pushing shoulders apart, telling the girls to leave room between them for the Holy Spirit. Sister Beatrice must have known all along how good this could feel. "Surprising", Marissa thought, "how Sister Beatrice left out all of the good stuff during her sex education classes".

Marissa then took her hands and put them behind Hans' neck gently touching his skin and stroking his hair softly. She felt so comfortable, so happy, so in love with Hans. Marissa had a hard time believing this was all real. Was it possible to be this much in love? In all the romantic movies she had seen, none had actually fully captured the essence of how wonderful this feeling of being in love was. She could not even think of how this feeling could be expressed completely using words. Then she realized some emotions had to be felt to be truly understood. Marissa asked her grandmother once how she would know when she was in love. Her grandmother answered, "When it happens you will know. It will be an experience like no other you have ever felt". Her grandmother was right, this was an experience she had never felt before, but one she wanted to continue feeling until the day she died.

In the cab ride on the way to her apartment Marissa sat quietly while Hans held her hand stoking her palm. Did he know how erotic it felt, she thought? How could such a simple gesture of slightly stoking the palm of her hand give her such sensual pleasure? He touched her this way before, each time with the same result. She wondered if this was a form of foreplay or was he merely touching her hand unknowing the power his touch commanded. Marissa kept her eyes closed, making a memory all the way home. These times were just too good to be true and she wanted to capture as many of them as she could. She knew as soon as they entered her apartment it wouldn't be long before he would be entering her. Foreplay for Marissa didn't start in the bedroom. It was the pulling out of the chair for her to sit, the way he held her hand at the table, the attention he paid to her, the way he caressed the palm of her hand in the cab and God yes, there was the dancing. She didn't realize when she bought the dress how much pleasure it would have given her. When she recalled how she haggled with the clerk to knock off five more dollars, she smiled, for if she had known the pleasure it would bring she would have gladly paid twice as much as she had for the dress.

Hans was as silent as Marissa during the cab ride home. But that was not unusual for Hans. It wasn't with words he spoke to her best. He spoke to her with the caring things he did and the way he acted and treated her when he was with her. When they in bed, that was when he spoke to her the loudest. That was when she heard him say how much he loved her. And it wasn't by his words, as he never spoke during sex, it was with his actions.

Day Eighth, Saturday, June 18th Hans' story

A delicious smell woke Hans from his sleep. When he opened his eyes he noticed Marissa was not in bed. He put on his boxers and followed the aroma to the kitchen. As Hans neared the kitchen he realized the volume of the music had covered the sounds of his footsteps making his arrival unnoticed. He leaned against the doorway and was mesmerized by how the music moved Marissa. He watched as her silk chemise moved with each sway of her hips to the rhythm of the music. One of her spaghetti straps had fallen off her shoulder while she was dancing, seeming to beckon him to kiss her shoulder. Hans controlled himself and would not allow his passion to win as he was enjoying her exhibition way too much, he had never seen her sexier. She was freely singing into the wooden spoon as if it were a microphone. With Marissa seductively shaking and swaying to the music it was making it even harder for Hans to not approach her.

When Hans was finally caught viewing Marissa's performance, fortunately she didn't seem upset with him. He walked over and kissed her shoulder from behind as she finished up the waffles. Hans had not expected Marissa to get up so early to prepare this wonderful breakfast for him. When she put the waffles on the bistro table piled high with fresh strawberries and whipped cream in front of him she said, "I hope you enjoy the whipped cream as much as you did the other night". Hans assured her he would thoroughly enjoy the homemade waffles she prepared but that the whipped cream would never taste better than when it was on her.

It was unusual for Hans to work on a Saturday. However, he had some investors arriving from Austria that insisted on this morning's meeting as they needed to be at another location by tomorrow. Hans believed the project they needed to discuss an important one, so he conceded, and agreed to the meeting. When Mrs. Hobes scheduled the meeting, she graciously offered to give up her Saturday as well. When he arrived at work, Hans was surprised to see his receptionist seated at her desk. "Good morning, Valerie", he said and continued on his way to his office. When he passed by Mrs. Hobes' desk he inquired why Valerie was working on a Saturday. He felt badly enough that Mrs. Hobes had given up her day, and didn't want another employee to suffer as well. She replied, "It doesn't look professional without someone at our front desk. Besides, Valerie can use the extra money." Hans shook his head in agreement and went into his office. He was surprised to see an agenda on his desk, as the meeting with the investors at 10:30 am was the only order of business for the day. He noticed Mrs. Hobes had scheduled him for a lunch meeting at 2pm.

Mrs. Hobes entered his office with his usual muffin and coffee that she would bring him each morning. She knew his Starbucks coffee would be done by the time he arrived to work and Hans always had a second cup of coffee while working in the morning. He thanked her for the coffee but told her he wasn't hungry because he had just eaten a stack of waffles. Mrs. Hobes asked which restaurant Hans had gone to, not looking up from the papers on his desk, he simply answered, "None." She now knew her hunch was correct; there was someone special in his life. Someone who cared enough for him that she would wake up early on a Saturday morning and make him a homemade breakfast.

While Hans reviewed the file on his desk he asked Mrs. Hobes if she would make reservations for him for dinner this evening. Mrs. Hobes told Hans of a wonderful place she had dinner last night. It seemed she had been seeing Mr. Huntzburg from the accounting office for a few months now, and he had taken her there dancing. Hans always thought Mr. Huntzburg to be an excellent accountant and a man of character. He was actually glad Mrs. Hobes was seeing someone. She had lived alone ever since her son, a Marine, had died in the "Dessert Storm" mission. She told Hans the new restaurant she went to in the city last night was named *The Cellar*. She said the ambiance was delightful and the food was excellent. They had an ensemble that played slow dancing music all night. "It's a nice place to sit and chat, and it's extremely romantic. I think your new lady friend would like it". When Mrs. Hobes called Marissa "his new lady friend" he was sure she knew that he in fact did have someone special in his life. Hans never gave away signals of his emotional state at work, or so he thought. Perhaps Mrs. Hobes had just known him too well, or perhaps it was borrowing the picnic basket that was the real give-away. Hans thought he would give the restaurant a try. After all Mrs. Hobes was a woman and if she thought it was a romantic place, so might Marissa. He asked her to make reservations for this evening at 8.

Hans then asked Mrs. Hobes why she scheduled a meeting for today at 2pm. She told Hans the meeting was with her. He wondered why she wanted a meeting. She told him she made fried chicken, potato salad and pie and they would be eating in. That is all she said as she turned and left his office. Hans hoped she was not going to tell him she was going to retire as she was irreplaceable.

The meeting with the investors went as smoothly as Hans had planned. After looking over the specs and hearing from the inventors they agreed to put up all the capital needed for the new venture. Hans was very pleased with himself. It always made him feel good helping establish new companies. And this one would create 250 new jobs in an area upstate where unemployment was on the rise. As he looked at his watch he noticed the time was 1:50 pm. How was it he wondered, how Mrs. Hobes would innately know how long to schedule meetings for. He left the conference room and returned to his office.

Promptly at 2pm, Mrs. Hobes came in with her picnic basket. Hans had fond memories of that basket. She set out the place mats, plates, silverware and food on a small conference table that was to the right of Hans' desk. Mrs. Hobes definitely had Hans' undivided attention. In all the years they worked together they never shared a meal, nor had she ever asked him to. She began, "Hans, long ago when you were just starting out I helped you navigate through the "dog eat dog" business you chose to work in. Now I see myself navigating in a field in which I am not familiar. I know you have been with many women. You are what I would call a lady's man. I, however, have only had one love in my life, Mr.Hobes. I have no expertise in the field of dating as you do. I am now seeing Arthur, and feel my lack of experience as a detriment. I know the world is a different place than when I dated years ago. I wondered if you might share the secret to winning a man's heart".

This was the first personal conversation the two had ever shared. Hans smiled. He thought, if she only knew the love of his life had no prior experience sexually with men and yet had totally had him under her spell, she would find that fact amusing. "Mrs. Hobes, I am surprised you would come to me for advice on matters of the heart, for as you say, I do have a reputation as a lady's man. All I am going to say on the subject is that you should do whatever your heart tells you. Yes, I have been with many women, but it did not prepare me for the one I am with now. She is totally different, unique, in a class of her own. Each moment I am with her is like no moment I have ever shared with another. So my advice to you is to be yourself. That is the key that will open his heart. Be yourself and if he is the one for you he will find your uniqueness captivating." Throughout the rest of their lunch, there was no more mention of the matter.

Their lunch conversation entailed Mrs. Hobes informing Hans of all the goings-on occurring at the office, all of which were news to him. The front receptionist it seemed, during her last vacation, had breast implants. One of his employees, Anne Fieldman, had a daughter who had just been accepted to NYU on a full scholarship. His top financial analysis, Bob White, who had recently moved out to the suburbs was getting a divorce. His wife left him for their pool cleaner. Hans thought, "How much am I absorbed in my work that I have no idea what's happening with my employees?" Mrs. Hobes assured him if anything were to occur that had any effect on the company she would always let him know and all these matters were just normal goings-on at any office environment. She then shared some information about the last company for whom they had both worked as employees and Hans was equally as oblivious to those goings-on as well.

As they finished up their lunch, Hans looked at his watch. It was 3:00 and he hadn't yet called Marissa to see if she was available for dinner. As soon as Mrs. Hobes left his office he immediately called Marissa. He smiled when Marissa said she would love to go to dinner with him. Actually every time he thought of her he would smile. Apparently, Mrs. Hobes had noticed he was in love, was it because she caught him smiling a lot? But he was sure no one else in the office had noticed. He certainly didn't want himself to be the topic of any inter-office conversations.

Hans, Mrs. Hobes and Valerie left the office at 3:30. He thanked them both for coming in as they entered the elevator. When he stood next to Valerie in the elevator, Hans could not help but notice she had in fact definitely had breast implants, and was surprised how he could have missed this. He remembered when he had hired her, he thought that on top of all the credentials she possessed for the position, it was her bubbly personality and friendly smile that won her the job. He really couldn't understand why she had done it, as she was a beautiful girl with a great figure. American culture at times perplexed him. He really was an outsider on so many of the things Americans did. Breast implants, the over use of tanning beds, monster truck competitions, fast food, faster sex, just to name a few. As the elevator doors opened to the lobby, he saw Valerie run over to a man and embrace him. He couldn't help but wonder if that man was the reason for the implants. What was this infatuation American men had with large breasts? Austrian men appreciated breasts in all sizes, to them size really didn't matter, as with each size held its own shape and beauty.

When he entered his apartment he put on some classical music, changed into his shorts and ran on the treadmill. Running after work would help clear his mind from all the business deals of the day, and help bring his level of intensity down a notch to a more relaxed state.

As he showered he couldn't help but think how nice it would be to have Marissa shower with him in his apartment as opposed to hers. His was much larger giving more options of positions to utilize for their play. One wall of the shower had a simulated waterfall spouting forth and he knew Marissa would absolutely love it.

He chose a darker colored suit for this evening. Although both his mother and his tailor told him he looked better in gray suits, he himself felt taller and more confident when wearing one of his darker ones. He was almost dressed when he received a call from Wolfgang. He had not heard from him in awhile and was happy to receive his call. Wolfgang said he would soon be visiting NYC on business. This could not have come at a better time. He told Wolfgang there was someone special he wanted him to meet. Wolfgang was speechless. He could hardly believe his ears. Hans' last "special" person was Gretchen and they had broken up when he was nineteen. Wolfgang could not have been happier for Hans as he listened to him list all of Marissa's amazing qualities. Wolfgang asked if Dr. Jane Phelps still lived on the third floor of his building. Hans answered yes, then inquired why he wanted to know. Wolfgang explained on his last visit to NYC, when Hans was away on business, and he stayed at Hans' apartment, he met the delicious blonde, Dr. Hayes in the elevator. He elaborated as to how she had made his week in NYC a memorable one. Wolfgang told her he would call her during his next visit. Wolfgang suggested perhaps all four could go out to dinner. Hans welcomed the idea and replied that it would be fine for him to invite Dr. Phelps. Hans informed him he had to make the conversation short as he was leaving to pick up Marissa. Wolfgang said "I'm glad to hear you're so happy Hans. It's about time. I will call you when I get the flight number and arrival time. Make sure you have plenty of Stolichnaya in the freezer" and hung up.

Hans noticed it was 7:30 pm. He called down to the door man to get him a cab. On the ride to Marissa's, Hans realized she made him feel like a teenager again. There was always that rush he would feel while getting ready to see her. Then the excitement would build on the way to her apartment. By the time he would actually lay his eyes on her he would hardly be able to contain himself. He had never felt this strongly about anyone, not even Gretchen.

As the cab pulled up in front of Marissa's building Hans paid the cabby and asked him to wait. When she would buzz him in the three flights of stairs to Marissa's apartment door always took only seconds as he would fly up them. When he knocked on the door he heard her say "Come in". As he entered he saw her coming out of her bedroom. The site of her took his breath away. There she stood in a black dress which tightly hugged every curve of her body. It was about four inches above her knees, and with one strand of pearls slightly hugging her neck while a second strand dripping down the front of the dress. She had a black shawl which fell off her shoulders that she had tucked under the bend of her arms. Her lips were the brightest red and had the appearance of being wet which beckoned them to be kissed. Her hair was swept up, exposing her neck, increasing his desire for her. She had on the highest black heels, which in themselves were very sexy, but these exposed her cute red toes nails, giving them an even sexier look. His sex drive now was in fourth gear. As she came towards him, the scent of freshly picked strawberries came with her reminding him of the whipped cream and strawberries they had shared that morning. She came in close to him and gave him a hug, giving him a stronger scent of the strawberries that surrounded her hair, and then she quickly backed away. He was glad she hadn't kissed him as he did not know if he could have resisted throwing her down on the floor right there and then. He needed to back down out of fourth gear and pull himself into neutral so he could make it through dinner.

Marissa said she was starving as she opened the door. Great he thought. They would be leaving quickly, giving him no time to try to delay their dinner plans. She walked ahead of him down the three flights of stairs, giving him time to compose himself. But it was difficult, as following behind her he, had the constant fragrance of her strawberry scent surrounding him. Her shawl dipped in the back revealing her naked neck and her shoulders, which seemed to shimmer as if she had added a shimmering powder to them.

During the cab ride to the restaurant, Hans couldn't help but hope Mrs. Hobes was correct with her choice of restaurants. The cab rides always seemed short when he was with Marissa as she always had something to talk about.

When they entered the restaurant he was skeptical as the door opened to nothing more than a hallway. He was pleasantly surprised however when they reached the bottom of the staircase. The room had a cozy, vintage feel to it. Hans gave his name to the maitre' de and they were escorted to a table nestled in a corner at the back of the room. The conversation, as always with Marissa was engaging, and the dinner was superb. Mrs. Hobes was definitely correct in her recommendation of this restaurant as a romantic place, Hans thought.

Hans could listen to Marissa talk for hours on any subject and not become bored but he broke the conversation to ask her to dance as he was feeling the urge to touch and hold her close. He didn't know if she enjoyed slow dancing and was delighted when she agreed. She slid off her shawl and put it onto the back of her chair as Hans took her left hand and led her through the array of tables to the dance floor. As he approached the dance floor, he stopped to allow Marissa to go in front of him and step onto it first. It was then that he saw the back of her black dress, or lack of it. It was a pleasant shock. As the lights over head shone on her bare back the shimmering glitter she had put on it glisten. He had never seen such an inviting dress. It was as if it were teasing him to follow the cut of the material to its final destination. He had not expected to be touching her bare skin as they danced. This was unquestionably a pleasant surprise. As he pulled her close to dance, his left hand made contact with her bare back. The mere touch of her back was such a sensual experience for him, and as they danced he envisioned touching all of her. He had never known such softness. Her skin was inviting itself to be caressed. He let his hand glide itself down to the lowest point of the opening of her dress. He couldn't help but toy with the edge of the lowest point of her dress with his fingers, allowing them to go even lower than the cut of the material had allowed for. He didn't know how long they had stayed on the dance floor, for whenever he was with her it was as if time were but a mere illusion. He held her closer than he had ever held anyone. It was as if his body was attracted to hers by some magnetic force field. Marissa followed his lead on the dance floor with such ease, as if she was an extension of his body.

The cab ride home was a quiet one, as neither one spoke. Hans held Marissa's hand gently stroking her palm and fingers with his fingertips. Even the simplest of touch with Marissa gave him such pleasure. When he was with her, it was as if he couldn't keep his hands off her. If they were walking he would have his arm around her waist or her shoulders and if they were sitting he would be holding her hand. He was at such ease when he was with her, even in the silence. It was effortless to be with her. There were no awkward silent moments, no desire to have to fill the air with conversation. He could just be himself. He had never known such contentment before. He was looking forward to arriving at her apartment, for he knew the best of the evening was yet to come.

DAY NINE

Day Nine, Sunday, June 19th Marissa's story

Marissa awoke to an empty bed as she rolled over she could smell Hans sent on his pillow. He had again crept out quietly and left her to sleep-in. She looked at the clock and it was 9 am. She couldn't believe Hans was working on a Sunday. He assured her it was an important meeting, but also promised her this was the last weekend he would work. She decided she would ask him to bring some clothes over to her place, to keep there, so he could shower and leave directly from her apartment to work. Her reasons were twofold. First he wouldn't have to leave before the sun came up and secondly, the subways were always so crowded during rush hour in the morning during the weekdays. For him to have him commute to his apartment first and then to his work seemed senseless.

Marissa then started to wonder why Hans hadn't yet brought her to his apartment. They could take turns sleeping at each other's apartments, she thought. She wondered if it wasn't in the best part of town and perhaps he was embarrassed by it. She enjoyed him staying at her place so she decided not to ask to see his place until he was ready to bring up the subject.

When she got out of bed she went directly to her dresser. She took out all of her clothes from her second dresser drawer and re-organized the other two drawers to accommodate the items. She then looked into her closet. Since she had just reorganized it, there was not much she needed to do but to rearrange one shelf to give Hans half of a shelf for his things. She had taken out a large amount of clothes to donate to Goodwill giving him plenty of room to hang some suits and shirts. She then went into the bath-room to clear out a shelf in her medicine chest. As she opened it, a tube of toothpaste and two tubes of lip stick fell into the sink. This would be the biggest challenge, as it was over its capacity with items. Long overdue, she thought, to clean out this cabinet. She first threw away all the medicine bottles that were outdated. She couldn't believe she still had pain medication from when she had her wisdom teeth extracted two and a half years ago. There was also expired medication from when she had her appendix removed. She tossed away bottles of near empty nail polish, an expired tube of antibacterial cream and moved her vitamins to the cabinet over the sink in the kitchen, which left one whole shelf for Hans. He is a man, so certainly he wouldn't need more room than that, she thought. She smiled to herself, thinking, who knows what the fu-ture holds in store for us, and decided she would call Hans later this afternoon to see if he wanted to bring some of his things over. If she called him now it would break the momentum she had going with her cleaning spree.

Marissa tried to do at least one productive thing each day. The bathroom medicine chest had only taken a half hour to clean out and she wanted to be more industrious than that. Since she was not working she wanted to still feel that she accomplished some-thing by the end of each day. So today she decided to go through her kitchen cabinets, put down some new shelving paper and organize them. She had found red and white diagonally striped shelving paper weeks ago, in a clearance bin near the checkout, quite by accident while food shopping. She knew this project would take most of the day, so she made a pot of coffee and got to work. She checked all cans and boxed foods in her cabinets for their expiration dates, and rearranged the items so they could be easily located. She tossed out cracked or chipped plates and cups. When that task was completed she scrubbed the kitchen from top to bottom.

When she stopped working for a lunch break at 1:00, she decided to call Hans. They hadn't made plans for this evening and she wanted to see if he would be coming over. When she called, the phone went directly to his voice mail, leaving Marissa to believe he must still be in a meeting. Unlike most people, Marissa never minded leaving a message. In fact, at times she talked for as long as it took for the machine to finally cut her off. She began, "Hi Hans, it's me, Marissa. I was thinking that you might want to leave some of your clothes here at my place so you don't have to go home each morning, before work. I cleared out a dresser drawer and a shelf in the medicine cabinet, and you have some room in the closet also. So, if you want....bring some stuff over tonight. That is, if you were planning on coming over tonight. We really hadn't made plans. Oh shoot, this message isn't turning out ... "BEEEEEEEEEEEEEEEEEEEEEEEP." The machine cut her off in mid sentence. She didn't know if she should call back, then decided to leave the message as is.

No sooner did she hang up the phone than she received a call from Rita. It seemed George had a business lunch and she was going to a movie to take her mind off how angry she was with him. She thought she'd invite Marissa to go with her. She was upset with George who agreed to work on a Sunday. Since she opened her boutique, it was the one day agreed upon by both, which was supposed to be all theirs. When Marissa told Rita Hans was working as well today, they both agreed that neither men should ever work Sundays, as they both worked hard enough all week. They both unquestionably agreed there were no financial matters, they could think of, that couldn't wait until a weekday. Marissa explained she was in the middle of a cleaning spree and didn't want to stop. She reminded Rita they would all be having dinner tomorrow night and they could certainly bring up the topic, making for an interesting evening.

She went back to cleaning the kitchen. Next on the agenda was to clean out under the sink. It was amazing the things she had put there and had forgotten about. Way in the back she found a sealed package of disposable latex gloves. They would have come in handy, had she remembered them, for the time she found a dead sparrow in the hall. Instead, she used three grocery plastic bags, one inside the other, to pick up the poor creature and toss it down the garbage shoot. She believed her neighbor's cat must have brought it in and left it there at her doorstep. A gift perhaps, in exchange for all the treats she had given it and for all the times she had let it back into the building on those cold nights when the neglectful owner left it outside. Marissa would feel badly for the cat when she would see the poor thing wondering alone in the hallways.

She also found a small spray can of lock- defroster. That would definitely have come in handy this past winter when she couldn't get her key into her frozen car door lock. If she had remembered it was there, she would not have had to stand out in the cold with her multi- purpose wand lighter which she used for unlit pilot lights, birthday cakes and fondues, looking like an idiot heating up her key before inserting it into the lock. She thought herself very resourceful at the time, and although many people walking by would laugh, she had been successful in gaining entrance to her car. The only casualty of the event was the singed mittens that she had to throw away. She also came across a large glass vase she had stuck under the sink in the back, to give her more cabinet space. She had never needed a vase that large, as no one brought her bouquets of flowers. She decided to wash it and leave it on the countertop; perhaps it would give Hans a hint to bring her flowers. And if it didn't prompt Hans to bring her flowers, it would still be useful to store her kitchen utensils in. The vase was made of the deepest red clear glass and fit perfectly as an accent piece with the kitchen decor. After cleaning out the cabinet under the sink, it didn't take long to polish the kitchen cabinet doors and wash the floor.

When she finished cleaning the kitchen, she decided to take a shower. As she left the kitchen she glanced over to the table near the rocker. There was her book with a collection of love poems by William Shakespeare. She was reading it before she went to the island last weekend and hadn't yet put it back on the book shelf. She walked over to it, and decided to finish reading it. She sat down in the rocker and began reading from the beginning. She could read his love poems a thousand times and still not tire of them. Now that she herself was actually in love, they took on a whole new meaning.

She became so engrossed in the book she forgot to keep track of the time. When she remembered to look at the clock on the mantel it was 7:00 pm. She realized she had put her phone on silence so she wouldn't be interrupted during her cleaning spree. She checked her cell phone and noticed she had missed a call. She quickly checked her voice mail. "Hi Marissa, it's Hans. When I come over later I will bring some clothes with me. Thank you for offering. I will get us some take out and come over at 8. If that is not an agreeable time for you, call or text me. See you soon."

It was already 7 pm. She didn't have much time to get ready. She put her book of poems on her nightstand underneath her paperback copy of <u>Romeo and Juliet</u>. She would read it just one more time before retiring it back to the book shelf. She barely had enough time to take a shower and get ready. She showered and washed her hair, in record time but still not giving her much time to decide what to wear. She could not be indecisive and take forever to pick an outfit as usual so she just threw on a pair of stonewashed jean shorts with her red cotton top. The shirt just barely hit the waist of her shorts, so if she were to move, Hans would be able to catch a slight peek of her waist. Her shirt was thick enough not to need to wear a bra. It had a low scoop neck and thin lacing around the edges. She put on her red sandals with the ribbons that strapped around her leg and meticulously tied each bow. She had just finishing applying some make-up when the buzzer rang. Just in the nick of time she thought, although her hair was still wet.

She opened the door and there stood Hans with a duffle bag over his shoulder carrying a shopping bag in one hand and flowers in the other. He handed her the flowers saying "They reminded me of the flowers we saw in the park during our lunch. I couldn't resist buying them for you, so you too could share in the memory". She wondered if all Austrian men had a way with words as he did. Was it a European thing? She didn't know but she liked the way he said things, much different than the guys she was used to dating.

He walked over to the coffee table and put down the shopping bag of take-out food. He sat his duffle bag on the floor and walked over to kiss her. He was wearing a pair of black leather boots, dark jeans and a baby blue shirt with the top two buttons undone and his sleeves rolled up twice. It was the first time he actually hadn't worn a tie. The blue shirt made his blue eyes more prominent than ever. He looked simply scrumptious. After he kissed her, he said, "Got your message this afternoon, tried to call you back, you must have been busy, it went directly to voice mail".

She explained she had turned her phone to silent so she could concentrate on her kitchen and forgot to turn it back on. She told him when she finished cleaning, she started to read some Shakespeare and lost track of the time. They sat down and ate by the fireplace. He told her he had bought the Hungarian food from a restaurant near his apartment. There was no logo or writing on the shopping bag or on any of the containers to give Marissa a clue as to where it was purchased, which would have given her a clue as to which neighborhood he lived in. The goulash was delicious and the dressing on the salad had flavors she wasn't familiar with, but were tantalizing to her taste buds.

After they ate Hans asked her where the napkins rings were kept so he could put them away. She said to him, "You know, I never gave you the twenty-five cent tour." He didn't understand the expression. Marissa explained it was what someone said when giving you a tour of their home. She laughed saying, "Although my apartment is small, it's more like a ten cent tour".

She took his hand, "Let's start at the front door". To the left of the door on the wall, she pointed to a draftsmen drawing which was in a mahogany frame with roses carved into it. "This is a design for a plumbing system for a ship that was one of the last projects my father was working on before he died. He was a plumbing engineer, designing systems for ships. This frame is not of my personal taste. I had the drawing framed for my aunt, thinking she would like it, but when she moved to Florida last year, she commented she had no room for it and offered it to me. I had a print, similar to this one, which I could not afford to have framed stored safely in the back of my closet, I said definitely "Yes." To the right of the door she pointed to a framed grouping of four 5x7 black and white photographs of the city saying, "Those were a gift from a friend who is an aspiring struggling photographer. He gave those to me as a house warming gift." When she pointed to the bedroom, she said smiling, "That recently has been my favorite room. I painted the walls red because red is my favorite color. Some people think it's too much red, but I like it. I decided to have black accent pieces in there, hence the black dresser and nightstand.

A family member had given me an old bedroom set that I painted black. The photos on the dresser are of my family and friends. Over my desk, is a reprint of a Norman Rockwell painting "Outside the Principal's Office", which I bought from an antique shop in Brooklyn. Rockwell had painted it for the cover of *The Saturday Evening Post* issue May 23rd, 1953. The Albert Einstein pen and ink is a copy I found in a shop in the East Village and framed myself. If you look closely you can see where I cut too deeply into the mat. And the photo of the woman next to my closet is a reprint of "The Migrant Mother" by Dorothy Lang.

Marissa walked him to the tiny kitchen, right before the entrance to the left, in the living room, was her bistro table and chairs. She pointed to a grouping of photos that hung on the wall above it. They were of three restaurants in the city that were now closed. She had found the photos in a thrift store. She explained the reason she purchased the bistro table was because of one of the photos. "The people looked so happy sitting in those chairs at the bistro table that the feeling seemed infectious", she said, and continued "Yes again, I spray painted the table and chairs red, because red just makes me smile." She continued with the tour, "The kitchen I painted yellow so I could wake up each morning to a sunny day. All the appliances are white so I threw a touch of red items here and there to wake it up. And in this drawer next to the sink is where the napkin rings go. The living room is white, boring I know but when the landlord saw the yellow and red walls he asked me to keep the living room white. The red loveseat and white fake bear rug are new. Over the fireplace, those two vases look similar to Egyptian ones I saw at Metropolitan Museum of Modern Art. I saw them at a garage sale in Brooklyn and got them really cheap. That large photo of the Brooklyn Bridge over the fireplace was a gift from George and Rita for my last birthday. It's a copy of an original photograph by Walker Evans. And the clock on the mantel was my grandmother's. It was a wedding gift she received from her mother. It is styled after a carriage clock, as you can tell by its shape and the brass handle. It's made of a rich mahogany wood, and if you look closely you can see the wooden rope molding that surrounds the convex glass which covers the face of the clock. It is one of my favorite items in my apartment. So that's it, that's the tour. I expect the same tour when we go to your place." It was 10:30 pm and Marissa was yawning so the two decided to go to bed. And tonight, they actually just slept. It seemed as if as soon as Marissa's head hit her special nook in Hans' arm, she was asleep.

Day Nine, Sunday, June 19th Hans' story

Hans awoke and left the apartment early. He made as little movement as possible as not to disturb Marissa. He turned to look at her before he left the bedroom. She looked so peaceful. He felt fortunate to have met her. He went to his apartment, changed and went to jog in the park. Since it was Sunday there were even less people than usual that he would pass. He enjoyed the peace and quiet it allowed him. As he ran by Wagner's Cove he thought of the lunch he recently had there with Marissa. He pushed himself harder than usual, speeding up his pace and lengthening his time running. He was upset with himself for having allowed a business meeting to be scheduled on a Sunday. He had told Mrs. Hobes yesterday this would be the last weekend he would work. He wasn't accustomed to working weekends, but due to scheduling conflicts with overseas clients it had started to occur a bit more often. But this would be the last one, he promised himself. He now had Marissa in his life and he was no longer going to live for work.

When he left the park he saw a man on the corner selling flowers out of the back of a truck. They were brilliant in color and the variety of flowers to pick from was numerous. They reminded him of the flowers that grew throughout the park. Hans had stuck money in his pocket to grab a coffee on his way back to his apartment. He was now glad he didn't have anything smaller than a 50 dollar bill in his money clip. He selected a beautiful bouquet then returned to his apartment to shower.

Not owning a vase, he took out a spaghetti pot, filled it half way with water and placed the flowers in it. He wanted them fresh for when he gave them to Marissa. He showered and readied himself for his lunch meeting. Wanting to be at his best, he wore one of his darker suits. Before gathering all his papers for the meeting, he called his driver to come pick him up. He then put the papers and folders into his briefcase and left his apartment.

He had always enjoyed eating at the "Daniel" restaurant. It was one of only five 4- star rated restaurants in Manhattan. As it was on 60 East 65th street, it was a short ride from his apartment. When he arrived, he was brought to a private room where the meeting was to be held. He was ten minutes early, yet the others were already there. While being introduced to the investors and their representatives, he shook hands with a gentleman named George Beck, an investment consultant whom had been hired by one of the potential backers of the project. There was something about this man that seemed oddly familiar. He felt as if he had known him, yet he was aware they had never met. The meeting was going well with all involved in agreement with the contracts at hand. Hans was a good judge of character and instantly liked George; he found him to be fair, ungreedy and had an honest quality about him. George had his client's interest at heart but, he was fully aware, and let it be known, how much percentage of the profits should be due to the inventors of this new technology with its endless list of possibilities of uses. Hans thought this man should be working for him. He jotted himself a note on the side of his folder to have Mrs. Hobes set up a meeting with this man. For he knew too well, an honest and caring men in this field of business were a rarity.

While at his lunch meeting, Hans found himself wondering what Marissa was doing. He couldn't believe his mind was actually wandering during a meeting where millions of dollars were being discussed. It was in the middle of a discussion on the possible number of products which could be developed using this new hologram technology, when his phone vibrated. He looked at the number, and realizing it was Marissa, excused himself from the meeting. By the time he arrived into the hallway, her call had gone to his voice mail. He listened to her message, called right back but got her voice mail as well. He was glad she had called him, as it was the first time she hadn't texted. He was delighted she wanted him to bring over a few things, not that it would save him time commuting, but it would give him more time in the mornings to be with her. But more importantly it meant she was letting him deeper into her life.

He realized the time had come to stop deceiving her and tell her the truth about his financial status. He could not withhold the information any longer. With having worked this weekend, he decided he would take Monday and Tuesday off, bring Marissa to his estate in the Hamptons where they could spend time together and he would tell her. Certainly she knew him by now. Surely she would understand his intentions were honorable. He thought better to tell her now then to have her find out by chance from another source. He would ask her tonight to go away with him. He would bring her to his estate, and lay all his cards out on the table.

On the cab ride back to his apartment he opened his photo app on his phone. He decided he would put an ID picture connected to Marissa's phone number so he would readily recognize she was calling and not have to rely on reading her number on the screen. He remembered she had sent him photos of herself the other night while out with friends and searched through them. As the photos ran across the screen, there it was. There was the reason George, whom he had just met at the meeting, looked so familiar. It was his face that was in the picture she had sent him with a photo of Rita. Marissa's friend George and George Beck were one in the same. It became so clear now as to why he had looked so familiar. There were many pictures of him on Marissa's fridge, not to mention on her bedroom dresser. Hans was relieved he had decided to tell Marissa about himself tomorrow. For he was cutting it too close, his secret might be revealed by another and not himself, as he had planned.

When he arrived at his apartment he sorted through the papers from the meeting, with his notes attached for Mrs. Hobes, and compiled a set to be sent to his lawyers' office on Monday. He put all the papers in a large envelope including a note for Mrs. Hobes asking her to set up a meeting with George Beck for the end of next week and placed them on his kitchen counter next to his keys. He would give them to the doorman to have them delivered to his office in the morning.

He went into his bedroom and changed out of his suit and into a pair of jeans and a shirt. He then started the task of packing a bag to bring to Marissa's. He could not bring his Tumi Bedford luggage, as he was sure Marissa would know its worth, so he dug through his closet and found an old duffle bag. He brought the barest of essentials respecting how limited her apartment space was. He then stopped at the Hungarian restaurant around the corner from his apartment, to pick up the dinner he had phoned ahead for. It was 7:30pm. He caught a cab and went to Marissa's apartment.

He enjoyed eating dinner by the fireplace as it was a relaxing way to end his day. He was pleased she enjoyed the Hungarian food as it was one of his favorite restaurants in the city. After dinner when Marissa gave Hans a tour of her apartment, he marveled how each piece of its contents had a special meaning for her. He especially liked the art work she had, the fact they were reproductions mattered not, he liked her taste. He had sat at Marissa's

bistro table many times and had never noticed the restaurant por-
trayed in the photo above it. During her twenty-five cent tour he
noticed the restaurant in the picture with the bistro table was
where he first worked when he arrived to America. He started out
busing tables, advanced to becoming a waiter, then bartender. With
his charm and good looks, he earned enough money for living expenses and to attend college. Marissa was unaware of the reason
for the restaurant closing. However, Hans was well aware why it
had closed. With his first job as an investment consultant, one of
the first items on his personal agenda was to find financial backers
to move the restaurant from the Bowery to a Park Ave address.
Marissa had no idea the meal she had just eaten was from that
very restaurant. But by tomorrow he would be able to tell her.

After she gave Hans the tour, Marissa was tired so they decided
to go to bed. Marissa went to brush her teeth and Hans decided he
would first put away the items which he brought over. When he
brought his duffle bag in from the living room and put it down
next to her dresser he noticed Marissa had removed some of her
photos to make room for him to add a few of his own. As he
looked at her dresser top, he saw many photos of Marissa's loved
ones, and right dab in the middle was group photo of her, Carter,
Rita and George. From what Hans had seen at his meeting today,
Marissa certainly was correct in knowing George was a man of
character. She certainly seemed to be able to read people. He
hoped she would not be angry when she learned he had deceived
her from the beginning. He decided not to wait until tomorrow. He
would tell her the truth right now. But as he looked over at her lying in bed, she was already dozing off.

When he opened the closet to hang his shirts he was amazed at
how organized it was, for the last time he had seen it, it was overrun with clothing. He hadn't expected her to make so much space
for him; he had absolutely nothing to put up on the shelf. When he
went into the bathroom to put away his shaving items he was

shocked when he opened her medicine chest. It was absolutely meticulously arranged. It was the first time nothing had fallen out of it when he opened its door. After brushing his teeth he joined Marissa in bed.

When Hans got into bed with Marissa, she rolled over and placed her head in her nook, as she called it. He realized she was not quite asleep yet and said "Marissa there is something important I need to discuss with you tomorrow. I am going to take off work. Do you want to spend the day with me"? She sleepily answered, "Ok Hans that sounds great, good night" and she drifted off to sleep.

As he laid there with Marissa asleep he couldn't help but wonder when he showed her his estate tomorrow what would he say while giving her a twenty- five cent tour? The only possible thing he could come up with was, "My designer decorated my apartment, and my designer decorated my estate, there is nothing in either of personal sentimental value". He realized that although he gave them a style and idea of what he wanted, he actually did not pick out a single item. That was, unless you counted the wine rack at his apartment and the wine cellar at the Hamptons. In that case he had chosen its entire inventory.

He laid there still awake while Marissa slept. He didn't know if he was over tired, or worried about Marissa's reaction to the truth tomorrow. There was light peeking in from her bedroom window from the moon. He noticed her copy of <u>Romeo and Juliet</u> on her nightstand. He decided to read it as it might help him to fall asleep. While he turned the pages he was fascinated by all of her- hand written notes she had filled to capacity along the edges of the pages. He fell asleep thinking about the pages he'd just read. I wonder if I could be her Romeo, but no, he thought, as he drifted to sleep, that tale had a tragic ending.

DAY TEN

Day Ten, Monday, June 20th Marissa's story

Marissa awoke with a vague memory of Hans saying he would not be going into work this morning. It was their first day together where he did not have to go to his apartment to retrieve fresh clothing. She slipped quietly out of bed, and went into the living room to start her computer. She wanted to check the internet for events occurring today in the city that would be of interest to them. After only twenty minutes, she had a long list of possibilities.

She quietly went back to bed trying hard not to waken her sleeping prince. She wanted to read him the list when he awoke but realized she had left it in the living room. As she gently rolled over to get up and retrieve it she heard Hans say "Where are you going without saying good morning first?" "Good morning" she said. "I didn't know you were awake". He pulled her closer to him and kissed her. "Care to take a shower with me?", he said with his adorable boyish grin. Remembering the last time they showered, she immediately replied yes. Hans got up and started to brush his teeth, Marissa did the same.

The quarters were close, but neither seemed to mind. She entered the shower first and he followed. As the water cascaded down her, he soaped up the washcloth and ran it across every inch of her. When he then started to lather himself, Marissa took the washcloth from his hand. She caressed his body with the soapy washcloth as gently as he had hers, lingering when she arrived at his most personal of places. As she purposely repeated her movements, she could hear his breathing change, making her obviously aware of his enjoying her touch. He then took the massage shower head off its base, and rinsed them both off. With his placement of the water massager, Marissa almost climaxed. When he returned the shower head to its base she noticed he turned it so the water ran down the tile wall. By the time he had her against the warm wet tile wall, she was ready to explode. As he entered her she knew she would not be able to sustain this height of excitement much longer. They both had been at the same level of excitement, she thought, as they came almost simultaneously, with him following right after her. He held her for a few minutes against the wall with the water still running down it keeping her back wet and warm while the steam continued to fill the air. She wished they could stay there forever.

When they got out of the shower, Hans wrapped Marissa in an oversized, soft, plush white towel. It was not her towel; she realized he must have brought it from his apartment. It felt so soft against her skin and its size was huge compared to her towels giving her plenty of room to easily wrap it around her body. While putting one of her towels around his waist, Hans asked "Do you mind if I shave?" She smiled and said, "Do anything you like", and left the room.

When he came into the bedroom Marissa was already dressed. She was looking into her dresser mirror putting on her make-up. She watched Hans get dressed from the reflection of her mirror, enjoying every stolen glance. She was so happy he was here in her apartment, and so much happier he was here in her life.

When Hans asked Marissa if she would go away with him for a couple of days she reminded him they had dinner plans this evening for him to meet her friends. Hans had forgotten that under one of the pictures she had sent him by phone from the restaurant, Marissa had texted him an invitation to dinner from George, Rita, Carter and Roberto. She could tell by the expression on his face, he was disappointed. She couldn't think of any reason why he would not want to meet her friends, or was it he had something special planned and since he worked this weekend had genuinely forgotten about the dinner. He hadn't mentioned where he had wanted to take her, but that was not surprising as he usually preferred to keep her in a state of anticipation. She was just about to ask him where it was he wanted to bring her, when she noticed his facial expression had changed. He appeared to be in a serious, somber mood and said "Marissa there is something of importance I need to share with you." Just as he finished his last word of the sentence his phone rang, and after looking at the number answered it. Marissa was certainly in a heightened state of anticipation now. What was it he wanted to tell her? She now remembered his saying last night before she fell asleep he wanted to discuss something with her. She wished now she had forced herself to stay awake to hear what he wanted to say.

Hans spoke in German on the phone so Marissa could not follow the conversation. She could however, deduce from the intonation in his voice and the look upon his face that he wasn't receiving good news. The conversation lasted a few minutes. When he hung up, he did not speak to Marissa, just immediately made a call. Again the conversation was in German, but this time his voice was different. It was curt, demanding and serious. Marissa was totally in the dark as to what was going on.

When he hung up the phone, he walked over and sat next to Marissa on the bed. "That call was from my Aunt Sophie. My mother is ill, her appendix has ruptured and is at this minute having surgery. I must go. I will call you when I land in Vienna." He grabbed his keys, money clip, and phone off her dresser and before leaving went over to her again saying, "I'm sorry I will miss the dinner this evening with your friends. I will make it up to you I promise. But I must leave now". Marissa totally understood for she would have reacted the same way.

As Marissa heard the door close behind him, she felt helpless. What could she do to help him? Hans would be so far away if his mother had complications, and she would not be there to give him support. She quickly called Rita but her call went directly to voice mail. She immediately then called Carter. He told her that Rita had left to visit a new factory in New Jersey that was getting a reputation for producing some of the finest made lace. Carter reassured her Rita would be back in time for their dinner that evening.

When Marissa explained the situation, Carter left the two clerks in charge of the boutique and quickly came to be with her. She was crying when he arrived, saying she had a feeling in her gut that something bad was going to happen. Carter assured her that she had not inherited her grandmothers' power of intuition and it was merely her being overly concerned. Carter asked if she knew which flight Hans would be taking so he could check when it landed safely. Carter also asked Marissa if she had Hans' address in Austria or the name of the hospital, so she could send flowers. She knew none of the answers to any of his questions. She only knew Hans' name.

Carter opened Marissa's laptop and immediately started to Google anything he could find with the name Hans Von Getz. After an inordinate amount of tries he came up with nothing. He could not believe there wasn't any information able to be found on Hans. Carter assured her everything would be OK. But in the back of his mind Carter knew that as soon as he left Marissa's apartment, he would call George to get his take on this situation. With George being in the same field of work, perhaps he could think of an organization they might have overlooked where Hans would be listed as a member. Or perhaps, he feared, Hans might not be who he says he is. To help calm her, he stated if Hans had told her he would call upon his arrival in Vienna, he was certain he would.

Carter stayed with Marissa all day. They called Rita several times but each time the call went to her voice mail. Carter hoped Rita would answer; as Carter was not good with emergencies and was not comfortable in the role of the person who was suppose to be in control. Carter was the one who was usually in a crisis. He was always looking to Rita and Marissa for help. It was never the other way around. Rita would know exactly what to do, and could guide him through this, but he couldn't get in touch with her.

Marissa and Carter went to the Guggenheim Museum to see an exhibit. It didn't help to keep her mind off Hans at all. After the exhibit they went to lunch. Marissa was very quiet at lunch, and Carter tried his best to do most of the talking. He talked about the dinner with Roberto's parents, and got Marissa to smile a few times at some of the antics which occurred that night. One such antic included an encounter at the rock garden in Roberto's parent's back yard.

After Marissa and Carter ate, he suggested a walk along the East River. Carter knew Marissa well enough to know that when she needed to calm down and think, she needed to be near a large body of water. It didn't matter if it was the East River, the Hudson River, the lake in Central Park or the beach; it just needed to be water. Marissa enjoyed her time with Carter but as it neared four o'clock she told him she wanted to be alone.

While they were walking to Marissa's apartment, Rita finally returned their calls. Rita had just returned to the boutique and realized her phone had been unknowingly on silent, she apologized profusely and wanted to come over to be with Marissa. Marissa explained she just wanted to go home and be alone. There was no need for her to come over now. Carter walked Marissa to her apartment, and when they arrived she did exactly as she said she would, she went upstairs alone.

When Marissa entered her apartment the first thing she did was to try to Google Hans name again. She had a hard time believing that nothing would come up with each attempt. How was it that an investment consultant would have no information about himself on the web. She Googled all the men she had dated from Wall Street. With each name, information would pop up. Then she Googled her mother's name. She couldn't believe it. Even her mother had information pop up on the internet, under a church group that she belonged too. She sat in her apartment wondering if Hans was who he said he was. It was not possible that he could work in the financial district of Manhattan and not have a web page or any association with some company which would come up if his name was Googled. Also, throughout the day Hans' sentence of "There is something important I need to discuss with you" kept running through her mind. What was it he wanted to tell her?

At 10:30 PM her phone rang. It was Hans. He told her he was on route to the hospital. He hadn't been given any new information about his mother. After he talked with the doctors he would know more and assured her he would call back. The car had just pulled up to the entrance of the hospital so he needed to hang up. Marissa wanted to ask Hans the spelling of his last name, as perhaps she had it wrong. She wanted his address or the name of the hospital. But she realized, now was not the time to mention it. She would ask him when he called her in the morning.

"Auf Wiedersehen", he said as he hung up.

Marissa couldn't sleep that night. She was worried about Hans and his mother. She tossed and turned all night. She tried to use

Han's pillow to sleep on because it still had a hint of his scent. It gave her some comfort, but, it didn't seem to help her sleep.

Day Ten, Monday, June 20th Hans' story

It was his first day of waking up at Marissa's when he did not have to return to his apartment for a change of clothing. Marissa asking him to bring over a few items, made him feel secure in the fact that she deeply cared for him. He decided he would make love to her and then ask her to go away for a couple of days with him. He would tell her all about his financial situation and then they would have no secrets between them. His plan was going well. He caught her before she got out of bed. Their showering together was as every encounter with Marissa, epic. He was sure she had no idea how excited he became with how she would respond to each and every touch of his fingers, hands, lips and tongue. He had never been with a woman before who had responded to him as she did. She was so totally uninhibited.

When he finally found the right moment to ask her to go away with him, he couldn't believe he had forgotten that tonight was the dinner to meet her friends. Hans decided right there and then would have to suffice as the correct time to tell her, as he would be meeting George tonight. He took a deep breath and said "Marissa there is something of importance that I need to share with you." No sooner did he get the sentence out of his mouth than his phone rang. He would have ignored it but it he noticed from the ringtone it was a call from Vienna. He looked at the number and noticed it was his Aunt Sophie. He immediately answered it, because in all the years he lived in America; she had never called him even once. She told Hans his mother was having emergency surgery. Hans hung up and called his pilot to have him ready his jet. Hans would meet him in forty-five minutes at LaGuardia airport. Hans left swiftly from Marissa's apartment, went to his apartment, got his passport, quickly packed some clothes in his luggage and took off for LaGuardia.

The flight did not leave as quickly as Hans had hoped as the pilot needed time to fill in and have approved the appropriate paper work before departure. While Hans sat on the plane as it taxied to the runway, he thought about how he had left Marissa's so abruptly. Hans hated how he mentioned he had something important to tell her, and then just took off. During the flight to Austria, Hans thought about his mother. He saw her last a little over a year ago. His last visit was last April when he flew over for the annual Vienna marathon. He would meet Wolfgang there each year for the marathon but this year it was an inconvenient time for both of them, so Hans did not attend. Hans called and spoke to his mother often but he had been working so many hours on so many different projects that he didn't want to leave for an extended period of time for a visit. He started to think how his priorities had not been what they should have been.

He thought about Marissa and realized he should have asked her to come. But since they had only known each other for a short period of time he wondered if she would have dropped everything and come with him. As much as he would think of his mother, his thoughts would keep returning to Marissa. He took out some paper and decided he would write to Marissa. Perhaps if he put down on paper how he felt, it would help.

Hans tried to call the hospital from the jet, however due to confidentiality rules; they refused to give out any information over the phone. Even with Hans' explanation that he was on his way from America, they would not change the decision. When Hans insisted on speaking with the supervisor in charge he was told he was not available at the moment. Hans attempted to call his aunt, whom he assumed must have been in the hospital with her phone turned off, because she did not answer his phone during any of his attempts.

When the jet arrived at Vienna International there was a car waiting for Hans to drive him to the hospital. After a few more futile attempts at reaching his aunt or reaching the supervisor in charge of the hospital, he called Marissa to tell her he had arrived. He apologized for not being able to meet her friends as she had wanted. He promised that upon his return he would surely meet them all. He assured Marissa he would call her later when he found out further information about his mother's condition.

When Hans reached the information counter he was both upset about not having knowledge on his mothers' condition and outraged at the fact no one would give him any information while he was in flight. He realized he should not take out his frustration on the woman at this counter, so he abruptly asked for his mothers' room number. When he received it, he swiftly found the elevator to hasten his visit with her. When the elevator doors opened onto the fifth floor he hurried down the hall looking for her room number. He could feel his heart racing in his chest. While entering room number 504, he thought he had the wrong room. What he saw before him was a grimly appearing older woman who looked frail, thin and pale with a scarf wrapped upon her head as if she had lost her hair from chemo treatments. If it weren't for the fact that his Aunt Sophie was sitting in a chair against the wall he would have left believing he was in someone else's room. It wasn't until he came closer to the bed that he recognized the gravely ill woman was his mother. Hans looked at all the monitors and machines she was hooked up to. He fought to hold back the tears as his inner child wanted to run out of the room screaming. How could she be this sick? He had seen her just a little more than a year ago and she was healthy and fine. Now before him laid a woman who seemed to be a shadow of whom his mother was. He pulled up a chair and sat by her bedside. How could all this be from a burst appendix? Something did not add up. His aunt looked seemingly tired as she must have been there for a long duration.

He was actually surprised to see her at all since his mother had not spoken to her in years.

Hans asked his Aunt Sophie if she would please let the nurse know that he wanted to speak with the doctor in charge of his mother's care. She left and did as he requested. He held his mother's hands watching her sleep and his hand brushed against the sheet. What was it about hospital sheets, he wondered, why were they always so stiff and so paper thin? And why was everything so white? And what was that odor he thought? Every hospital he had ever been in seemed to have that same odor. It was a unique smell but one he could not identify.

Hans sat with his mother, as she slept, for about half an hour before the doctor arrived. The doctor asked Hans to come into the hallway. It was in the narrow hallway, with the pale blue wall papered speckled with tiny green leaves and visitors and nurses hustling about, where Hans learned that his mother had ovarian cancer. She had been ill for some time now and she was nearing the end. Hans could not believe what he was hearing. How was it that his mother never told him she was sick? How could his Aunt not have contacted him earlier? Why had she called and lied to say her appendix had ruptured. He was told by the doctor there was nothing that anyone could do but make his mother as comfortable as possible. There was nothing he could do; nothing that all the wealth he possessed could do to help his own mother, he thought. Hans felt flushed and paced the hallway for a bit. He realized he needed to get out of the hall. He needed to think! He didn't know what to do. He went down to the first floor to the atrium. As he opened the heavy metal door that led to the seating area in the neatly kept garden, he felt a bit relieved as the fresh air swept across his face. He sat on a bench by a tree and tried to clear his head. He realized he wanted Marissa there so he took a chance and called her.

She was asleep and groggy when she first answered. Hans didn't even say "Hi", he immediately asked her if she had a passport. When she replied that she had, he then asked her if she'd be willing to come to Austria to be with him as his mother was dying. She instantly responded "Yes". As soon as she did, Hans told her he would have someone call with information on her flight. "It will be all set. You need only to pack. There will be a ticket sent to your apartment in the morning. There will be a car to take you to the airport and a car to pick you up when you arrive". She agreed. As soon as Hans hung up he immediately called the States and spoke to Mrs. Hobes. It was the middle of the night but he knew she'd understand and agree to take care of all the details for Marissa. Hans asked Mrs. Hobes to text him the information so he would know what time to pick Marissa up. She agreed. Mrs. Hobes was glad Marissa would be meeting him in Austria so he would have someone by his side to go through this with.

Hans returned to his mother's room. He decided he was definitely bringing her home. He had to rescue her from this place. This room was too starch and disinfectant smelling, too much for her to have to bear. The room seemed depressing and he wanted his mother back in her own bedroom with its pink- flowered wallpaper, oak bedroom set, soft chenille bedspread, and her scented candles that she would burn in the evenings. The view from her hospital room looked out to a stark towering black glass building with no view of life. It was no comparison to her oversized French doors in her own room with the view of the vineyard that she loved.

Hans held his mother's frail hand attached to the IV, with skin so transparent that her veins were easily visible and softly kissed it. The kiss seemed to have awakened her from her slumber. When she opened her eyes, they still possessed the sparkle that Hans remembered. Her voice was weak when she said, "I knew you would come". "Of course I would come, I would have come earlier had I only known", he answered. He then asked why she hadn't told him she was ill, as there had been so many phone calls when she could have mentioned it. She explained she didn't want to worry him. She wanted him to go about and live his life, as there was nothing he or anyone could do to change the situation. She told him it was not to be discussed any further as she refused to waste her precious time with him talking of her illness. He then told her he would be taking her home. He was going to have the doctor discharge her and get her medication ready so they could leave. She refused saying "I don't want each time you walk into our home for you to remember that it was where I died. The nurses here are kind and I'm not in any pain. It's all right Hans. I am in good hands here. This is where I want to be". Hans knew his mother was stubborn and he was not going to go against her wishes, especially as it would be her last.

His mother wanted to hear more about the girl he had told her about when he called her last week. Her first question was, "Capture her essence to me in one word". Hans answered instantly "Verzaubert", enchanting. She asked him question after question about Marissa until she tired. After about an hour of talking she told him she needed to take a short nap.

She napped and awoke on and off all during the night and the next day. He sat there by her side, never leaving. His Aunt Sophie never returned, and he did not call her. He decided not to confront his aunt with any questions. There would be time enough for that later, he thought. For now he wanted to be by his mother's side for as long as he could.

DAY ELEVEN

Day Eleven, Tuesday, June 21st Marissa's story

When Marissa hung up with Hans, she realized she still didn't have an address in Austria. She jumped out of bed and started to pack. Her passport was just where she left it, in the side pocket of the luggage she had purchased for Rita's bachelorette party. Carter persuaded the group to have the party in Canada. It wasn't until the strippers were totally naked shaking all that God had given them when the group realized why he had chosen Canada. Apparently, New York has a state code that insists all dancers' genitals be covered and in Canada that piece of fabric was not a requirement. As Rita had only "been with" George, Carter thought she should at least see a few more genitalia before her wedding night, and he certainly got his wish that night.

She was glad she purchased the new luggage for that weekend getaway or else she would be going to Austria with a duffle bag. She was packed and ready to go by 4am. She tried to sleep but couldn't. She received a phone call from a Mrs. Hobes at 6am. She introduced herself as Hans' secretary. She offered Marissa two choices of flights to Austria. Since Marissa was ready to go so she picked the first flight available. Mrs. Hobes gave her the flight information and time of arrival in Austria. She asked if Marissa could be ready by 8am to be picked up by a car and Marissa assured her she was ready. Marissa inquired if she might have Hans address in Austria to give the information to her mother. Mrs. Hoges gave Marissa his home address in Vienna and the hospital name and address as well. Marissa knew that her mother, George, Rita and Carter would be more comfortable if they had an address where she would be staying. Marissa opened her laptop and emailed them with the news of her departure, the flight information and the addresses. She stated in her emails the reason for her not calling personally was due to the early hour. Actually, she was afraid if she called any one of them they would have tried to stop her from going to be with a man she barely knew and to a foreign country to boot.

The car arrived promptly to drive Marissa to the airport. As the driver opened the car door for her to enter, he handed her a plane ticket. Marissa was nervous. She never liked flying. Carter had given her some pills when they had flown to Canada to assist her on getting through the flight. She was glad there were still some in the zipper pocket of her carry on that she neglected to remove as she planned on using them this morning. Once she settled into her seat on the plane she took one of the pills. She forgot how powerful they were until she awoke four hours later. The rest of Marissa's flight was uneventful, thankfully no turbulence.

She grabbed the travel guide she purchased in the airport while waiting for the plane to board. She read that Vienna had the oldest zoo in the world, and read a list of all the animals it owned including pandas. It made her nervous when she read they had wild boars in their woodlands. It interested her when she read that Austria was the homeland of Mozart, Beethoven, Strauss and Brahms. It only seemed natural now why Hans would be so into classical music. It's from his roots. She also read and reread the English to

German dictionary that Carter gave her. She went over some key phrases in her head that she felt might come in handy. "Where is the bathroom?" is the first phrase she memorized. She listened to her I Pod Nano and prayed for Hans' mother to have a peaceful death and for Hans to have the strength needed to endure it. When the pilot announced they would be landing in Vienna shortly, Marissa freshened up. Marissa was so glad she was going to be with Hans shortly. She wanted to be there to comfort him in whatever way she could.

When Marissa went to pick up her luggage she walked past several men in black suits lined up holding signs with various people's names written on them. It was like a scene out of a movie. There was a gentlemen holding up a sign that read, "Marissa Molinari". She hoped he understood English, and he did. He carried her luggage and while putting it into the trunk, told her not to concern herself with it as it would be brought to the house. When she entered the car at the airport, Hans was not in it. The driver told her that Mr.Von Gleirscher would meet her at the hospital. So that was Hans' real name, Von Gleirscher. She decided when she saw him she would not ask him why he had not told her his real name, as now was not the time. Surely, he had a good reason for it. She would ask him later, when they returned to the States. But she would later email Carter with the discovery of Hans' real last name, to ease her friend's mind.

As Marissa rode in the limo to the hospital, she started to concern herself over the possibility of Hans maxing out his credit cards on cars and flights. She had only a small amount of money with her that she had taken out at the ATM in the airport. She realized this flight was expensive and decided she would pay him back, a little at a time, of course. When Marissa arrived at the hospital, Hans was leaning against the marble wall at the main entrance waiting for her. She could tell he hadn't shaved or slept since she last saw him, since he was still in the same clothes that she had last seen him in. When he opened the door of the car she couldn't get out fast enough. She just stood there holding him as tightly as she could. He looked at her and said "Thank you for coming". She kissed him and told him there was no other place she'd rather be.

The hospital looked newly built. The outside of the building was marble with a lot of glass walls and brass sculptures in the entryway. It was a very modern looking building, unlike the baroque buildings and statues she had passed along the way. They had driven past buildings looking hundreds of years old, with statues with such intricate details everywhere, even some carved out of the sides of the walls of buildings. She passed magnificent fountains with sculptures of such magnitude. Some were as tall as two story buildings. Marissa was impressed with the architecture; she had never seen so many baroque-style buildings before. The buildings in Hans' city certainly were much more ostentatious than in her own.

As they exited the elevator to the fifth floor, Marissa thought to herself, "What was that smell? How is it, whether you are in NY or Austria, hospitals always have the same smell?" It momentarily brought her back to when her father was ill and hospitalized. Hans held her hand tighter as they entered his mother's room. She walked in and saw a frail, older woman, sleeping peacefully. His mother had IV's in both hands, what seemed to be a heart monitor attached to her and one other machine which Marissa was not familiar with, which constantly beeped. When Marissa looked into his mother's face she could see the resemblance. Hans moved a chair near the bed, next to his, so Marissa could be near him. Marissa wondered if Hans had eaten or slept. When she asked him, he replied he had eaten some. He ate from the tray they continued to bring his mother, though she had no appetite and he had slept a bit in the chair. He told her his mother has lucid moments and then sleeps. He wanted to be with her for her waking moments as much as possible.

Just as he said that his mother's eyes opened. Hans spoke to her softly in German. He introduced Marissa to his mother. At least she thought that was what he was saying. Although she was frail and sick, Marissa could tell she was a beautiful woman. She had a warm smile, when she looked at Marissa. Marissa could see by her facial expression that she approved of her. His mother talked to Hans again in German. He seemed a bit annoyed with her but said "Da". Marissa knew that meant "Yes", she had been studying the English to German dictionary a little bit each day, ever since Carter had given it to her. Hans explained his mother wanted him to go home to shower, shave and change as she said "he looked a mess". He told Marissa he agreed to his mother's request but would only do so when she fell back to sleep again. The three had a nice conversation, with Hans interpreting. His mom inquired about Hans' life in NY. Marissa wondered if Hans was interpreting everything or filtering it a bit. When she asked Marissa questions about herself, Marissa was sure Hans interpreted that part exactly as she had spoken it, as she could see in his mother's eyes she was pleased with her answers. After every answer, Hans' mother would give Marissa a beautiful smile. That smile was a familiar sight to Marissa for Hans had his mother's smile. Marissa was thrilled that his mother seemed to like her. After about an hour his mother drifted off to sleep. Hans and Marissa left the hospital. A black car was out front waiting for them.

It wasn't a long drive to Hans' house from the hospital. When the driver pulled the car up in front of Hans' house, it was picturesque. It was just how she imagined a house in the Austrian countryside would look like. It was a modest sized home, surrounded by a white picket fence. The house was made of cobblestone, with a winding slate walkway leading to a bright red front door. It was such a charming entrance with a small pebble bed on both sides of the slate walkway near the doorway filled with pansies and violets. To the left of the door was a huge bay window. A cobblestone chimney ran up the left side of the house, as did crawling ivy. There were flower beds scattered all about the front yard that gave splashes of colors everywhere. There were rhododendrons, irises, poppies, lavender and hydrangeas. There were also tiny white flowers throughout the garden. It was apparent that his mother loved to garden. When they entered the home Marissa marveled how quaint it was. The driver brought their luggage into Hans' room and put it on the floor near the dresser. It was then she noticed, she had been correct, he hadn't been home yet. There was his luggage being carried it right along with hers. He had never left his mother's side. When Hans announced he was going to take a shower, Marissa noticed the size of the tub in the bathroom and suggested a bath. It was a 2-step-down tub that was at least twice the width of her tub. As he undressed, Marissa ran the water. She undressed and entered the tub first. She rested her back against the back of the tub and instructed Hans to get in. He laid his back against her chest. She had her arms around him. She washed his chest and arms with the washcloth as he lay against her. Her legs were wrapped around him as well. She could feel him relaxing. He was breathing easier. She just laid there holding him. They stayed in the tub for about an hour, from time to time adding hot water. When they were ready to leave the tub, Hans drained the water then turned on the shower. Marissa rinsed off and got out. Hans stayed in the shower to shave.

Marissa was in Hans' bed when he came out. As he stood there in his towel she told him to come to bed to rest. He removed his towel then laid his head on his pillow. He looked exhausted. Marissa kissed him softly on his cheek. She then moved to his lips, neck, and chest. She met no resistance when she held down his hands. She caressed and kissed his chest feeling each ripple of muscle on his chest and enjoyed the salty taste of his skin. Marissa started to make love to Hans orally, every inch of him, as he did the first night when he first made love to her. It was the first time Hans just laid there accepting all the pleasure that were being given to him, without reciprocating. He allowed Marissa to please only him. After he climaxed Marissa told Hans to roll onto his stomach. She put some lotion onto his back and gave him a long hard massage. She could feel the tension in his muscles. She tried to work out the knots to help him relax. During the massage, he drifted off to sleep, just as she had hoped he would. Marissa laid there awake for awhile looking around Hans' bedroom, then drifted off to sleep.

A few hours later Marissa was woken by a gentle touch on her shoulder from Hans. He was fully dressed. He asked her if she minded being left alone because he wanted to go and be with his mother. He told her there was a car in the garage and the keys were on the kitchen counter. He insisted she call him if she needed anything. Marissa told Hans she would be fine and she understood. And as she heard the key lock the front door Marissa could feel herself falling back to sleep.

Day Eleven, June 21st Hans' story

Hans was glad that Marissa's flight would be arriving soon. He was the most concerned when his mother slept. Each time she closed her eyes, he feared it would be the last. When his mother awoke he told her of Marissa's upcoming arrival. His mother seemed pleased and was happy she would get to meet the woman who brought the sparkle back to her son's eyes.

When she was awake they talked, and when she became tired of talking he would read to her. When she would fall asleep he would continue to read aloud to her. Even though she slept he wondered if perhaps she could hear his voice and if it would somehow bring her comfort. He brought with him from America the book that his mother had snuck into his backpack when he left Austria, what now seemed a lifetime ago. It was a book with several of Shakespeare's plays. She knew he loved the English literature class he had taken in high school so she thought he would enjoy reading it on his plane ride. He read it to her, translating it into German so she would understand. When he received the call of Marissa's car approaching the hospital he went downstairs to meet her. When she got out of the car and flung her arms around him, he felt so comforted. He was so glad she had finally arrived.

He knew his mother would like Marissa. Hans did not translate every word his mother spoke. His mother told Marissa she had heard many things about her from Hans, but Hans shortened her remarks. He didn't think Marissa needed to know how he jogged every day on the beach hoping to catch a glimpse of her, or that he hadn't yet told her of his successes. There would be time to tell her of these things later, he thought. Hans enjoyed the conversation the three shared. He was glad his aunt had not returned, as he cherished the time he was spending alone with his mother and now that Marissa had arrived he wanted the privacy for the two to meet. There would be time for Marissa to meet his family later. He wanted her to be alone with his mother and himself for awhile. His mother insisted Hans go home to shower and shave since his girlfriend was here now and it wasn't acceptable for him to look as he did. Hans agreed only to appease his mother knowing he would return shortly.

When Hans returned home and entered the warm water of the tub he felt his body relaxing. He was apprehensive that he might fall asleep in the tub, as he had never felt such exhaustion. Hans suggested they shower off the soap, as if he made the shower cool enough he believed it would wake him up just enough to give him the energy to shave. When his head hit the pillow he felt as if he were already asleep. When Marissa started to kiss him, he was already in a dreamlike state. He could feel everything she was doing to him but it was as if he was unable to move. Each caress, each kiss, every sense of her breath touching his body gave him immense pleasure like he had never known before. As she was bringing him to orgasm he could feel his whole body trembling. When she started to massage his back his dreamlike state became even more intense and he felt himself losing consciousness. She gave him such pleasure, such comfort. It was at that moment he realized what the feeling he had for her was. He hadn't been able to put his finger on it before. But now, in his dreamlike state when things should be obscure, it was as clear as glass. It was love. He knew he loved Marissa.

DAY TWELVE

Day Twelve, Wednesday, June 22nd Marissa's story

Marissa awoke alone. She opened her eyes to the unfamiliar room she was reminded instantly of the situation at hand. She then immediately said a quick prayer that Hans' mother would pass peacefully, without pain and for Hans to have strength to endure this impending ordeal. She wondered what time it was when Hans had left for the hospital. She got up, showered and dressed. She wasn't going to venture to the hospital as she realized Hans wanted to be alone with his mother. So she did the one thing Italian's do best when they want to express their emotions, whether it is in celebration, sympathy or their love – she cooked. She went to the kitchen to assess what foods were in the house that she had to work with. She had decided she wanted to make an Austrian dish for Hans for when he arrived home. She thought it might bring him some comfort to eat a familiar food at this time of stress. She had her laptop in her luggage, so decided to check out recipes online. But when she realized she didn't have an electrical plug converter with her, she searched for a cookbook. She found some cookbooks on the top shelf of one of the kitchen cabinets. She went to retrieve her English/German translation dictionary from the front pocket of her carry-on luggage to help her navigate through the recipes. She found one cookbook whose pages seemed to just fall open without effort and whose pages appeared to have the most wear. She decided to use those recipes thinking they must have been the ones most often used. She had all the ingredients in the kitchen to bake an apple strudel, so she started to bake. Not being in her own kitchen it was a more difficult task, trying to find where his mother kept the bowls, utensils, measuring cups, rolling pin, and knives. It was however a labor of love and Marissa put her whole heart into making it the best strudel she could.

She was busy making the strudel when someone knocked at the door. When she opened the door, there stood a gray haired man about fifty years old in overalls carrying a large tool box in one hand and several boxes of door locks in the other. He spoke to her in German and she did not understand one word. Not wanting to call Hans and bother him, she retrieved her English to German dictionary and handed it to the man with paper and a pen. He fumbled through the pages and wrote "Mr. Von Geirscher want change locks all". From the amount of locks she could see the man carrying she guessed that Hans had ordered all locks to be changed on the outside doors. So, unlike her Brooklyn native gut feeling of mistrusting strangers, Marissa continued to cook, while allowing the gentleman to change all the outside locks. He finished his work before Marissa was finished with the completion the second strudel. He handed her what appeared to be a bill and a handful of keys. She smiled at him as he left. Marissa left the bill and the keys on the counter, next to the car keys Hans had left for her.

She was pleased with herself when the delicious aroma of the strudel started to fill the house making it feel more like a home to her. She was glad there were enough apples to make two strudels, in case someone stopped to visit Hans. Marissa was taking the second apple strudel out of the oven when Hans appeared at the front door. He walked over to her just as she had finished laying the two dishes on the counter. As she turned to him, he held her for what seemed a very long time without saying a word. She was still in his embrace when he whispered in her ear, "She's gone". Marissa held him tighter, saying nothing; realizing nothing she could say would ease his pain. While they stood there in the kitchen against the counter, Marissa could feel Hans trembling as she cried.

Marissa composed herself and broke the silence "Hans I am so sorry for your loss. Is there anything I can do"? Hans reluctantly broke their embrace, told her he had arrangements to make and left the kitchen. As he walked by the counter, he nonchalantly picked up the keys with the bill, saying nothing. Marissa continued to cook, for that was one of the ways she had learned over the years to bear heartfelt pain. The other was extreme house cleaning but with his mother being an impeccable house keeper, that was not an option. She came across a stroganoff recipe from one of the easily-opened pages and began the search the ingredients and cooking utensils she needed. That kept her busy while Hans made the arrangements for the funeral. She heard him making several phone calls speaking in German so she wasn't sure what he was saying. But, since she had lost both her father and grandmother, she knew there were a lot of details to take care of. She thought he might be hungry but didn't think he'd sit for anything substantial to eat. She put a slice of warm apple strudel on a plate and brought it in to him with a tall glass of ice cold milk. He smile and leaned over and kissed her cheek, then continued with his conversation.

People came in and out all day bringing over food and offering their sympathies. Amazingly, most of those who came to pay their respects spoke English. It was about 10 pm when there was a knock on the door. Hans opened the door and Marissa saw two men standing there. She could see by the way they acted that those were the two friends Hans had told her about from the Navy. They had two unopened bottles of Vodka with them in hand. Hans introduced them to Marissa. After about ten minutes of Marissa joining them in conversation, she thought they should be alone to console Hans. She believed that men had their own way of showing condo-lences amongst themselves. Marissa excused herself and said she needed to send some emails to her family back home.

Hans followed her into the bedroom explaining she was more than welcome to stay with his friends. He attached an electrical converter to the outlet and connected her laptop to the internet. He left the room but not before he kissed her. She could hear low voices with serious tones as she sat at her computer. After about an hour she assumed that the vodka had kicked in, as she could overhear the men telling Navy stories and laughing. She was glad to hear Hans laughing. Even in moments of despair, laughter is helpful, she thought. Marissa remembered bursting into laughter outside the funeral home at her father's viewing when Carter mis-judged a puddle and was ankle deep in water. As she laughed, Carter and Rita laughed along with her. Carter then told her a quote by Charlie Chaplin, "Laughter is the tonic, the relief, the surcease for pain". Marissa believed that to be true and it made her happy to hear Hans laugh.

Marissa responded to emails she received from Carter, Rita and her mom. They were all irritated that she hadn't called them before leaving for Austria. She realized they saw through her charade of using the early hour as an excuse for having not called. She was fully aware they knew the truth that she didn't want to hear a lec-ture or be told not to go. She loved Hans and knew she needed to come to Austria to be with him. But since only knowing him for such a short time, she didn't think they would have approved. How could they have when she herself couldn't understand how fast and how hard she had fallen in love with him. She wrote to them explaining about her flight, the friendliness of the people in Aus-tria, the hospital visit, and of Hans' mother's condition. At the end of Carter's email she added Hans' real last name. It seemed as if no sooner did she send one email than she would receive a response. Their replies were all very supportive.

Marissa's emails to Rita were the most in depth. She stayed on-line a couple of hours corresponding with her. She knew Rita would understand the depth of the love she felt for Hans, for Rita herself was in love. Rita, in several of her emails, suggested she come over to be with Marissa. But each time it was mentioned, Marissa would assure her she was fine. Marissa finally needed to end their conversation as she was growing increasingly tired. As she drifted off to sleep, she could hear the laughter of the men in the other room. Tomorrow would be the viewing. She knew that Hans could use laughter tonight.

Day Twelve, Wednesday, June 22nd Hans' story

Hans awoke in a cold sweat. He had a strange feeling sweep over him that his mother needed him. He called for a car to pick him up and then quickly got dressed to go back to the hospital. He went into the kitchen to look for his mother's car and house keys; she always left them on a hook near the refrigerator. He didn't want to leave Marissa in the house feeling stranded. He put the keys on the kitchen counter so they would be easily found. He woke her gently to tell her of his departure. She looked so peaceful sleeping, he hated to disturb her. When his limo pulled up to the hospital, the gut feeling he felt when he had first awoken grew stronger. A wave of nausea hit him as he opened the main door to the hospital. The realization that his mother would soon be gone finally sunk in. The elevator didn't come fast enough so he has-tened up the five flights of stairs.

When he entered her room she was awake. "You look remark-ably better", she told him. "See what wonders a shower and only a few hours of sleep can do?" His mother was totally lucid. She pat-ted the bed and said, "Come son, come sit by me." She seemed energetic and extremely talkative. They had a wonderful conversation, with his mother speaking of things which were never shared before. She told him how she had fallen in love with his dad. She recalled stories about himself as a boy he had long forgotten or was too young to remember. She told him stories about his dad, before they had married. Hans sat there fully engaged, hanging on her every word, as the stories unfolded before him. She answered many questions he had wondered about over the years. She answered them all, all but one.

They sat for a few minutes in silence. Hans thought perhaps his mother was tired, but then she spoke. "Hans I have a will. Our lawyer has a copy. I am leaving all that I own to you. Please promise me that if your Aunt Sophie asks you for anything, you will say no. Promise me you will not give your Aunt Sophie one item from our home. Do not give her as much as a piece of thread from a curtain. You told me she was in this hospital room and I am concerned she may have taken the key to our front door. Hans please change the locks to all of our entrances. I do not want your Aunt Sophie to ever step foot into our home. And when you go to the lawyers' office to settle my will, please make sure you have him add to your will that she does not get any of our property or possessions. Promise me Hans!" His mother seemed quite upset and Hans wanted her to be as calm as possible. Hans promised her he would take care of it immediately. He made two phone calls by her bedside, one to their lawyer at his home to explain the situation and make an appointment to meet with him in the morning and one to find a locksmith. He wanted her to hear that he was taking care of what she had asked so she would be comforted and realize her last wishes were being fulfilled.

When the calls were finished Hans sat next to his mother in silence. She seemed to be more relaxed now. Looking up at him with a smile she said. "Now tell me more about Marissa." He shared with his mother how deeply in love he was with Marissa. He gave details of her tiny apartment and explained how it was filled with so much love. He mentioned that Marissa had brought him to church; a fact which he knew would make his mother beam with delight. He told her of the interesting walking tour Marissa took him on to see the unique architecture which was purely American. His mother was intrigued when he told her of the Thinnest house. She could not imagine living in such cramped quarters. He assured his mother that Marissa was a woman of character and one whom he knew would be faithful. He wasn't sure how long he had talked about Marissa, but when he looked at his pocket watch he realized it had been almost two hours.

His mother looked like she was beginning to tire. She then held his hand tightly and told him how much she liked Marissa. Although the time she spent with Marissa was short, she assured him Marissa had a look in her eyes of sincerity and love. She was positive Marissa was deeply in love with him. "It's always in the eyes" she said. She asked him when he was planning on proposing to her. Hans was surprised his mother had guessed that he would, and assured her it would be soon. His mother was pleased with the news. "Promise me, you will always treat her kindly and with respect" she said. "Of course I will mother" Hans replied. She said, "I have seen it time and time again. You have two young people in love. Then with time, children arrive, and the man begins to have more responsibilities than he had imagined. He wants a distraction, so he cheats. Women are very strong Hans. We can bear a heavy load, but when a man cheats on us it breaks us right down to our core. So treat her with respect Hans, the way I raised you." Hans agreed. He couldn't help but wonder if his father had cheated on his mother. Could that be why their home was so cold? Was that the reason she hadn't cried at his funeral?

Hans sat next to his mother, holding her hand and stroking it, for a very long time with both of them in silence. He wanted to ask her why she hadn't told him of her illness, but he didn't want to upset her. Realizing if he didn't ask he might never know, so he inquired, "Mother, why did you not mention to me in any of our many phone calls that you were sick? Why when I told you I could not come for the marathon last April did you not insist I come home? His mother answered in a quiet voice, "Hans, I did not want you to see me like this. I wanted your memories of me to be of me healthy and full of life. It would have broken my heart to have seen your face look at me while I was going through the chemotherapy and losing my hair. I love you Hans and wanted to spare you the pain of watching me die. I asked the nurse to call you near the end and tell you I had a burst appendix so you would have the plane ride home to prepare for the possibility of my dying."

There was one more question to ask, one he had pondered over often through the years. He wasn't going to ask, but with the insistence of his Aunt being left out of the will, he had to ask. Hans took a deep breath and asked, "Mother, why was it you never spoke to your sister?" His mother replied, "I did not know she was here in my hospital room. Had I known, I would have asked the nurse to have her leave. I know I have not always been the best mother. I should have been warmer with you. Sometimes it was hard for me to look at you as you were the spitting image of your father. When your father died, it was then I learned he was having an affair with my sister Sophia. He was in her bed when he had his heart attack and died. It broke me, Hans. I should have been stronger for you; I am so sorry that I wasn't. I do love you so much Hans, but fear I never really let you know how much." He replied instantly, "Mother you have nothing to be sorry for." He could hear his mother's breathing change. It became weaker and shallow. He continued, "You did the best you could. We didn't make such a bad team, you and I. We worked the land well together for many years. I am sorry for all the trouble I put you through when I was a teenager". His mother replied, "You were no trouble Hans. Boys will be boys. It was in your nature to be devilish, after all you were your father's son. Always remember Hans, I love you." As he bent over to kiss his mother he said, "I love you too, Mom" and he noticed a slight smile came across her face. When he kissed her forehead, a machine started to beep loudly without stopping. As he looked down at his mother she looked so peaceful and serene.

Nurses came running into her room, pushing Hans aside. The doctor quickly followed. He took her vital signs, then turned to Hans and said "She's passed". As the nurses and doctor left the room, Hans sat down again in the chair next to his mother bedside and reverently held her hands. He brought her hands to his face and lovingly kissed them. These were the hands that for years had washed his clothes, cooked his meals, bandaged his cuts, held him when he got stitches and put cool wash clothes on his forehead when he had fevers. Did he ever thank her, he wondered? Her hands looked so frail now, but he remembered a time when they were strong. She worked the field with him side by side carrying heavy crates, and they were certainly strong enough to smack his face when he was disrespectful. Those were the hands that cradled him when he was a child and applauded him when he walked across the high school stage to get his diploma. Hans just sat there holding and starring at her hands for hours thinking of all the things they had done for him during his life. He held her hands until they turned cold. Hans could not get himself to let go of her hands.

A nurse finally came in and informed Hans they needed to get his mother ready to be picked up by the funeral home and he would have to leave soon. He realized he only had minutes left to be with her. He looked down and noticed her wedding band and engagement rings was not there. He was surprised he hadn't noticed it before. He wondered if possibly the nurse had given them to his Aunt Sophie for safe-keeping. He would certainly find out and get them back if she had. Ahhh, his Aunt Sophie, now so many questions were answered for him. Now he knew why his mother would never speak her name, and why she would not go to any family functions if she were to be there. His poor mother, he thought, her only sister having an affair with her husband and the whole town knowing that he died in her bed. It was clear to him now why his mother had been cold all those years. It was as she said, she was broken.

The nurse came in again one final time. "Would you like a lock of her hair?" she asked. Hans had not thought of it, and said "Yes, thank you". She gently cut a piece of her hair and placed the lock in an envelope and handed it to Hans. "It's time for you to go now" she said. Hans bent over to kiss his mother one more time. Her cheek was so cold. He tucked in her blanket as to keep her warm. He kissed her hands and placed them gently back upon the bed and turned to leave. He could not look back. He was afraid if he did, he would not be able to walk out the door. So without turning back he left the room. As he walked towards the stairway the nurse yelled" Mr. Von Geirscher, please wait a minute". She caught up to him and gave him a small envelope. The nurse said "Here sir, your mother gave this to me last night to give to you, when you left with your girlfriend. She made me promise to wait until she passed before giving it to you." Hans took the envelope and thanked her and opened the door to the stairwell. He looked down at the white envelope. On it his mother had written. "Hans you know who to give these to" as he peeled open the seal he saw his mothers engagement and wedding rings. Tears ran streaming down his face as he leaned against the concrete wall of the stairwell. He was always composed and in control of his emotions. The last time he had cried was when Gretchen had broken his heart. He realized he could not stop the tears, as hard as he tried. He put the envelope into his breast suit pocket, and stood in the stairwell until he could regain control.

His driver was outside waiting for him when he left the hospital. As he sat in the back seat, still dazed with the whole situation feeling surreal, he asked the driver to drive around the city for awhile before heading home. He knew he needed to talk to Wolfgang. When Wolfgang first picked up the phone, Hans could not speak. His throat had the feeling it was closing up. When Wolfgang inquired, "Hans, is that you? Are you alright?", he realized his name had appeared on his friend's caller ID. The sound of Wolfgang's voice was comforting, as he was like a brother to him. Trying to get the words out, "My mother is dead", was hard. In a soft, almost whisper Hans proceeded to inform his friend of the events that led to his call. Wolfgang was pleased to hear that Marissa was already there, so Hans would not be alone. He had been aware while growing up that Hans was not close to his relatives and knew they would be of no comfort for him during this crucial time. Wolfgang explained he was in Bangkok on business but assured Hans he would be on the next flight home and would get to him as soon as he possibly could.

When Hans opened the door to his house the aroma of freshly baked apple strudel welcomed him. It was as if he was in a dream, reliving his childhood, returning from school to find his mother had made his favorite dessert. She often gave him a piece of apple strudel with a tall glass of milk while he worked on his homework on the kitchen table. Hans closed his eyes for just a moment and savored the memory. He saw that Marissa was in the kitchen. He walked over to her but he could not speak. He just wanted to be held. Such a new relationship, he thought, and yet she had now seen him at his weakest. She was the first girl since Gretchen that he had let in.

Hans made all the arrangements. He called the funeral home, florist, church, and his Aunt Sophie. He was not looking forward to talking with his Aunt Sophie, now knowing how she had hurt his mother. But there were relatives and his mother's friends to contact and he was not up to the task. He also knew that if he footed the bill, she would have a reception after the burial at her home, another task he was not up for. He decided he was going to make it perfectly clear to her during their conversation, that after tomorrow she was to have no contact with him. A fact he believed would not upset her, as he barely knew her and would only see her briefly at weddings or funerals.

Friends and relatives came in and out of his home all day bringing food and their sympathies. By 9 pm the last visitors left. As Hans was trying to rearrange the refrigerator and freezer to accommodate all the food that had been brought over, there was a knock on the door. Hans was pleasantly surprised when he opened the door. Standing there were his two his best friends from the Navy, Clint and Jethro. They were the kind of friends that although it had been years since they had last seen each other, it was as if it had been yesterday since they had last met. He learned that Mrs. Hobes had contacted both of them alerting them of the impending death of his mother. A fact which made Hans aware that she had gone through his address book, leaving him to wonder whom else, if anyone, she might have contacted.

Hans understood why Marissa went to the bedroom to do some correspondence. She stayed a respectable amount of time to be polite to meet his friends, before excusing herself to the other room. She put up with visitors coming and going all day and night. She was the perfect hostess, getting drinks, serving food, doing dishes and all while trying the best she could to break the communication barrier. Hans never expected so many people to stop by his house. If he had an inkling of the number of people that would show up he would have hired help for the day. Each time he attempted to help Marissa she demanded he visit with his company insisting she had everything under control. Actually, she did have everything under control. However, Hans hated the inordinate amount of work she had done today. It was not what he wanted or expected her to do today. He was sure she was indeed in need of a break. He appreciated the time he spent alone with Jethro and Clint. It had been far too long since they had last met, and Hans promised the length of time between visits would be shortened. When his friends left, Hans walked to the bedroom thinking perhaps Marissa hadn't left because she needed a break , perhaps she knew he needed time to be alone with his friends. And if that was the case, he thought, she was perfectly correct.

DAY THIRTEEN

Day Thirteen, Thursday, June 23rd Marissa's story

When Marissa awoke Hans was still asleep. This was a rarity, so she assumed its cause must have been the vodka. She quietly went into the kitchen to prepare breakfast. She was putting the breakfast on the table, and just about to awaken Hans, when he walked in. She didn't know if it was the smell of bacon wafting throughout the house or the sounds of pans and dishes that had awoken him. The baby blue robe he wore to the table complimented his eyes, although they looked so weary this morning. He didn't say anything, looking extremely tired and just sat at the table. After his first bite he announced "This is delicious!" It was only omelets, home fries and toast so Marissa didn't see the big deal. Hans informed Marissa he did not want her to do any more work. She had done more than enough already. He mentioned that he was planning on taking her out for breakfast this morning. Marissa said "It's no bother at all Hans, did you forget, I'm Italian, that's what we do, we cook". He smiled. It was a refreshing sight, as she missed seeing it. She got him a second helping of everything as he still seemed hungry. He obviously didn't have a hang-over she thought, or he would not have been able to eat so much.

During breakfast he told her that he needed to pick out a casket, go to the lawyer's office to settle his mother's affairs and he would be back later. It surprised her how he just blurted it out so matter of fact, "I have to pick out a casket." She thought, I guess there is no other way of saying it, but he seemed to have listed off his "to do" list so robotically. It was then she realized he must have been suppressing his emotions to enable him to get through this ordeal. It also was clear this was something he wanted to do alone. Marissa was relieved, because she did not want to go with him when he picked out a casket. She was certain she would lose control of her emotions and a hysterical woman was something he didn't need right now.

He showered, dressed and was out the door before she had finished cleaning up the kitchen. He kissed her softly before he left and said, "I won't leave you alone too long I promise. The car keys and new house keys are on the counter if you want to go out. If you need me, don't hesitate to call". She assured him she would be fine and he should do whatever needed to be done and take as much time as he wanted to do it. When he left she decided to take a long relaxing bath. She didn't think Hans would mind, so she went into his mothers' bathroom to look for bath salts. Marissa found four bottles of bath salts with pictures of different flowers on each. The labels were written on in German, so it was much easier to open and smell each bottle than to look up each word in the dictionary. The bath salts she decided to use smelled delicious. She soaked in the hot bath for at least an hour trying to relax both her body and her mind. She realized she might have stayed in there a bit too long, when upon leaving the tub she realized her finger tips were all wrinkly.

After drying off she looked in Hans' dresser for something to put on, as she had left her bathrobe at home. In one of his drawers she found some old T-shirts. She picked a black one with the words "4 Non Blondes" written on it and made a mental note to ask him what it meant. She then went online to email Rita, Carter, and her mom. She was extremely pleased at how well Rita and Carter were at accepting the fact she had come to Austria with a man she had only recently met. One of Carter's emails struck her as extremely interesting. He had actually taken the time to calculate how many hours she had spent with Hans since they first met. He then formulated the amount of time spent on a regular date, and adding the time on an average of two dates per week, informed her that in actual dating time they had actually been seeing each other for months. She thought his logic was a bit bazaar but if it helped him and Rita accept this whirlwind romance she was in, she was all for it.

It was getting close to 1:30 pm so she decided to get dressed. She recalled Hans had said the viewing hours would be from 4-9 pm. She put on her simple black dress and black heels. She was glad she remembered to pack her black stockings as well, although she neglected to pack her black waist length short sleeve cardigan to wear over it. If it got chilly tonight she would be cold but she was going to have to tough it out. There was no way that she was going to wear the red cardigan that she did pack. She was upset with herself for not remembering in her haste to pack her *Obsession*. But she thought, at least she would smell delicious from the bath salts she had soaked in.

Hans returned just as she had finished dressing. He told her she looked lovely. As he walked closer to her he stopped for a brief second and then continued to approach her. She thought she detected a tear in his eye. He said he needed to get ready and went into the bathroom. Marissa went into the living room to give him privacy. She felt he needed to be alone. When he came out into the living room he looked as if he had just stepped off a cover of <u>GQ</u> magazine. His black suit fit him impeccably. He wore a gray shirt and gray silk tie. You could see in his face that he was grieving. As they were about to leave, Hans mentioned to Marissa she might need a jacket if it became cooler later in the evening. She explained she only had her red cardigan with her and it would not be appropriate to wear. She assured him she would be fine without any jacket. Hans went into his mother's bedroom and returned with a shawl. He wrapped it around her shoulders. It with the most beautiful, softest, black silk shawl she had ever seen. "She'd want you to have it", Hans said, as he kissed her cheek.

The funeral home was packed. It was obvious how well-liked his mother was by the turn out. She missed much of what was being said as it was mostly in German. Hans stood in a receiving line next to his uncle, his aunt and a few cousins as the visitors paid their respects. Marissa sat on a love seat against the wall that was opposite the receiving line. Hans stopped by and sat with her on and off during the calling hours. He introduced her to many people, too many to remember most of their names. Marissa kept herself occupied by studying the English to German dictionary that she kept in her bag.

Towards the end of the calling hours Marissa noticed an extremely stunning, tall, lean, toned, blonde woman enter the room with the swagger of a runway model. As if she wasn't tall enough already, her stilettos made her appear well over six feet tall. Her short hair was slicked back on the sides and spiked up on top, with a few strands down over her forehead. She had 2 inch long, thin, spiral gold earrings drawing attention to her long neckline. She was so absolutely striking that Marissa wondered if she were a model. It was the first time Marissa understood the term "drop dead gorgeous". The woman appeared to be wearing the same black dress as Marissa. However, it was apparent how much better it looked on the icy hot blonde than on Marissa. The dress clung closely to the blondes every curve as if it were a second skin, was about 2 inches shorter than Marissa's dress and exposed more of her cleavage than Marissa thought appropriate for an occasion such as this. As she entered the room all eyes were on her, both women and men alike.

Marissa noticed as the blonde walked towards the receiving line, Hans immediately left the line walking into the hall. The blonde changed direction and walked towards the hall as well. Marissa had a great vantage point from the love seat. She could see by Hans' facial expression he was not happy with the blonde's arrival. She couldn't help but wonder who she was. Marissa was considering the possibilities when one of Han's cousins, whom she had met the night before, came to sit next to her. Pointing to the blonde she said in English, "Ignore that situation. They have been done for years. Hans wants nothing to do with her". And as quickly as she had sat down she had left. Marissa noticed Hans walking towards her, with the blonde following closely behind him. He sat down next to Marissa and asked her if she would like to leave. Marissa told him she was ready to leave whenever he was. The blonde interrupted and said something to Hans in German. Hans looked annoyed and then looking at Marissa said "Marissa this is Gretchen, she is nobody. Gretchen this is my girlfriend Marissa from NY. If you are to speak any further use English, but I prefer you not to speak". He took Marissa's hand and said "I'd like to leave now please Marissa". The blonde tapped on Hans shoulder and said in English "You know where you can find me Hans". Hans without looking at her said "I'm not a kid anymore; I don't look under rocks, so I won't be seeing you. You can slither back from where you came from". She started speaking angrily and loudly in German while following Marissa and Hans towards the door. From out of nowhere a strikingly handsome, tall, blonde man, who looked to be about the same age as Hans, grabbed the woman's arm and veered her away from Hans. Marissa heard him say, "Awww Gretchen, are you finished fucking, I mean fucking over every man in Paris? Is that why you are home, to see if there are any Austrian men you haven't fucked with yet"?

When they arrived out front there was a car waiting to bring Hans and Marissa home. They didn't speak on the way home. Marissa did not believe it was the proper time to bring up any questions of past girlfriends, as it was obvious the blonde was an ex-girlfriend of Hans. She knew Hans would tell her in his own time, just as he would tell in his own time why he had lied about his last name.

When they entered the house Hans went into his mother's bedroom. Marissa watched as he took the crucifix off the wall over her bed, took her jewelry box from her dresser, then went into her night stand and took out her blue rosaries and a journal. As he put them into his suitcase, she noticed him gently wrap them to prevent them from being damaged.

They both changed for bed in silence. Hans made love to Marissa tenderly that night. His hands were ever so gentle with each caress. Whenever he brought her to orgasm orally, he actually sent shivers up her spine and tonight was no exception. She equally enjoyed bringing him pleasure orally as well. Although she was quite a novice at this activity, she was beginning to feel quite accomplished as it seemed to come natural to her. When she bent over him, softly touching her bare breast against his check and as she lightly scratched his chest on the way down to her play ground she knew exactly what effect she was having on him. She could sustain his pleasure for as long as she desired. She had learned by acutely paying attention to his every movement when he was about to climax, and could adjust her pace to delay its arrival. And tonight she wanted to prolong his pleasured state for as long as he could bear it.

Day Thirteen, Thursday, June 23rd Hans' story

Hans awoke to the aroma of bacon cooking. He was extremely hungry although he didn't understand why as he had certainly overeaten the day before. There had been so much food brought over by visitors, plus the food Marissa had prepared. When he entered the kitchen Marissa was just putting breakfast on the table. He was amazed how well she timed its preparation. It was as if she knew when he would awaken.

Hans could not stop thinking about how he needed to pick out a coffin this morning. He had told the funeral director he would be in early so preparations could be completed in time for the service that evening. He did not want to do it, but it had to be done. He wished Wolfgang was in town so he could accompany him, but he was in Thailand on business and would not be arriving until late afternoon at best. He did not want Marissa to accompany him, as he was not sure what his reaction would be, plus he had to stop by his lawyer's office. There was paper work to be filed on his mother's behalf and also paperwork to be notarized on a personal matter as well. He didn't quite feel like himself. He felt as if he was just going through the motions void of emotion.

When he arrived at the funeral home the owner showed Hans into his office and handed him a catalog of caskets. Hans put the catalog on the desk and stated he wanted to see the caskets not merely look at pictures. When they entered the display room Hans noticed a white casket in the far corner. It was white with brass handles, with hand painted edelweiss flowers along the trim. It reminded him of the white edelweiss that covered the front of his home in every patch of earth where there wasn't a flower bed. Pointing to it, he told the funeral director he wanted that one. He explained to Hans the ones on the other side of the room were of better quality and a bit more costly. Hans walked over to the white casket and opened it, touching the white lining which was the softest of silk. "This is the one I want" he said in a demanding voice. Just then, something Hans' mother had told him years ago popped into his memory. His parents had taken him to a toy store for his 7th birthday. For his gift, his parents were letting him pick any toy he wanted. Hans went up and down each aisle, painstakingly checking out each toy that was being considered. Then he spotted the perfect toy, a truck. It was a red truck with a flat bed just like the one his dad drove. That was the one he wanted. He loved it! He ran to his mother and handed it to her saying he had made his decision. The clerk had obviously overheard the conversation Hans had with his parents regarding the fact that price was not an issue. When his mother put the red truck on the counter to pay for it, the man started to show Hans a more expensive truck. The man said "This one is a bit more expensive but look it has lights that actually turn on and off and a horn that beeps". It was a very nice truck and Hans did like it, but not as much as the red truck. Even without the lights that worked or a horn that beeped, Hans' favorite was the red truck. It was then his mother turned to him and said "Hans just because something is more expensive doesn't mean that it's better. Get what you like, don't be swayed by the price. The best isn't always the most expensive." Hans remembered his parents had bought him the red truck and how he had spent many hours playing with it in the dirt pile he built in his back yard. He wondered what ever happened to it.

Just then he heard a voice from the front doorway of the room that startled him, "You heard the man, he wants the white one. Done"! Hans turned around and there stood Wolfgang with luggage in tow. The two embraced. Hans had never been happier to see him. Wolfgang explained, "Sorry it took so long for me to get here Hans. The flights were all booked. I went to the airport to see if I could bump someone off a flight but no one would give up their seat. I had to bribe some guy with my Rolex, and then pay him full price for his ticket with him knowing I was coming to attend a funeral. It never ceases to amaze me how incredibly shameful people can be. I came directly from the airport. Something told me this would be the first place you would be this morning. So here I am, what can I do?" Hans replied, "You're doing it, you're here."

After putting Wolfgang's luggage into the trunk of the car which was waiting for Hans outside the funeral home, the two got into the back seat. When the driver asked, "Where to?", Hans gave him the name of a small jewelry store in town. Wolfgang looked at Hans with a puzzled expression. Hans explained to Wolfgang that he wanted to marry Marissa. Wolfgang couldn't help but wonder if the urgency was in some way related to the recent death of Hans' mother. But after listening to him talk about Marissa with such excitement and hope in his voice, during the fifteen minute ride to the store, he realized Hans was truly in love. Hans asked Wolfgang to go along with his charade of being an investment consultant and nothing more as Marissa was still not aware of his financial situation. Wolfgang agreed. However, he warned Hans he needed to tell her soon, for if she found out from another source, she would feel deceived. Wolfgang listened as Hans told him of his future plans. He gave Hans his vote of support with each step of the plan that was discussed.

Entering the jewelry store, the manager recognized Hans and walked up to him. He welcomed him back home to Vienna asking, "What can I do for you today sir?" Hans replied, "I am in need of a Rolex and an engagement ring". Hans looked at Wolfgang and they both started laughing.

He remembered when Marissa spoke of her grandmother's jewelry, she had mentioned how she preferred jewelry from Europe, as it tended to have more filigree and the gold had a pinkish tint to it. He looked into each case scrupulously looking for just the right one. He finally found the one he thought she would like and it seemed perfect. He showed it to Wolfgang, who gave him a thumbs-up. He pulled out the small white envelope from his breast pocket. He asked the jeweler to remove the diamond from his mothers ring and place it into the setting he had just picked. He also insisted it needed to be done today and asked the jeweler if that would be possible. Hans was a faithful customer, always stopping in whenever he was in town to buy something for his mother. "Of course", he said, "I will do it right away. Can you come back in a few hours?" Hans was thrilled it would be done today. As he turned to leave the store, the jeweler asked, "Would you like the Rolex gift wrapped?" Hans smiled and said "No, thank you", and handed the box to Wolfgang. As the two walked out of the store laughing, Hans realized how much he had missed his friend's company. He could always be himself with Wolfgang. He now realized, with such clarity, that life with both its rewards and challenges was much better when shared with people you love.

As they entered the car, Hans gave the lawyer's address to the driver. On the way to the office, Hans decided to inform Wolfgang he had finally learned the reason for the feud between his mother and his aunt. Wolfgang couldn't believe what he was hearing. He replied "Well that is one scenario neither one of us came up with as a reason for the feud when we were kids. This is going to be one interesting funeral Hans because I also heard the She-Devil is in town. I will try to keep the wolves at bay"?

The office visit with the lawyer went quickly. Hans had to sign some papers as executor of his mother's will. Wolfgang was surprised when he learned he was also mentioned in her will. She had left him a substantial amount of stock which she owned in a lucrative company located in America. Hans was not even aware that his mother owned this stock. It was a company he had mentioned to her years ago and had attempted to convince her to invest in. She always was stubborn, and apparently didn't want Hans to know she had heeded his advice and purchased the stock on her own. Hans looked at Wolfgang and reaffirmed, "I told you she always liked you". To which Wolfgang smiled and replied, "She's probably just paying me back for all the free labor she got from me working in your fields". A smile came across Hans' face. The lawyer also had already drawn up the papers of a personal matter which he had discussed with Hans yesterday. All that needed to be done was to add signatures and to have them notarized. It worked out perfectly that Wolfgang had arrived when he did, as being the executor of Hans' will he was there for the explanation of the changes and also for his signature as witness. Not to mention the best part for Wolfgang, which was he finally realized what Hans had told him all along was true. Hans' mother really did feel he was family. Hans took notarized copies of everything for his own records and put them into his breast pocket of his suit jacket.

There was one place left to go on Hans' list, the church. He asked the driver to drive to Christ Church. As they walked towards the church to meet the priest Wolfgang said, "Of all the things we have done Hans, we have never lied to a priest. This possibly could be the worst stunt we've pulled off, in God's eyes that is. Not mine, I'm fine with it". Hans assured him that it would be fine as he felt in his gut it was the right thing to do.

Father Enise was pleased to see both boys as he hadn't seen either of them in church since high school. He informed them both that Hans' mother had kept him abreast as to how well both boys had been in their careers. However, she prayed for both to one day return to the church. "And here you both are, fine young men, standing again in my church. Why is it that it takes a wedding or a funeral to get people to come back to the church"? Father Enise asked. Wolfgang and Hans had no answer. They just flashed their impish smiles to the priest.

Hans explained what he wanted the priest to do the day after the services for his mother had been completed and Father Enise happily agreed. He consoled Hans with the knowledge that his mother was prepared to die. He told Hans his mother spoke of him often after Mass, and had just recently told him about Marissa. He was looking forward to meeting her. As they walked back to the car Wolfgang said, "Only you could come up with this one Hans, let's see what tomorrow brings".

The errands were completed fairly quickly, leaving some time before the ring would be ready. Wolfgang said "Let's get a drink. I could use one, how about you?" Hans looked at Wolfgang and said, "Check your watch, how much time do we have till we pick up the ring?"

Wolfgang looked at his Rolex and said, "It's not set, I haven't a clue what time it is". They both started laughing as Hans pulled out his pocket watch to check the time saying, "Only you would wear a $7,000 watch and not set the time." Wolfgang replied, "Come on Hans, for $7,000 don't you think it should come already set?" The two walked to the cars laughing, the kind of laugh that makes your stomach hurt. Hans so needed this. He needed the diversion, he needed to laugh, he needed to forget for awhile.

They decided to stop at the first pub they saw and grab a beer. Wolfgang caught Hans up on what was going on with his newest business venture, and with stories of the newest women in his life. Wolfgang showed him some photos of his newest love interests on his smart phone. Hans was shocked that women would actually send photos such as these to him. Wolfgang replied, "They weren't sent, I took them". Again the two laughed. With Wolfgang here, the day certainly hadn't turned out as he had expected. Wolfgang had made it all, somehow, tolerable.

Upon arriving back at the store Hans was impressed to see how beautiful the diamond looked in the setting he had chosen. The jeweler put the engagement ring into a black velvet box which was a beautiful contrast for the brilliance of the diamond; for it let the colors it reflected seem more vibrant. He put his mother's empty setting and the engagement ring into the breast pocket of his suit jacket. Looking at Wolfgang, Hans asked "Hey what time is it?" As

Wolfgang went to look at his Rolex he realized he had forgotten to set the time while at the pub. The two walked out of the store laughing once again.

On the drive to Wolfgang's parents house Hans expressed to him how much he appreciated his dropping everything to come to Vienna. Wolfgang stopped him and said, "Hans words aren't necessary. I haven't done anything that you wouldn't have done for me." Then he noticed a cabinet in the back seat of the car and opened it. It was a mini-fridge. As he took out a beer he replied, "Hans we have had cold beer in here the whole time and you didn't tell me". And as he took a swig he said, "And I thought we were friends". Again the two started laughing.

After dropping off Wolfgang, Hans didn't want to go back home just yet. He asked the driver to drive around for a bit. Hans was not looking forward to the impending event that was to occur shortly. He never understood the need for the body of the deceased to be displayed for all to view. He could not comprehend the reasoning behind this barbaric ritual. And most importantly, he did not want to have to see his mother in a casket, dead, while people paraded by her extending him their condolences. He did not want nor need their commiseration. The only reason he was going through with this barbaric custom was out of respect for his mother. If he did not attend this evening's event, the whole town would be talking about it. And after learning about his father's indiscretion with his aunt, he knew they had already been talking about her for years. He refused to give them another story to tarnish her reputation.

When the car pulled up in front of his house, Hans couldn't help but wish there was some valid reason he could use not to attend the wake. He sat for a moment and prayed. Praying was something he hadn't done since his childhood, and yet since being with Marissa, this was his third time. He prayed for the strength to get through the evening while being in total control of his emotions.

He prayed that he could restrain himself from telling his aunt how he truly felt about her betrayal to his mother. He prayed that the She-Devil would not show up. And he prayed that his mother could look down and see him and be proud.

As he opened the front door to his home, he looked at the grandfather clock against the wall, and realized he hadn't left himself much time to get ready for the viewing. When he entered his bedroom, he saw Marissa looking beautiful. As he neared her he was taken aback by her scent. He recognized it as his mother's favorite. It was the only fragrance his mother would wear. It was called *White Orchids*. He composed himself and then hugged Marissa. While he hugged Marissa, memories of his mother started flooding his mind. Marissa would have had no way of knowing how that scent held so many memories for him, he thought.

Hans was glad Marissa hadn't expected him to talk with her in the car on the way to the funeral parlor. He was using the time to mentally prepare himself, as if one could actually prepare themselves for an event such as this. He stood in the receiving line with the visitors giving their condolences, while reminding himself of why he was there, otherwise he would have fled. He was thankful Marissa was there to sit with, even if only to hold his hand, when he would almost reach a breaking point. Hans knew how Wolfgang felt about viewings, and sharing in his belief, did not expect his arrival tonight. He would see him at the interment tomorrow.

With only a short time left for the calling hours, Hans noticed Gretchen walk in. Making an entrance as only she could. She had been a runway model for a short time and would always enter a room with the confidence that all eyes would be on her. And to ensure that being the case she would dress so provocatively that it would even be hard for a priest to deny his eyes from gazing upon her. Why would she come, he thought? As if she hadn't caused him enough pain in his life already, why would she come at this vulnerable time? Was it to plunge the knife deeper into his heart, he thought. His mother would not have wanted her there and he believed she was being disrespectful by her mere presence. He decided to go to the outer hall to avoid her in the receiving line. When Gretchen followed him, Hans was taken aback. She started to tell him how sorry she was for his loss and that she was there should he need comforting. He disregarded all she said and replied "You are not wanted here, please leave!" She continued talking to him, giving the name of the hotel she was staying at and her room number as he was walking away. When Gretchen relentlessly continued to follow him, he decided to discretely introduce Marissa to her leaving an explanation of their relationship for a later time.

On the way home, Hans was more quiet than usual. He had told his aunt at the viewing he had changed all the locks to his home, had ordered an alarm system to be installed, and that she was not to set foot into his mother's house. He stated he would be back in a month or two to pack up his mother's belongings, but would not be seeing her then or ever again. Immediately after entering his house, he remembered there were three personal items from his mother's bedroom he wanted to bring back to NYC. He took the cross over her bed, which his mother had received as a wedding gift from her mother. He took her jewelry box from her dresser, where she kept all her sentimental treasures, like his first tooth, his high school ring, his grandmother's broach and all the jewelry he had purchased for his mother over the years. And then he opened the drawer to her nightstand and removed the rosaries that she would use every night while saying her prayers before she went to sleep. Next to the rosaries he noticed a journal, and he decided to take that also. He wondered if perhaps it would give him a better insight to his mother's last days.

When he was making love to Marissa that night, Hans was tempted to ask her to marry him, but decided to wait until they were on the flight home. Whenever they made love it was as if she could read his mind. There was never an awkward moment; every movement flowed into the next as if it were synchronized. Marissa definitely had read his mind tonight. She had brought him to a heightened level of excitement several times during their love making. Just when he believed he would climax, she would slow down at the precise moment to ensure his lasting much longer than he believed he could have ever sustained. As they fell asleep in each other's arms, he knew he had made the right decision. He was going to marry her. He hoped his mother was correct in believing Marissa felt the same way, for now having met her, he could not imagine life without her.

DAY FOURTEEN

Day Fourteenth, Friday, June 24th Marissa's Day

As Marissa left the house she could feel the dampness in the air and was glad she had Hans' mother's shawl. The sun was shining, but from the feel of the air she could tell rain would soon be on its way. When she entered the limo, three of Hans' friends were already inside. There were his two friends from the Navy, whom she had met, and the man who had firmly escorted Gretchen from the funeral parlor last night. None of them spoke in the car, not a single word. The men all sat there gazing out of the limo windows. Marissa dared not break the silence; so she sat quietly holding Hans' hand.

Fortunately, the uncomfortable ride to the church was a short one. She learned from one of Hans' cousins the night before, the Mass was being held at his mother's parish Christ Church. She was surprised when the limo pulled up to such a small building. It was not a magnificent structure ornately decorated with statues carved into its façade nor did it have many steeples, or fashion itself in the baroque styles as all the other churches she had seen as they drove through the city. Instead, it was a modestly sized church with a narrower interior than any she had ever visited. The oak wooden pews to the left and to the right of the main aisle were short in length, each not allowing for more than the seating of eight people. At the end of each pew were simple carvings etched into the wood. The ceiling was high and constructed of dark wooden exposed beams. There were several arched wooden supports attached to the main beams, made of the same dark wood, which were beautifully hand- crafted. They were attached to the stark white walls, and just as paintings hung in a museum, it offered a beautiful background for the magnificent carvings to be viewed. The one thing which stood out most among the plainness of the church was the magnificently crafted stained glass windows, behind the altar, that were made of the richest and deepest of colors. The windows faced east allowing the sun in, all its brilliance, to shine in blanketing the interior of the church with such an array of vibrant hues which mimicked the splashes of colors that adorned Hans mother's front garden. A perfect decoration, added by the angels, Marissa thought, to guide his mother's way to heaven.

There was standing room only in the small crowded church. When Marissa and Hans started down the aisle to their seats she could feel the hundreds of pairs of eyes looking at him, and she could feel his hand starting to sweat. It was then she realized this was the first time she had visited this church and she had three wishes. Her eyes gazed up to the heavens and she prayed silently, "Dear God, please give Hans the strength to bear his pain with total control of his emotions today, for I fear that his dignity would be in jeopardy if he had to share his anguish in full view of so many staring eyes. My second wish is to be Hans' wife. Only You and I know how intense my love is for him. He is the greatest gift you have ever bestowed upon me. And thirdly, I pray You bless us with a child." Just as she finished asking for her three wishes, they had arrived to their designated pew. As she settled into her seat,

Hans reached for her hand, only letting it free later during the service when Marissa went to the altar to receive Communion.

Although German was the language being used during the service, being a Catholic church, Marissa could follow along as she knew the liturgy well. She would have liked to have understood what the priest was saying when he spoke at the pulpit. She could tell by the tone of his voice and how it cracked several times that he had been close to Hans' mother and was grieving as well as those attending the Mass. During the liturgy he made eye contact with Hans several times. She wasn't sure if it was to console or to engage him. When the priest came by with the incense to adorn the casket, Marissa felt a wave of nausea come over her. Memories of her father and grandmothers funerals were reemerging from deep within her, where she had safely tucked them away.

Marissa was glad when the Mass was finally over as she was in need of fresh air. However, when Hans stood up to leave the pew to carry out his duties as pallbearer, Marissa forgot about her nausea as she noticed his pale and grief stricken face. She watched as he took the brass handle with one hand and lovingly lifted the casket with his other onto his shoulder. She was relieved she did not have to bear that honor when her father or grandmother had died.

She did not think the ride to the cemetery could have been any more uncomfortable than the ride had been to the church, however, she was mistaken. It was a painfully long ride as she watched Hans eyes glued to the hearse that rode in front of them, which was easily visible from the front windshield. She remembered how agonizing it was to follow a hearse. She wondered why the custom had been for the immediate family to follow behind their loved one being transported in a hearse. She felt the departed should already be at the grave site awaiting the family's arrival. She believed the procession of following the hearse only extended the painful aching they felt in their hearts. As she watched his eyes, she wondered what thoughts were going through his head. Was he thinking of his childhood? Was he having fond memories? She hoped whatever thoughts he was having, they were all happy ones of his mother.

When they finally arrived at the cemetery Marissa was impressed with the beautiful landscaping and the amount of large lush trees that were sprawled throughout. The old headstones, some blackened and bent over with age, and the small hills with grave markings gave it an antiquated appeal. The sky had started to darken and it was imminent rain was on its way. When the driver opened the door to the limo, Hans' three friends exited, with Hans remaining entranced in his seat. Marissa had not expected this reaction from Hans and didn't know how to respond. She sat quietly next to him, while still holding his hand, praying he would have the strength to get out of the car. "It's almost over. You can do this Hans", she kept repeating silently to herself.

She had no idea how long they had stayed in the car, as time seemed just as frozen as Hans was in his seat. Finally the car door opened. There stood the man, whose name she had not yet known, who rode with them in the limo. Her eyes gazed upward and she silently thanked God for Hans' friend who came back to help. He spoke to Hans in German, took hold of Hans' arm and led him out of the car. After Hans exited the car, the friend took Marissa's hand to help her out as well. And the three walked on the path to the tent, with Marissa on Hans' left side holding his hand, while his friend was at his right side holding onto his arm.

Marissa was surprised to see so many people in attendance at the interment. She had no idea who most of these people were as only some looked familiar from the viewing. She did notice that Gretchen wasn't there. There was a large white tent with about thirty white folding chairs, near the family mausoleum where the casket had been placed. Along the path which led to the tent, there was a young boy handing out white roses. When he attempted to give Hans and Marissa a rose Hans responded "Nein", and they continued their walk without receiving one.

The priest spoke softly and lovingly as he sprinkled the casket with holy water. Marissa could hear people crying in the background. His aunt, who was in the row behind them, was loudly sobbing. Marissa sat there holding tightly onto Hans' hand. He had shown great restraint, he had not cried, he was staying in control. There was a light mist of rain when they arrived, but by the ending of the ceremony it had started to pour. As the priest finished his eulogy each person came up one at a time to place their white rose onto the casket. They then turned away and one by one they left the cemetery. Marissa, Hans and his friend were the only three remaining when all the others had left. They sat for about twenty minutes in total silence. Hans then turned to his friend and after speaking to him in German, his friend stood up, placed his rose onto the casket and left.

Hans and Marissa sat for a minute longer when Hans took out two flowers from his breast pocket. He handed one to Marissa. She followed behind him as he put the edelweiss on his mother's casket, and she placed her flower on it as well, all the while he never let go of her hand. He bent over, put his hand on the casket and kissed it. She heard him say, "Auf Wiedersehen Mutter" then whispered something softly to his mother and turned and they walked away. Marissa could not hold back her tears any longer. She tried as hard as she could, for Hans' sake, but she lost control. The tears were streaming down her face as they walked to the limo. In the car she put her head on Hans' chest and sobbed all the way home. He held her tightly, saying nothing. Even with her head buried into his chest and his arms around her, she could hear the loud thunderous roars in the distance and the pounding of the intense rainfall on the roof top.

When they arrived at the house Marissa quickly tried to pull herself together, for she knew there was food to be heated up for the guests that would be coming. As she was readying the food, she noticed from the view of the kitchen into the bedroom that Hans was changing into his jogging clothes. He came out of his room and announced he was going for a run. She was confused. "Won't there be people coming over?" she asked. Hans explained he had reached his limit and had asked his aunt yesterday to host the reception. He told her he was done, and could not bear anymore. Marissa could see that he needed to be alone. She did not ask him if he wanted her to join him, so she stayed back at the house while he ran.

She watched him leave through the front door and could see the streaks of lightning dancing across the sky like a light show. The thunderous sounds were deafening as well as frightening to Marissa. She was concerned for his safety as his house was surrounded by wooded areas and she had read in the visitors guide she purchased at the airport that wild boar lived in Vienna's wooded areas. She wondered if there were any where he was going to run, as she knew in Central Park he always went off the beaten path. She watched him from the kitchen window as he started his run down the street. She could see by the intensity of the movements of his swaying arms that he was pushing himself hard. She realized his pace was too fast for the wetness of the road. The relentless pounding of the rain onto the road caused the water to rush down the sides of the curbs as if gushing streams. Within an hour so much rain had fallen the storm drains stopped accepting water. The street outside of Hans' house was starting to flood.

About an hour and a half after Hans had left the wind started to pick up. Marissa looked out of the window fearful, as the trees were bending to such a degree she believed some might break. She then noticed with the force of the wind the flowers had bent over in the front yard to the length that each flowers' petals were touching the earth. It was as if Mother Nature was demanding each flower to bow in honor of her power. She watched as she saw the wind carrying branches down the street. She was worried about Hans being out in this weather alone, and she was worried about herself being alone as well. There was always the possibility of a power outage or that a limb might crash through a window.

She had been trying to keep her mind preoccupied by making some brownies. She was on her third batch when she heard clashes of thunder lapping over each other. She was fearful for Hans being among the trees during this lightning storm when she heard a large cracking sound coming from the front of the house. She looked outside the window and noticed the tree in front of Hans' house had been stuck by lightening and was split in half.

Marissa started to panic. She hated thunderstorms and that was when she was in the city surrounded by millions of people. Here, alone, isolated, she did not even know what direction to walk in to arrive at the nearest house to safety. She dialed Hans' phone and heard it ringing in the bedroom. "Shit", she thought, "he had forgotten to take his phone". She went into the bedroom and picked up his phone. Looking at it she realized his contact numbers might have someone in the area that she could call. She opened his contact list looked for his "in case of emergency" numbers, while continuing to hear the roars of thunder in the background. There it was, Wolfgang, the name of the man who Hans had told her was his best friend. She noticed it was an Austrian phone number. She hit send and prayed he would answer. When he answered she heard, "Hallo ist Hans dieser Sie?" Marissa started to cry. She started to talk to herself rambling, "Shit, what do I do now? I can't speak German. Where is Hans? I can't do this. I'm so scared." She then heard on the other end "Marissa is this you? Are you using Hans phone, is he not there?" She then explained that Hans left for a run two hours ago and she hadn't any idea where he was. While telling him of the tree which was struck by lightning she started to break down and started sobbing. While Wolfgang tried to calm her, telling her he would come right over, Hans walked in.

As she ran to him she could see the water dripping off his drenched hair and running down his face. His clothes were soaking wet and were making a puddle on the floor. When she reached Hans she held onto him tightly. He held onto her with one hand and with the other took the phone from her hand and very briefly spoke to Wolfgang in German. Marissa calmed down after several minutes of being held by Hans. She stopped shaking and felt more at ease. She had been so frightened and anxious that she hadn't even noticed he was cold and shaking. His eyes were red and she could see he had been crying.

Hans apologized for leaving her alone for so long. He had lost track of time. When he realized how bad the weather had become he immediately turned around, but she was a good distance away by then. He decided to call her and then became aware that he left his phone at home.

Marissa demanded he get into a hot shower so he wouldn't become sick. Hans suggested she join him. Marissa agreed as she was still a bit anxious from being left alone and wanted to be close to him. They were just about finished with their shower when she heard a voice yelling out in German. She could see by Hans' facial expression he instantly recognized the voice. Hans looked at Marissa and said "It's Wolfgang", as he left the shower. Hans was dressed and in the living room before Marissa had even dried off. Marissa could hear the two talking in German. She dressed and came into the living room. Hans introduced his childhood friend Wolfgang to Marissa. Wolfgang spoke in English saying, "I hadn't realized until you called a little bit ago, that last night when we first met during an awkward situation at the funeral home, and then in the overwhelming somberness of today, I was never introduced to you, I apologize." Marissa apologized also for calling him in a panic, but Wolfgang assured her there was no need to apologize and that she could call him anytime she wanted.

Marissa watched Hans face as he spoke with his friend and he was more relaxed now. Marissa was as well as the storm had passed. The two friends talked for hours, sometimes speaking in English then changing unconsciously it seemed to German. She thought it best to leave the old friends to themselves and went into the bedroom. She went online to check out a web site she had recently discovered that translated common German phrases to English. She had a list of phrases she had written down phonetically she heard during the past few days and was interested in learning their meaning.

It was nearing dinner time and Marissa asked Hans if he would like something to eat. Wolfgang remarked how shocked he was that Hans would make such a lovely creature cook. Wolfgang insisted on buying dinner, suggesting they could go to the restaurant Korso, one which he knew was Hans' favorite. Hans declined the offer saying he would rather stay at home. Wolfgang apologized for his insensitivity saying he would go pick up something and bring it back. Hans opened the refrigerator and showed the contents to Wolfgang. They both laughed. There was enough food from neighbors and Marissa to feed the whole town. Wolfgang said to Marissa, "I am sure you have done enough since you've been here, you sit. Hans and I can manage a microwave". It was a bit comical as she watched the two of them cutting and making salad while trying to figure out which containers of food should be eaten together.

Hans seemed more comfortable with Wolfgang than any other person she had seen him with. Marissa enjoyed the fascinating dinner conversation. Wolfgang told such colorful tales of childhood memories of himself and Hans. She hadn't realized that Hans had been such a rabble-rouser in his youth, until Wolfgang told of many schemes the two shared in. Marissa was thrilled to learn more about the man she had fallen in love with, and it only en-

deared him more to her. After dinner Wolfgang insisted on cleaning up, adding that Hans would help as well.

Hans went into the kitchen, to attempt to rearrange the leftovers
back into the refrigerator, so he and Wolfgang would have room
on the counter top to work. He was well out of range of hearing
when Wolfgang told Marissa an extremely interesting story. It
seemed when he and Hans had reached their junior year of high
school they concocted a scheme to attempt to get all of the junior
class girls to have sex with them. He explained that at age sixteen
a strong wind could give them an erection. They were sexually
frustrated so they knew they would have to come up with a plan.
They had successfully pulled off many schemes before and realized
anything was possible with a well thought out strategy. He continued with his explanation, "We realized the girls in our class were
significantly different than the boys. The girls worried about their
sexual reputations, and also about not losing their virginities,
while the total opposite was true for the boys. Hans and I had absolutely no experience with girls and we had nothing to lose and
everything to learn. We discussed the situation for days until we
came up with a plan we believed would be feasible. Our plan was
so simple yet we believed it to be genius, but you have to remember we were only sixteen years old. We would go out on a date and
when that crucial moment occurred when you want to go from
second to third base, we would simply explain to our date we had
no intention on pursuing the act of sexual intercourse. The girls,
we had hoped, would be intrigued and would allow us to continue
with our well rehearsed script. We would promise them that at no
time would we undo our pants; we assured them our gratification
came solely in pleasuring them. We had taken out every book on
women's anatomy we could find in the library and had scrupulously studied it. We read every science journal with reference to
the female anatomy, and had located a copy of the Kinsey report
written in1953. We definitely were traveling in uncharted waters.

What we discovered was that the junior girls were just as sexually frustrated as we were but they were not willing to take the chance of getting pregnant or at acquiring a bad reputation. We dated as many girls as we could for months. After our dates we would get together to compare our notes to see what did and didn't work. We had a code between us, to never divulge names. By senior year, girls were calling us for dates, and by then we had become quite skillful at our trade."

It was then Marissa learned of Hans' relationship with Gretchen. Wolfgang continued, "Our plan ended when Hans took out Gretchen. Before Hans could get his hand up her shirt she already had hers down his pants pleasuring him. No more dry humping for Hans but his poor heart, it..." but before Wolfgang could finish his sentence Hans had returned from the kitchen. Having heard the last part of the conversation he looked furious. It was the first time Marissa had seen him angry. He spoke to Wolfgang in German, using a loud, stern voice. The two went into the kitchen. Marissa thought this would be a good time to exit. She could tell by Hans' facial expression and tone of voice he was embarrassed, but she was glad that Wolfgang had shared the story with her as it was her favorite one of the evening. It was getting late so Marissa decided it would be a good time to leave the two alone. She yelled into the kitchen, "It was nice meeting you Wolfgang" and went into the bedroom.

She opened her emails and answered ones from Rita and Carter. She could hear Hans and Wolfgang talking loudly, and was glad when their argument ended shortly. It was comforting for her when she began to hear them laughing. After about an hour on the internet she became tired and went to bed. As she laid there trying to fall asleep she couldn't help but think about Gretchen. She must have been Hans' first love, she thought. Then she started to think about all the girls in his junior year class that he had gone out with. She couldn't help but wonder how many girls he had pleasured. She wondered if Hans would have ever told her that story himself.

The day had been full of strong emotions and she couldn't seem to turn off her mind. She couldn't fall asleep, no matter how hard she tried. Then she had an idea. If she could smell Hans' scent it would be as if she was lying in the nook of his arm. She saw that he laid his clothes from the funeral across the chair. She got up took off her chemise and put on his shirt. She could smell his scent. She was right, as it did relax her. She breathed easier and fell asleep wondering what other devilish deeds the two of those boys could have gotten into when they were younger. It was those thoughts that lingered in her mind as she fell asleep, as it was so much more interesting than counting sheep.

Day Fourteenth, Friday, June 24th Hans' story

Hans awoke to the sound of birds chirping outside his bedroom window, a pleasant change from the banging of garbage cans into garbage trucks, traffic, and taxi horns he had become accustom to hearing in the mornings waking up in Manhattan. The sun was shining brightly, but he had seen on the weather channel the night before that rain was in the forecast. He was glad he had requested a tent to be put up at the cemetery as he didn't want people, who were there to pay their respects, getting drenched. It was such a beautiful day, he hated that the expected clouds and gray skies would make the already gruesome day bleaker.

As he stood in front of his window he realized it had been a long time since he gazed out onto the beautiful view. In his youth when he looked out his window he would be wishing he could be in New York City, the Big Apple, where he could make his fortune. He believed if your goal was to work in the financial world then NYC was the place to be. As he looked out of his window today, it was different now. He wasn't looking at the view with the eyes of a boy but with the insight of a man. It was a beautiful view, equal in beauty to the skyline view from his penthouse apartment.

The vineyard beyond his house held fond memories for him, as he had spent many hours toiling in those fields with both his mother and Wolfgang. As teenagers, whenever Wolfgang and he would get caught doing something wrong, which was frequent, his mother would put them to work in the fields as a consequence. If either boy had a problem to work out, his mother put them to work in the field telling them manual labor would clear their minds. Wolfgang teased Hans telling him his mother really only wanted the free labor. But Hans knew better. He knew his mother believed if the two boys worked enough hours out in the field they would be too tired to get into any further mischief. He was also aware of his mothers' belief that working with your hands in the earth gave you a sense of belonging to something much bigger than yourself, a connection to the universe which made you aware of just how small your problems truly were.

He remembered when he was a young boy about ten he helped his mother plant seeds. He asked her how it was possible that those tiny little seeds would grow into big plump strawberries. His mother replied, "A man more knowledgeable than me, Albert Einstein, said 'that there are two ways to live. You can live as if nothing is a miracle or you can live as if everything is a miracle'. I believe that everything is a miracle Hans. You need to think about it for yourself and see how you view it."

Hans walked over towards Marissa. She was still asleep and looked so peaceful. How nice it was of her, he thought, to come all this way to be with him to help him get through this ordeal. As he moved the hair from her face she awoke. "You sleep longer if you want", he said, "I'm going to take a shower and get ready." He knew she would realize he needed to be alone, for there had never been a time when he hadn't invited her into the shower with him. She stayed in bed until he finished, just as he knew she would.

When he came out of the shower, with his towel wrapped around his waist, she got up. As she walked by him, he grabbed her pulling her close saying, "I'm so glad you that came, Marissa". She kissed him saying there was no other place she would rather be than by his side. When Marissa took a shower Hans dressed then went out onto the front porch. His mother's flowers were in full bloom and the gardens had never looked as vibrant with color as they had today. As he stared out at the flower beds to the left of his house, with its heather, roses, carnations and hyacinths he could almost see his mother kneeling near her flowerbeds, wearing her over sized yellow straw hat, with the green ribbon tied under her chin, tending to their needs. He walked over to a patch of edelweiss, bent over and took some putting them into his breast pocket. Even though the house was surrounded by beautifully colored flowers, those tiny white ones were always his mother's favorite.

By the time they left for the church the sun was still shining. Hans knew the small church would be packed with his mother's friends, as she was very popular in town. During the drive to the church, Hans was flooded with memories of his childhood. He tried to only remember the good times, but he had to live with the realization of his decision. The decision to stay away so long from home was his and his alone.

Hans felt unnerved as he walked down the aisle of the church. He wished they had arrived earlier so he would not to have the look into the saddened eyes of his mother's friends who were also grieving. Having Marissa by his side, gave him great comfort and strength. It was hard for Hans to sit and listen to the priest speak about his mother. He didn't want to be there. He wanted to be any-where else. His mother would have been the one person who would have understood that, he thought.

As he stared at the casket in the front of the church he realized it was not his mother who was in there. There was nothing in the casket but rotting flesh and bones. The essence of who she was had left when she took her last breathe at the hospital he believed. Hans never really believed one way or another about the existence of a God. He told his mother he was an agnostic, as he did have his doubts. But, whenever he told her that fact she would have a fierce reaction. She would lecture him on the Bible until he left and she would end up going to church to light candles. Sitting in the church, with Marissa by his side, he couldn't help but believe there was a God. Perhaps his mother was looking down on him right now. He thought she'd be saying "Hans I am glad you wore your new dark gray pin stripped suit. It looks good on you. I always thought you looked your best in a gray suit, it really brings out your blue eyes. I like the casket you picked out for me; you know how I love edelweiss." He remembered the day he had called her to inform her he had a job interview with an important firm in Manhattan. She insisted he wear his gray suit. She believed it made him look more distinguished. All sorts of memories went rushing through his mind as he starred at the casket. Although his childhood had been a cold one, his mother had changed after the years he been had gone and their relationship had grown warmer. He always thought it odd how they were at their closest when they were at the farthest in distance.

The time had come for him, as one of the pallbearers, to carry his mother out of the church. He could feel his palms become sweaty, he could feel his heart racing, and he felt nauseous. When he touched the cold brass handle to lift the casket he was reminded of how cold his mother's hands were when they last touched. He looked to his right and there was Wolfgang holding onto the brass handle on the opposite side. His two friends Clint and Jethro were directly behind him. It gave him strength to look into the eyes of his best friend Wolfgang and knowing his other two friends were right behind him.

The ride to the cemetery was not long in distance but it was long in torment, for Hans had full view of the back window of the hearse driving directly in front of them. Hans invited Wolfgang, Clint and Jethro into the limo with him and Marissa. No one spoke. Not a single word. When they arrived at the cemetery everyone got out of the limo. Hans just sat for awhile, not knowing if he could get out. He contemplated for a moment on leaving. At that moment his friend Wolfgang came back, opened the door to the car and said "Its time Hans. We can do this, come sit by me. We'll get drunk later and we'll throw up together, and we'll figure it out in the morning". Hans remembered the last time Wolfgang said that to him. It was when Gretchen had broken their engagement. Hans was heartbroken, his core shattered. He couldn't eat, sleep or function and refused to see anyone. After a few days, Wolfgang came over to his house with a bottle of Vodka banging on his bedroom window. When Hans opened the French door, Wolfgang took hold of his arm, held out the bottle of vodka and said "We can get through this. We'll get drunk and then throw up together and we'll figure it out in the morning".

Hans held Marissa's hand tightly. When the service was over he was frozen in his chair. He didn't know how long he had sat there but he did notice that everyone else had left. He knew he could not stay any longer as he could feel Marissa shivering from the cold morning air. If Marissa hadn't been shivering, he might not have been able to leave. He walked slowly over to the coffin. He touched it, noticing how cold it was. How cold she must be inside it, he thought. He placed the edelweiss on her coffin and said "Good-bye Mother. I love you. Every time I see the edelweiss I will think of you".

By the time Hans reached his house he feared he would no longer be able to contain his emotions. The rain was coming down extremely hard and he noticed the lightning, but he needed to be out in the wide open space, alone. He needed to run. He needed the release of the rush of endorphins to help calm his emotionally overcharged body. He needed to clear his thought from the events which had just occurred. He grabbed Marissa's I Pod Nano he saw laying on the bedroom dresser, while he was changing, to bring with him on his run.

He turned on the music, with its volume as high as he could stand it to help discourage any thoughts of the day from entering his consciousness. He was surprised when he learned that Marissa had downloaded some classical music to her playlist. It brought a short lived smile to his face when he wondered if her first intro-duction to classical music had been her incentive for adding those pieces to her selections. He ran faster and harder than he ever had, purposely pushing himself to his limit. He paid close attention to every breath he took in trying to calm himself. The rain hurt as the wind whipped it across his face, yet he was thankful for the rain as it masked his tears.

Hans had not realized the severity of the weather until a branch from a tree fell in front of him. It was then that he was shaken back to reality. He had left Marissa alone in this storm. As he turned to head back, he realized he had left his phone at home and was not able to reach her. On his run back he noticed some streets were flooding, and broken tree limbs and debris were being whirled about by the wind. He could not return at the same speed as he had departed for exhaustion was hitting him. But he pushed himself as hard as he could.

When he returned home, he noticed the tree outside his house had been hit by lightning and was split in half. Hans opened the front door and saw Marissa standing there sobbing holding his cell phone. She ran to him and held him tighter than she had ever be-fore. He was angry with himself for having not thought of her first and staying at the house. When he took the phone from her hand he realized she had called Wolfgang for help. He was pleased she had chosen the one person that would have come to help her no matter the weather conditions.

He wondered if his body was reacting from the events of the day or from his clothing being soaking wet when he started to shiver uncontrollably. Marissa suggested a hot shower and he agreed, hoping just the chill of the rain was its cause. His shivering continued even after the water should have warmed him. It was not until Marissa held him for several minutes that his body seemed to calm. He loved when they showered together. She would always lather him up with such affection and attention. Just as they were rinsing off the soap he heard Wolfgang's voice. It was a pleasant sound for Hans. He immediately left the shower to welcome his friend. He introduced Wolfgang to Marissa as he realized he hadn't done this when the two had first met. It was such a comfort for Hans to have Wolfgang around. They reminisced during dinner and it seemed to be just what Hans needed.

With dinner finished, Hans cleared off the counter and put all the food away as he didn't want Marissa to do any further work. When he returned to the living room, he was stunned to hear Wolfgang telling of their junior year scheme. He couldn't believe Wolfgang would share that story with Marissa. Hans tore into the living room and into Wolfgang. He demanded to know why Wolfgang would divulge such personal and sensitive information to Marissa. Wolfgang explained if this was the girl he was planning to marry, he didn't think Hans would be keeping any secrets from her. Wolfgang was the one person who knew some of the deepest and most personal information about Hans. Wolfgang apologized profusely and Hans forgave his indiscretion and they continued with their reminiscing.

They started to clear the table and fill the dishwasher. As Hans went into the dining room to retrieve more dishes he could hear Wolfgang laughing, and repeating sexual phrases in both English and German. He entered the kitchen to find Wolfgang reading

Marissa's English/German translation dictionary. As Wolfgang continued to read some of the yellow highlighted sexual phrases Hans attempted to grab the dictionary from his hands. Wolfgang raised the book above his head saying, "I found this book next to the microwave. It seems this dictionary opens itself to Chapter Three, as if it has been opened to that chapter a thousand times. Now I see why you are in love Hans, I am noticing some selections in this chapter on sexual phrases which are highlighted that even I have not attempted yet." Hans did not look amused. Hans said in a demanding voice "I am counting to three Wolfgang and if you do not give me the book by then, I will assume you do not value your life". Wolfgang, not wanting to anger his friend, handed it back to him saying, "I am only giving this back to you for Marissa's sake. If she is in need of giving you direction she might need it as a reference". As Hans left the room he could hear Wolfgang yelling to him in German, "You're getting old Hans; you're losing your sense of humor".

Hans brought the dictionary to his bedroom, reading some of the highlighted phrases as he walked. Marissa was busy on the internet when he entered. Placing the dictionary on the desk next to her, he said, "Marissa, here is your dictionary. Wolfgang found it next to the microwave. I am interested in some of the phrases that are highlighted. Perhaps at a later date we could discuss the one you have highlighted on page 42". Hans smiled, and he could see Marissa was blushing. She replied, "This is the translation dictionary that I mentioned Carter gave to me. He highlighted some phrases thinking he was being humorous". Hans could see Marissa was embarrassed. Turning to leave the bedroom Hans flashed her his boyish grin and said, "Very disappointing Marissa, I was looking forward to the highlighted section on page 42". He turned his head back to look at her and saw that a smile had come across her face and he couldn't help but laugh a bit as he walked away.

Approaching the kitchen Hans could hear Wolfgang saying some odd phrases, "A little to the left. A little to the right. You are missing it completely. You are almost there. Too hard. Slow down. Did you ever take anatomy in high school? No, I will not do that! You are missing it entirely". He entered the kitchen and saw Wolfgang with a pen and pad writing these phrases down in German". Hans asked, "Wolfgang what are you doing?" He replied, "Hans I noticed there were a few important phrases in Chapter Three that were missing. I thought perhaps I could jot some down for Marissa so she could help you navigate and satisfy her better." The two broke out into laughter and then spent the next hour laughing while coming up with some phrases that were not in the book but should have been. With one of the suggestions Wolfgang had given, Hans remarked "Is that legal in this country?" To which Wolfgang replied, "It is here but I'm pretty sure it's illegal in New York". When they were done Wolfgang jokingly suggested they contact the author of the dictionary to see if perhaps he wanted to add their list to his next addition, and then said, "Hans we should write our own book". Hans laughed, realizing he had been laughing so hard that his sides actually ached.

The two continued to clean up from dinner, discussing how they would never again let this much time lapse between visits. They vowed to reprioritize their lives, and not allow their jobs to consume their time. As Wolfgang left he said, "See you tomorrow at church, call me before you leave".

While walking to his bedroom, Hans wondered how he should approach the story of his junior year, which Wolfgang had freely shared, with Marissa. Or, perhaps he shouldn't even mention it. Well, he thought to himself, it could have been worse. Wolfgang could have told her how we would measure our penises each month during puberty to see if they were growing. Then Hans had an awful thought, perhaps Wolfgang had told her that story. Hans realized that he was in the kitchen a pretty long time alone. Wolfgang could have told her a number of stories from his youth which he wouldn't have wanted shared. He realized Wolfgang knew more about him than anyone should know about another. He made a mental note that when he called Wolfgang the next day he would ask if there were any other stories shared that he should be aware of. Wolfgang was a good friend indeed and Hans felt extremely fortunate to have him in his life.

When Hans entered his bedroom, Marissa was already fast asleep. He noticed she was wearing one of his dress shirts. He wondered why she was wearing it and was amazed how sexy she looked in it. She had the top three buttons undone exposing part of her breast, and the blanket had been thrown aside leaving her bare legs exposed as well. He dared not wake her as it had been a long emotional day, and he knew what they both needed was sleep, so he curbed his desire to ravish her.

DAY FIFTEEN

Day Fifteen, Saturday, June 25th Marissa's Day

Marissa awoke realizing she had forgotten to ask Hans what time their flight would be leaving in the morning. Aware that Hans would have set the alarm, she rolled over to check what time it set for and her stirring in the bed woke Hans. He told her it was still dark outside, too early to get up and suggested she should go back to sleep. When she asked what time they would be leaving for the airport, he assured her it wasn't until the afternoon.

Marissa nestled back into her nook thinking how thankful she was Hans had come into her life. She had finally found a man who loved her and he was perfect. She laid there listing in her head, all the things she was grateful for. She knew Hans could tell she was not asleep, although she did not know how, as she was purposely staying very still. She felt him as he moved closer to her. She could feel that he was aroused. She couldn't think of a better way to start their day. She felt his hand move slowly up her shirt. She loved the way his hands caressed her, always taking his time, never hurrying. Hans unbuttoned the shirt and kissed her breast ever so softly yet holding them firmly. He never needed to prolong foreplay for her body to be ready for him to enter her, for her body was instantly ready whenever he was near, but he still always did. He seemed to enjoy his exploration of her body as much as she did. He would take hours pleasuring her. When Hans finally penetrated her she was already near climaxing. He always instinctively seemed to know when to go faster, slower, deeper or to withdraw. She was amazed how well he had come to know her body in the short time they were together. She loved the feel of his starched shirt against her body as they made love. It made her feel as if he surrounded her. He always brought her to heights of pleasure she never had known attainable each time they made love.

When they finally got out of bed, they took a lengthy relaxing hot shower together. Marissa decided to make waffles with whipped cream and strawberries. She had noticed the other day on Hans' back porch sat two large clay handmade pots with strawberries growing in them. The clay pots had beautiful drawings of grape leaves painted in thin black lines that encircled them. Marissa went out to the back porch and picked some fresh strawberries to put on the waffles. As she plucked them from their stems she realized their fragrance was stronger and their size much larger than any strawberry she had ever picked from her grandmother's garden.

Hans was quiet during breakfast, but he did mention they would leave for the airport at 1:30 pm, with one slight detour. She couldn't help but wonder what detail he needed to finish before leaving, but Marissa was sure it had something to do with the closing of the house or perhaps his mother's will. After cleaning up the breakfast dishes with Hans helping, Marissa then packed. With the packing finished she went onto the back porch to sit and take in the beauty of the land before having to leave it. As she sat on the handmade wooden bench, she marveled at its construction void of any nails or screws. The wooden slats appeared to have been cut to fit together tightly like a puzzle. It seemed to be made of a much stronger wood than the bench she sat on near the Brooklyn Bridge, or perhaps it was that the strips of wood were cut thicker. Although it had apparently seen many years of use, the bench had been taken care of. It was well preserved, as if it had been coated with a fresh sealant each year.

At the end of the porch was an area in the back yard about a twenty foot square, with slabs of black slate arranged in the dirt with a wrought iron table and six chairs which sat upon it. To the left of the house, just behind the table was a stone wall, made of large stones of various shades of blue gray, about six feet high and about one hundred feet long. In the stone wall was built a small fountain that flowed into a coy pond. Beyond the table was a large flowerbed. She marveled at how his mother had planted such an array of colors so pleasing to the eye. Amidst the flowers stood a simple concrete birdbath, which several birds were partaking in. The back yard was shaded by large lush trees that protected it and the house from the harsh heat of the beating sun. As Marissa sat with her eyes closed she focused on the sounds of the soothing melodic tunes from the wind chimes which his mother had scattered about the back yard and the rippling sounds of the falling water from the stone wall as it entered the coy pond. She felt a feeling of calm as she sat on the bench. She imagined how peaceful it must have been for Hans sitting there in that very seat when he was a growing boy.

She sat there admiring the beautiful vineyard behind his house. There were rows and rows of vibrant grape plants whose colors ranged from pale green to royal purple. The soil appeared dark and fertile. She wondered if Hans knew the owners of the vineyard, under what label they sold their wine and if it was available for purchase in NY.

Hans seemed busy. After he finished packing, she could hear him speaking in German to someone on the phone while walking through the house making sure all windows and doors were securely locked. She decided that when she returned to NY she would take German lessons as the language was such a big part of Hans' life and she wanted to be able to share it with him. Not to mention, it was killing her not knowing what he was saying half the time.

It was 1:25 pm when Hans came out to the back porch and asked her if she was ready to leave. She patted the bench and asked him to sit down. He obliged and sat putting his arm around her shoulders. She asked him if the vineyard had been there when he was a little boy. Hans told her the vineyard was older than he was. When she inquired if they could purchase the wine from that vineyard in NY he assured her he would procure some upon their return. She was surprised when he suddenly gave her a long and feverishly intense kiss. If it hadn't been for the fact they had to leave for the airport, she would have thought he was going to make love to her right then and there.

As they left the house Marissa felt a bit saddened. She turned and gave the house one last glance. She was going to miss it. She really loved the rustic feel it had and all the memories it held for Hans, some memories she had already learned and some that were yet to be discovered. She felt Hans could somehow see in her face that she wanted to stay a bit longer. As they walked to the car, he assured her he would bring her back again for a visit, soon.

A car was out front to take them to the airport. Don't they have regular taxis over here in Austria, Marissa thought? It seemed every time they went somewhere there was a black car waiting for them. As they drove to the city Marissa took note of the majestic mountains that scraped the sky. As they drove by city hall, she couldn't help but notice its five pillars, standing so regal, magnificently built similar to Vienna's churches. They passed huge water fountains with the most beautiful sculptures. There was one fountain in particular she liked. Hans told her the name was the Donner fountain. In the middle stood a giant statue of a woman who was surrounded by four cherubs spewing water into the fountain. On each of its four corners stood huge statues about two stories high. They passed too many buildings with Corinthian columns to even count. The architecture in the city was surpassed by none that she had ever seen in person or in books.

When the car stopped in front of the church where the service had been held the day before, Marissa was surprised. Hans looked into Marissa eyes as he took a ring out of his pocket and handed it to her. It was a thin gold band, beautifully etched with tiny leaves. Hans told Marissa as proof of his commitment to be faithful in their relationship he wanted to give her this ring. As Marissa had told Hans that her cross necklace had been blessed by a priest and her rosaries, which had belonged to her grandmother, had been blessed by the pope, he wanted to have this ring blessed before she wore it. Marissa's excitement over receiving a ring from Hans was intensified with his caring gesture of having it first blessed by a priest. As they entered the church, she noticed Wolfgang sitting in the first pew with an older woman. Upon approaching the pew Wolfgang introduced his mother to Marissa explaining she only spoke German. Hans walked to the back vestibule. Wolfgang mentioned he wanted to see Hans before he left for New York and knew he would be coming to the church before he left for the airport. He brought his mother along with her insistence on saying goodbye to Hans as well.

As the priest entered the church with Hans, Marissa went up to meet them. Hans stood next to Marissa while Wolfgang and his mother stayed in the pew. As the priest blessed the ring, he asked Marissa a question. Hans interpreted, "He asks if you love me and want to be faithful to me while we are in this relationship?" Marissa nodded her head and replied "Yes". The priest and Hans spoke in German, with the priest then speaking for about three minutes alone. Finally, he made the sign of the cross over the ring, blessing it. Hans put the blessed ring on Marissa's right ring finger.

Marissa was impressed how embellished their blessings were. Although, she thought, as the churches in Vienna were overly ornate, it was only fitting their blessings of objects, such as rings, be equally as overstated.

Wolfgang and his mother hugged them saying their goodbyes, and then remained in the church when Marissa and Hans left. As they walked out of the church there was a gardener trimming some bushes in front of the building. Hans spoke to him in German and took his clippers from him. Hans explained to Marissa of an old custom in Austria, where it was good luck or a couple to cut wood together. Marissa thought it was a cute custom and helped Hans as they trimmed a large branch. Marissa was used to different cultures having their own beliefs in what brings good luck. In her own family, it was believed good luck would be bestowed upon a person, if while holding a baby's its diaper leaked and urinated on you. Marissa always thought that to be a strange one, at least with the Austrian custom she didn't have to be peed on to have good fortune.

On the way to the airport Marissa could not help but admire what a beautiful ring Hans had just given her. She was certain he must have picked it out at a vintage jewelry store in Vienna as it had a European look to it and he knew she loved vintage jewelry from hearing her talk of her grandmother's jewelry. When they arrived at the airport they boarded a private jet. Marissa wondered if perhaps the company Hans worked for owned it.

As they were settling into their seats an attractive blonde stewardess asked them if there was anything she could get for them. Marissa had never seen so many attractive blonde people in her whole life as she had seen while being in Vienna. It seemed as if everyone in this country was blonde and all somehow genetically destined to be gorgeous.

Marissa began to think perhaps Hans was much more successful with his investments than she had previously believed. They had never really talked about his work. She decided that during the plane ride there would certainly be time to bring up the subject. They had only been in the air for a few minutes and Marissa was looking out the window at the impressive view when Hans said, "Marissa there is something important I want to ask you. I realize this is sudden as we have only known each other for a short time. But I don't want to ask you this question years from now after we have gotten to know each other better. I want to ask you this question now and then we can learn more about each other as we go through life together". Hans got down on one knee. Marissa could not believe it, Hans was going to propose. He said "Marissa you have opened my eyes as well as my heart. I have never known such happiness or contentment as when I am with you. I love you. Will you allow me to be your husband to cherish you until the day I die?" She got down on the floor next to him, feeling happier than she had ever felt in her life saying "Yes". He took a box from his breast pocket. As he opened it, Marissa viewed the most beautiful engagement ring she had ever seen. As he handed it to her it reflected the sun's rays coming in through the window scattering magnificent colors across the interior of the plane. The setting had beautiful filigree with a slight pinkish tinge to the gold which resembled her grandmother's jewelry. As he slipped it onto her finger they passionately kissed and that was when Marissa joined the Mile High Club.

When they finally returned to their seats, Hans asked Marissa if she liked the ring. Marissa explained she couldn't have picked a more beautiful ring herself. Hans told Marissa about the conversations he had with his mother about her. He then showed her the envelope where his mother had placed her rings and had written in German "you know who to give this to". Hans said he believed it was fitting to give her his mother's diamond but insisted that if she wanted her own, he would buy her a new one, a bigger one perhaps if she'd like. Marissa looked up at Hans so adoringly and said

"Hans, I want THIS diamond. It has such sentimental value for both you and I. I don't want a bigger stone. Just because something is more expensive doesn't mean that it is better."

The plane was going through some turbulence and Marissa decided to take one of the pills Carter had given her. She fell asleep in her favorite nook as she snuggled close to Hans, with thoughts of wedding plans whirling through her mind.

Day Fifteenth, Saturday, June 25th Hans' story

Marissa's tussling around awoke Hans. She had woken way too early to get up, Hans thought. He tried to convince her to go back to sleep, but as he laid there next to her listening to her breathing, he could tell, even though she laid motionless, she was still awake. Hans also could not fall back to sleep. He waited for a few more minutes to see if Marissa would drift off. He then decided since they were both awake, he would see just how awake she actually was. He moved in closer to her. It never ceased to amaze him how her body would instantly reacted to his mere proximity to hers. As his hand slid down her body and went between her thighs, he reveled in delight each time at the wet welcome he would encounter. Feeling her so aroused always heightened his desire for her. Her body's response to his every touch fueled the fire that already was burning within him. He realized with Marissa he was not just having sex, he was making love. What a difference the two acts were, he thought, and he much preferred the latter.

After packing, Hans called Wolfgang. He wanted to check on the time to meet at the church, but mostly he wanted to see if Wolfgang had divulged any other boyhood memories that he might have to explain in more detail with Marissa at a later date. Wolfgang assured him no other secrets were exposed. He told Hans he would be leaving for New York later in the day. If it weren't for the fact that Hans was planning on proposing to Marissa on the plane, he would have insisted Wolfgang join them. Hans did, however, insist they meet at a restaurant for drinks and dinner in NYC. Hans was planning on calling Marissa's friends Rita and Carter to meet them after they had arrived and wanted Wolfgang to be there also. Hans was looking forward to meeting those whom Marissa held dear. He told Wolfgang he would text him later with the name of the restaurant and the time to meet. Hans saw Marissa's phone charging by the bed the night before and had retrieved Rita's cell phone number from it and added it to his contact list.

Hans walked out to the front yard of his home. He looked at all the flower beds with their bright array of colors and realized they would never again have the loving care of his mother's hands. He realized that every time he came home, as he walked up the path to his front door, they would be there in her stead to welcome him, a constant reminder of her. He sat in the white wicker chair near the yellow rose bush and phoned Rita. He no sooner introduced himself than Rita interrupted and started talking. He was surprised to learn that Rita had already known all about him. She let Hans know as soon as they learned he had swept Marissa off to Austria, Carter had come to her home to help in deciding what should be done about the situation. They had no idea who Hans was, and Rita was not about to let Marissa go off with a stranger. Rita was in the middle of packing her bags to fly to Vienna to find Marissa at the hospital when Carter arrived at her home. However, when Carter showed George and Rita a picture he had taken of Hans through *Antonio's* restaurant window, their fears were put to rest. George recognized Hans from prior investment deals and assured Rita he was a man of character. They decided, knowing how Marissa felt about men who worked in the financial district, that Hans had his reasons for hiding his real identity from her. She further explained that neither she nor Carter had exposed Hans' true identity to Marissa during any emails. Rita insisted Hans tell Marissa before she returned to NYC. Rita informed him that she would no longer conceal his secret once Marissa was home. Hans was truly impressed how much her friends cared for her. He said he was looking forward to dinner and drinks with her, George, Carter and Roberto after their arrival later that day. He mentioned he wanted the dinner to be a surprise for Marissa. When Hans said he would make the arrangements, Rita insisted it would be easier for her to make the reservations and contact Carter from New York. Rita assured him she would text him with the restaurant name and time of the reservation. Her voice had a hint of scolding in the beginning of the conversation but her voice softened as the dialog continued. The chat was short but Hans could tell by Rita's tone of voice that she approved of him. With the dinner plans for that evening being taken care of Hans started the ordeal of closing up the house.

Closing up the house took longer than Hans had anticipated as while making sure each window and door was secure memories would bombard his mind. He knew he would be back in a few months to go through the house and pack up his mother's belongings, but the thought of leaving home was hard. He wondered if it was realization that upon his return his mother wouldn't be there to welcome him as she always had. He had to fight back the tears so many times as he would go from one room to the next securing each window.

When Hans finished locking up, he noticed Marissa sitting on the bench on the back porch. That was his favorite place in his home because it held such powerful memories for him. He remembered helping his father make it now realizing his father had wanted to share his love of carpentry with Hans. He showed Hans how to work with the grain of the wood and not against it and how to connect the pieces of wood without the use of nails or screws. His father worked many hours on that bench with Hans by his side. Hans would hand him saws, sandpaper, glue, clamps and whatever else his dad needed, the whole time taking in every lesson that was to be learned. Upon the bench's completion Hans was amazed how strong it was with the use of only hand tools and glue. After all these years it still held tight. When he was a teenager he would sit there on many nights looking out into the vineyard. It was especially beautiful at sunset, he recalled. The beauty of the sunset there was never matched by any other sunset in all of his travels.

Hans remembered as a little boy sitting on this bench with his parents in the evenings, listening to them share their dream of making the best wines in the whole of Austria. His father would have been proud he thought, if he could see the numbers of distributers they now had and how many countries carried their label.

After his father died it was on that bench where his mother gave Hans his father's pocket watch. His grandfather had given it to his father when he turned sixteen. It had been in his family for several generations. His mother's picture was on the inside cover, but under it were his grandmother's picture, and his great grandmother's picture. He remembered that after his father's death, his mother would sit there alone looking out onto the vineyard, her face weary and void of expression. He could recall like it was yesterday, sitting on that bench with his mother, when she told him they might lose the house and the land after his father had died.

It was on that bench at the age of fourteen where he and Wolfgang had gotten drunk for the first time on a bottle of Russian vodka which Wolfgang had stolen from his parent's home. And it was on that bench where his mother had found them both passed out the next morning.

When his father completed the bench, Hans watched his father carve a heart with his parent's initials into it. There was also a burn mark on that bench from when Hans attempted to blow torch off the heart with his and Gretchen's initials on it. It was on that bench where Gretchen had given Hans back her engagement ring. Hans had thrown it so far out into the vineyard that night, he never knew if it was still there buried deep in the soil or if it had been found by one of their workers. He wondered if it sunk straight down to hell where it belonged or if it was later dug up with the tilling and caught up on a broken twig and tossed away. Even the event of that night couldn't take away the special place in his heart for that bench. Too many good memories overcame it.

It was on that bench where Hans told his mother he was leaving for America. And it was on that bench, with each return home where he sat and watched the sunset with her. That was the view of his childhood. Sitting on the bench always brought him peace. When he went out to get Marissa to leave, she asked him to sit on the bench with her. As he sat there with his arm around her, he re-alized he wanted to make a new memory with Marissa on his bench. When he kissed her a warm feeling swept over him. He re-alized that wherever she was, would be home. And with that thought, it made it easier to lock the front door behind him.

When they pulled up to the airport, Hans had yet to tell Marissa they were not taking a commercial flight. As they neared his jet, he realized he probably should have mentioned it to her earlier, but he was concerned she would have asked him why. And as he wanted to wait until they were in flight before explaining his ca-reer, his success and his love for her, he decided to wait until re-vealing it. Marissa seemed puzzled while boarding the jet but didn't question Hans about it. Hans was glad she was not inquiring yet but he could tell by the look on her face she would soon be asking lots of questions.

They had barely taken off when Hans decided to propose to Marissa. He watched her face as she was enjoying the view from the window. He then had a thought come to him that he hadn't thought of before, what do I do if she says "No"? He felt he hadn't planned this out very well, if she turned down his proposal he had nowhere to go to regroup. He also realized he hadn't prepared what to say. So there he was with no plan and no script, so he spoke from the heart. Hans wanted to do this right, so he got down on one knee. He knew at that moment she would be aware of what he was about to ask. When Marissa said yes, he was relieved that she accepted. It was proof for him that she loved him as much as he loved her. He felt extremely fortunate that he had told the stewardess not to come into the seating area unless he called for her, as he hadn't anticipated the reaction that was to take place. Making love to Marissa was not planned but was surely a welcomed surprise.

Hans thought perhaps he had made the wrong decision in giving Marissa his mother's diamond. He thought it possible she would prefer a new diamond, one of her very own, perhaps a bigger one. When he suggested this idea to Marissa, her answer brought him back to the toy store he had gone to on his seventh birthday, when he bought his red toy pickup truck. Marissa had some of the same core values his mother had taught him. One value being that just because something is more expensive doesn't mean that it is better. With that thought in mind he realized he hadn't told Marissa yet of his career, his success and his wealth. He was so caught up in the moment he forgot that she needed to know. Just as he was about to bring up the subject, the plane hit some turbulence. Marissa became anxious and took some medicine which made her drowsy. He missed the window of opportunity, now he would have to wait until they landed. He was concerned with the prospect that she might feel deceived and give him back the ring. He decided to have a glass of wine and put the thought out of his mind. He knew she loved him, and he would hold onto that thought.

Day Fifteen, Saturday, June 25th Marissa's story

Marissa awoke to the sound of Hans speaking German on the phone. "Did you sleep well? We will be arriving in NYC shortly."

he said. Marissa went to the bathroom to freshen up. She looked in the mirror and noticed she looked a fright. Her hair was all messed up and she had pillow face. It was all crinkly from learning on Hans' shoulder for hours. How is it she thought that he looked as fresh as when they had left Austria? She felt better after putting some water on her face and brushing her teeth. When Marissa returned to her seat Hans had a pot of coffee waiting for her. As she drank her coffee she noticed Hans had a look of concern on his face. She wondered what he was thinking of. Could it be thoughts of his mother, she wondered, or perhaps all the work that had been piling up for him at his office waiting for his return. After two cups of coffee, she felt like herself again.

She decided she was going to ask Hans about the private jet, his work, and the Armani suit and the Italian-made shoes he wore at the funeral. But before she could get out the question, Hans looked at her with such sincerity and said "Marissa there is something I must tell you about myself". Marissa panicked. "Shit ", she thought, "I knew this was too good to be true. Something is terribly wrong. Perhaps, he is an ex-addict, a felon, an inside trader, already married, has had a vasectomy, hates children". Her mind went wild with tons of thought whirling through her head, of possible things that could be wrong. He took her hand and said, "We have never talked in detail about what I do for a living. You know that I work with investment dealings, but that's all. When you first met me I was dressed in not the best of attire. I learned during our first lengthy conversation you disliked men whom were financially successful. You had seemed quite adamant on the subject. I did not want you to prejudge me. I wanted you to get to know me for myself and judge me for my character and not my financial situation. I deceived you and for that I am sorry. But my only deception was on the amount of my success and not in any other matter. I led you to believe I was not as successful as I truly am. I am the sole owner of an investment company in which I have been very successful. I own an apartment on Park Ave. and a house in the Hamptons. I love you Marissa. Can you forgive me for not disclosing this information to you sooner and understand why I was not forthcoming with all the facts?"

For the first time in Marissa's life she decided to think before she answered. She sat there frozen in her seat. She was numb. She didn't see this one coming. She loved him so much. He was nothing like the egocentric, money mongers she had known from Wall Street. He was kind, sensitive, romantic, handsome, thoughtful, compassionate and generous with both his time and money. Having gone through the ordeal on the beach and then the loss of his mother with him, she was sure he had showed his true character. And then as she looked at him she noticed something familiar. She noticed how Hans was looking into her eyes. She had seen that look before, many times. It was how George always looked at Rita. George loved Rita so intensely that it showed every time he looked at her. Every time she entered a room his eyes would light up. He looked at her with such love that any girl around would be envious. She could see that same look in Hans' eyes. She was so happy. She had finally found someone who truly loved her. She knew it was real. She knew it didn't matter how much money he possessed, what mattered was that he possessed her heart.

Minutes had gone by without Marissa uttering a single word. When she did speak she could see Hans was totally attentive to what she was about to say. "Hans I love you. I do want to be your wife. I guess it wasn't fair of me to be so judgmental of those who are financially successful. I never thought of myself as judgmental before, but I guess I am. I'm sorry I made you feel that you needed to hide your success from me. I do, however, want to be clear on one fact. I have no intention of changing any aspect of my personality or my life due to your financial success. I refuse to become one of those Upper East Side women who cares only about themselves. I also insist on us signing a pre-nuptial agreement. If we should break up, I take nothing of yours. I will not have people believe that I married you for your money. If you agree to this, then, yes, I will marry you". With that being said, she kissed him. As they kissed the pilot announced they would be landing momentarily.

Marissa was excited to be home. She had so much to tell her mom, Rita and Carter that she was about to burst. When they got into the limo, Hans said to the driver, "Park Ave, please". Marissa realized she was finally going to see where Hans lived. As they pulled up to the front entrance to his Park Ave address Marissa was uneasy. She didn't know what to expect. When the driver opened the door, in front of her stood the most magnificent building. She must have walked passed it a thousand times before, never really taking notice of it. As she looked up she saw the elegant architecture of the building with its exquisite gargoyles sitting on the ledge above, seemingly staring down upon her, as if they were innately aware she did not belong there. The lobby was larger than her whole apartment, with its beautiful pink and rose streaked marble walls and floor. The wall across from the elevator was mirrored expanding the sense of space. The elevator doors were made of highly polished brass. As she stood in front of them, there staring back at her was Hans looking comfortable and poised while she looked quite nervous and out of place. When they entered the elevator Hans put his key into the numbered panel and pushed the button for the Penthouse. She could feel her heart begin to race.

Hans opened the door to his apartment; the scene of the skyline was instantly in view from his living room windows. It was one of the most spectacular views she had ever seen of her city. He had a corner apartment so one wall of windows overlooked the park, while the other over looked the city skyline. The walls of the living room were continuous ceiling to floor windows with no coverings so there was nothing to disrupt the magnificent view. His living room resembled a page right out of Architectural Digest, with its highly polished hardwood floors, black leather furniture with silver metal framing, a large white area rug, an extremely oversized flat screen TV, with track lighting strategically placed, and an oval glass top coffee table with accent pieces which appeared to be merely for decorative purposes and of no sentimental value. Between the living and dining room was a 360 degree totally enclosed glass fireplace from which both rooms shared a full view of. His apartment had such an expansive feeling of space, due to the enormous footage, floor to ceiling windows and the lack of walls allowing the living room and dining area to flow into each other. The dining room furniture was made of a beautiful ebony wood so bold and masculine. On the dining room table sat a beautiful orchid plant in a red gloss pot, the same type of orchid that Hans had given to Marissa on their first date. The oversized oval shaped mirror which hung over the buffet reflected the impressive view of the city. Off the dining room was the kitchen, all the appliances were stainless steel and of restaurant quality. The counter top was made of beautifully rich black granite with specks of white throughout it. It was the most beautiful kitchen Marissa had ever seen. The apartment was certainly elegantly furnished but lacked the feeling of a home.

Marissa could feel herself becoming flushed and overwhelmed. Hans seemed to notice it also, as he asked her if she would like a glass of water. As he handed her the glass she started to cry. "What's the matter?" he asked. "This is so much to take in all at once. I don't know if I can do this?" Hans took the glass from her hand and placed it onto the countertop. He held her tightly and told her to close her eyes saying, "You are with me. It doesn't matter where we are. We can live in your apartment if you'd like. I just want to be with you. Don't look at this stuff and think it's me. You know me. I'm a boy who grew up with parents who worked hard for a living, just as yours did. I worked my way through college the same as you. None of this means anything to me, they are merely material objects. You said if we break up you don't want anything of mine. If you should leave me you will take the most valued possession I own, my heart. Please Marissa, it's going to be ok, I promise."

She opened her eyes and looked up at Hans. His warm smile melted away her apprehensions and they walked to the entrance to his bedroom. Marissa could see it was decorated very masculine, with brown hues. It also had ceiling to floor windows, but she noticed these windows had blinds that could be drawn. She saw the leather headboard to his bed with its brass fasteners shaped as buttons, his treadmill that faced his window and a roll top desk in the corner of his room. When Hans had given her the tour he didn't mention any personal statements about anything. He was so matter of fact about everything. As she entered the bedroom with him she wondered if there would be pictures of his family, something that would give her a glimpse of his life, but there was nothing. She saw the most beautiful quilt on his bed. The stitching was comparable to ones she had seen while driving through Amish country in Pennsylvania once. The colors were so rich and vibrant. The combinations of the fabrics were so intriguing and different than any other quilt she had ever seen. It was certainly handmade, but by whom she wondered.

Off the bedroom was Hans' bathroom. She had never been in such a large and luxurious bathroom before. It was enormous. Marissa's bathroom in her apartment could have easily fit into the spacious shower area of the room alone. The walls were a beautiful gray marble with streaks of white running through it. The sunken tub with a Jacuzzi had plenty of room for two. There was a walk in shower with no door. The three walls of the shower were made of the same gray marble with each of its walls having a shower head attached to it. The gray marble countertop held two glass sinks. The wall over the countertop had mirrors that reached to the ceiling. The brass faucets, towel bars and accessories gave the bathroom a masculine feel to it. The bright white plush towels that were piled on two shelves helped to pull out the white streaks which ran through the gray marble. In the raised ceiling was an opaque skylight that diffused the natural light which softened it as it entered the room.

Marissa was still feeling beset when Hans took her hand and led her to the bed. As they sat on the bed he told her he had brought the quilt from Austria. Finally, something personal in his apartment, she thought. Hans began to open up to her as he shared stories about his past. She was learning more about what laid deep within his heart. When he pressed his body on top of hers she had hoped he was going to make love to her. For whenever they made love it was as if he was truly inside her, not merely physically, but it was as if he was touching her very soul. It was hard for her to believe it had only been two weeks since they had first met since now she could not imagine life without him. She smiled at the thought of how one day could change your life forever and how two weeks could define it.

Day Fifteen, Saturday, June 25th Arriving in NYC Hans' story

Hans decided when Marissa awoke he would tell her of his financial situation and be done with it. It was getting harder to try to conceal it. When they arrived at the airport his car would be waiting for them, and he didn't want to have to explain the reason for yet another limo. When Hans felt Marissa stirring he looked down at her. Her side bangs were covering her face. He thought she looked so absolutely adorable when she slept as her hair would always be tossed about. He hadn't slept during the flight. He had gone to brush his teeth and freshen up about an hour earlier without waking Marissa. She was so sound asleep he easily placed her head on his shoulder again, without disturbing her slumber when he returned to his seat.

Hans received a text from Rita alerting him of the name of the restaurant and the time of their reservation. He then called Wolfgang leaving him a voicemail to the time of the reservation and the address to the Riingo restaurant, which was in the Alex Hotel at 205 E. 45th Street. As he hung up from calling Wolfgang he felt Marissa stir, he feared that his talking had awoken her. When Marissa awoke she left for the bathroom. Hans tried to build up his confidence to tell her about his financial situation when she returned. Surely, he thought, she would understand and not break up with him due to his innocent deception.

He had coffee waiting for her so she would be totally alert to hear what he had to say. After her second cup he decided the time was right. He had gone through his speech in his head, a hundred times. He knew what he wanted to say but as he started to speak he felt as if it was coming out all wrong. When he finished telling her, she sat there in silence. He didn't know why. Was it because she was appalled that he had deceived her and was going to break up with him? When she finally spoke he was relieved to hear her say she wasn't angry with him. He could not have been happier.

When they exited the plane Boris was there waiting. He drove them to Hans' Park Ave apartment. He had called ahead to make sure the apartment was freshly dusted, linens changed and for a special plant be placed on the dining room table. He wanted Marissa to like his apartment and wondered if she would like the décor. He knew it didn't appear as comfortable as her apartment did. It wasn't full of personal items and photos like hers was. It did have expensive furniture and paintings but he was aware that it lacked the sense of being a home.

When they arrived at his apartment Marissa was quiet, not her effervescent talkative self. As he walked her through the apartment he realized he didn't have a twenty-five cent tour to give her as she had given him at her apartment. His apartment had been decorated by someone he didn't even know, nor who knew him.

When Marissa started to cry Hans could see she was over-whelmed. He tried to calm her. While he was holding her he could see into his bedroom. He realized that he did have something to share with her. He did have a twenty-five cent tour for her.

He took her hand and brought her into the bedroom. After showing her his bathroom he walked her towards his bed and he could see that she noticed the quilt. As they neared the bed he asked her to sit down and he sat on the bed next to her. He told her the day he had left for America his mother had given him this quilt. His mother told him that for years she had been saving pieces of fabric to make a quilt for him, for when he grew up and left home. She said she wanted him to always have a piece of home with him wherever he was. She gave it to him as they were sitting on the bench on their back porch looking out into the sunset the night before he left for America.

Hans told Marissa what his mother had said to him that night, "Do you see those purple grapes over there? The first time we tried to transplant them from Italy they died. We realized we hadn't brought enough of the earth that had originally surrounded them. The second time we tried to transplant them we were successful. We brought a much larger amount of the earth that they had been growing in. It was as if the soil that surrounded them was home and with enough of it surrounding them there were not homesick and therefore flourished. I want you to be surrounded with your soil, the memories of where you are from, so that you, like those grapevines, will flourish. So if ever you miss home, you can wrap yourself with this quilt and you will be surrounded with your memories of home."

One by one he went through each patch on his quilt and ex-plained its origin and what it represented. Hans explained, "The yellow cotton fabric square was made from my first nightgown when I was an infant. The green fuzzy square was cut from my fa-vorite baby blanket. The red terry cloth square was from my mother's bathrobe she wore on cold nights when she nursed me. The blue shiny square was from my first snowsuit. The plaid square was from the shirt I wore on my first day of kindergarten. The several denim squares that are scattered around the quilt were from my father's work jeans. My mother told me when I was young I used to ride on my father's lap while he worked the machinery and those were the jeans he had worn most often on those days. The poppy flower cotton print square was from my mother's apron. Apparently, when I was a toddler I was constantly tugging on it to get her attention. The brown corduroy square was from the couch in our living room. When it was recovered she saved a square in her box of scraps. It was on that coach, where I first had sexual intercourse. I am sure my mother was not aware of that fact, but couldn't help but wonder when it turned up in the quilt if possibly she had. The dark blue linen square was from the jacket that I wore when I made my First Communion. The flannel square with the blue checks was from a nightgown that belonged to my maternal grandmother. The bright, shiny red satin square was from my favorite football jersey, the real football that you Americans call soccer. The white lace fabric with the eyelets was from my mother's wedding dress. When my aunt got married she wanted to wear my mother's dress but, because she was shorter it had to be altered. My mother had put a scrap of it into the box. The white cotton square with the red trucks on it was from the pajamas I had worn when I had the chicken pox. The baby blue cotton fabric was from the shirt I wore on my graduation from High School. The bright red linen square with the embossed flower print was from a napkin set my mother only used on Christmas day. The slightly larger middle square of royal purple satin with the grapes embroider on it is my favorite. My mother bought the fabric and embroidered grapes on it so I would always remember my home. The baby blue cotton backing on the quilt was made from one of my sheets that had been on my bed the night I told my mother I was moving to America. The boarder of the quilt with it light green colored cotton, was made from a pair of curtains which hung in my parent's bedroom when I was very young."

Hans had told his mother in the month of April he would be moving at the end of the summer to go to America. His mother had worked all summer on the quilt, surprising him with it when he left for America in September. Hans was happy that he did have a twenty-five cent tour to give Marissa as she looked pleased with his story.

Hans looked deep into Marissa's eyes. When he looked at her he felt as if he could see right into her soul. She gave herself so freely to him in every way. He didn't plan on making love to her, it just seemed to always occur. As he pressed her against the bed he could smell her natural scent. What was it about her scent that was so intoxicating to him? He loved touching her body. Hans gently caressed every inch of her and he savored every moment he spent with her. When he was making love to her, time stopped. He had no thoughts other than to please her. She somehow could make his mind drift far away from any thoughts other than of her and take him away from reality. As he made love to her he looked down at her and realized that his whole past was beneath her, and beneath him was his whole future.

Day Fifteen, Saturday, June 25th (Later That Day)
Marissa's Story

Marissa looked at the clock by the side of the bed trying to figure out what time it would be in Vienna. She remembered they hadn't eaten on the plane and she was starving. She wondered if Hans had anything in the kitchen she could quickly whip up for the two of them. As Marissa got out of bed she told Hans she was going to scout out his kitchen for food. He told her she would be disappointed because he hadn't any food in the house. He added they had reservations for dinner and they should start getting ready now. She wondered how he could have made reservations when he hadn't left her side upon arriving at La Guardia Airport. When she inquired as to where they were going, he replied, "Isn't a little mystery good in a relationship?" Marissa asked for a hint but all he would say was "It's near Park and 45th St." Marissa started running through her mind all the restaurants she knew in that part of town trying to figure out which one it could be.

Marissa was looking forward to taking a shower in Hans' bathroom because she wanted to check out the three different shower head designs. When she asked him to join her he said "Yes, but remember we have someplace to be so it won't be as memorable as your next shower in there will be". Marissa smiled. Hans did give her a kiss here and there during the shower, but as promised it was "just a shower". One shower head was similar to Marissa's with its changeable pulses. Another of the shower heads was rectangular in shape with the water cascading out of it as if it were a waterfall. The third one looked like a huge sunflower and when you stood under it the water hit you as if you were in a rainfall.

Marissa loved the double sink. They could simultaneously brush their teeth and Hans could shave while she applied her makeup and did her hair. Hans finished before Marissa and left to go into his spacious walk- in closet. As she applied her make-up she could see the reflection of Hans getting dressed and she did steal a peek here and there, trying to be nonchalant. It excited her just as much to see him dress as undress. She watched him as his slipped on his black underwear over his calves then over his thighs. She enjoyed watching him adjust himself into them. Then he put on his black socks, first his left then his right. His black shirt was next and she watched as he buttoned each button, thinking how much fun she would have later unbuttoning it. She thought he looked sexy as he slipped on his black suit pants tucking in his shirt before zipping up and putting on his belt. She controlled herself from running over and unzipping him as she knew he wanted to make the reservation on time. She enjoyed watching him tie the Windsor knot in his black silk tie, as he painstakingly made sure the knot was perfect. Hans slipped on his black suit jacket and Marissa noticed how impeccably tailored it was. The last item he put on were his black Italian- made shoes with tassels. He was dressed in total black, very New York looking, she thought to herself. She really didn't like the tassels on his shoes, but she kept that fact to herself. For everyone had a flaw she thought, he couldn't be totally perfect. But for the exception of those tassels, he was perfect, at least to her.

She luckily had all she needed to get ready with her, already in her suitcase. She wore her strapless white dress with the large red poppies, her red cardigan and her red sandals with the ribbons that wrapped around her calf. She wore her large gold hoop earrings and her grandmother's small cross around her neck. After she flat ironed her hair, she was all set. She looked for her small red clutch and took out the strap from the inside wearing it over her shoulder and across her chest so that it fell onto her hip. She didn't want to have to carry around a purse all night.

When she entered the living room Hans was standing at the window gazing out at the city skyline. "Amazing", he said as he turned and looked at her, "I had always thought this to be the most beautiful view I had ever seen, that is until I met you". Marissa could feel his eyes look right through her and she knew that he meant it.

Hans grabbed his keys, money clip and phone from the kitchen island and then took Marissa's hand. As they walked towards the door Marissa felt as if she could not be any happier. "Prayers are answered", she thought, "just like my grandmother told me".

There was a black car waiting for them outside Hans' building. Due to traffic the ride down Park Ave. was slow. They were nearing the entrance to Grand Central Station when Marissa asked

Hans if he had ever been there. When he said no, she insisted they stop and see it saying, "You said the restaurant is near Park and 45th Street. That's a short walk from here. We can go inside of Grand Central, take a peek and walk the rest of the way to the restaurant". Hans agreed and they got out of the car to tour Grand Central Station. While walking to its entrance Marissa was bombarding Hans with as many facts as she could recall about the building. She told him its interior was 275 feet long, 120 feet wide and 125 feet high and that it took ten years to build. She added that each of the six arched windows were 60 feet high. When they entered the building she remarked how the double marble staircase was modeled from the Paris Opera house and the two chandeliers that hung from the ceiling were made of nickel and gold plating. She pointed to the clock and remarked how it was the largest Tiffany clock ever made. Marissa informed Hans the floor was made from Tennessee marble. She smiled as she told him her favorite little known fact about the building, the Kissing Room. In the 1940's there was a special train the "20th Century Limited" which traveled from the West Coast and arrived at a room known as the Kissing Room. Back in the 1900's the Biltmore Hotel stood above that room. When soldiers returned home they met their loves and kissed in that room before taking the staircase up to the hotel. Hans inquired as to how she knew so much about the building. Marissa had written a report on the building in her senior year in high school for an English project, as it was one of her favorite pieces of architecture in the city. The facts had just seemed to stay with her, but she told Hans with a smile, "It is my city, I should know some interesting facts about it to tell people who aren't from here, don't you think?

Two Marines, who were walking behind them, were listening to Marissa as she was spouting out facts about the station. One Marine asked her "Miss, you seem to know a lot about this building. Do you know about other parts of NYC?" Marissa asked him what information he needed. He told her that he and his friend were meeting up with a buddy coming in by train and they wanted to celebrate before they went overseas on Monday morning with their unit. Marissa told them it would be cheaper to celebrate in Brooklyn for the drinks were quite pricey in Manhattan. She wrote down the address to her cousin Joey's bar in Brooklyn. She told them it was only two train stops outside of Manhattan and wrote down which subway trains to take. She then wrote down her phone number in case they got lost or needed any further help. She told them her cousin Joey was a former Marine who had done two tours in Iraq. She assured them once Joey learned they were shipping off on Monday, between the patrons and himself they would not be paying for any of their drinks. The Marine thanked her and added "You mentioned your cousin "used to be" a Marine. Once a Marine, always a Marine, Mam". As they hurried past Marissa and Hans to get to the track in time, Marissa could detect a look of concern on Hans face. Marissa smiled at him and said "And who is it that says New Yorkers aren't friendly? We need to break that myth". She continued listing more facts about the station as they neared the information booth.

The station was crowded with commuters and those shopping on the second floor, but Marissa had one more thing she wanted to show Hans. She brought him near the information booth. Standing in front of it she told him to look up at the ceiling. There, painted on the ceiling was a massive mural of the constellation. She told him that it was painted backwards on purpose. The artist wanted to portray the stars as God would view them from heaven. As they finished looking at the mural, Marissa could hear a man chanting something in what seemed to be Arabic. It was loud and seemed to echo from the ceiling. But being a New Yorker, she was used to unusual things occurring and having it seem perfectly normal. It was a common occurrence to walk down a street and pass by someone talking to themselves, so shouting to themselves seemed not out of the ordinary.

When they started to walk away from the information booth, Hans tightened his grip on her hand. "Marissa we need to get out of here now", Hans said and he pulled her and they started to run. Just as they neared the stairs Hans pushed Marissa against the wall. He told her to cover her ears. He then put his forearms tightly against both sides of her head. He was pressed against her so closely she could feel his heart beating, and it was racing. Her heart was racing as well. She did not feel confined by his body against hers, rather she felt protected.

Marissa was frightened. She was pressed hard against the cold marble wall wondering what Hans had seen to make him react this way. It was then she heard the explosion. Its force pressed Hans even closer against her body. She could hear the screams and chaos of what surrounded her but Hans' body was shielding her eyes from viewing it. After a moment Marissa could feel Hans push his weight off her. She looked up at him, frightened. She noticed blood running down his face. The muscles on his face seemed to be clenching, as he was grimacing in apparent pain. The sight of this produced within her a sense of fear that overtook her whole body. She had never experienced such fear. She started to feel herself tremble. Hans looked down at her and said, "Don't be frightened Marissa. Everything's going to be all right. I am right here with you. I will always be right here with you". As she was looking into his eyes, his head fell onto her shoulders. Marissa could feel the weight of his body against hers as it became limp and started to fall. She tried with all of her might to hold him up, but he was too heavy. Hans was still in her arms when they both fell to the floor. Without his body to shield Marissa's eyes, she for the first time saw the aftermath of the destruction and witnessed the mayhem that lay before her.

As she looked around the station, in total disbelief, it seemed so surreal. Her eyes scanned her surroundings through a haze of smoke and all that she saw seemed to be happening in slow motion. She looked up and saw the chandeliers were gone, the clock was gone, and the magnificent arched windows that adorned the station previously allowing for the brilliance of the sun rays to enhance the beauty of the Tennessee marble floor, were now shattered and mere holes in the walls whose sole purpose was as an escape route for the bellowing smoke.

She could see people running towards the exits screaming. Bodies of men, women and children lay haphazardly across the marble floor. There were scattered body parts, pieces of metal and thousands of pieces of broken glass from the windows reflecting the color of the freshly spilled pools of blood. As Marissa looked to the left she saw a small child about five years old sprawled out face down on the floor. The child lay lifeless in a plaid dress with her white blood-splashed stockings, black patent leather shoes with her pigtails neatly combed, covered in her own blood. Her one arm was outstretched and she could see that the other had been clutching a stuffed animal, as she could see its tiny brown ear peeking out from under her shoulder. Marissa witnessed people trampling on this child body as they were scrambling, searching for safety. Marissa was so repulsed by the sights she was encompassed in that she turned her head away from Hans and threw up.

She could not bear to see any more deplorably graphic images so she looked back down at Hans. She was horrified to see a shard of glass was protruding from his neck, which was spilling blood profusely covering his body. "No, this can't be happening" she screamed. She tried to think of what she could use to stop the bleeding. She decided to use her cardigan. In her haste to remove it quickly, she hit her head hard against the marble wall. She felt a sudden sharp pain on the back of her head. She instantly felt lightheaded and nauseous. As she lifted her head she saw the two

Marines she had just spoken to only moments before, running towards her. As her eyes closed and she fell into unconsciousness, the darkness was a welcome respite from the carnage and destruction that her eyes had been forced to record.

Day Fifteen, Saturday, June 25th (Later That Day) Hans' Story

Hans had forgotten to keep track of the time. When Marissa mentioned she was hungry he looked at the clock and realized they needed to be leaving within the hour to be on time to meet their friends. Her invitation to have him shower with her was tempting, as he knew it would save time. He also knew they didn't have time to have their usual playful shower, lest they be even later than he had already anticipated they would be.

Marissa was the first woman to ever use his shower as Hans had never before brought a woman to his apartment. His home was where he worked and where he relaxed, not where he played. He had never been close enough to a woman to want to share that part of his life before. He enjoyed having Marissa next to him at the sink while getting ready, it felt natural. His bathroom was much more comfortable than the tight squeeze when the two were in her bathroom. As he shaved he peeked over at her in the mirror and watched her when he thought she wouldn't notice. She didn't need makeup and he wondered why she even bothered with it. He watched her put on her mascara and couldn't believe that she didn't poke out an eye. He was glad when she only used a slight brushing of blush and no foundation as he believed it would only hide her real beauty. He liked the pink gloss she put on her lips. He noticed the label read "bubblegum flavor" on the tube and wondered what it would taste like later when he kissed her. He wondered why she straight ironed her hair at all because her curls were so soft and inviting to touch. But either way, straight or curly, he thought her to be absolutely gorgeous.

Hans was texting Wolfgang to let him know they were running a bit late, but, out of the corner of his eye, he watched Marissa as she slipped her dress over her head. It seemed that everything she did he found sexy. He was glad when he noticed when she put on her sandals that she wasn't wearing any stockings, because he wanted to touch her bare skin as they drove to the restaurant. Those sandals were one of his favorite pairs, he liked the way the ribbons caressed her calves. Hans was ready first and he went into the living room, enjoying the view from the window while he waited for Marissa.

When Marissa entered the living room, Hans saw her reflection in the window. He turned and looked at her, reveling in the idea that he would be spending the rest of his life with her. As Hans closed the door behind him to the apartment, he realized that if all the pain and struggles he had to go through in life was to bring him to this moment in time, to be with Marissa, then it had all been worth it.

Traffic was usually heavy in the city, but tonight it seemed to be even more congested than usual. When they were just approaching Grand Central Station the car seemed to have not moved for at least ten minutes. His driver had mentioned there appeared to be an accident up ahead. When Marissa suggested giving him a tour of Grand Central Station, he was calculating in his head how much later it would make them in meeting their friends. She seemed eager to show off her city and Hans didn't want to disappoint her. The traffic had come to a standstill, so walking to the restaurant did seem to be a quicker route. He quickly texted Wolfgang before leaving the car, alerting him of their approximate time of arrival. Wolfgang returned with a text informing Hans that he had met up with Marissa's friends at the restaurant and was enjoying their company immensely so he wasn't to worry.

Hans marveled at how much information Marissa knew about the station. When they entered the building Hans could see it was as spectacular as she had led him to believe. When the Marine spoke to Marissa he could see warmth in her eyes. It seemed to give her pleasure to help out someone in need. He was a bit concerned however of her giving her number to a total stranger. She seemed a bit under cautious, he thought, especially for a New Yorker. He would have preferred if she had given him his number instead.

Upon entering the station Hans could see why she loved this architecture feat. Grand Central was indeed excellently designed. He had always preferred European architecture to American architecture; however he thought perhaps he had just not seen the right buildings in America. As they walked down the staircase Marissa's enthusiasm for showing Hans the station seemed to increase. Hans could hear someone speaking in Arabic. It was faint at first and he couldn't understand it clearly until they finished looking at the ceiling mural. He had learned enough of the language while in the Navy Seals to know the man was shouting "Death to America". When Hans turned to the man who was shouting, he noticed the man was wearing enough plastic explosives on his chest to blow up the whole building. Hans quickly tightened his grip on Marissa and tried to get her to safety. When Hans heard the man shout "You will die NOW", he pushed her against the wall as he believed there was not enough time to exit the building.

Hans could feel the explosion push his body deeper against Marissa. He suddenly felt something hit both his back and his neck, causing severe pain and realized he had been struck with some debris from the explosion. He pushed himself off from Marissa as he didn't want his weight, which had been pressed into her, to cause any discomfort. He looked down to see if she was all right and noticed she was still holding her ears. He gently removed her hands from her ears, he could see the look of extreme fear in her face. He had seen that look before in the faces of men with whom he had served with on missions overseas. He wanted to reassure her that she would be safe. He tried to console her, but as he tried a feeling of weakness was overcoming him. He could feel his strength leaving his body. He loved her and wanted to protect her, but he didn't know if he could. He wasn't sure what his injury was but he knew he was becoming lightheaded and not able to think clearly. Hans' weakness became greater he could feel himself falling to the floor. He was looking into Marissa's eyes when her face started to become out of focus. He realized then his injury was grave and instantly prayed to God for Marissa's safety. If there were such things as guardian angels, he prayed that one would guide Marissa out of the station and out of harm's way.

It was then when Hans noticed, out of nowhere, the station suddenly became illuminated with a brightness of which he had never seen before. He could no longer attempt to focus on Marissa's face or any other object, as he seemed to be blinded by the light that enveloped him. Its appearance perplexed him. The sun had not been brilliant when they entered the station, nor had it ever been so brilliant. Certainly, if a police helicopter had been summoned to access the damage and were hovering overhead, they possessed no search light with this degree of intensity of light. Strangely, with the powerful strength of the illumination, his eyes were not forced to close. As each minute passed, the illumination appeared to be growing in intensity. He felt he was being drawn to it by some unseen force. It was as if the light was beckoning him to discover what lay beyond it. He had within him the most profound sense of peace and calm that he had ever known. It seemed as if the light was compelling him to locate its origin and as he left to pursue it he innately knew Marissa would be all right.

Day Fifteen, Saturday night, June 25th

Marissa started to awake from her unconscious state, before her eyes opened, she noticed a familiar odor and she knew she was in a hospital. In the background she could hear the scurrying of feet and a voice over the intercom paging for doctors and listing off codes, "Dr. Delancy please report to the ER front desk, Dr. Elliot please report to the counseling room, Code Red in room 203". She opened her eyes and saw rows of florescent lights leading down the narrow hallway ceiling. Her eyes then lowered, she saw the gurneys lining the walls with the injured that were crammed into the narrow hallway and her memory was jogged back into reality. She was recalling the events in her mind which were the catalyst for her being in a hospital, but she could not remember how she got here.

Marissa looked to her left she saw Rita at a doorway complaining to a nurse that her friend needed attention now. When Rita turned and noticed Marissa was awake, her face lit up. Rita ran over to Marissa asking how she was feeling and if anything hurt. Actually she had a terrible pain in the back of her head, but her main concern was Hans. Rita promised she would get a doctor to see Marissa as soon as possible. But, due to the number of injured Rita did not know how long it would take. Marissa was in a state of confusion and still dazed. Marissa's first words were, "Where is Hans? Where are we?" Rita explained that after the explosion two Marines had carried her and Hans out of the station. After flagging down a car they brought Hans and Marissa to the closest hospital, Belleview. One of the Marines found Marissa's cell phone in her purse. After checking for the emergency contact person, he called Rita. "Where is Hans?" Marissa demanded. When tears started to run down Rita's face Marissa knew the news would not be good. "What happened to him, where is he? Say he's all right, please!" she insisted. Rita held Marissa's hand tightly and said, "Marissa, I'm sorry. They did everything they could. But he didn't make it."

Marissa felt as if she were in a dream. This certainly could not be true. Perhaps the pill she had taken on the plane to ease her nervousness had her in some horrific nightmare and she would shortly wake up. Marissa broke free from Rita's clasp and started to run out of the Emergency Room on uneasy footing. She entered the waiting room noticing it was packed, there seemed to not be a space where there wasn't someone standing, laying or sitting. She saw the forlorn look in the faces of those waiting to hear news of their loved ones' condition. In the corner near the coffee machine, she saw George and Carter. Marissa ran to George, pleading "Bring me to Hans, please. I must see Hans!" George looked puzzled and looked at Rita for clarification. Rita said, "She knows. I told her, but she refuses to believe me and wants to see him".

As Marissa buried herself into George's chest in tears, she heard him say he had noticed the gurneys that were covered with sheets being brought down to the basement by the elevators marked "Service Elevator". George took Marissa's hand and they all walked towards the service elevator. There was such chaos on the floor that no one even noticed their entering it. As the elevator descended, George warned Marissa this might not be the best time for her to see Hans. But despite his attempt at persuading her, she still insisted. So as she held George's hand and with Rita's arm around her shoulder, and Carter quietly crying, they continued their descent to the basement. In their search of the morgue they passed several orderlies, but again, with the urgency of their duties, no one stopped them.

As they turned a corner, Marissa spotted Wolfgang. He was at the end of the hall with his back against the wall, his head down holding onto a white plastic bag. She broke free from George and Rita and ran to him. "Where is Hans?" she asked. As he lifted his face she could see the anguish in his eyes while tears were running down his cheeks. "Marissa you don't want to see him like this, wait until they've cleaned him up", Wolfgang pleaded. "I want to see him now!" she insisted. George took the white plastic bag, with "Patient Belongings" printed on it, from Wolfgang's hand and Wolfgang brought Marissa beyond the doors labeled "Morgue".

When Marissa entered the morgue, the room was crammed wall to wall with body-ladened gurneys. The feeling of confinement was intensified by the reflection of the gurneys from the polished stainless steel refrigerated cubicles which covered the wall opposite the entrance. She had a steady stream of tears that had not ceased since she had heard of Hans' demise. As she looked across the sea of blood stained sheets, she couldn't help but think how each sheet represented someone's loved one. She remembered a saying her grandmother once told her when she was a little girl. "You might be one person to the world, but to one person you might be the world". She didn't know why that quote popped into her mind, except that as she was squeezing through the rows of gurneys accidently bumping into some of the bodies she couldn't help but wonder just who all these people might belong to. They were each someone's mother, father, sister, brother, husband, wife, lover, friend or child. With all these bodies, she thought, how was she to know which was Hans. Just then her eyes spotted the black Italian leather tasseled shoes. Those tassels which she disliked so much earlier in the evening now were so dear to her.

Wolfgang took her hand to help navigate her through the rows of gurneys. It was hard not to brush up against the rows of bodies as they walked through the tight-spaced path. As she approached Hans' gurney she gently touched the tassel. She then gently removed the sheet from his face. A wave of nausea hit her. His bright blue eyes that would light up a room were closed. As she looked at his lifeless face, covered in blood, it became real to her that he was gone. When she gently brushed his hair from his forehead with her fingers and stroked his hair, she noticed his hair was hardened from dried blood. She gently kissed his lips; they were not the lips she remembered. They had turned ice cold. She asked Wolfgang if he could look for a blanket for Hans. Wolfgang realizing a blanket would only serve the purpose of warming Marissa's heart not Hans' left in search of her request.

Marissa noticed there was a large deep metal sink on the wall to the left of the refrigerated cubicles. Above it were shelves filled with stacks of green linen towels. Marissa walked over and took four towels from the shelf, soaking them with warm water then wringing them out tightly. She saw a radio on the shelf besides the towels. She turned it on and fumbled as she looked for a classical music station. It was an older model radio with a knob for tuning in on a station, which required steady hands, something that she didn't posses at the moment. When she finally found a station, it took a minute to get it tuned in clearly. She did not know what piece they were playing, she only knew Hans loved classical music, and she wanted it on for him. She brought the wet towels over to Hans' gurney. She softly wiped the hardened dried blood from his face, ears and hair and attempted to talk with him. She tried three times, but with each attempt, her throat seemed to tighten up and the words would not come out. She got out as much of the dried blood as she could. She needed to retrieve more wet towels to clean up, what seemed to be, an endless amount of blood. As she rinsed out the towels the smell of the dried blood overcame her and she threw up. She tried keeping it together as she wanted to finish removing as much of the blood off of Hans as she could. The music must have calmed her a bit for as she tried to speak to Hans a fourth time, her throat seemed to have loosened and the words came out. She wanted to tell him one last time that she loved him. "Hans I love you" but with that said a release of emotions rushed through her body and she could hear herself sobbing loudly and seemingly out of control. She had never experienced such heartache as this before. She felt actual pain in her chest, as if her heart was truly breaking. Realizing this would be the last time she would be able to speak with him she tried as hard as she could to pull herself together, so she would be able to speak. "I hope that you know how much having you in my life has meant to me. I will remember every day and night we spent together. I hope you like this piece of music. I think I remember hearing something like this on your Smart Phone." As she started to clean the left side of his neck, she saw the huge gash from where the shard of glass had hit him. Her crying became more intense. It became harder for her to catch her breath. As she spoke, her voice cracked. "Hans, why did you have to protect me? If you hadn't then we would still be together. I would be with you in heaven instead of this hell on earth you have left me in. I wish we had stayed in the shower longer. I wish I hadn't asked you to see Grand Central Station. It's all my fault Hans. If only I hadn't..." Wolfgang at that moment had just returned from his search for a blanket, walked up behind her, interrupting her saying, "Marissa it's not your fault. You did nothing wrong. Things happen that we don't understand the reasons for". He put his hand on her shoulder. "I could not find any blankets. The hospital is full of injured people from the explosion and supplies are limited." She insisted they find something to put over Hans as he was ice cold. Wolfgang realized there were no blankets to be found in the hospital, and wanting Marissa to be comforted, took off his jacket and laid it over his best friend's chest.

Wolfgang stayed by her side, as she bent over laying on Hans chest weeping. The music filled the air with its soothing notes, but it didn't muffle the sounds of her anguish. Wolfgang told Marissa the name of each selection of music as it was being played. He told her a story of how Hans and he had come to appreciate classical music. It seemed they had both taken private piano lessons from a teacher who was in her late 20's, gorgeous, tall, blonde and built. He added how the teacher always wore low cut blouses and short skirts. Wolfgang was sure their love of classical music was probably heightened by their having this particular teacher, as they were both in puberty and in constant states of excitement during their classes.

Wolfgang realized perhaps Marissa wasn't really listening to him but he was trying to get through this ordeal the best he could.

Talking of happy times he had shared with Hans was the only way he could think of to endure the pain of standing next to his best friend's cold and lifeless body. Wolfgang was trying to console Marissa the best he could, but he himself was holding on to his composure by a thread. He wanted to be strong for Marissa, because he knew that was what Hans would want him to do.

They had been in the morgue for about an hour, with Wolfgang telling stories, when a nurse came in. "You should not be in here! How did you even get in? You have to leave, now!" the nurse demanded. As Marissa looked up from Hans' chest, her face clearly expressed her agony. The nurse changed her tone after looking into Marissa's eyes and said, "I am so sorry for your loss but we have to get these bodies ready to move, as we have more in the halls. I am truly sorry, but you have to leave".

Marissa could not believe that only hours ago Hans was with her in his apartment alive and making love to her. She didn't want to leave; she just wanted to hold onto him forever. Letting go of Hans was the hardest thing she ever had to do. She realized that when her fingers left his hands they would never touch him again. She was supposed to spend a lifetime with him, not two weeks. When she finally released his hands, she couldn't look back. She clung to Wolfgang's shirt, and he held her tightly as they left the morgue. As the morgue doors opened, she could see that Rita, George and Carter had been waiting for her in the hallway. Rita opened her arms and Marissa fell into them sobbing. They stood there a moment, and then started down the hall. The nurse ran up after them and handed George Wolfgang's jacket which was covered in blood. George opened the white plastic bad and added it to its contents.

In the elevator Marissa could hear the conversation between her friends trying to decide where they should go, but she couldn't seem to speak to offer an opinion. She clung to Rita and didn't let her go until they entered the cab. Her friends were still discussing in the cab whose apartment they should take her to, when Marissa's voice cracked and said "Hans' apartment on Park Ave." Wolfgang agreed as it was the closest to the hospital of any of their homes. It had ample room for all to sleep comfortably and he knew they were all well passed exhaustion.

DAY SIXTEEN

Day Sixteen, Sunday, June 26th

As Marissa stepped out of the cab looking up to the Penthouse apartment, she felt her knees give way. Luckily, George was there to catch her. He picked her up and she buried her face in his chest, trying to hide from the world, as he carried her into the lobby. She heard the doorman ask Wolfgang if everything was all right. Wolfgang asked if Dr. Phelps was in. The doorman said she had left hours ago to help with the emergency at the hospital due to the bombing. Wolfgang asked the doorman to have her contact him when she returned. Marissa could hear the elevator doors open. She couldn't believe that just yesterday she and Hans were there together, with her anticipating her first look at his apartment. There was no anticipation now, for now the apartment held nothing for her. She nuzzled her face deeper into Georges' chest, as she was hesitant to return to the Penthouse.

As Wolfgang outstretched his arm to unlock the door, the sleeve of his shirt rose up revealing his Rolex. He had looked at it many times since its purchase without a single thought of it. But now as he looked at it he had to fight back the tears, and yet a small smile came across his lips as he recalled the fun he had shared with Hans on the day it was given to him. He unlocked the door to the apartment with his key which had remained on his key fob since the day he received it from Hans. Wolfgang frequently stayed with Hans whenever he was in town, and often without notice. As Hans was a bit of a lady's man, and not always at home or available to answer his phone, Hans has given him a key so he would never have to stay in a hotel due to his inability to reach him. Wolfgang felt his hand tremble as he turned the key, realizing this would be the first time he would be staying there without his friend returning home. As he opened the door he took a deep breath before entering.

When Rita entered Hans' apartment she didn't take notice of its extravagant size or its exquisite furnishings. Her only concern was to get her friend cleaned up and put to bed. With George still carrying her, Wolfgang escorted them to Hans' bathroom. Upon entering she checked for shampoo, soap, towels and wash cloths, everything she would need. She noticed Marissa's luggage when they walked through the bedroom. It still had the same black and white stripped ribbon tied into a bow that Marissa had attached to it when they had gone to Canada, for its easily being spotted on the conveyer belt at the airport. When George put Marissa down, Rita asked if he could find something for Marissa to sleep in from her luggage and then to please leave it on the bed. Rita asked Wolfgang to please have Carter check the kitchen to see if there was any soothing herb tea he could make for Marissa.

Rita then closed the door leaving the two friends alone. She looked at Marissa who was standing in front of the mirror with her eyes glazed over. She wondered if perhaps she was in shock. She was glad Wolfgang knew a doctor in the building because she was not comfortable with the fact Marissa had left Belleview without first being checked by medical personnel. When Rita spoke to Marissa she reacted as if she couldn't hear her. Marissa wasn't responding to any attempt to get her undressed and into the shower. Rita looked at Marissa staring into the mirror; and wondered what horrors her friend might be replaying in her mind. Rita was concerned Marissa might be in some kind of catatonic state. Rita knew Marissa would not be able to shower alone.

When Marissa saw her own reflection in the bathroom mirror she was horrified. She had not noticed before that she herself was covered in blood. Her favorite color was now tainted by the overwhelming dark crimson that seemed to have been scattered all over her clothing, arms, legs and hair. How had she not noticed this before, she wondered? The images of the carnage that she had witnessed were replaying in her mind and seemed to have frozen her in time. She seemed for some reason, unknown to her, not able to speak or move. She just stood there staring into her own reflection, seeing image after image of the aftermath of the explosion over and over again. It seemed as if the night was replaying itself in her mind frame by frame, horrific scene by horrific scene. As she continued to stare into the mirror the images of the carnage she had witnessed were presenting themselves in front of her as if they were in present time. She tried to close her eyes to escape them, but they continued to play out in her head. She couldn't shake the visions of the teddy bears' ear, the destruction, the mayhem and Hans laying on the gurney covered in blood. Marissa's face has splashes of blood across it. Her hair was separated into strands hardened with dry blood. There were strange pieces of something in her hair that she couldn't identify, they looked similar to some dried out pieces that were stuck to her red stained dress as well. They shockingly resembled what Marissa had believed to be pieces of flesh she had seen stuck on the marble walls of the station after the explosion.

Marissa wanted to help Rita undress her, but she felt dead inside, lifeless. Marissa felt as if life was occurring around her, but she was unable to participate in it. She felt Rita's hand guide her to the shower. Rita removed her own shoes and went into the shower with Marissa. The warm water felt soothing to Marissa as it flowed down her body. As the cleansing waters flowed over Marissa's hair a familiar odor was apparent. The mystery was solved. She now knew what the eerie odor that was apparent in all hospitals which she had ever visited was. The smell was of dried blood and flesh. She watched as the crimson colored water swirled down the drain. A color she had loved, but tonight she had begun to hate the sight of. She could taste the blood as the water ran from her hair and swept over her lips. She wondered just whose blood she was tasting. Was it only Hans', or perhaps did it belong to others who were near them during the explosion. When Rita applied the shampoo to Marissa's hair, it was a welcome relief from the wretched smell of the dried blood and flesh. Marissa just stood there, with her eyes closed trying to fight away the memories of the evening, as Rita carefully wiped off the blood and then washed Marissa's body.

When the blood was finally washed away, Rita left the shower. Marissa remained in the shower longer, letting the warm water run over her body hoping it would help her troubled mind. After changing into dry clothes, Rita returned and turned off the faucets to the shower. After toweling Marissa dry, Rita picked up the nightgown George had left on the bed and slipped it over Marissa's head. She led Marissa over to the bed and sat her on it. As she looked into Marissa's eyes they were barren. In all the years she had known her, Rita had never seen her friend in such distress. She thought perhaps some tea would help to sooth her friend and went to the kitchen to see if any had been brewed.

Carter felt useless. He was never any good during a crisis. He always looked to Rita for help in that department. It didn't help that Roberto had left the day before on a business trip and wouldn't be back until tomorrow, for Carter could surely use his support right now. Rita gave him the task of making tea. He could not believe Hans had actually lived in this apartment as it seemed to be void of any normal persons stocked food items. There wasn't any teas, coffee, cans of soup, *Bisquick*, cereals, pastas or any item one would find in an inhabited dwelling. Carter, therefore, went to the store around the corner to buy some tea. He found a section in the back of the store stocked with Celestial Seasons Teas and bought some chamomile, sleepy time, vanilla, and green raspberry teas. He also found another brand of teas he was not familiar with and bought some Kava tea as well. He recently read an article in a magazine stating that Kava could be used to reduce stress. And he couldn't think of a more stressful situation than the one they were all in at the moment. He also purchased coffee, sugar, milk, a few boxes of cereal, a loaf of bread, eggs and butter as he knew they all would be in need of those items in the morning. Carter was pleased that Marissa hadn't finished with her shower before he returned, giving him time to make the tea before it was needed.

When George left Rita and Marissa in the bathroom to clean up, he felt powerless. He didn't know what he could do for Marissa. George knew Marissa always looked to him for guidance, but he hadn't a clue what he could do to help ease her pain. He entered the living room and noticed that Wolfgang had changed out of his blood stained clothing and was getting out a bottle of Stolichnaya from the freezer. Wolfgang looked at George saying, "Hans never had any food in this place, but he always had vodka in the freezer, and a full wine rack. Would you care to join me?" George thought it was the perfect beverage for the situation. He thought it might help take the edge off the tension he was feeling from this horrific evening. Wolfgang handed him a pair of pants and shirt for him to change into saying, "Your glass will be waiting here for you when your return".

When Carter arrived back from the corner store, he put away the groceries, made the tea for Marissa and then joined the men with their bottle of vodka. George was sensitive to the fact that Wolfgang had just lost his best friend, and tried to console him as best he could. He listened attentively while Wolfgang told stories of his and Hans' antics during their teenage years. The conversation then turned to a more serious note as Wolfgang mentioned the need for making funeral arrangement. As executor of Hans' will, he had been privy to the details of what kind of viewing Hans had wanted when he died, which was none. Apparently, he only wanted an interment service, and that was all, no viewing was to be held. Hans had told Wolfgang that since he would not die until much later in life there was no hurry to decide what to do with his remains. So the decision for his final resting place lay in the hands of his friend. Wolfgang felt a cemetery in Long Island would be nice, as Marissa could easily visit. He told George he would not make any final decision until he spoke with Marissa, but in her current state he wasn't quite sure when he would be able to bring up the subject with her. Wolfgang had called his mother when he left the morgue to tell her of Hans' passing. She assured him she would immediately call Hans relatives to inform them as well. Wolfgang decided he would wait a week for the burial to take place, giving family members ample time to take care of their affairs before traveling to America. Wolfgang would send Hans' jet to Vienna for their transportation. George sat there attentively listening, as he realized his newly made friend needed someone to share his thoughts with. Carter was glad the sleeping arrangements had been previously made for he needed to excuse himself not only due to the fact of his becoming intoxicated from the shots of vodka, but more for the fact of all this talk of funerals was making him quite anxious.

Marissa was sitting on the side of the bed when Rita left the room. She began to feel a chill in the air and could feel herself starting to tremble. She wished Hans could be there to hold her, as that wasn't possible she decided if she had his scent it would help to calm her. She went over to his suitcase and took out the shirt he had worn at his mother's funeral. Since it hadn't yet been laundered his scent still lingered on it. She changed out of her night-gown and put on his shirt. She pulled the top of the shirt up to her nose, closed her eyes and inhaled his scent as deeply as she could. She sat on the bed, her hands touching the smooth materials of the quilt beneath her. She started to recall the story Hans had told her of each square. She wrapped herself in the quilt and laid down on his bed. She tried to lay on her back but the bump on her head was quite sore and was accompanied with a fierce headache.

As she laid in Hans' bed wrapped in his quilt, memories of times they had spent together flooded her consciousness. With each breath she took, she inhaled his scent from his pillow. She played and replayed in her mind every time they had made love, trying to recall every detail no matter how finite. She had made many mem-ories, just as her grandmother had taught her, which gave her vast information to draw upon. Marissa was glad she had made so many memories. She would have never believed they would be all that she would have of Hans to last her a lifetime.

When Rita returned with the tea, she could not convince Marissa to drink any of it. Rita laid down next to Marissa holding her, and did not leave her side all night. As they laid there, Marissa could hear from the sound of her breathing that Rita had fallen asleep. Marissa laid there awake for hours praying to God to awaken her from this nightmare she had seemed to be stuck in. When sleep finally arrived it was a respite for Marissa, for in her dreams Hans was alive and well. In her slumber she could once again taste his kisses and feel his body close to hers.

DAY SEVENTEEN

Day Seventeen, Monday, June 27th

Marissa awoke to the sound of murmuring outside the bedroom door. Her friends were discussing the events of the prior evening. So it wasn't a dream, Marissa thought, it was real, it did happen. She overheard her friends say a radio station had just reported that the suicide bomber at Grand Central Station had acted alone. She couldn't help wonder if that were the case, or had it been a story concocted by the FBI to ensure that panic not run wild in the streets of Manhattan . Apparently, a note was found at the suicide bombers home stating the reason for choosing Grand Central Station. The bomber had picked it for its thousands of daily commuters, hundreds of guests dining at restaurants at the station's upper level and the many shoppers who would frequent the specialty shops at the station. "Surprisingly only 500 people were killed, with no number yet mentioned of how many injured" she overheard Rita say. A chill went up Marissa's spine hearing this news and she ran to the bathroom to throw up.

When Rita entered the room, she was carrying a cup of coffee and breakfast, an omelet and buttered toast for Marissa. She was surprised to see Marissa throwing up, and was concerned about her concussion. She placed the breakfast on the dresser and helped Marissa back to bed. Despite her insistence, Marissa refused to eat, drink or see anyone, including her mother. She returned to the co-coon of the quilt with its scent of Hans and slept the day away, with Rita checking in on her every hour. Fortunately, Wolfgang's friend, Dr. Phelps, arrived and checked on Marissa about 3 pm. She apologized for not arriving sooner but explained that she had been detained at the hospital.

When the doctor entered the bedroom, escorted by Rita, Marissa at first refused to be examined. But with Rita's insistence she finally agreed. After the doctor's examination, she explained to Marissa that she had a concussion and nausea was a common occurrence with it. She added that if the nausea didn't stop within a day or two to call her back and she left her business card on the nightstand. She then asked Marissa "Is there any possibility that you could be pregnant? Have you had any unprotected sex, as I would like to prescribe some medicine to help you relax?" Marissa responded, "No and thank you anyway, but I do not want any medicine. I just want to be left alone."

When Dr. Phelps entered the living room she assured Rita that Marissa would be fine, all she needed was some rest. The four friends stayed together the rest of the day, checking in on Marissa and watching coverage on CNN. There were reports on the bombing and coverage of the life of the suspected suicide bomber. Rita, Carter and George left about 9PM but not before Rita made a schedule for each to stay at the apartment, to make sure Marissa would not be left alone. Rita made the schedule for the next five days, as she didn't want to leave it to happenstance. Rita was hesitant to leave but Wolfgang assured her that if Marissa needed them, he would call instantly. Rita would be back in the morning for the early shift; Carter would then come from noon to 5 pm. George would arrive at 5pm after work, with Rita meeting him there after Carters' arrival back to the boutique. They would then stay until Wolfgang returned from work. As Wolfgang was staying at the apartment there was no need for the others to stay overnight. With Hans appointing Wolfgang the position of CEO in his will, Wolfgang needed to see that everything was running smoothly during the transition. Wolfgang also worked as an investment consultant, but independently on a contractual assignment basis. This left him the flexibility to be able to, if he chose, to handle Hans' company.

DAY EIGHTEEN

Day Eighteen, Tuesday, June 28th

Marissa sequestered herself in Hans' bedroom. With blinds drawn, she hid in the darkness isolating herself from the world. Enveloped in the darkness, with the sounds of symphony's emitting loudly from her ear buds and the scent of Hans surrounding her she found some comfort.

When Wolfgang returned from work, Rita had an enormous dinner waiting for him. There was an abundance of foods made for Marissa, to coax her to eat, which was left untouched. After Rita and George left, Wolfgang changed into his sweatpants and T-shirt to work out in his room. He had a set of free weights that he kept there for when there wasn't time to go to the gym located on the third floor in Hans' building. Just as he picked up a dumbbell, he heard Marissa screaming for Hans. He quickly ran to her room and sat on the bed to awaken her from what seemed to be a nightmare. She awoke in a fright and held onto him crying. He tried his best to calm her. When her trembling subsided, he asked her if there was anything he could do for her. She looked up at him, with tears streaming down her face and asked if he would stay with her. He kicked off his sneakers and sat on the bed with his back against the thick brown leather headboard. Marissa sat up, still wrapped in the quilt, and leaned against Wolfgang's shoulder. He was the only one, she believed, besides herself who felt the deep sense of loss and emptiness. Only he shared in her anguish and lamented over Hans' passing. She asked him if he would tell her a story of when Hans was a boy. He knew that she hadn't eaten for days and thought perhaps he could entice her to eat in exchange for a story. With her nausea, the mere thought of food would upset her stomach, so they agreed she would at least have a cup of broth. Wolfgang went into the kitchen and retrieved some chicken soup, which Rita had made, from the fridge. He carefully removed the chicken, vegetables and noodles. After heating it up, he brought it to Marissa. She sat there sipping the broth as he told her stories of Hans as a boy. When she finished the broth he took the cup from her and sat back against the headboard with Marissa again leaning against his shoulder. Wolfgang spent hours reminiscing, with Marissa intently hanging on to his every word. She finally drifted off to sleep during one of his stories. When Wolfgang left the bedroom he looked back at her realizing that Marissa was all that he had left of his lost friend. He wondered if she realized that he needed her as much as she needed him during this time of suffering. Marissa was helping him through his grieving, but Wolfgang couldn't help but wonder what he could do to get her through hers and out of that bed.

DAY NINETEEN

Day Nineteen, Wednesday, June 29th

With each day that passed Rita had the apartment full of the most delightful aromas, making all of Marissa's favorite foods, stuffed shells, raviolis, lasagna, chicken pot pie, chicken noodle soup and baked ham. Each attempt to try to get Marissa to eat was futile. The four friends could only eat so much, so Hans' freezer was fast becoming full to its capacity. Carter went to Marissa's favorite bakery and bought her red velvet cupcakes, but she turned her head to those as well. George brought loaves of freshly baked Italian bread sending the most inviting smell wafting throughout the air, but Marissa again would refuse. Her mother came several times to try to console Marissa, but with each visit she was turned away.

Marissa's friends would come into the bedroom with attempts to comfort her, but each visit proved unsuccessful. She loved her friends and appreciated their effort, but she believed they could not comprehend the severity of her suffering. When each friend would come into the bedroom Marissa would simply put her head under the quilt and tell them she wanted to be left alone.

Ever since arriving from the hospital, sleep was Marissa's respite from reality. When she awoke her only thoughts were of Hans, playing and replaying every moment she could remember of their time together. She refused to see her friends, refused to eat, remaining alone in the darkened bedroom all day, wrapped in Hans' quilt. But in the evenings when all would leave, she would patiently wait for Wolfgang to come and sit on the bed to tell her more childhood stories of Hans. Each night the ritual would be the same. Wolfgang would bring Marissa some broth and while she sipped it, he would tell her stories of his and Hans' childhood. It was as if hearing stories of Hans was keeping him alive within her. And each night she would fall asleep against Wolfgang's shoulder.

DAY TWENTY

Day Twenty, Thursday, June 30th

Marissa awoke feeling the same as yesterday, hopeless. She wondered when her heart would stop aching and when her tears would subside. She laid in bed making a mental list of all the things she would miss about Hans. When she thought about it, it was the simple things she'd miss the most. Things she'd miss, that until three weeks ago, she wasn't even aware of their existence. She would miss his playful boyish grin, and his beautiful smile. She would miss the brushing of the hair from his forehead with her fingertips, and of his coming up behind her when she was cooking and kissing her neck. She would miss looking at him from across the breakfast table, the feeling of being safe in his arms, sleeping in her special nook, the excitement she felt when she received a text from him and the excitement of waiting for his arrival. But MOST of all, she would miss the look in his eyes whenever he looked at her. The look that told her she was loved, truly loved.

Carter felt inadequate as a friend, as with each attempt to console Marissa, he failed. He wanted to do something for her but he seemed incapable of coming up with anything that had been successful. Then as he was searching for lace for a design he was working on at the boutique, an idea came to him. If Marissa decided to attend the interment she would need a veil. Marissa being a very private person would surely want to conceal her pain from view. He searched the storage room for the softest black lace he could find. It was thicker than the usual lace he worked with, perfect for Marissa's grief to be her own. He worked on the design most of the day. He knew it had to be elegant, sophisticated yet possess something which made it unique, as it was for Marissa, one of the most unique women he had ever met.

When Wolfgang returned from work, as usual, there was a feast to be had. Rita seemed to not be able to stop herself from cooking. At this point she wasn't quite sure if it was because she wanted Marissa to eat, or because she needed to be doing something, anything. Or else she would be left alone with her thoughts, which would go directly to her friend in the next room, whose suffering she couldn't seem to console.

That night when Wolfgang came in carrying his usual broth he brought in some strawberry jello as well. He put the cup of broth on the night stand and handing the jello to Marissa he said, "I made this myself. I remembered you mentioned how you enjoyed the strawberries from Hans' back porch. I went to the store and bought the jello and the best strawberries I could find. I cut the strawberries into tiny pieces so they'd be easier to swallow. I used the fast method using ice cubes so I hope it tastes alright". Wolfgang stood there so proudly holding his cup of jello that Marissa couldn't help but smile. She took the jello from his hand and ate a spoonful. As it melted in her mouth it brought her back to her childhood. As a youngster when she was nauseous or throwing up her grandmother would always make her strawberry jello. It was a comfort food she had long forgotten that she loved, for it had been years since her grandmother had made it for her.

Wolfgang again comforted Marissa with stories of Hans. During the telling of one of his stories while he was still speaking, he heard Marissa starting to talk. In her dreamlike state she had mistaken Wolfgang for Hans. As she leaned closer to his chest she shared a concern that she had been having dry heaves all week and she believed something might be seriously wrong with her. After Wolfgang put her head softly onto the pillow, he left the room to call Dr. Phelps. The doctor told Wolfgang she would come to see Marissa in the morning. Wolfgang was concerned about Marissa's health but didn't want to call Rita and alarm her. He would wait until the morning when Rita arrived to tell her, to not add any additional stress on her.

DAY TWENY-ONE

Day Tweny-one, Friday, July 1st

When Rita was taking the subway to visit Marissa, she realized it was the fifth day of Marissa's secluding herself in Hans' bedroom. Hans' funeral was tomorrow, and no one had been able to discuss with Marissa whether or not she would attend. Wolfgang had made all the arrangements, but had yet to speak to Marissa of it. Every time he attempted to bring up the subject Marissa would insist that he stop. When Rita arrived at Hans' apartment, she wondered if it would be another day of Marissa never venturing out of the bedroom. Upon entering the bathroom, she found Marissa kneeling on the floor in front of the toilet bowl with dry heaves. Rita went into the living room and mentioned to Wolfgang that she was worried that Marissa was making herself actually physically sick with her grieving. Wolfgang told her he had called Dr. Phelps last night and she would check on Marissa this morning. Wolfgang was slowly working his way into Rita's heart as a friend. She was so pleased at how well he looked after Marissa, and she realized how much Marissa needed him now. He did for

Marissa what Rita couldn't; truly empathize in the loss of a shared loved one.

Marissa was aggravated when she learned her friends had called a doctor. "I'm fine", she shouted at the doctor, who was sitting at the edge of Hans' bed. Marissa finally agreed to let the doctor check her over, as it seemed the only way the doctor would agree to leave. Dr. Phelps persuaded Marissa to let her take a blood sample. Because Marissa had been overseas, there were a variety of things which she could have been exposed to. Before leaving ,the doctor reassured Rita that she would run tests to confirm or eliminate some possibilities of out what might be causing Marissa's nausea. Rita went into the bedroom and pleaded with Marissa to take a shower and a Marissa again pleaded with Rita to leave her alone. Although she constantly refused to allow her friends to stay with her in Hans' room, it was reassuring for her to know that they were just outside the door if she needed them.

That night as Wolfgang entered the room with his usual cup of broth, he reminded Marissa tomorrow was the day of the interment. For the first time, Marissa didn't interrupt him and forbid him from mentioning it. He told her he had picked a cemetery in Long Island with beautiful landscaping and an abundance of flowering plants. He mentioned that Hans' family members had arrived for the service and were staying at a hotel in the city. He didn't want to upset her, but he needed to go through Hans's closet to find a suit to give to the undertaker.

Marissa unwrapped herself from the quilt and went into Hans' suitcase. She gave Wolfgang Hans black suit with the blue pinstripes. "Here, this was one of his favorite suits, I think." She then went to Hans' closet to find a fresh shirt and matching tie. She opened his drawer and picked a pair of black boxers, and a pair of black socks. She then noticed a pair of black Italian shoes with tassels in the corner of his closet and picked them as well. Marissa was sure that Hans must have loved the tasseled shoes if he owned two pairs of them. She put the items in a neat pile and handed them to Wolfgang.

Marissa tried to explain to Wolfgang how she didn't feel she was emotionally strong enough to attend the service in the morning. Wolfgang assured her it would be all right and that Hans would have understood. He informed her all the arrangements had been made. George, Carter and Roberto would be attending in her stead and Rita would be staying back with her during the service. Wolfgang told Marissa he would put a flower on Hans' casket from her. Marissa then recalled how Hans had put edelweiss on his mother's casket as it was her favorite flower. And, for the first time in five days she stepped outside of Hans' bedroom. She went into the dining room and picked up the potted orchid plant which sat on the table. It had eight beautiful flowers on its stem. She lifted the flowers to her nose and inhaled their sweet fragrance of raspberries and cream, reminiscing of the night when she had first breathed in their scent. As she set the pot on the dresser, she said, "Break off this stem tomorrow. These are the flowers I want you to put on Hans' casket. He will know they are from me." Wolfgang handed her a cup of broth. They sat on the bed with Wolfgang leaning up against the leather headboard and Marissa leaning against his shoulder, sipping her broth. But, tonight there were no stories, tonight there was only silence.

When Wolfgang left Marissa's bedroom, he brought the pile of clothes with him. George had offered to bring them to the funeral parlor and would be stopping by shortly to pick them up. When the doorbell rang, Wolfgang was expecting to see George, but when he opened the door Dr. Phelps was standing there. It was the first time they had been alone since Wolfgang's last trip to NYC. Dr. Phelps expressed her sympathy for the loss of his dear friend. Then as she softly kissed him, she let him know she would be attending the interment tomorrow. She invited him to stay over at her apartment tomorrow night, saying, "It will be an emotional day for you Wolf. You have been so busy taking care of Marissa that you haven't been taking care of yourself. Why don't you let someone take care of you for awhile? I took a few days off from work and would love to spend them with you." Wolfgang thanked her for the offer. Before making a decision he would have to see what tomorrow would bring. When the doctor asked to see Marissa, he told her she had just fallen asleep. She opened her briefcase and wrote a note attaching it to Marissa's blood test results then sealed them into an envelope. She took out a white bag from her briefcase which was stapled closed at the top. She handed the envelope and bag to Wolfgang saying, "Will you please make sure Marissa gets this when she wakes up?" Wolfgang assured her that he would. As she opened the door to leave she said, "Remember my offer Wolf". He replied with a lingering kiss, "Let's see how things go tomorrow".

Wolfgang wondered if Marissa was sick with more than her grief. When he was handed the white bag he could hear pills rattling. He suspected it was medicine, but respecting Marissa's privacy, he did not open it to reveal its contents. About an hour had passed when Wolfgang heard the toilet flush in Hans' bathroom. He went into the bedroom to give the envelope and bag to Marissa. As he handed them to her, he was surprised to see her put them on the nightstand. "Aren't you going to open the envelope?" he inquired. "Yes, later", Marissa replied as she put her head under the quilt. As she closed her eyes, inhaling Hans' scent from his quilt, she prayed once more to be able to dream of Hans. Sleep was her only relief these days, for it gave her back her Hans. In her dreams she could still see him, hold him, touch him and kiss him. In her dreams he was alive; it was that reality which was so dear to her and the one she desperately wanted to hold onto.

When George arrived to retrieve the suit for the funeral parlor, he left some items for Marissa. He asked Wolfgang to put them in her bedroom saying, "Carter asked if you would put these in

Marissa's room so she would have them in the morning in case she decides at the last minute to attend Hans' service. He doesn't want her to have stress over thinking about what to wear". When George left, Wolfgang quietly walked into the bedroom and placed the items on the chaise lounge. He was careful not to waken Marissa, for as the light from the opening of the door shone across her face she looked at peace. In her sleep the look of suffering seemed to have left her face. He understood why she hid into slumber to escape her shattered life, but knew she needed to pick up the pieces and rearrange them so she could fit into the world again.

About 2 am Marissa awoke feeling quite nauseous. She wondered if possibly the doctor was correct and she had caught something from being overseas. She went into the bathroom, thinking she might throw up. As she turned on the light she caught a glimpse of herself in the mirror. She hardly recognized herself. She had dark circles under her eyes that were prominent due to her pale appearance, and a sullen look on her face. She had to pull herself together, she was certain, but she didn't know how. She splashed some water on her face and returned to the bedroom. Instead of climbing back into the bed she walked over to the window and opened the vertical blinds that had helped shut her out from the world. She stood there gazing out upon the beautifully lit up city skyline wondering when everything she saw would stop reminding her of Hans. When would this ache in her heart lessen, and when would the emptiness that depleted her very being be filled? she wondered. The one thing she did not want to lose was the feeling of Hans' presence. Sometimes when she closed her eyes and thought of Hans she could actually still feel him right next to her. That was what made her believe he was still there with her in his bedroom. As long as she could keep her eyes closed, he was there. But she knew she couldn't keep her eyes closed forever, at some point she needed to open them and reenter the world.

She looked at the brown leather chaise lounge across the room and noticed that her black dress was lying across it in a dry cleaner bag. At the foot of the chaise lounge, were her black patent leather heels. As she walked over to it, she noticed a few other items that also had not been there earlier. There was a package of black stockings, her small black beaded clutch and a unique pair of black lace gloves with just a hint of a ruffle at the wrist. She picked them up and felt how soft the lace was. She observed there was no tag inside. It was obvious they were hand-made, and instantly she knew that Carter had made them for her. It was then when she noticed the black lace veil, which had been placed besides them. It was also apparent that it too was the handy work of Carter. The veil's lace pattern design was large enough to give privacy for its wearer while still enabling the wearer a clear view. The veil had an avant-garde look to it and was extremely stylish. It was made with five small black feathers, about three inches in length, arranged in a fanned out fashion, affixed to a comb. The comb was attached to the veil, but set off to the side allowing for the comb to be secured to the left side of the head. As she tried on the veil attaching the comb to the hair on the left side of her head, the veil stopped just short of touching her shoulders. It was perfect. But of course it would be, as Carter had exceptional taste and was an excellent fashion designer as well. She thought to herself, "He has been helping me put together my outfits for years; of course he would help me with an outfit for tomorrow, knowing I would be under an extreme amount of stress". She couldn't help but think of how sweet Carter was. He must have used her spare apartment key to get her dress and shoes. He then had gone to the dry cleaners to have her dressed cleaned, bought her stockings and made the veil and gloves to put this all together for her. She had decided she wouldn't be attending the service tomorrow. But Carter having all this ready for her, had she decided to go, confirmed Marissa's belief that the genuine love she felt for him was mutual.

As Marissa sat there trying on the veil, looking into the mirror, she realized how truly blessed she was to have such good friends as she did. She needed to pull herself together, not only for herself, but for them. How much longer could they hold a vigil outside Hans' bedroom? Although, during the day, though her friends were just outside her door, Marissa felt so terribly alone. Hans' dying left such a void in her heart that she feared it would never heal. She took off the veil and decided to return to bed. She started to re-think whether or not she should attend the funeral the next day. She thought she would wait until the morning to decide. "Yes, tomorrow" she thought, "I will make my decision tomorrow. I don't have the strength to think any more tonight." Just before closing her eyes to sleep, she noticed the envelope from the doctor, sitting on the nightstand. "Tomorrow", she said to herself, "there is nothing that can't wait till the morning."

DAY TWENTY-TWO

Day Twenty-two, Saturday, July 2nd

Marissa had forgotten to close the blinds prior to returning to bed last night so the rising of the sun awoken her. Feeling quite sick, she hastened to the bathroom just making it before the dry heaves started. She then went to the nightstand where Rita would leave a bottle of water for her each night before she would go home. After picking up the bottle she noticed the envelope from the doctor. She brought the envelope with her as she walked to the window and stared out admiring her beautiful city. The sunrise was remarkable, reflecting the sunlight softly from the windows and steel frames of the buildings. It wasn't the harsh, bold, light that emanated from the billboards and skyscrapers that crossed the night time sky. As she looked out the window she couldn't help but think, "So this was the view Hans awoke to each morning". She felt the warmth of the sun upon her face as it shone through the window. Being bathed in the morning sun was refreshing. And as the sun's rays entered they set free the darkness that had permeated the room for six days. The soft morning light of the day inhabited the room and seemed to breathe life back into it and into Marissa as well as if releasing her from her self-imposed tomb.

She tore open the envelope and removed the contents. She read the hand written note first.

Dear Marissa,

Congratulations! You are pregnant! I believe this is the reason for your nausea and dry heaves. You will need to start taking better care of yourself. I have put some prenatal vitamins in the accompanying paper bag for you. Please see your gynecologist as soon as possible so she can give you suggestions or possible medication for your morning sickness. If you look at your blood test results you will see that your HCG levels are higher than they should be if you are only a few weeks pregnant. This could indicate you're carrying twins. Again, Congratulations.

Sincerely,
Dr. Phelps

Marissa felt a wave of emotions rush throughout her body, over-whelming her. She put her left hand against the window to help keep her balance as she felt as if she was going to faint. She clutched the papers in her right hand pressing them close to her heart. The reason for the dry heaves was not her grieving, but morning sickness. She was euphoric, yet at the same time dis-traught. How was it possible for her heart to be aching with devas-tating pain and swelling with euphoric happiness at the same time? How two emotions of such powerful opposite extremes could be occurring within her simultaneously seemed impossible. She remembered a conversation she had with her grandmother the day her father died. She had asked her grandmother how she was able to survive the pain of losing a husband and a son, just how much could a heart bear. As she looked deeply into Marissa's eyes, her grandmother answered, "The heart can bear a tremendous amount of pain and still hold an abundance of happiness. My son has just died and my heart aches and yet when I look into your eyes and see the reflection of your love, happiness enters it. As you experience more of life's intense pleasures and extreme depths of despair you will learn just what the heart can hold". Marissa finally understood what those words meant.

Marissa looked out the window to the new day that was breaking, with a new sense of purpose. As she closed her eyes, she concentrated on the moment. She allowed herself to feel every emotion that was running through her body, both the happy and the sad. Her thoughts drifted to Hans. She could smell his scent as strongly as if he were standing right next to her. She felt as if she could feel his body come up behind her and press it against her own. She savored the moment, realizing that what she was physically feeling was not possible. She was quite aware her mind was somehow playing a trick on her. But she lingered with her eyes closed enjoying the sensation, for she did not know how much longer her mind would be playing these tricks on her. Would it be another day, a month, a year...a lifetime she hoped. As she opened her eyes and started to remove her hand from the window, she noticed a handprint to the left of her own. It was larger than her own handprint; it was Hans' handprint she was sure. "He WAS here, he WAS standing right behind me", she thought. She felt a chill run through her, the hair on her arms actually raised. When she had gazed out the window the night before, she would have surely noticed the handprint, had it been there. With both the reflection of the window from the lit skyline in front of it, and the lights coming from the bathroom behind it, the handprint would have been clearly visible for sure.

There was an antique oak roll top desk in the corner of the room. Marissa rolled opened the cover and found some paper, a pen and an envelope. She walked towards the window to sit on the landing to write Hans a letter. As she neared the window she noticed the hand print was gone. That was all the proof she needed. Hans had sent her a sign. He was here and he would always be with her. She started to write.

Dear Hans,

I just learned we are going to be parents, possibly of twins. I know you are as happy as I am about the pregnancy. I guess when Sister Beatrice told us in sex education class that prophylactics only had a 98% success rate; she was actually giving us one bit of information which was accurate. I cannot tell you how ecstatic I am! For the first time in my life I am thrilled to be in the failing percentage rate of an equation. I promise you I will be the best mother I can possibly be. I will teach our child or children all about you. I will tell them about your character, courage, kindness, and how deeply you loved. I will learn German, the best that I can, and have them learn it as well. I will teach them about your heritage. I will ask Wolfgang to be their Godfather and Rita to be their Godmother. I want to thank you for this gift. This is the most treasured gift you could have given me. This baby is a part of you and now I will always have a part of you here on earth until we meet again in heaven. I love you now and I will love you forever.

Love, Marissa

She put the letter and blood test into the envelope and held it close to her heart. She decided she would be attending the interment. She opened her clutch to put in the envelope and noticed that Carter had put in a small pair of pearl earrings and her long faux pearl necklace into it for her to wear as well.

Rita, George and Carter arrived early, 7:30 am, at Hans' apartment. Roberto would be leaving from his own apartment later to go to Brooklyn. Roberto would be going to Marissa's mother's house to be with her while she waited to be picked up by the limo. The limo would not be arriving at Hans' apartment until 11am, but Rita wanted to arrive early in case Marissa decided to attend and needed her help getting ready. When Rita saw Wolfgang take a bottle of Stolichnaya from the cabinet she attempted to get him to eat something, but he refused. He explained the vodka was not for him to drink, but rather, he would be placing it into Hans' casket. He opened the cabinet and retrieved two lead crystal rock glasses as well. He put them on the counter next to his keys and sat on the couch next to George. Rita and Carter were making coffee when they heard the shower running in Hans' bathroom. They looked at each other in amazement; for this meant Marissa was cleaning up. Rita went into the room and knocked on the bathroom door, "Are you ok?" she asked. Marissa assured her that she was fine, and told her she would be accompanying them to the interment. Rita was thankful her prayers had been answered, for Marissa had found a way out of her despair.

While Marissa took a shower, she stood under the flow of water enjoying the warm sensation that caressed her entire body. Marissa was filled with a new sense of hope; it was replacing the feeling of desolation she had for many days. Hans had not left her alone, just as he had promised. He had left a part of himself behind. As she touched her lower abdomen she felt blessed that a part of him would always be with her.

Standing in her towel still wet from the shower, Marissa remembered the reason Hans had worn his gray suit at his mother's funeral. It was because it was his mother's favorite. She wondered what she could wear today that was Hans' favorite. She went over to her suitcase and opened it. She noticed that Rita had washed everything in it and had neatly repacked it. Marissa took out a red bra and red panties. These were Hans' favorite, her red underwear, and she would wear them for him. She fixed her hair, put on her make-up, and went over to the chaise lounge to get all the items Carter left for her and readied herself for the interment. When she was all dressed she went back to the suitcase and took out a second pair of red underwear. She took off the pair she was wearing and slipped them into her clutch purse, knowing where she would later be placing them, and slipped on a fresh pair. She looked in the mirror. Something was missing, but she didn't know what. Then it came to her. She needed something of Hans' to hold onto during the ceremony. She went into the living room looking for Wolfgang.

When she entered the living room, all eyes were upon her. It was the first time in six days that her friends had seen her leave Hans' bedroom. Carter, Rita, George, and Wolfgang were shocked to see she was dressed and ready to go. Rita was thankful that she herself had dressed appropriately in the hopes that Marissa would change her mind and attend the interment. Marissa asked, "Wolfgang where is the white plastic bag that we brought from the hospital with Hans' belongings?" Wolfgang replied, "It's over here. I didn't go through it. I thought we could go through it together. There are some things I need to go over with you". Actually, Wolfgang had already gone through its contents. He had taken out the money clip, tie tack, Navy ring, and pocket watch and cleaned off the dried blood. He had removed the blood stained dollar bills and replaced new ones in Hans' money clip, then returned all the items back into the bag. There was nothing he could do with the blood stained documents and paper that had been in Hans' breast pocket of his jacket. Those he removed from their original envelopes and just left out to dry. When they were completely dried he then placed them into fresh envelopes.

"I want to put Hans' pocket watch on my necklace", Marissa said, as she opened the bag looking through its contents. She looked up at Wolfgang and in a cracked voice said "I haven't yet thanked you for letting me and my friends stay here during this distressing time. I want you to know how much I have appreciated it and how close I feel that I have become to you." She felt tears welling up in her eyes, but took a deep breath and tried to compose herself. She removed the pocket watch from the bag, unclipped her pearl necklace and attached the watch to it. She attached the tie tack onto the left side of her black dress, and put Hans' Navy ring on the middle finger of her left hand, leaving the money clip untouched.

She picked up the envelopes from inside the bag and asked, "What are these Wolfgang?" Wolfgang opened the first envelope and removed the blood stained documents that were written in German saying, "The information in these papers is what I need to discuss with you, Marissa". Wolfgang opened the first document and said, "Marissa it is I who should be thanking you for letting me stay here this last week. While Hans was in Austria he had a new will drawn up. I was with him when he went to his lawyer's office to sign it. This is his copy of the will; it is signed, witnessed and notarized. He left all of his earthly belongings to you Marissa."

Marissa was shocked. "What does that mean?" she asked. Wolfgang replied, "That means you own his company, his apartment, his estate in the Hamptons, his home and vineyard in Austria and all of his money." Marissa sat there momentarily speechless, and then asked, "The vineyard behind his house is his?" Wolfgang replied, "Yes Marissa, it was his parent's property since before he was born. The wine rack over there is full with its harvest".

Marissa just sat there trying to take all this in. George took hold of Marissa's hand and softly said, "His family will probably contest this will in court because whenever there are large sums of monies involved families come after each other for blood. It will take years for you to see any of the money or property, if at all". Marissa got up and started to walk towards the kitchen to get herself a glass of water. Wolfgang said, "Marissa you need to sit down. I have to explain further. There is another document." Marissa returned to the living room and sat down on the couch in between Wolfgang and

George, holding George's hand tightly and said "Wolfgang I don't want his money or his property. I have no intention of fighting his family in court over it. His pocket watch, Navy ring and tie tack are all I want." Wolfgang replied, "That is probably why he left it all to you Marissa. Hans knew you loved him for himself and not his money. Do you remember when you and Hans went to have your friendship ring blessed"? he asked. She lovingly touched the ring that sat on her right forefinger, and said, "Of course I remember. Hans knew I had my cross and my grandmother's ring blessed years ago by a priest and asked if I would like to have our promise ring blessed. The blessing only took a couple of minutes". Wolfgang turned and looking at George said "George, you needn't worry that anyone will contest this will in court. This document I hold in my hand is Hans' and Marissa's marriage license. My mother's and my signatures are here on the bottom of this document as we were at the ceremony as witnesses." Marissa could not believe her ears. They were married! She didn't understand why Hans would have them married secretly without her knowledge. But she wasn't angry, for now the child she had within her would carry his name. She wondered if perhaps he had a premonition and that was the reason he had arranged the marriage. When she inquired if Wolfgang knew why Hans did it, his reply was, "Hans was the happiest I have ever seen him. He told me he loved you and didn't want to spend another day without you being his wife and asked me to help him carry out his plan. Hans even arranged for the church's gardener to be outside, so you two could cut a piece of wood together. It's an Austrian tradition to bring good luck to the bride and groom. You looked to be so in love with him, and he had told me of his plan to propose to you on the plane ride home, so I saw no harm in it."

Marissa just sat there on the couch, numb, going over in her head the unbelievable information she had received this morning. First, she learned that she was pregnant, and then she learned she no longer needed to worry about how she would be able to afford to raise their child, and now she learned that she is married. All this was almost too much for one day. Marissa sat motionless and speechless trying to soak it all in. She held onto Hans' pocket watch tightly. She felt its smooth texture. She had seen it in the watch pocket of his vests but had never seen him check the time with it. The watch seemed to be an antique and she assumed it had sentimental value and no longer worked.

Marissa realized the bottom line for her was that she could not care less about the money, she was just thrilled her child would bear Hans' name. Marissa then asked Wolfgang, "Is it still a legal marriage if I did not know I was getting married?" Wolfgang replied, "Yes Marissa, because the only people who are aware of that are those of us in this room, and none of us would ever divulge that information."

Wolfgang then handed Marissa the second envelope saying, "I don't know when he wrote this, but this paper was in his pocket as well". As she opened the envelope she saw a poem on blood stained paper written in Hans' handwriting.

To My Juliet,

Distance has not erased the image of thy face,
but has etched it deeper into my memory.

Thou may be not within my reach,
but willst never be far from my heart.

Fear not fair maiden, for my
love for you will never die.

For can the moon command
the stars not to shine?

Can the oceans will the tides to
cease from reaching the sands?

Can the branches of the trees not
reach themselves towards the sky?

For when you first did touch me,
you also touched my heart.

Feelings you have released within me,
do not allow me to sleep.

For fair maiden, it is only with
you where I find my true peace.

Love always,

Your Romeo

Marissa felt the tears fall down her cheeks. She did not share the poem with anyone, merely held it close to her heart. She would tuck it in her favorite copy of <u>Romeo and Juliet</u> and would cherish that poem forever.

Marissa knew Wolfgang would be going alone to the funeral parlor when they sealed Hans' casket as she was awake the night Wolfgang had called the funeral director to make the arrangements. She could hear his voice through the door as he paced by when he talked on the phone. It was then she had learned Hans did not want a wake, only an interment service, and that he only wanted Wolfgang present when his casket was sealed. She had overheard Wolfgang attempting to convince the funeral director to allow him to drive the hearse alone to the cemetery. Wolfgang's voice became irate as he expressed how cold hearted people could be, and was appalled how money seemed at times to be the only persuader in having someone do the right thing. When there was an offer of a large sum of money, she knew from his reply the funeral director had accepted.

When Marissa asked Wolfgang if she could ride up front in the hearse with him to the ride to the cemetery, Wolfgang agreed saying, "I think that Hans being driven to his final resting place, with his two favorite people in world is the perfect way to do it." Marissa replied, "I must see him before they close the coffin. I have an envelope I want to put into his hand and something I have to slip into his front jacket pocket." Wolfgang told her he would escort her to the room where Hans was laid out and she could have as much time with him as she wanted before they left for the cemetery.

Wolfgang said it was time for them to leave. Marissa asked him to please give her a few minutes as she needed to put on her veil. When she entered the bedroom she went over to the desk and got a new envelope and pen. She opened her letter to Hans and added to the bottom of her note, P.S. Thanks for marrying me, you always did enjoy surprising me. Love, Mrs. Christian Hans Von Geirscher.

She got out a second piece of paper and sitting at the desk, wrote from her heart.

To My Dearest Romeo,

My pillow weeps and is saddened
for it is your comfort that it seeks.

For me sleep does escape
and hide as memories arise.

Thy scent still lingers although it be faint.

The sense of you remains abound
whirling throughout the room.

If I close my eyes it is as if you never left.

But, alas when eyes do open, reality returns.

And there is but a memory,
where did thou head once lie.

Love forever, Your Juliet

Just as she slipped the papers into the envelope and put it into her clutch, Carter walked into the bedroom. He looked at Marissa and asked, "Would you like me to put your hair up and put on your veil?" Marissa replied, "That would be nice. Thank you Carter." She sat at the chair in front of the desk as Carter worked on her hair. And with a tear running down her face she said, "You fixed my hair for my first date with Hans, it's only fitting that you fix it for my last date with him".

So with tears welling up in his eyes, Carter put Marissa's hair up in a French twist with whips of hair draping down her neck, just as he had done for their first date. After attaching the veil to her hair, he gently put his hand on her shoulder and said with tears streaming down his face, "Marissa, I can't take my eyes off of you, and I'm gay, so imagine what effect you will have on him?" She remembered Carter had said that the night he helped her get ready for her first date with Hans. He slipped his hand into his pocket and pulled out a bottle of *Obsession*. Handing it to her he said, "Here you go, I forgot to put this with the other items for you to wear today". She looked up at him trying to hold back the tears, and gave him a slight smile. That smallest of smiles was all Carter needed to see, to know that his friend would be all right. Just before Marissa left the bedroom she went over to Hans' desk and retrieved a pair of scissors. She then walked over to the orchid plant on the dresser and cut the stem off with the blooming flowers and brought it with her.

As she walked down the hall to the living room Marissa was thinking about the three people whom she had loved the most in her life, her dad, her grandmother and Hans. They were all now in heaven looking down and watching over her. When she entered the living room and looked into the faces of her friends, Carter, Rita, George, and Wolfgang, she knew there would be four down here on earth looking after her as well. She knew it was somehow going to be all right.

She walked over and hugged Rita, as she did the clasp was released on the pocket watch and it opened. As Marissa looked down at it she smiled. She realized now why she had never seen Hans open his pocket watch; it wasn't because it was broken. She recognized the photo of herself in the inside cover of the watch. It was one that had been on her refrigerator door. She never noticed that it was gone as there were too many photos to have missed just one. She lovingly closed it, and told Wolfgang she was ready to leave.

She momentarily felt nauseous. Her morning sickness made her feel as if she had just gotten off from a whirling amusement park ride. The queasiness reminded her of something her grandmother had once said, "Life is like a roller coaster. You don't want to just stand at the gate and watch all the other people having fun. You want to get on the coaster and enjoy every twist, turn, incline and descent. You might get sick on the ride and throw up, but at least you experienced it. If you don't feel, you're not living". The past three weeks had certainly been like a roller coaster ride she thought. She was glad she took the chance and went on the ride, although she felt the deepest despair she had ever known, it had also given her the most euphoric times as well. And this feeling now, of being pregnant with Hans' child, this was the best feeling of them all. This child would be proof of their love having existed. Marissa thought to herself, no other child had been conceived in more love and no other child would ever be more loved....or would that be two?

Her friends had a bit more time to wait before the limo would arrive to take them to the cemetery. Wolfgang and Marissa were leaving ahead to go to the funeral home. Wolfgang opened the apartment door and as Marissa neared the door she hesitated. Wolfgang looked at her and said "There's a German expression that says "The greatest step is out the door'. We can do this Marissa, together". Marissa took his hand and they left the apartment. She looked up at Wolfgang with a small smile, holding her clutch and flower with one hand and with her other hand on her abdomen saying, "You gave me two big surprises this morning. During the ride to the cemetery I have one for you". As the door closed gently behind her she realized the events that had taken place in the last three weeks had changed her life forever, and for the better.

ABOUT THE AUTHOR

A Tree Grows In Brooklyn and so did I. Proudly I admit from the Park Slope area. It is there where my roots began and where my personality and values developed. It's there were I learned the true meaning of friendship and of love. It is also where I learned the importance of laughter and where I formulated my sense of humor. I was fortunate to have been raised by parents so deeply in love that I became a hopeful romantic.

Brooklyn is a cauldron of diversity, but when introduced to the Italian culture at a young age by my friend Marie, I was fascinated with it. I was drawn into it with its deep family loyalties, the tightness of the extended family ties, the acceptance of true friends as family and of course the food. In my twenties was the first time I had met anyone who was Deaf. We become friends and she introduced me to the culture of the Deaf world. Intriguingly it is with this culture where I have focused most of my career. I have worked with the Deaf community in a variety of capacities, two of my favorites being the teaching of American Sign Language and Interpreting.

I currently live in upstate New York with my two daughters who attend college and my Yellow Labrador Retriever. My true passion is writing. I've seen bumper stickers that say "I'd rather be sailing, fishing, skiing" or some other activity. If I could find one I'd put on my bumper: "I'd rather be writing".

I hope that you enjoy the journey where my books lead you as I enjoyed the journey where my characters brought me. Please visit my website: www.charlottesymonds.com